Dante born 1265

THE DIVINE COMEDY OF DANTE ALIGHIERI

rivers of Hell: Acheron, Styx, Phlegethon (blood) pg. 191.

I INFERNO

uniform with this volume

PURGATORIO

PARADISO

THE DIVINE COMEDY OF DANTE ALIGHIERI

WITH

TRANSLATION AND

COMMENT BY

JOHN D. SINCLAIR

INFERNO

OXFORD UNIVERSITY PRESS

NEW YORK

OXFORD UNIVERSITY PRESS
Oxford London Glasgow
New York Toronto Melbourne Wellington
Nairobi Dar es Salaam Cape Town
Kuala Lumpur Singapore Jakarta Hong Kong Tokyo
Delhi Bombay Calcutta Madras Karachi

First published by Oxford University Press, New York, 1939
First issued as an Oxford University Press paperback by special arrangement with THE BODLEY HEAD, 1961

printing, last digit: 29 28 27

PRINTED IN THE UNITED STATES OF AMERICA

TO

M. O. S.

PREFACE

THE translation of the *Divine Comedy* into English prose seems, on the face of it, a singularly gratuitous form of failure, and how far, if at all, I have succeeded in my aim of combining a close rendering of the Italian with the requirements of a credible English, it is not for me to estimate. I am so far qualified that I know something of the magnitude of the task and of how limited a portion of Dante's substance and quality it is possible, at the best, to convey. I have tried to serve readers who have little or no knowledge of Italian and who wish to know the matter of Dante's poem. The requirements of some to whom the whole medieval outlook is strange and many of the classical references unfamiliar may excuse the number and the simplicity of the annotations, which are intended merely to make the narrative intelligible. In these I have erred, like the warder of the gate of Purgatory, 'rather in opening than in keeping locked'.

I have used the critical text of the *Società Dantesca Italiana* as revised by the late Professor Giuseppe Vandelli, and for their courteous consent to this I have to thank the publishers, Messrs Ulrico Hoepli, of Milan. The few departures I have made from that text are limited to readings adopted either in Moore's or Casella's texts. I have found suggestions for interpretation in some of the current English versions and have borrowed an occasional phrase from one or other of them. In passages where Dante seems to have had the language of the Vulgate in mind I have adopted, as far as possible, that of the Authorized Version.

In the comments on the cantos I have gone on the view, confirmed all through with closer knowledge of the poem, that Dante is constantly and closely concerned with the moral and spiritual system and consistency of the whole, his imagination working habitually *within* that system; that one of his most distinguishing qualities—in his imagery, his epithets, his choice of *dramatis personae*, his mythological and historical illustrations, his astronomical way of telling the time of day or night, his frequent harping on words, phrases, and ideas, his curious verbal devices, his varying moods as a pilgrim—is the quality of *relevancy*, relevancy, that is, to the moral and spiritual matter in hand, and that these features as they come are not merely decorative, they are integral and are to be so interpreted. Their relevancy *is* their meaning. The elaborateness and the obscurity of much of Dante's symbolism have given rise, on the one hand, to volumes of forced and fantastic interpretation and to the valuation of mere ingenuity of invention as itself the product and the proof of his imagination and, on the other hand, to a critical reaction which tends to limit the value of the poem to its 'poetic' qualities and even to its outstanding passages of lyrical and dramatic beauty, and to regard the general scheme as little more than a framework for these. The one bias seems to me as mistaken as the other. The famous passages, the great lines, would be great even if they were isolated and anonymous, but they are far greater and more significant because they are part of the whole and because they are Dante's. In nothing is Dante more 'classical' and in nothing does he tower more above his medieval predecessors than in this high quality of sustained relevancy, and in commenting on the text I have tried to keep it in view as the main criterion and guidance. The question is always, What does this passage mean, not merely in itself as a form of words, but concretely as an occurrence in the mind of Dante as it comes to him and comes from him in this situation and context?—a question, plainly, which it is not always possible to answer, but, for interpretation, the only question that matters. Dante did not merely inherit the theology and cosmology of the Middle Ages along with his generation and then take them for granted; he re-imagined them and peopled them and made them the matter of his thought and of his song. He was not, indeed, an original and authoritative thinker, that is not his greatness. He was a great interpreter and a supreme imaginer, bodying forth the abstractions of scholastic thinking, turning them to shapes and giving them a local habitation and a name, and it is only as we provisionally accept the ethical and theological system and standards of the thirteenth century and hold in mind its conceptions of the world and life and eternity that we can enter into the mind and imagination of its poet. 'But Dante is not the man to accept submissively the thoughts and convictions of other men, above all in his poetic constructions and imageries; everything may help to an understanding of his writings, but the key of real comprehension is to be sought, not so much in Saint Augustine or the Abbot Joachim or Saint Thomas—or Ubertino da Casale—as in the inner life and the work of the poet himself' (*M. Barbi*). In some passages any interpretation is fairly open to debate, but it is by that standard of relevancy that it must be judged, and a poet is to be known from within or not at all.

I should perhaps note that although in debatable cases I have given my own view dogmatically and without discussion, it has not been without consideration of the alternatives and of the reasons given in support of them, nor always with as much assurance as may appear; and also that in such comments as I make on the work of some of Dante's literary predecessors and contemporaries I do not mean to pretend, as I may seem to do, to an independent judgment of my own.

I have not thought it necessary to offer any general introduction to the subject in futile competition with the masterly essays of Church (the best) and Lowell and Symonds. Along with one or all of these the English reader who is new to the subject should have Gardner's *Dante* in the *Temple Primers* and either Rossetti's or Norton's version of the *Vita Nuova*. So much being assumed, I have tried to make the comments on the cantos sufficiently explanatory as they come. In the brief notes dates are mentioned, as a rule, only when they fall within or near Dante's lifetime (1265–1321).

I have to acknowledge my large indebtedness to the commentaries of Scartazzini (revised and largely replaced, in the latest editio s, by Vandelli), Casini (revised by S. A. Barbi and quoted as '*Casini-Barbi*'), Torraca, Grabher, and, in the *Inferno*, Rossi; to many of the *Lecturae Dantis* delivered in

Florence, Genoa, and Rome (quoted here as '*L.D.*'); and to the writings of De Sanctis, D'Ovidio, Zingarelli, Parodi, M. Barbi, Torraca, Rossi, and Croce, and I have quoted these the more freely because they are not generally available in English. Every English student of Dante must be indebted to Moore's three volumes of *Studies in Dante* and his *Textual Criticism of the Divine Comedy*, and to Toynbee's *Dante Dictionary*, and I have made use of Carroll's three volumes on the *Comedy*, Gardner's *Dante's Ten Heavens*, Vossler's *Die Göttliche Komödie—Mediæval Culture* in the English version—and the annotations by Vernon, Plumptre, Butler, Tozer, Grandgent, and the *Temple* editors.

The version of the *Inferno* is published along with that of the *Purgatorio*. Too many of Dante's readers know him only as 'their Dante of the dread Inferno', and therefore do not know him; for all the essential, larger meaning of the *Inferno* lies in its relations with the rest of the poem, and primarily with the *Purgatorio*. The result of Dante's experience in Hell was that he was able 'to see again the stars' and prepared 'to course over better waters', and the experience without the end in view would have been, for him, meaningless melodrama.

I hope the version of the *Paradiso* may follow later.

J. D. S.

Edinburgh
March, 1939

My version of the *Paradiso* was published, uniform in format, during 1946. I have now been given the opportunity of making some emendations in all three versions and in the notes for this new printing.

J. D. S.

Edinburgh
April, 1948

CONTENTS

CONTENTS

CONTENTS

DANTE'S HELL

In Dante's cosmology the earth is at the centre of the universe and Hell a vast funnel-shaped cavity or reversed cone reaching from near the earth's surface to the centre, which is the centre of the universe, the farthest point from God. The sides of the cavity form a succession of concentric levels in diminishing circles as they approach the central depth, and on these levels the successive classes of the impenitent are punished, each lower circle punishing more severely a worse offence. Jerusalem, as the place of the Crucifixion, is the centre of the land hemisphere, in the line of the central axis of Hell. The other hemisphere is all water except for the island-mountain of Purgatory, at the antipodes of Jerusalem. Dante's journey is from the edge of the pit—we are not told where or how he enters it—down to the centre, and then, continuing in the same direction, up the bed of a subterranean stream to the shore of Purgatory.

It should be noted that in Dante's narrative 'here' means this present world, in which he tells his story, and 'there' the world of the dead. In dialogue, of course, this usage is reversed.

THE SYSTEM OF DANTE'S HELL

	Circle		
		Neutrals	
	Circle 1.	Virtuous Heathen	
Incontinent	„ 2.	Lascivious	
	„ 3.	Gluttons	
	„ 4.	Avaricious and Prodigal	
	„ 5.	Wrathful	
	„ 6.	Heretics	
Violent	„ 7.	(1) Violent against others	
		(2) „ „ self	
		(3) „ „ God, nature, and art	
Fraudulent	„ 8.	Simply Fraudulent	(1) Panders and Seducers
			(2) Flatterers
			(3) Simonists
			(4) Diviners
			(5) Barrators
			(6) Hypocrites
			(7) Thieves
			(8) Fraudulent counsellors
			(9) Makers of discord
			(10) Falsifiers
	„ 9.	Treacherous	(1) to kindred
			(2) to country and cause
			(3) to guests
			(4) to lords and benefactors

INFERNO

INFERNO

NEL mezzo del cammin di nostra vita
mi ritrovai per una selva oscura
che la diritta via era smarrita.
Ah quanto a dir qual era è cosa dura
esta selva selvaggia e aspra e forte
che nel pensier rinova la paura!
Tant' è amara che poco è piu morte;
ma per trattar del ben ch'io vi trovai,
dirò dell'altre cose ch'i' v'ho scorte.
Io non so ben ridir com' io v'entrai, 10
tant'era pieno di sonno a quel punto
che la verace via abbandonai.
Ma poi ch' i' fui al piè d'un colle giunto,
là dove terminava quella valle
che m'avea di paura il cor compunto,
guardai in alto, e vidi le sue spalle
vestite già de' raggi del pianeta
che mena dritto altrui per ogni calle.
Allor fu la paura un poco queta
che nel lago del cor m'era durata 20
la notte ch' i' passai con tanta pièta.
E come quei che con lena affannata
uscito fuor del pelago alla riva
si volge all'acqua perigliosa e guata,
così l'animo mio, ch'ancor fuggiva,
si volse a retro a rimirar lo passo
che non lasciò già mai persona viva.

CANTO I

The dark wood; the sunny hill; the three beasts; Virgil

IN the middle of the journey of our life[1] I came to myself within a dark wood where the straight way was lost. Ah, how hard a thing it is to tell of that wood, savage and harsh and dense, the thought of which renews my fear! So bitter is it that death is hardly more. But to give account of the good which I found there I will tell of the other things I noted there.

I cannot rightly tell how I entered there, I was so full of sleep at that moment when I left the true way; but when I had reached the foot of a hill at the end of that valley which had pierced my heart with fear I looked up and saw its shoulders already clothed with the beams of the planet that leads men straight on every road.[2] Then the fear was quieted a little which had continued in the lake of my heart during the night I had spent so piteously; and as he who with labouring breath has escaped from the deep to the shore turns to the perilous waters and gazes, so my mind, which was still in flight, turned back to look again at the pass which never yet let any go alive.

Poi ch'èi posato un poco il corpo lasso,
  ripresi via per la piaggia diserta,
  sì che 'l piè fermo sempre era 'l più basso. 30
Ed ecco, quasi al cominciar dell'erta,
  una lonza leggiera e presta molto,
  che di pel maculato era coverta;
e non mi si partìa d' innanzi al volto,
  anzi impediva tanto il mio cammino,
  ch' i' fui per ritornar più volte volto.
Temp'era dal principio del mattino,
  e 'l sol montava 'n su con quelle stelle
  ch'eran con lui quando l'amor divino
mosse di prima quelle cose belle; 40
  sì ch'a bene sperar m'era cagione
  di quella fera alla gaetta pelle
l'ora del tempo e la dolce stagione;
  ma non sì che paura non mi desse
  la vista che m'apparve d'un leone.
Questi parea che contra me venesse
  con la test'alta e con rabbiosa fame,
  sì che parea che l'aere ne temesse:
ed una lupa, che di tutte brame
  sembiava carca nella sua magrezza, 50
  e molte genti fè già viver grame.
Questa mi porse tanto di gravezza
  con la paura ch'uscìa di sua vista,
  ch' io perdei la speranza dell'altezza.
E qual è quei che volontieri acquista,
  e giugne 'l tempo che perder lo face,
  che 'n tutt' i suoi pensier piange e s'attrista;
tal mi fece la bestia sanza pace,
  che, venendomi incontro, a poco a poco
  mi ripigneva là dove 'l sol tace. 60
Mentre ch' i' ruvinava in basso loco,
  dinanzi alli occhi mi si fu offerto
  chi per lungo silenzio parea fioco.
Quando vidi costui nel gran diserto,
  'Miserere di me' gridai a lui
  'qual che tu sii, od ombra od omo certo!'

CANTO I

After I had rested my wearied frame for a little I took my way again over the desert slope, keeping always the lower foot firm; and lo, almost at the beginning of the steep, a leopard light and very swift, covered with a spotted hide, and it did not go from before my face but so impeded my way that I turned many times to go back.

The time was the beginning of the morning and the sun was mounting with those stars which were with it when Divine Love first set in motion those fair things,[3] so that the hour of the day and the sweet season moved me to good hope of escape from that beast with the gay skin; but, even so, I was put in fear by the sight of a lion which appeared to me and seemed to be coming against me holding its head high and furious with hunger so that the air seemed in dread of it, and of a she-wolf which appeared in its leanness to be charged with all cravings and which has already made many live in wretchedness. This last put such heaviness on me by the terror which came forth from its looks that I lost hope of the ascent; and like one who rejoices in his gains and when the time comes that makes him a loser has all his thoughts turned to sadness and lamentation, such did the restless beast make me, coming against me and driving me back step by step to where the sun is silent.

When I was rushing down to the place below there appeared before my eyes one whose voice seemed weak from long silence, and when I saw him in the great waste, 'Have pity on me, whoever thou art,' I cried to him 'shade or real man!'

Rispuosemi: 'Non omo, omo già fui,
e li parenti miei furon lombardi,
mantovani per patrïa ambedui.
Nacqui *sub Julio*, ancor che fosse tardi, 70
e vissi a Roma sotto 'l buono Augusto
al tempo delli dei falsi e bugiardi.
Poeta fui, e cantai di quel giusto
figliuol d'Anchise che venne da Troia,
poi che 'l superbo Iliòn fu combusto.
Ma tu, perchè ritorni a tanta noia?
perchè non sali il dilettoso monte
ch' è principio e cagion di tutta gioia?'
'Or se' tu quel Virgilio e quella fonte
che spandi di parlar sì largo fiume?' 80
rispuos' io lui con vergognosa fronte.
'O delli altri poeti onore e lume,
vagliami 'l lungo studio e 'l grande amore
che m' ha fatto cercar lo tuo volume.
Tu se' lo mio maestro e 'l mio autore;
tu se' solo colui da cu' io tolsi
lo bello stilo che m' ha fatto onore.
Vedi la bestia per cu' io mi volsi:
aiutami da lei, famoso saggio,
ch'ella mi fa tremar le vene e i polsi.' 90
'A te convien tenere altro vïaggio'
rispuose poi che lagrimar mi vide
'se vuo' campar d'esto loco selvaggio:
chè questa bestia, per la qual tu gride,
non lascia altrui passar per la sua via,
ma tanto lo 'mpedisce che l'uccide;
e ha natura sì malvagia e ria,
che mai non empie la bramosa voglia,
e dopo 'l pasto ha più fame che pria.
Molti son li animali a cui s'ammoglia, 100
e più saranno ancora, infin che 'l Veltro
verrà, che la farà morir con doglia.
Questi non ciberà terra nè peltro,
ma sapïenza, amore e virtute,
e sua nazion sarà tra Feltro e Feltro.

He answered me: 'Not man; once I was man, and my parents were Lombards, both Mantuan by birth. I was born *sub Julio*,[4] though late in his time, and I lived at Rome under the good Augustus, in the time of the false and lying gods. I was a poet and sang of that just son of Anchises[5] who came from Troy after proud Ilium[6] was burned. But thou, why art thou returning to such misery? Why dost thou not climb the delectable mountain which is the beginning and cause of all happiness?'

'Art thou then that Virgil, that fountain which pours forth so rich a stream of speech?' I answered him, my brow covered with shame. 'O glory and light of other poets, let the long study and the great love that has made me search thy volume avail me. Thou art my master and my author. Thou art he from whom alone I took the style whose beauty has brought me honour. See the beast for which I turned; save me from her, famous sage, for she sets the pulses trembling in my veins.'

'Thou must take another road' he replied when he saw me weeping 'if thou wouldst escape from this savage place; for this beast on account of which thou criest lets no man pass her way, but hinders them till she takes their life, and she has a nature so vicious and malignant that her greedy appetite is never satisfied and after food she is hungrier than before. Many are the creatures with which she mates and there will yet be more, until the hound comes that shall bring her to miserable death.[7] He shall not feed on land or pelf but on wisdom and love and valour, and his country shall

Di quella umile Italia fia salute
  per cui morì la vergine Cammilla,
  Eurialo e Turno e Niso di ferute.
Questi la caccerà per ogni villa,
  fin che l'avrà rimessa nello 'nferno, 110
  là onde invidia prima dipartilla.
Ond' io per lo tuo me' penso e discerno
  che tu mi segui, e io sarò tua guida,
  e trarrotti di qui per luogo etterno,
ove udirai le disperate strida,
  vedrai li antichi spiriti dolenti,
  che la seconda morte ciascun grida;
e vederai color che son contenti
  nel foco, perchè speran di venire
  quando che sia alle beate genti. 120
Alle qua' poi se tu vorrai salire,
  anima fia a ciò piu di me degna;
  con lei ti lascerò nel mio partire:
chè quello imperador che là su regna,
  perch' io fu' ribellante alla sua legge,
  non vuol che 'n sua città per me si vegna.
In tutte parti impera e quivi regge;
  quivi è la sua città e l'alto seggio:
  oh felice colui cu' ivi elegge!'
E io a lui: 'Poeta, io ti richeggio 130
  per quello Dio che tu non conoscesti,
  acciò ch' io fugga questo male e peggio,
che tu mi meni là dove or dicesti,
  sì ch' io veggia la porta di san Pietro
  e color cui tu fai cotanto mesti.'
Allor si mosse, e io li tenni retro.

1. Dante's 35th year, A.D. 1300. 'The days of our years are three score years and ten' (*Ps.* xc. 10).
2. The sun, the symbol of God.
3. Creation was supposed to have taken place and the stars to have been 'set in motion' in spring, when the sun was in the Ram, on the same date as the Incarnation and the Crucifixion. It was the morning of Good Friday.

> 'Of all things the beginning
> Was on an April morn;
> In spring the earth remembereth
> The day that she was born.'
> (From a medieval song translated by Helen Waddell)

be between Feltro and Feltro;[8] he shall be salvation to that low-lying Italy for which the virgin Camilla and Euryalus and Turnus and Nisus died of their wounds;[9] he shall hunt her through every city till he has sent her back to Hell whence envy first let her loose.[10] Therefore, considering what is best for thee, I judge that thou shouldst follow me, and I shall be thy guide and lead thee hence through an eternal place where thou shalt hear the despairing shrieks of the ancient spirits in pain who each bewail the second death.[11] Then thou shalt see those who are contented in the fire[12] because they hope to come, whensoever it may be, to the tribes of the blest, to whom if thou wouldst then ascend there shall be a spirit fitter for that than I; with her I shall leave thee at my parting. For the Emperor who holds sway there above wills not, because I was a rebel to His law, that I come into His city. In every part He reigns and there He rules. There is His city and His lofty seat. O happy the man He chooses to be there!'

And I answered him: 'Poet, I entreat thee by that God whom thou knewest not, in order that I may escape this evil and worse lead me where thou hast said, that I may see Saint Peter's gate[13] and those thou makest so sorrowful.'

Then he set out and I came on behind him.

4. Under Julius Caesar; Virgil was born in 70 B.C.
5. Aeneas.
6. The citadel of Troy.
7. Probably Can Grande della Scala, afterwards Lord of Verona.
8. Probably Verona, between the towns of Feltro and Montefeltro.
9. Four who fell in the Trojan-Latin War.
10. 'Through envy of the devil came death into the world' (*Wisd.* ii. 24).
11. 'The lake which burneth with fire and brimstone; which is the second death' (*Rev.* xxi. 8).
12. The pains of Purgatory.
13. The gate of penitence admitting to Purgatory proper.

NOTE

The directness, speed, and energy of the narrative in the opening canto are eminently characteristic of Dante and seize and hold us from the first words. We are at once in the midst of things and follow the quick succession of his moods—distress, bewilderment, relief, fear, astonishment, confidence,—a tumult of experience marking a crisis in the soul, an end and a beginning. 'It was characteristic of Dante's thought—rather of medieval thought in general—to proceed from the reality to the symbolical meaning, and not to sing in his lines of simple abstractions' (*F. Pellegrini, L.D.*), and it is as impossible to ignore the autobiographical elements in the *Divine Comedy* as it is easy to overstress them. Dante in the poem is at once Dante Alighieri of Florence and Everyman, reporting at once his own inner experience and the way of man's salvation. When he dates his story expressly from 'the middle of the journey of our life' we must recall his leading place during part of the year 1300 in the civic life of Florence, the outbreak there of civil strife, and eighteen months later his exile, which broke his life in two. In Dante, being such as we come to know him, these events were the setting and the occasion of a moral turmoil, a losing and finding of himself, which is pictured in the dark wood, the sunny hill, the threatening beasts, and Virgil's summons.

The first step in Dante's salvation was his discovery that he was lost, when he came to himself in a dark wood. He recovered so far as to realize the condition of sin and ignorance into which he had fallen as if in his sleep, by lethargy and acquiescence. His attempt to climb the hill with the morning sunshine on it represents his hopeful aspirations after a better way of life, possibly in the serene consolations of philosophy, possibly in an honourable and successful earthly career, for the symbolism of the sunny hill is one of the debated problems of this canto.

Perhaps it may be taken for the pagan conception of the earthly life. It is, at any rate, his attempt to escape from evil by reforming his way, the good which he would but does not, because of 'another law in his members, warring against the law of his mind, and bringing him into captivity'.

He is foiled by three beasts, by the main forces of evil in the world,—the leopard, or lust, the lion, or pride, and the wolf, or covetousness. They were doubtless suggested by the same three beasts in *Jer.* v. 6, and the ideas correspond with those in 1 *John* ii. 16,—'all that is in the world, the lust of the flesh, and the lust of the eyes, and the pride of life'. These forces of evil are not conceived merely as personal to Dante himself, but also, if not chiefly, as forces in the world about him, but pressing in on him and claiming the mastery of him. In his poem he confesses both to lust and pride, and though he would have repudiated the charge of covetousness it was on that charge—specifically the charge of corruption in public office—that he was banished from Florence.

If there is ambiguity and perplexity in the imagery here it is because Dante is recalling at once his outer and inner experience, both his term of high office in the government of Florence in 1300, when the forces were gathering which were soon to defeat all his personal hopes and to drive him into exile, on the one hand, and, on the other, the turmoil and bewilderment belonging, in such a soul as his, to spiritual conversion. For Dante it was one experience and the conflict and confusion of motives are an essential part of it.

In the moment, it seemed, of his final defeat he was confronted with Virgil, historically his ideal poet, the model and inspiration of his verse, and symbolically his reason and conscience, the primal authority for man's earthly life. Virgil's 'voice seemed weak from long silence', for both the world and Dante himself had long given little hearing or heed to the voice of the higher reason and it seemed at first as if reason could hardly get utterance at all either in the world or in Dante's own soul. His re-discovery to the world of Virgil's poetic greatness is wholly in accord with this representation of him.

It is Virgil, at once the prophet of the Roman Empire and the supposed foreteller of Christ, who foretells the coming of a deliverer of the world from the power of covetousness, the wolf that came so persistently against Dante. The identity of 'the hound' that is to hunt the wolf to Hell has been the subject of much debate and many guesses, but Can Grande—the name means Great Dog—is the commonest interpretation. He was a boy of nine at the assumed date of the poem—perhaps ten years older when this was written—and later the chief representative in Italy of the Imperial cause, that is, for Dante, the cause of all social order and civic righteousness. In his exile Dante found a home in Can Grande's court at Verona for a time and he held him always in the highest honour and dedicated the *Paradiso* to him. He appears to have hoped that Can Grande would effectively establish the Imperial authority in Italy and deliver the country from the fierce party strife which was rending the life of the cities and especially from the greed and worldliness of the Papacy. The passage is an instance, thoroughly characteristic, of the crossing and mingling in Dante's story of the personal and the public spiritual interest; for him they were essentially one. It is also one of various utterances, all intentionally cryptic, in the course of the poem of his undying hope for the advent of a heroic deliverer of the world from the present powers of evil.

But as things are, and as Dante is, there is no deliverance for himself by the mere study of philosophy or by the way of an honourable and successful public career; he 'must take another road' and there must be shown to him by Virgil 'the eternal roots of misery and of joy' (*J. A. Carlyle*). Virgil is to be his guide through Hell and Purgatory, which are, so to speak, within the range of reason, and for Paradise there will be the higher guidance of Beatrice. Nothing else will serve to liberate him wholly from the forces of evil about him and from the fear of them but to see their final issues, what ultimately they mean for the human soul. And for that understanding he must follow where his reason will lead him; that inner obedience is the first condition of his salvation.

There is a curious example of Dante's fondness for verbal device in the 'there—there—there' at the beginning of the canto, in reference to the dark wood, and again at the end 'there—there—there', with the Italian adverb in its fuller, more emphatic form, in reference to the divine city which is his goal. The end of the journey is set before him by Virgil at the very beginning.

These are some of the leading ideas of the canto; but, like all the other cantos, it is greater than its ideas. It is the passionately imagined record of a great experience.

It is usual to regard this canto rather as an introduction to the whole poem than as a part of the *Inferno* proper, a reckoning which suits the studied symmetry of the *Comedy*, making thirty-three cantos in each of its three parts and completing the whole in a hundred.

INFERNO

Lo giorno se n'andava, e l'aere bruno
toglieva li animai che sono in terra
dalle fatiche loro; e io sol uno
m'apparecchiava a sostener la guerra
sì del cammino e sì della pietate,
che ritrarrà la mente che non erra.
O Muse, o alto ingegno, or m'aiutate;
o mente che scrivesti ciò ch' io vidi,
qui si parrà la tua nobilitate.
Io cominciai: 'Poeta che mi guidi, 10
guarda la mia virtù s'ell' è possente,
prima ch'all'alto passo tu mi fidi.
Tu dici che di Silvïo il parente,
corruttibile ancora, ad immortale
secolo andò, e fu sensibilmente.
Però, se l'avversario d'ogni male
cortese i fu, pensando l'alto effetto
ch'uscir dovea di lui e 'l chi e 'l quale.
non pare indegno ad omo d' intelletto;
ch'e' fu dell'alma Roma e di suo impero 20
nell'empireo ciel per padre eletto:
la quale e 'l quale, a voler dir lo vero,
fu stabilita per lo loco santo
u' siede il successor del maggior Piero.
Per questa andata onde li dai tu vanto,
intese cose che furon cagione
di sua vittoria e del papale ammanto.

CANTO II

Discouragement; Virgil and Beatrice; the start

THE day was departing and the darkened air releasing the creatures on the earth from their labours, and I, alone, was preparing to endure the conflict both of the way and of the pity of it, which memory that does not err shall recount. O Muses, O lofty genius, aid me now! O memory that noted what I saw, here shall be shown thy worth!

I began: 'Poet, who guidest me, consider my strength, if it is sufficient, before thou commit me to the hard passage. Thou tellest of the father of Sylvius that he went, still subject to corruption, tc the eternal world and was there in the flesh.[1] Bu if the Adversary of all evil showed him this favour, taking account of the high consequence and who and what he was that should spring from him,[2] it does not seem unfitting to one that understands; for in the heaven of the Empyrean[3] he was chosen to be father of glorious Rome and of her Empire, and both of these were established—if we would speak rightly of them—to be the holy place where sits the successor of the great Peter. By this journey for which thou honourest him he heard things which fitted him for his victory and prepared for

Andovvi poi lo Vas d'elezïone,
per recarne conforto a quella fede
ch' è principio alla via di salvazione. 30
Ma io perchè venirvi? o chi 'l concede?
Io non Enëa, io non Paulo sono:
me degno a ciò nè io nè altri crede.
Per che, se del venire io m'abbandono,
temo che la venuta non sia folle:
se' savio; intendi me' ch' i' non ragiono.'
E qual è quei che disvuol ciò che volle
e per novi pensier cangia proposta,
sì che dal cominciar tutto si tolle,
tal mi fec' io in quella oscura costa, 40
perchè, pensando, consumai la 'mpresa
che fu nel cominciar cotanto tosta.
'S' i' ho ben la parola tua intesa'
rispuose del magnanimo quell'ombra
'l'anima tua è da viltate offesa;
la qual molte fïate l'omo ingombra
sì che d'onrata impresa lo rivolve,
come falso veder bestia quand'ombra.
Da questa tema acciò che tu ti solve,
dirotti perch' io venni e quel ch' io 'ntesi 50
nel primo punto che di te mi dolve.
Io era tra color che son sospesi,
e donna mi chiamò beata e bella,
tal che di comandare io la richiesi.
Lucevan li occhi suoi più che la stella;
e cominciommi a dir soave e piana,
con angelica voce, in sua favella:
"O anima cortese mantovana,
di cui la fama ancor nel mondo dura,
e durerà quanto 'l mondo lontana, 60
l'amico mio, e non della ventura,
nella diserta piaggia è impedito
sì nel cammin, che volt' è per paura;
e temo che non sia già sì smarrito,
ch' io mi sia tardi al soccorso levata,
per quel ch' i' ho di lui nel cielo udito.

the Papal mantle.[4] Later, the Chosen Vessel went there,[5] that he might bring thence confirmation of that faith which is the beginning of the way of salvation.

'But I, why should I go there, and who grants it? I am not Aeneas; I am not Paul. Neither I nor any man thinks me fit for this, so that if I commit myself to go I fear lest my going be folly. Thou art wise; thou understandest better than I speak.'

And as one who unwills what he willed and with new thoughts changes his purpose so that he quite withdraws from what he has begun, such I became on that dark slope; for by thinking of it I brought to naught the enterprise that was so hasty in its beginning.

'If I have rightly understood thy words,' replied the shade of that great soul 'thy spirit is smitten with cowardice, which many a time encumbers a man so that it turns him back from honourable enterprise, as a mistaken sight a shying beast. That I may deliver thee from this fear, I shall tell thee why I came and what I heard at the time when I first took pity on thee. I was among those who are in suspense,[6] and a lady called me, so blessed and so fair that I begged her to command me. Her eyes shone brighter than the stars, and she began to speak to me with angelic voice in sweet, low tones: "O courteous Mantuan soul, whose fame still endures in the world and shall endure as long as the world lasts, my friend, who is no friend of fortune, is so hindered on his way on the desert slope that he has turned back for fear, and from what I have heard of him in Heaven I fear he may already be so far astray that I have risen too late

Or movi, e con la tua parola ornata
e con ciò c' ha mestieri al suo campare
l'aiuta, sì ch' i' ne sia consolata.
I' son Beatrice che ti faccio andare; 70
vegno del loco ove tornar disio;
amor mi mosse, che mi fa parlare.
Quando savò dinanzi al signor mio,
di te mi loderò sovente a lui."
Tacette allora, e poi comincia' io:
"O donna di virtù, sola per cui
l'umana spezie eccede ogni contento
di quel ciel c' ha minor li cerchi sui,
tanto m'aggrada il tuo comandamento,
che l'ubidir, se già fosse, m' è tardi; 80
più non t' è uo' ch'aprirmi il tuo talento.
Ma dimmi la cagion che non ti guardi
dello scender qua giuso in questo centro
dell'ampio loco ove tornar tu ardi."
"Da che tu vuo' saper cotanto a dentro,
dirotti brievemente" mi rispose
"perch' io non temo di venir qua entro.
Temer si dee di sole quelle cose
c' hanno potenza di fare altrui male;
dell'altre no, chè non son paurose. 90
Io son fatta da Dio, sua mercè, tale
che la vostra miseria non mi tange,
nè fiamma d'esto incendio non m'assale.
Donna è gentil nel ciel che si compiange
di questo impedimento ov' io ti mando,
sì che duro giudicio là su frange.
Questa chiese Lucia in suo dimando
e disse: 'Or ha bisogno il tuo fedele
di te, ed io a te lo raccomando.'
Lucia, nimica di ciascun crudele, 100
si mosse, e venne al loco dov' i' era,
che mi sedea con l'antica Rachele.
Disse: 'Beatrice, loda di Dio vera,
chè non soccorri quei che t'amò tanto
ch'uscì per te della volgare schiera?

to succour him. Haste then, and with the beauty of thy speech and whatever is needful for his deliverance give him such help that I shall be comforted. I am Beatrice who bid thee go. I come from the place where I desire to return. Love moved me and makes me speak. When I am before my Lord I will often speak to Him in praise of thee."

'Then she was silent, and I began: "O lady of virtue, through whom alone the human kind surpasses everything within the smallest circle of the heavens,[7] so grateful to me is thy command that my obedience, were it given already, is late; there is no need for more than to declare thy will to me. But tell me the reason why thou dost not shrink from descending into this central depth from the spacious place where thou burnest to return."

' "Since thou wouldst know so deeply," she answered me "I shall tell thee shortly why I do not fear to enter here. Only those things should be feared that have power to do us ill, nothing else, for nothing else is fearful, and I am made such by God of His grace that your misery does not touch me nor a flame of the fires here assail me. There is a gentle lady in Heaven who is so moved with pity of that hindrance for which I send thee that she breaks the stern judgement there on high;[8] she called Lucy[9] and gave her her behest: 'Thy faithful one is now in need of thee and I commend him to thee.' Lucy, enemy of all cruelty, rose and came to the place where I was seated beside the ancient Rachel and said: 'Beatrice, true praise of God, why dost thou not succour him who so loved thee that for thy sake he left the vulgar herd? Hearest thou

non odi tu la pièta del suo pianto?
non vedi tu la morte che 'l combatte
su la fiumana ove 'l mar non ha vanto?'
Al mondo non fur mai persone ratte
a far lor pro o a fuggir lor danno, 110
com' io, dopo cotai parole fatte,
venni qua giù del mio beato scanno,
fidandomi nel tuo parlare onesto,
ch'onora te e quei ch'udito l' hanno."
Poscia che m'ebbe ragionato questo,
li occhi lucenti lacrimando volse,
per che mi fece del venir più presto
e venni a te così com'ella volse;
d' innanzi a quella fiera ti levai
che del bel monte il corto andar ti tolse. 120
Dunque che è? perchè, perchè restai?
perchè tanta viltà nel cuore allette?
perchè ardire e franchezza non hai?
poscia che tai tre donne benedette
curan di te ne la corte del cielo,
'l mio parlar tanto ben t' impromette?'
Quali i fioretti, dal notturno gelo
chinati e chiusi, poi che 'l sol li 'mbianca
si drizzan tutti aperti in loro stelo,
tal mi fec' io di mia virtute stanca, 130
e tanto buono ardire al cor mi corse,
ch' i' cominciai come persona franca:
'Oh pietosa colei che mi soccorse!
e te cortese ch'ubidisti tosto
alle vere parole che ti porse!
Tu m' hai con disiderio il cor disposto
sì al venir con le parole tue,
ch' i' son tornato nel primo proposto.
Or va, ch'un sol volere è d'ambedue:
tu duca, tu segnore, e tu maestro.' 140
Così li dissi; e poi che mosso fue,
intrai per lo cammino alto e silvestro.

not his pitiful weeping? Seest thou not the death which combats him on the flood that is not less terrible than the sea?' Never were men on earth so swift to seek their good or to escape their hurt as I, after these words were spoken, to descend here from my blessed seat, trusting to thy noble speech which honours thyself and them that have heard it."

'When she had talked with me thus she turned away, with tears, her shining eyes; which made me haste the more to come, and so I came to thee as she wished. I delivered thee from that beast which deprived thee of the short way to the beautiful mountain. What then? Why, why dost thou delay? Why harbourest such cowardice in thy heart? Why art thou not bold and free, when three such blessed ladies care for thee in the court of Heaven and my words promise thee so much good?'

As little flowers, bent down and closed with the chill of night, when the sun brightens them stand all open on their stems, such I became with my failing strength, and so much good courage ran into my heart that I began as one set free: 'O she compassionate that succoured me, and thou who of thy courtesy wast quick to obey the true words she spoke to thee! Thou hast so disposed my heart with desire for the journey by thy words that I have returned to my first intent. Now go, for but one will is in us both, thou leader, thou lord and master.'

Thus I spoke to him, and when he set out I entered on the deep and savage way.

INFERNO

1. Aeneas's visit to the dead (*Aeneid* vi).
2. Aeneas, ancestor of the Emperors.
3. The highest of the heavens, the immediate presence of God.
4. The founding of Rome prepared for the Papacy.
5. St Paul. 'He is a chosen vessel unto me' (*Acts* ix. 15). 'He was caught up into paradise, and heard unspeakable words, which it is not lawful for a man to utter' (2 *Cor.* xii. 4).
6. The virtuous heathen in Limbo (Canto iv), suspended, as it were, between torment and bliss.
7. Within the circuit of the moon.
8. The Virgin, through whom 'mercy rejoiceth against judgment' (*Jas.* ii. 13).
9. St Lucy of Syracuse, 3rd century martyr.

NOTE

Dante spent the night before Good Friday in the dark wood; he attempted the sunny hill on Good Friday morning and in the course of the day was driven back by the three beasts; it was only on the evening of Good Friday, after his talk with Virgil, that he was ready to start on the great journey, the first part of which is to end on Easter morning,—for so we learn from a later canto to date his story. The whole story of the *Inferno* passes, so to speak, in the time between the Crucifixion and the Resurrection. It was during these days and nights of sin's apparent victory—when Christ Himself, in the language of the creed, 'descended into Hell'—that Dante was led to search out sin and to know the worst of it; and the canto begins with the solemn and testing isolation of his soul when darkness fell and 'he, alone, was preparing to endure the conflict' of the way.

Before setting out Dante puts himself expressly, critically, into comparison with Aeneas and Paul, with the representatives, that is to say, of the Empire and the Church, who have their high historical place in relation to the divine counsel and the eternal world of spiritual things. For him, a mere man among men, only a baffled human soul, 'why should he go there, and who grants it?' What was his warrant? Only the grace and the calling of God. For all the great place given to Church and Empire and their institutions in human order and fellowship and intercession, the essential and primary operations of grace are always, for Dante, unofficial, inward, personal, in principle prior and superior to all institutions.

And yet, along with that personal humbleness, there is in Dante—and it is an essential factor in the *Divine Comedy*—the pride of a great calling. 'Three blessed ladies care for him in the court of heaven, protecting him in the fearful enterprise which the wise leader holds to be necessary for his deliverance. The poet thus places himself third alongside of the father of the Roman line and the convert of Tarsus. A representation of cowardice is resolved into an affirmation of great-hearted pride; it is the first instance of the heroic poetry of that moral and civil apostolate which is the *Divine Comedy*' (*V. Rossi*).

The linking together of the names of Aeneas and St Paul is the first of many instances in the poem of Dante's practice of balancing examples from Scripture with others from classical paganism, scriptural and pagan history being taken as complementary elements of divine providence. As the mystic journey of Aeneas prepared for the Empire and thus for the Papacy, so Paul's made plainer the way of salvation for men, and together they served one end.

A small instance of Dante's habitual relevancy to the matter in hand in his language is his naming of Aeneas 'the son of Anchises' in the first canto, when the reference is back to Troy, and here 'the father of Sylvius', when it is forward to the royal line and Rome.

When Dante shrank from the journey Virgil's rebuke was not sufficient to change him. It needed a deeper appeal and assurance than that of reason itself to make him obedient to reason, and Virgil had to show Dante a warrant higher than his own, that he had been sent by her who was for Dante the embodied revelation of the truth of God, her 'through whom alone the human kind surpasses everything within the smallest circle of the heavens'. Reason or conscience—the two are one in Virgil—is but the messenger and the vicegerent of revelation and only in so far as it is that, and more than a mere private prompting, has it authority.

Beatrice, the personal embodiment of heavenly truth, is in a sense the representative of the ideal Church, as Virgil of the ideal world-Empire, so that her prompting of Virgil here for Dante's deliverance suggests that co-operation of Church and Empire to which Dante looked for all human well-being. It is at the bidding, so to speak, of the true Church and Empire that he sets out on his pilgrimage.

To Virgil it was a wonder that Beatrice should come so low as Limbo for Dante's help, for such reasons as moved Beatrice are strange to natural reason and even Beatrice gave a reason that was beyond herself. The Virgin was the fount of grace, and grace works by reasons which are in itself, not waiting for the desert or the petition of the soul; that is grace by definition. St Lucy seems to have been in some sense Dante's patron saint, perhaps as the saint of enlightenment (*luce*, light), helpful to one troubled with his eyes. At any rate this spirit of enlightenment is the medium between grace and revelation; Lucy brings the message of the Virgin to Beatrice. The symbolism of the 'three blessed ladies' is in itself arid and formal, but the late Professor Rossi rightly noted 'the serenity and sweet intimacy of all this scene in Paradise'. That fragrant breath, as if from the pages of the *Vita Nuova*, brings to Dante the sense of a precedent grace which takes and keeps the initiative with him, the assurance of a love beyond reason, all that was meant for him by the revived memory of Beatrice, and it renews his purpose and makes him obedient to his reason and ready now to follow Virgil, 'leader, lord, and master', through the gates of Hell.

3 ladies:
Virgin ?
Beatrice
St. Lucy

INFERNO

PER ME SI VA NELLA CITTÀ DOLENTE,
PER ME SI VA NELL' ETTERNO DOLORE,
PER ME SI VA TRA LA PERDUTA GENTE.
GIUSTIZIA MOSSE IL MIO ALTO FATTORE:
FECEMI LA DIVINA POTESTATE,
LA SOMMA SAPÏENZA E 'L PRIMO AMORE.
DINANZI A ME NON FUOR COSE CREATE
SE NON ETTERNE, E IO ETTERNA DURO.
LASCIATE OGNI SPERANZA, VOI CH' ENTRATE.
Queste parole di colore oscuro 10
vid' ïo scritte al sommo d'una porta;
per ch' io: 'Maestro, il senso lor m' è duro.'
Ed elli a me, come persona accorta:
'Qui si convien lasciare ogni sospetto;
ogni viltà convien che qui sia morta.
Noi siam venuti al loco ov' io t' ho detto
che tu vedrai le genti dolorose
c' hanno perduto il ben dell' intelletto.'
E poi che la sua mano alla mia pose
con lieto volto, ond' io mi confortai, 20
mi mise dentro alle segrete cose.
Quivi sospiri, pianti e alti guai
risonavan per l'aere sanza stelle,
per ch' io al cominciar ne lagrimai.
Diverse lingue, orribili favelle,
parole di dolore, accenti d' ira,
voci alte e fioche, e suon di man con elle

CANTO III

The gate of Hell; the Neutrals; the Acheron; Charon

THROUGH ME THE WAY INTO THE WOEFUL CITY,
THROUGH ME THE WAY TO THE ETERNAL PAIN,
THROUGH ME THE WAY AMONG THE LOST PEOPLE.
JUSTICE MOVED MY MAKER ON HIGH,
DIVINE POWER MADE ME AND SUPREME WISDOM
AND PRIMAL LOVE;
BEFORE ME NOTHING WAS CREATED BUT ETERNAL
THINGS[1] AND I ENDURE ETERNALLY.
ABANDON EVERY HOPE, YE THAT ENTER.

These words I saw inscribed in dark characters over a gateway; therefore I said: 'Master, their sense is dreadful to me.'

And he said to me, like one experienced: 'Here must all distrust be left behind, here must all cowardice be ended; we are come to the place where I told thee thou shouldst see the woeful people who have lost the good of the intellect.'[2] And when he had laid his hand on mine with cheerful looks that gave me comfort, he led me in to the things that are hidden there.

There sighs, lamentations and loud wailings resounded through the starless air, so that at first it made me weep; strange tongues, horrible language, words of pain, tones of anger, voices loud and hoarse, and with these the sound of hands,

facevano un tumulto, il qual s'aggira
 sempre in quell'aura sanza tempo tinta,
 come la rena quando turbo spira. 30
E io, ch'avea d'orror la testa cinta,
 dissi: 'Maestro, che è quel ch' i' odo?
 e che gent' è che par nel duol sì vinta?'
Ed elli a me: 'Questo misero modo
 tengon l'anime triste di coloro
 che visser sanza infamia e sanza lodo.
Mischiate sono a quel cattivo coro
 delli angeli che non furon ribelli
 nè fur fedeli a Dio, ma per sè foro.
Caccianli i ciel per non esser men belli, 40
 nè lo profondo inferno li riceve,
 ch'alcuna gloria i rei avrebber d'elli.'
E io: 'Maestro, che è tanto greve
 a lor, che lamentar li fa sì forte?'
 Rispuose: 'Dicerolti molto breve.
Questi non hanno speranza di morte,
 e la lor cieca vita è tanto bassa,
 che 'nvidïosi son d'ogni altra sorte.
Fama di loro il mondo esser non lassa;
 misericordia e giustizia li sdegna: 50
 non ragioniam di lor, ma guarda e passa.'
E io, che riguardai, vidi una insegna
 che girando correva tanto ratta,
 che d'ogni posa mi parea indegna;
e dietro le venìa sì lunga tratta
 di gente, ch' io non averei creduto
 che morte tanta n'avesse disfatta.
Poscia ch' io v'ebbi alcun riconosciuto,
 vidi e conobbi l'ombra di colui
 che fece per viltà il gran rifiuto. 60
Incontanente intesi e certo fui
 che questa era la setta de' cattivi
 a Dio spiacenti ed a' nemici sui.
Questi sciaurati, che mai non fur vivi,
 erano ignudi, stimolati molto
 da mosconi e da vespe ch'eran ivi.

made a tumult which is whirling always through that air forever dark, as sand eddies in a whirlwind.

And I, my head encircled with horror, said: 'Master, what is this I hear, and who are these people who seem so mastered by their pain?'

And he said to me: 'This miserable state is borne by the wretched souls of those who lived without disgrace and without praise. They are mixed with that caitiff choir of the angels who were not rebels, nor faithful to God, but were for themselves. The heavens drove them forth, not to be less fair, and the depth of Hell does not receive them lest the wicked have some glory over them.'[3]

And I said: 'Master, what is it that is so grievous to them, making them lament so sorely?'

He replied: 'I will tell thee in few words. They have no hope of death, and so abject is their blind life that they are envious of every other lot. The world suffers no report of them to live. Pity and justice despise them. Let us not talk of them; but look thou and pass.'

And I looked and saw a whirling banner which ran so fast that it seemed as if it could never make a stand, and behind it came so long a train of people that I should never have believed death had undone so many. After I had recognized some of them I saw and knew the shade of him who from cowardice made the great refusal,[4] and at once and with certainty I perceived that this was the worthless crew that is hateful to God and to His enemies. Those wretches, who never were alive,[5] were naked and sorely stung by hornets and wasps that were

Elle rigavan lor di sangue il volto,
  che, mischiato di lagrime, ai lor piedi
  da fastidiosi vermi era ricolto.
E poi ch'a riguardare oltre mi diedi, 70
  vidi genti alla riva d'un gran fiume;
  per ch' io dissi: 'Maestro, or mi concedi
ch' i' sappia quali sono, e qual costume
  le fa di trapassar parer sì pronte,
  com' io discerno per lo fioco lume.'
Ed elli a me: 'Le cose ti fier conte
  quando noi fermerem li nostri passi
  su la trista riviera d'Acheronte.'
Allor con li occhi vergognosi e bassi,
  temendo no 'l mio dir li fosse grave, 80
  infino al fiume del parlar mi trassi.
Ed ecco verso noi venir per nave
  un vecchio, bianco per antico pelo,
  gridando: 'Guai a voi, anime prave!
Non isperate mai veder lo cielo:
  i' vegno per menarvi all'altra riva,
  nelle tenebre etterne, in caldo e 'n gelo.
E tu che se' costì, anima viva,
  pàrtiti da cotesti che son morti.'
  Ma poi che vide ch' io non mi partiva, 90
disse: 'Per altra via, per altri porti
  verrai a piaggia, non qui, per passare:
  più lieve legno convien che ti porti.'
E 'l duca lui: 'Caron, non ti crucciare:
  vuolsi così colà dove si puote
  ciò che si vuole, e piu non dimandare.'
Quinci fuor quete le lanose gote
  al nocchier della livida palude,
  che 'ntorno alli occhi avea di fiamme rote.
Ma quell'anime, ch'eran lasse e nude, 100
  cangiar colore e dibattìeno i denti,
  ratto che 'nteser le parole crude:
bestemmiavano Dio e lor parenti,
  l'umana spezie e 'l luogo e 'l tempo e 'l seme
  di lor semenza e di lor nascimenti.

there; these made their faces stream with blood, which mingled with their tears and was gathered at their feet by loathsome worms.

And then, directing my sight farther on, I saw people on the bank of a great river, so that I said: 'Master, now grant me to know who they are and what law makes them so eager for the crossing as they seem by what I discern through the dim light.'

And he said to me: 'These things will be plain to thee when we stay our steps on the sad shore of Acheron.'[6]

Then, my eyes bent down with shame, fearing lest my words had displeased him, I kept from speaking till we reached the river. And lo, coming towards us in a boat, an old man, his hair white with age, crying: 'Woe to you, wicked souls, hope not ever to see the sky. I come to bring you to the other bank, into the eternal shades, into fire and frost; and thou there that art a living soul, take thyself apart from these that are dead.'

But when he saw that I did not go, he said: 'By another way, by other ports, not here, thou shalt come to the shore and pass. A lighter vessel must carry thee.'[7]

And my Leader: 'Charon, do not torment thyself. It is so willed where will and power are one, and ask no more.'

On that the shaggy jaws of the pilot of the livid marsh, about whose eyes were wheels of flame, were quiet. But those souls, which were weary and naked, changed colour and gnashed their teeth as soon as they heard his cruel words; they blasphemed God and their parents, the human kind, the place, the time, and the seed of their begetting and of

Poi si raccolser tutte quante inseme,
forte piangendo, alla riva malvagia
ch'attende ciascun uom che Dio non teme.
Caron dimonio, con occhi di bragia,
loro accennando, tutti li raccoglie; 110
batte col remo qualunque s'adagia.
Come d'autunno si levan le foglie
l'una appresso dell'altra, fin che 'l ramo
vede alla terra tutte le sue spoglie,
similemente il mal seme d'Adamo
gittansi di quel lito ad una ad una,
per cenni come augel per suo richiamo.
Così sen vanno su per l'onda bruna,
e avanti che sien di là discese,
anche di qua nuova schiera s'auna. 120
'Figliuol mio,' disse 'l maestro cortese
'quelli che muoion nell'ira di Dio
tutti convegnon qui d'ogni paese;
e pronti sono a trapassar lo rio,
chè la divina giustizia li sprona,
sì che la tema si volve in disio.
Quinci non passa mai anima bona;
e però, se Caron di te si lagna,
ben puoi sapere omai che 'l suo dir sona.'
Finito questo, la buia campagna 130
tremò sì forte, che dello spavento
la mente di sudore ancor mi bagna.
La terra lagrimosa diede vento,
che balenò una luce vermiglia
la qual mi vinse ciascun sentimento;
e caddi come l'uom che 'l sonno piglia.

1. Angels, the heavens and primal matter.

2. The knowledge of God.

3. 'Because thou art lukewarm, and neither cold nor hot, I will spue thee out of my mouth' (*Rev.* iii. 16).

4. Probably Pope Celestine V; elected in 1294 at the age of 80 he resigned 5 months later.

their birth, then, weeping bitterly, they drew all together to the accursed shore which awaits every man that fears not God. The demon Charon, with eyes of burning coal, beckons to them and gathers them all in, smiting with the oar any that linger. As in autumn the leaves drop off one after the other till the branch sees all its spoils on the ground, so the wicked seed of Adam fling themselves from that shore one by one at the signal, as a falcon at its recall. Thus they depart over the dark water, and before they have landed on the other side a fresh crowd collects again on this.

'My son,' said the courteous Master 'all those that die in the wrath of God assemble here from every land; and they are eager to cross the river, for divine justice so spurs them that fear turns to desire. By this way no good spirit ever passes, and therefore if Charon complains of thee thou canst well understand now what his speech imports.'

When he had ended, the gloomy plain shook so violently that the remembrance of my terror bathes me again with sweat. The tearful ground gave forth wind and a red blaze flashed which overcame all my senses, and I fell like one that is seized with sleep.

5. 'Thou hast a name that thou livest, and art dead' (*Rev.* iii. 1).

6. The classical river of death.

7. As a penitent Dante is to go after his death to Purgatory, by a way described in *Purg.* ii.

NOTE

The abrupt opening of the canto—'Through me the way' ('*Per me si va*'), three times, like strokes of doom,—arrests us as Dante was arrested with its 'dreadful sense'. He is faced with the nature and significance of Hell, of sin, that is, in its fulfilment, a 'way' whose end cannot be missed by those who follow it. It is the refusal of God, and all that God is—power, wisdom, love, the special attributes in medieval theology of Father, Son, and Spirit—is involved in that estrangement. Hell has not been from eternity but was 'prepared for the devil and his angels' after Lucifer's rebellion in Heaven and before the creation of man; but it 'endures eternally', for in sin is neither resource nor hope.

Here Virgil's first charge to Dante is his warning against cowardice; for it belongs to Dante's salvation and is the special contribution to it of this stage of his journey that he should be delivered from the fear of what sin can do against the powers and the authority of grace, from all respect for it and delusion about it as if it were inevitable and irresistible, and should come to know it for what in fact it is, the soul's loss and bondage and disaster.

The first class of the lost, the Neutrals, angels and humans, is an original and most characteristic invention of Dante's, outside of all the traditional systems. For him, especially after Virgil's admonition, they are the object of a peculiar contempt; and here, as so often in the poem, there is an unmistakably autobiographical note in the words of Dante's reason about them: 'Let us not talk of them; but look thou and pass.' These innumerable seekers of safety first, and last, who take no risk either of suffering in a good cause or of scandal in a bad one, are here manifestly, nakedly, that which they were in life, the waste and rubbish of the universe, of no account to the world, unfit for Heaven and barely admitted to Hell. They have no need to die, for they 'never were alive'. They follow still, as they have always done, a meaningless, shifting banner that never stands for anything because it never stands at all, a cause which is no cause but the changing magnet of the day. Their pains are paltry and their tears and blood mere food for worms.

Dante recognizes some but does not name any of them, not even 'him who from cowardice made the great refusal'. It was a description not to be mistaken by the contemporaries of Pope Celestine V, and the absence of his name, with the assumption that everyone would know who was meant, makes the reference the more scathing and contemptuous. He is the type and frontispiece of the whole crowd, enabling Dante 'at once and with certainty' to identify them as 'the worthless crew that is hateful to God and to His enemies.' The aged hermit had allowed himself to be raised to the supreme office by those who thought to restore the character and credit of the Papacy, and then was persuaded to resign, as was believed, by the man who succeeded him as Pope Boniface VIII and who then kept him in prison till his death in 1296. Boniface, in Dante's view, was the shameful opposite of all the Papacy should stand for, so that Celestine's 'great refusal' had brought moral disaster on the Church and on Christendom. The facts that Celestine's resignation was taken by many as evidence of his devout humility and that he was afterwards canonized only throw into stronger relief Dante's judgement of such a dereliction of public duty.

The word used with reference to Celestine and rendered here cowardice (*viltà*) means, more strictly, pusillanimity, littleness of soul, the meanness of nature by which a man refuses his calling and misses his mark, the character directly opposite to that of the *magnanimo*, the 'great soul'; in the previous canto and this Dante is three times warned by Virgil against it, and the warning is now enforced by his sight of the vast aimless troop of the Neutrals whose common offence is *viltà*.

The grim and violent figure of Charon, the classical ferryman of the river of death, and his summons to the crowd, represent the horror of death for the reprobate, and it comes to us, as it

Charon

came to Dante, as a surprise that the lost on the shore of Acheron are so spurred by divine justice that they are eager for the crossing and their 'fear turns to desire'. It is not that they care for the divine justice, but that the divine justice operates in their perversity; they work out their own damnation and are headlong and eager in it and cannot now be otherwise, for their sin is their doom.

Here as elsewhere in Hell Dante is distinguished as a 'living soul' from the dead souls there,—not merely, that is, as one still in the earthly life, but as one living by hope in grace and coming here by a warrant higher even than that of his reason: 'It is so willed where will and power are one.' So too he passes the river, not by Charon's boat, but by a mystic and soul-shaking experience which leaves him stunned and from which he recovers to find himself at a new stage of his journey.

This canto has been described as 'the most Virgilian in the whole poem' and anyone who compares it with the sixth book of the *Aeneid*, telling of Aeneas's visit to the world of the dead, will recognize in how many features Dante follows his acknowledged master. But all the more marked for the likeness of their stories is the difference, and this difference in particular, that the whole magical apparatus of Aeneas's journey—the spells, the ceremonies, the tokens—is absent here, and its place is taken by wholly moral and spiritual forces—the soul's life, the voice of reason, the will of God.

INFERNO

RUPPEMI l'alto sonno nella testa
  un greve truono, sì ch' io mi riscossi
  come persona ch' è per forza desta;
e l'occhio riposato intorno mossi,
  dritto levato, e fiso riguardai
  per conoscer lo loco dov' io fossi.
Vero è che 'n su la proda mi trovai
  della valle d'abisso dolorosa
  che truono accoglie d' infiniti guai.
Oscura e profonda era e nebulosa, 10
  tanto che, per ficcar lo viso a fondo,
  io non vi discernea alcuna cosa.
'Or discendiam qua giù nel cieco mondo'
  cominciò il poeta tutto smorto:
  'io sarò primo, e tu sarai secondo.'
E io, che del color mi fui accorto,
  dissi: 'Come verrò, se tu paventi
  che suoli al mio dubbiare esser conforto?'
Ed elli a me: 'L'angoscia delle genti
  che son qua giù, nel viso mi dipigne 20
  quella pietà che tu per tema senti.
Andiam, chè la via lunga ne sospigne.'
  Così si mise e così mi fè intrare
  nel primo cerchio che l'abisso cigne.
Quivi, secondo che per ascoltare,
  non avea pianto mai che di sospiri,
  che l'aura etterna facevan tremare.

CANTO IV

The First Circle; the Virtuous Heathen; the four poets; Limbo

A HEAVY thunder-clap broke the deep sleep in my head so that I started like one who is waked by force, and, my eyes being rested, I stood up and looked about me, then set my gaze steadily to know where I was. I found myself in fact on the brink of the abysmal valley of pain, which resounds with noise of countless wailings; it was so dark and deep and full of vapours that, straining my sight to reach the bottom, I could make out nothing there.

'Now let us descend into the blind world down there,' began the Poet, deadly pale; 'I will be first and thou second.'

And I, who noted his colour, said: 'How shall I come if thou art afraid who, when I am in doubt, art wont to be my strength?'

And he said to me: 'The anguish of the people who are down here paints my face with that pity thou takest for fear. Let us go, for the long way urges us.'

So he went on and made me too enter into the first circle that girds the abyss. Here, so far as I could tell by listening, was no lamentation more than sighs which kept the air forever trembling;

Ciò avvenìa di duol sanza martìri
ch'avean le turbe, ch'eran molto grandi,
d'infanti e di femmine e di viri. 30
Lo buon maestro a me: 'Tu non dimandi
che spiriti son questi che tu vedi?
Or vo' che sappi, innanzi che più andi,
ch'ei non peccaro; e s'elli hanno mercedi,
non basta, perchè non ebber battesmo,
ch' è porta della fede che tu credi.
E se furon dinanzi al cristianesmo,
non adorar debitamente a Dio:
e di questi cotai son io medesmo.
Per tai difetti, non per altro rio, 40
semo perduti, e sol di tanto offesi,
che sanza speme vivemo in disio.'
Gran duol mi prese al cor quando lo 'ntesi,
però che gente di molto valore
conobbi che 'n quel limbo eran sospesi.
'Dimmi, maestro mio, dimmi, segnore,'
comincia' io per volere esser certo
di quella fede che vince ogni errore:
'uscicci mai alcuno, o per suo merto
o per altrui, che poi fosse beato?' 50
E quei, che 'ntese il mio parlar coperto,
rispuose: 'Io era nuovo in questo stato,
quando ci vidi venire un possente,
con segno di vittoria coronato.
Trasseci l'ombra del primo parente,
d'Abèl suo figlio e quella di Noè,
di Moïsè legista e obediente;
Abraàm patriarca e Davìd re,
Israèl con lo padre e co' suoi nati
e con Rachele, per cui tanto fè; 60
e altri molti, e feceli beati;
e vo' che sappi che, dinanzi ad essi,
spiriti umani non eran salvati.'
Non lasciavam l'andar perch' ei dicessi,
ma passavam la selva tuttavia,
la selva, dico, di spiriti spessi.

these came from grief without torments that was borne by the crowds, which were vast, of men and women and little children.

The good Master said to me: 'Dost thou not ask what spirits are these thou seest? I would have thee know, then, before thou goest farther, that they did not sin; but though they have merits it is not enough, for they had not baptism, which is the gateway of the faith thou holdest; and if they were before Christianity they did not worship God aright, and of these I am one. For such defects, and not for any guilt, we are lost, and only so far afflicted that without hope we live in desire.'

Great grief seized me at the heart when I heard this, for I knew people of much worth who were suspended in that Limbo.

'Tell me, my Master, tell me, sir,' I began, seeking to be assured of that faith which overcomes every doubt,[1] 'did ever anyone, either by his own merit or another's, go out hence and come afterwards to bliss?'

And he, who understood my veiled speech, replied: 'I was new in this condition when I saw a mighty one come here, crowned with a sign of victory.[2] He took from among us the shade of our first parent, of Abel his son, and of Noah, of Moses, law-giver and obedient, of the patriarch Abraham, and of King David, of Israel with his father and his sons and Rachel, for whom he did so much,[3] and many others, and he made them blest. And I would have thee know that before these no human souls were saved.'

We did not cease to go on for his speaking, but continued all the time passing through the forest —for such it seemed—of thronged spirits; and we

Non era lunga ancor la nostra via
 di qua dal sonno, quand' io vidi un foco
 ch'emisperio di tenebre vincìa.
Di lungi v'eravamo ancora un poco, 70
 ma non sì, ch' io non discernessi in parte
 ch'orrevol gente possedea quel loco.
'O tu ch'onori scïenzia ed arte,
 questi chi son c' hanno cotanta onranza,
 che dal modo delli altri li diparte?'
E quelli a me: 'L'onrata nominanza
 che di lor suona su nella tua vita,
 grazia acquista nel ciel che sì li avanza.'
Intanto voce fu per me udita:
 'Onorate l'altissimo poeta: 80
 l'ombra sua torna, ch'era dipartita.'
Poi che la voce fu restata e queta,
 vidi quattro grand'ombre a noi venire:
 sembianza avean nè trista nè lieta.
Lo buon maestro cominciò a dire:
 'Mira colui con quella spada in mano,
 che vien dinanzi ai tre sì come sire.
Quelli è Omero poeta sovrano;
 l'altro è Orazio satiro che vène;
 Ovidio è il terzo, e l'ultimo Lucano. 90
Però che ciascun meco si convene
 nel nome che sonò la voce sola,
 fannomi onore, e di ciò fanno bene.'
Così vidi adunar la bella scola
 di quel signor dell'altissimo canto
 che sovra li altri com'aquila vola.
Da ch'ebber ragionato insieme alquanto,
 volsersi a me con salutevol cenno;
 e 'l mio maestro sorrise di tanto:
e più d'onore ancora assai mi fenno, 100
 ch'e' sì mi fecer della loro schiera,
 sì ch' io fui sesto tra cotanto senno.
Così andammo infino alla lumera,
 parlando cose che 'l tacere è bello,
 sì com'era 'l parlar colà dov'era.

had not gone far from where I slept when I saw a blaze of light which was enclosed in a hemisphere of darkness. We were still a short distance from it, yet not so far but that I partly made out that an honourable company occupied that place.

'O thou who honourest both science and art, who are these who have such honour that it sets them apart from the condition of the rest?'

And he said to me: 'Their honourable fame, which resounds in thy life above, gains favour in Heaven which thus advances them.'

At that moment I heard a voice: 'Honour the lofty poet! His shade returns that left us.'

When the voice had paused and there was silence I saw four great shades coming to us; their looks were neither sad nor joyful. The good Master began: 'Mark him there with sword in hand[4] who comes before the three as their lord; he is Homer, the sovereign poet. He that comes next is Horace the moralist, Ovid is the third, and the last Lucan. Since each shares with me in the name the one voice uttered they give me honourable welcome, and in this do well.'

Thus I saw assemble the noble school of that lord of loftiest song who flies like an eagle above the rest. After they had talked together for a time they turned to me with a sign of greeting, and my Master smiled at this; and then they showed me still greater honour, for they made me one of their number so that I was the sixth among those high intelligences. Thus we went on as far as the light, talking of things which were fitting for that place and of which it is well now to be silent.[5]

Venimmo al piè d'un nobile castello,
sette volte cerchiato d'alte mura,
difeso intorno d'un bel fiumicello.
Questo passammo come terra dura;
per sette porte intrai con questi savi: 110
giugnemmo in prato di fresca verdura.
Genti v'eran con occhi tardi e gravi,
di grande autorità ne' lor sembianti:
parlavan rado, con voci soavi.
Traemmoci così dall'un de' canti,
in luogo aperto, luminoso e alto,
sì che veder si potean tutti quanti.
Colà diritto, sopra 'l verde smalto,
mi fur mostrati li spiriti magni,
che del vedere in me stesso n'essalto. 120
I' vidi Elettra con molti compagni,
tra' quai conobbi Ettòr ed Enea,
Cesare armato con li occhi grifagni.
Vidi Cammilla e la Pantasilea
dall'altra parte, e vidi 'l re Latino
che con Lavina sua figlia sedea.
Vidi quel Bruto che cacciò Tarquino,
Lucrezia, Julia, Marzïa e Corniglia;
e solo in parte vidi 'l Saladino.
Poi ch' innalzai un poco più le ciglia, 130
vidi 'l maestro di color che sanno
seder tra filosofica famiglia.
Tutti lo miran, tutti onor li fanno:
quivi vid' ïo Socrate e Platone,
che 'nnanzi alli altri più presso li stanno;
Democrito, che 'l mondo a caso pone,
Dïogenès, Anassagora e Tale,
Empedoclès, Eraclito e Zenone;
e vidi il buono accoglitor del quale,
Dïoscoride dico; e vidi Orfeo, 140
Tullio e Lino e Seneca morale;
Euclide geomètra e Tolomeo,
Ipocràte, Avicenna e Galïeno,
Averoìs, che 'l gran comento feo.

We came to the foot of a noble castle, encircled seven times with high walls and defended round about by a fair stream; this we passed over as on solid ground and through seven gateways I entered with these sages. We came to a meadow of fresh verdure, where were people with grave and slow-moving eyes and looks of great authority; they spoke seldom, with gentle voices. Then we withdrew on one side to an open space, bright and high, so that we could see every one of them.

There before me on the enamelled green were shown to me the great spirits by the sight of whom I am uplifted in myself. I saw Electra with many in her company, of whom I knew Hector and Aeneas and Caesar, in arms and with his falcon eyes;[5] I saw Camilla and Penthesilea on the other side, and I saw the Latian king, who sat with his daughter Lavinia; I saw that Brutus who drove out Tarquin, Lucrece, Julia, Marcia, and Cornelia; and, by himself apart, I saw the Saladin.

When I raised my eyes a little higher I saw the master of them that know sitting amid a philosophic family, all of them regarding him and all showing him honour.[6] There I saw Socrates and Plato in front of the rest and nearest to him, Democritus, who ascribes the world to chance, Diogenes, Anaxagoras, and Thales, Empedocles, Heraclitus, and Zeno; I saw the skilled collector of simples—I mean Dioscorides—and I saw Orpheus, Cicero, Linus, and Seneca the moralist, Euclid the geometer, and Ptolemy, Hippocrates, Avicenna, Galen, and Averroes, him who made the Great Commentary.

Io non posso ritrar di tutti a pieno,
  però che sì mi caccia il lungo tema,
  che molte volte al fatto il dir vien meno.
La sesta compagnia in due si scema:
  per altra via mi mena il savio duca,
  fuor della queta, nell'aura che trema;
e vegno in parte ove non è che luca.

1. Christianity, with the statement of the Creed that Christ 'descended into Hell'.

2. Probably the traditional crossed halo of Christ. Virgil died in 19 B.C., 53 years before the Crucifixion and the Harrowing of Hell.

3. 'Jacob served seven years for Rachel, . . . and he served yet seven other years' (*Gen.* xxix. 20, 30).

4. Homer, as the poet of war.

I cannot give full account of them all, for the length of my theme so drives me on that many times my words come short of the fact.

The company of six falls off to two and my wise Leader brings me by another way out of the quiet into the trembling air and I come to a part where no light shines.

5. Electra, mother of Dardanus the founder of Troy, accompanied by the chief heroes of Troy and Rome; the names just following are prominent in the same story, Lavinia Aeneas's wife, Lucius Brutus founder of the Roman Republic. 'The Saladin', Sultan of Egypt and Syria in the 12th century, famed for his munificence.

6. Aristotle, with famous Greek and Roman philosophers and scientists; Orpheus and Linus, mythical Greek poets; Avicenna and Averroes, Moslems of the 11th and 12th centuries, and Averroes, author of the *Great Commentary* on Aristotle.

NOTE

It is a thunder-clap, as if following immediately on the red flash reported at the end of the third canto, that breaks Dante's swoon, and it is so he tells of the first of his unconscious transits from one stage to another of his mystic journey.

The Limbo or 'border' of Hell was an early invention of the Church Fathers, logically required by their doctrines of human salvation. Between the Fall of Adam and the Crucifixion of Christ there could be no salvation; but the Old Testament saints, being Christian believers by anticipation, were held there only in reserve for their final deliverance by Christ when, before His Resurrection, 'he went and preached unto the spirits in prison' (1 *Peter* iii. 19). It provided a place, also, for unbaptized infants, incapable alike of sin and of faith, for whom the Fathers could conceive of no other destiny. It is to this orthodox doctrine of Limbo, so limited even by Aquinas, that Dante makes the bold and characteristic addition of including among its inmates the virtuous souls of all times and races who were neither Jews nor Christians.

The relation of virtuous pagans to the Christian scheme of salvation was a matter of acute and peculiar difficulty for Dante. With his deep conviction of the divine ordering of secular history (represented mainly by the story of Troy and Rome) as a kind of parallel and complement of sacred history (represented by the Old and New Testaments and the Church), with his strong sense of the unity of humanity and of all its spiritual values, and with his profound reverence for all that was best in what he knew of pre-Christian paganism, the exclusion of the virtuous heathen from salvation, inevitable as he conceived it to be, put a great and painful strain on his mind. He recurs to the subject again and again, and even in the Heaven of Justice, described in the *Paradiso*, he finds only imperfect relief from 'the great fast that has long kept him hungry, finding no food for it on earth'. Here that exclusion is simply set forth as a fact, and the absence of question makes the fact seem the more inevitable. It should be remembered that here as elsewhere Dante is giving his picture not only of the future but of the actual condition of these souls in the earthly life, 'having no hope, and without God in the world'.

In seeking from Virgil confirmation of the accepted Christian doctrine of the Harrowing of Hell, a very familiar subject of medieval sculpture and painting, Dante has to use 'veiled speech', for Christ is unknown and cannot be named in Hell, and verisimilitude is given to the event in a way most characteristic of Dante, by Virgil's testimony, a report as it were disinterested and detached. He speaks of that coming of 'a mighty one, crowned with a sign of victory', as of an event strange and hardly accountable, belonging to a sphere of things beyond his comprehension.

The vague and tremulous life of the thronging souls in Limbo is utterly inadequate to the 'people of much worth' who must, he knows, be there, and he represents the life of the greatest among the non-Jewish and non-Christian races, naming the heroes and heroines of Troy and Rome, three famous Moslems, and the chief poets, philosophers and scholars of antiquity, such as were known to him, as a life full of nobleness and dignity and great compensations. In the account of it the word 'honour', in itself and its derivatives, is used eight times, and honour here is not merely fame but the deserving of it. Their castle, representing natural human genius and wisdom, is surrounded by seven walls, probably representing the three intellectual and the four moral virtues of ancient ethics, and by a stream, generally taken to mean eloquence, which the wise cross dry-shod. They walk on a fresh meadow, to suggest their unfading fame, and their place makes a great hemisphere of light in the enclosing darkness. Dante's description of them is a reminiscence of Aquinas's account of Aristotle's 'magnanimous'—great-souled—man: 'his temper demands gravity of voice and slow speech and movement.'

They live in a light which is *enclosed* by the dark. For the canto is filled with Dante's sense at once of the greatness of human reason and genius and of their insufficiency for the problems of destiny and the requirements of the soul. There is a diffused melancholy throughout the canto and the words *sighs*, *grief*, *lost*, *without hope*, give their colour to it all. It is Dante's version of

'the pain
Of finite hearts that yearn'.

The occupants of Limbo cannot, of course, have been among the 'wicked souls' of Charon's cargo on Acheron, and we are left with one among the many minor inconsistencies and unexplained elements in Dante's scheme.

The five poets who enrolled Dante in their company were in his estimation the greatest poets of antiquity—though in the case of Homer this estimation was merely traditional for Dante, who knew no Greek,—and the whole scene is Dante's proud assertion to his countrymen and to the world of the height of his own calling and of his fitness for it, and in particular of his revival in verse of the classical standards of order, elevation, and dignity. But it is also much more than that. Everything possible is added to mark the dignity of the meeting and mutual greeting of the six poets. 'The voice'—presumably Homer's, but the impersonal word is used three times,—breaks in unexpectedly and with authority. Virgil accepts and approves the greeting which the others give him, not as mere personal compliment, but expressly on the ground that he and they share the high name of poet, and the six converse by themselves, as on themes beyond the crowd. For poetry is more than the poet; it is the utterance in terms of the imagination of truth which cannot otherwise be known or told and its functions are the loftiest of all that belongs to human speech. 'For Dante and his contemporaries, poetry was wisdom' (*V. Rossi*), and he pleads here, partly for himself, but far more for poetry.

INFERNO

Così discesi del cerchio primaio
  giù nel secondo, che men luogo cinghia,
  e tanto più dolor, che punge a guaio.
Stavvi Minòs orribilmente, e ringhia:
  essamina le colpe nell'entrata;
  giudica e manda secondo ch'avvinghia.
Dico che quando l'anima mal nata
  li vien dinanzi, tutta si confessa;
  e quel conoscitor delle peccata
vede qual luogo d'inferno è da essa; 10
  cignesi con la coda tante volte
  quantunque gradi vuol che giù sia messa.
Sempre dinanzi a lui ne stanno molte:
  vanno a vicenda ciascuna al giudizio;
  dicono e odono, e poi son giù volte.
'O tu che vieni al doloroso ospizio,'
  disse Minòs a me quando mi vide,
  lasciando l'atto di cotanto offizio,
'guarda com'entri e di cui tu ti fide:
  non t' inganni l'ampiezza dell'entrare!' 20
  E 'l duca mio a lui: 'Perchè pur gride?
Non impedir lo suo fatale andare:
  vuolsi così colà dove si puote
  ciò che si vuole, e più non dimandare.'
Ora incomincian le dolenti note
  a farmisi sentire; or son venuto
  là dove molto pianto mi percuote.

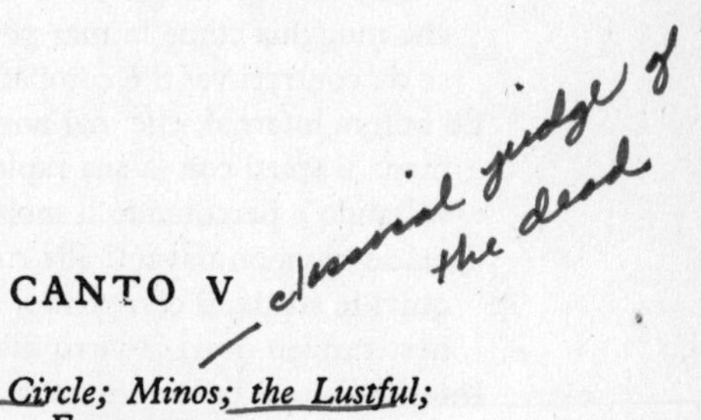

CANTO V

The Second Circle; Minos; the Lustful;
Francesca

THUS I descended from the first circle down into the second, which bounds a smaller space and so much more of pain that goads to wailing. There stands Minos,[1] horrible, snarling, examines their offences at the entrance, judges and despatches them according as he girds himself; I mean that when the ill-born soul comes before him it confesses all, and that discerner of sins sees what is the place for it in Hell and encircles himself with his tail as many times as the grades he will have it sent down. Always before him is a crowd of them; they go each in turn to the judgement; they speak and hear and then are hurled below.

'O thou that comest to the abode of pain,' Minos said when he saw me, leaving the business of his great office, 'look how thou enterest and in whom thou trustest; let not the breadth of the entrance deceive thee.'

And my Leader said to him: 'Why dost thou too make an outcry? Hinder not his fated journey. It is so willed where will and power are one; and ask no more.'

Now the notes of pain begin to reach my ears; now I am come where great wailing breaks on me.

Io venni in luogo d'ogni luce muto,
che mugghia come fa mar per tempesta,
se da contrari venti è combattuto. 30
La bufera infernal, che mai non resta,
mena li spirti con la sua rapina:
voltando e percotendo li molesta.
Quando giungon davanti alla ruina,
quivi le strida, il compianto, il lamento;
bestemmian quivi la virtù divina.
Intesi ch'a così fatto tormento
enno dannati i peccator carnali,
che la ragion sommettono al talento.
E come li stornei ne portan l'ali 40
nel freddo tempo a schiera larga e piena,
così quel fiato li spiriti mali.
Di qua, di là, di giù, di su li mena;
nulla speranza li conforta mai,
non che di posa, ma di minor pena.
E come i gru van cantando lor lai,
faccendo in aere di sè lunga riga,
così vidi venir, traendo guai,
ombre portate dalla detta briga:
per ch' i' dissi: 'Maestro, chi son quelle 50
genti che l'aura nera sì gastiga?'
'La prima di color di cui novelle
tu vuo' saper' mi disse quelli allotta,
'fu imperadrice di molte favelle.
A vizio di lussuria fu sì rotta,
che libito fè licito in sua legge
per tòrre il biasmo in che era condotta.
Ell' è Semiramìs, di cui si legge
che succedette a Nino e fu sua sposa:
tenne la terra che 'l Soldan corregge. 60
L'altra è colei che s'ancise amorosa,
e ruppe fede al cener di Sicheo;
poi è Cleopatràs lussurïosa.
Elena vedi, per cui tanto reo
mpo si volse, e vedi il grande Achille,
che con amore al fine combattèo.

I came to a place where all light was mute and where was bellowing as of a sea in tempest that is beaten by conflicting winds. The hellish storm, never resting, seizes and drives the spirits before it; smiting and whirling them about, it torments them. When they come before its fury there are shrieks, weeping and lamentation, and there they blaspheme the power of God; and I learned that to such torment are condemned the carnal sinners who subject reason to desire. As in the cold season their wings bear the starlings along in a broad, dense flock, so does that blast the wicked spirits. Hither, thither, downward, upward, it drives them; no hope ever comforts them, not to say of rest, but of less pain. And as the cranes go chanting their lays, making of themselves a long line in the air, so I saw approach with long-drawn wailings shades borne on these battling winds, so that I said: 'Master, who are these people whom the black air so scourges?'

'The first among those of whom thou wouldst know' he said to me then 'was Empress of peoples of many tongues, who was so corrupted by licentious vice that she made lust lawful in her law to take away the scandal into which she was brought; she is Semiramis, of whom we read that she succeeded Ninus, being his wife, and held the land which the Soldan rules.[2] The next is she that slew herself for love and broke faith with the ashes of Sychaeus, and then wanton Cleopatra; see Helen, for whose sake so many years of ill revolved; and see the great Achilles, who fought at the last with

Vedi Parìs, Tristano'; e più di mille
 ombre mostrommi e nominommi a dito,
 ch'amor di nostra vita dipartille.
Poscia ch' io ebbi il mio dottore udito 70
 nomar le donne antiche e' cavalieri,
 pietà mi giunse, e fui quasi smarrito.
I' cominciai: 'Poeta, volontieri
 parlerei a quei due che 'nsieme vanno,
 e paion sì al vento esser leggieri.'
Ed elli a me: 'Vedrai quando saranno
 più presso a noi; e tu allor li priega
 per quello amor che i mena, ed ei verranno.'
Sì tosto come il vento a noi li piega,
 mossi la voce: 'O anime affannate, 80
 venite a noi parlar, s'altri nol niega!'
Quali colombe, dal disio chiamate,
 con l'ali alzate e ferme al dolce nido
 vegnon per l'aere dal voler portate;
cotali uscir della schiera ov' è Dido,
 a noi venendo per l'aere maligno,
 sì forte fu l'affettüoso grido.
'O animal grazïoso e benigno
 che visitando vai per l'aere perso
 noi che tignemmo il mondo di sanguigno, 90
se fosse amico il re dell'universo,
 noi pregheremmo lui della tua pace,
 poi c' hai pietà del nostro mal perverso.
Di quel che udire e che parlar vi piace
 noi udiremo e parleremo a vui,
 mentre che 'l vento, come fa, ci tace.
Siede la terra dove nata fui
 su la marina dove 'l Po discende
 per aver pace co' seguaci sui.
Amor, ch'al cor gentil ratto s'apprende, 100
 prese costui della bella persona
 che mi fu tolta; e 'l modo ancor m'offende.
Amor, ch'a nullo amato amar perdona,
 mi prese del costui piacer sì forte,
 che, come vedi, ancor non m'abbandona.

love; see Paris, Tristan,—' and he showed me more than a thousand shades, naming them as he pointed, whom love parted from our life. When I heard my Teacher name the knights and ladies of old times, pity came upon me and I was as one bewildered.

I began: 'Poet, I would fain speak with these two that go together and seem so light upon the wind.'[3]

And he said to me: 'Thou shalt see when they are nearer us, and do thou entreat them then by the love that leads them, and they will come.'

As soon as the wind bent their course to us I raised my voice: 'O wearied souls, come and speak with us, if One forbids it not.'

As doves, summoned by desire, come with wings poised and motionless to the sweet nest, borne by their will through the air, so these left the troop where Dido is, coming to us through the malignant air; such force had my loving call.

'O living creature gracious and friendly, who goest through the murky air visiting us who stained the world with blood, if the King of the universe were our friend we would pray to Him for thy peace, since thou hast pity of our evil plight. Of that which thou art pleased to hear and speak we will hear and speak with you while the wind is quiet, as here it is. The city where I was born[4] lies on the shore where the Po, with the streams that join it, descends to rest. Love, which is quickly kindled in the gentle heart, seized this man for the fair form that was taken from me, and the manner afflicts me still. Love, which absolves no one beloved from loving, seized me so strongly with his charm that, as thou seest, it does not leave me yet. Love

Amor condusse noi ad una morte:
  Caina attende chi vita ci spense.'
  Queste parole da lor ci fur porte.
Quand' io intesi quell'anime offense,
  china' il viso, e tanto il tenni basso, 110
  fin che 'l poeta mi disse: 'Che pense?'
Quando rispuosi, cominciai: 'Oh lasso,
  quanti dolci pensier, quanto disio
  menò costoro al doloroso passo!'
Poi mi rivolsi a loro e parla' io,
  e cominciai: 'Francesca, i tuoi martiri
  a lacrimar mi fanno tristo e pio.
Ma dimmi: al tempo de' dolci sospiri,
  a che e come concedette amore
  che conosceste i dubbiosi disiri?' 120
E quella a me: 'Nessun maggior dolore
  che ricordarsi del tempo felice
  nella miseria; e ciò sa 'l tuo dottore.
Ma s' a conoscer la prima radice
  del nostro amor tu hai cotanto affetto,
  dirò come colui che piange e dice.
Noi leggiavamo un giorno per diletto
  di Lancialotto come amor lo strinse:
  soli eravamo e sanza alcun sospetto.
Per più fïate li occhi ci sospinse 130
  quella lettura, e scolorocci il viso;
  ma solo un punto fu quel che ci vinse.
Quando leggemmo il disïato riso
  esser baciato da cotanto amante,
  questi, che mai da me non fia diviso,
la bocca mi baciò tutto tremante.
  Galeotto fu il libro e chi lo scrisse:
  quel giorno più non vi leggemmo avante.'
Mentre che l'uno spirto questo disse,
  l'altro piangea, sì che di pietade 140
  io venni men così com' io morisse;
e caddi come corpo morto cade.

brought us to one death. Caina waits for him who quenched our life.'[5] These words were borne from them to us. And when I heard these afflicted souls I bent my head and held it down so long that at last the Poet said to me: 'What are thy thoughts?'

When I answered I began: 'Alas, how many sweet thoughts, how great desire, brought them to the woeful pass!' Then I turned to them again to speak and began: 'Francesca, thy torments make me weep for grief and pity, but tell me, in the time of your sweet sighing how and by what occasion did love grant you to know your uncertain desires?'

And she answered me: 'There is no greater pain than to recall the happy time in misery, and this thy teacher knows; but if thou hast so great desire to know our love's first root, I shall tell as one may that weeps in telling. We read one day for pastime of Lancelot,[6] how love constrained him. We were alone and had no misgiving. Many times that reading drew our eyes together and changed the colour in our faces, but one point alone it was that mastered us; when we read that the longed-for smile was kissed by so great a lover, he who never shall be parted from me, all trembling, kissed my mouth. A Galeotto was the book and he that wrote it;[7] that day we read in it no farther.'

While the one spirit said this the other wept so that for pity I swooned as if in death and dropped like a dead body.

1. Judge of the dead in classical mythology.

2. Semiramis, legendary Queen of Assyria, supposed to have legalised incest,—Babylon, her capital, confused with Babylon of Egypt; Dido, mistress of Aeneas, unfaithful to her husband's memory; Cleopatra, mistress of Julius Caesar and of Antony; Helen of Troy, mistress of Paris, cause of the Trojan War; Achilles, killed, according to the medieval story, in consequence of his love for the Trojan Polyxena; Paris, Prince of Troy, killed in the war; Tristan, lover of Yseult, killed by her husband.

3. Paolo and Francesca of Rimini.

4. Ravenna.

5. Caina, in the deepest circle of Hell (Canto xxxii).

6. Lover of Queen Guinevere.

7. Galeotto, the intermediary between Lancelot and Guinevere; his name became the synonym for a pander.

NOTE

The figure of Minos in the place of judgement at the entrance to the true Hell of unrepented sin is an image of remorse, bad conscience, cruel, implacable, grotesque, judgement as it appears to impenitence and despair. It is one among many examples in the *Inferno* of the Christian transformation of divine and other dignified figures of paganism into devils. Minos is judge in the Tartarus of the *Aeneid*, but with no other likeness besides his name and office to Minos here.

There is nothing in Dante's treatment of these carnal sinners of the false and unchristian condemnation of sexual motive which has sometimes obtained in the Church's teaching. Their offence is not at all the natural impulse of sex, but that they 'subject reason to desire'. Three times in the canto they are compared with birds, for their light passage through the air. They are 'borne on', 'driven', 'brought'; the words deliberately chosen give a cumulative effect of passivity and helplessness. They have given rein to their natural passion and have lost the power of restraint; they have allowed the inner order of their life to be subverted; they have sown the wind and forever reap the whirlwind. Sexual wantonness is a fitful, violent, disorderly vice, throwing human relationships into confusion, driving souls helpless before it in alternating passion and lassitude, in the continual inconstancy and agitation figured in the battling winds.

Dante wrote when the literature of French chivalry, the tales of love and war which were the precursors of modern fiction, had an immense vogue in Italy; and he shows here, on the one hand, how he responded to their appeal and thrilled at the names of 'the knights and ladies of old times' whose wars and loves were the subjects of that literature, and, on the other, how perilous he knew the spirit of romance, uncontrolled, to be, and how in the greater world of ultimate realities the soul must submit to a severer measure. It was the story of Lancelot and Guinevere, the best-known love-story in the Arthur Cycle, that Dante's lovers read together and of which Francesca says: 'A Galeotto was the book and he that wrote it.' The judgement is Dante's own, and its significance is strengthened rather than weakened by the fact that some of Francesca's most impassioned lines—spoken in mitigation, almost in justification, of their sin—are like an echo of Dante's own earlier verse, the sonnet, for example, in the *Vita Nuova:* 'Love and the gentle heart are but one thing.' For it is in that union of tenderness and severity—and these not in alternation but together in spiritual tension—in his profound human sympathy along with his unflinching moral realism, according to the necessities of his thinking, that much of Dante's power consists; and nowhere are that combination and that spiritual tension more moving than here.

There is an obvious and intentional contrast between the crowd of souls that is compared to 'a broad, dense flock' of starlings and those other like cranes 'making a long line in the air' while they 'chant their lays',—the contrast between the common mass of wanton livers, none of them named, and the great succession of famous lovers, and as they leave this second troop Paolo and Francesca are distinguished from it by the comparison to doves 'borne by their will through the air'. It is an example of Dante's studied and discriminating imagery.

There is no more profoundly imagined scene in the *Divine Comedy* than that of Dante's meeting with the two lovers, and the infinite gentleness and tenderness of it, his own overwhelming pity for the lovers and the poignant sense in Francesca's words of their love as a kind of fate that seized them unawares and holds them still, with the absence in the whole incident of any word or hint of reproach, make their story the more appalling and the judgement expressed in it the more inevitable. It was their fateful, unrepented commitment to an unlawful love that was their doom. 'Can an eternity of floating on the wind in each other's arms be a punishment for lovers? That is just what their passion, if left to speak for itself, would have chosen. It is what passion stops at and would gladly prolong for ever.

Divine judgement has only taken it at its word. . . Abandon yourself, Dante would say to us,—abandon yourself altogether to a love that is nothing but love, and you are in Hell already' (*G. Santayana*).

In three of her lines Francesca sums up their story,—'Love, which is quickly kindled in the gentle heart',—'Love, which absolves no one beloved from loving',—'Love brought us to one death.' 'She repeats still down there in Hell, with the unconsciousness of an echo, the maxims she has learned in elegant court assemblies and in the melodious love-songs which perhaps she used to sing' (*E. G. Parodi, L.D.*). When Dante sees the two 'that seem so light upon the wind' Virgil bids him 'entreat them by the love that drives them, and they will come.' 'One word only has power to attract these two souls, *Love*. They had nothing else in common with the company among whom they passed, nothing to make them capable of understanding or of being understood except the omnipotent thought of love, which has absorbed every other thought and instinct and desire of theirs and like wings bears them lightly on the violence of the tempest and leaves them, as it were, lost and unaware in a desolate eternity. . . . The love, blind and exclusive, that dominates Francesca admits of no accompaniment save, perhaps, of a hatred no less blind than her love' (*E. G. Parodi, L.D.*),—'Caina waits for him who quenched our life.' When Dante, after bending his head in thought till Virgil questions him, says: 'Alas, how many sweet thoughts, how great desire, brought them to the woeful pass!', 'the wonderful lines are like the sigh of a man wise and pitiful who understands and excuses, but passes judgement' (*E. G. Parodi, L.D.*).

The story, of which Dante is the sole contemporary witness, was that Francesca da Polenta of Ravenna was married to Giovanni Malatesta, the cripple son of the Lord of Rimini, that his younger brother Paolo became Francesca's lover, and that her husband, taking them by surprise, killed them both together. The additional facts, known otherwise, that Paolo was then a married man with two children and that Francesca had been married for ten years and had a daughter nine years old, may dim the romance for us as a matter of history. On the other hand, Dante must have been familiar with the handsome and gallant figure of Paolo, who was Captain of the People in Florence a few years before the tragedy when Dante was a sensitive and romantic youth of seventeen in the city, so that he would receive the shock of the news of the double murder at Rimini in its full horror; and it is easy to suppose that he had knowledge which is lacking to us on which to base his portraiture of Francesca. Later, at any rate, he was on very friendly terms with some members of her family and he spent his last years under the protection of her nephew, then Lord of Ravenna.

In any case our concern is with the Francesca, not of history, but of Dante's imagination. 'All the details of the episode, as we note them carefully, reveal the purpose of creating in this canto a great scene of pity, and the very survival of their love in Paolo and Francesca beyond their death and their condemnation is offered as a sign of the power of that love and to show how hard it was to resist it. . . . The fundamental sentiment of the canto is a great commiseration for the frailty of human nature' (*M. Barbi*).

INFERNO

AL tornar della mente, che si chiuse
dinanzi alla pietà de' due cognati,
che di trestizia tutto mi confuse,
novi tormenti e novi tormentati
mi veggio intorno, come ch' io mi mova
e ch' io mi volga, e come che io guati.
Io sono al terzo cerchio, della piova
etterna, maladetta, fredda e greve;
regola e qualità mai non l' è nova.
Grandine grossa, acqua tinta e neve 10
per l'aere tenebroso si riversa;
pute la terra che questo riceve.
Cerbero, fiera crudele e diversa,
con tre gole canina-mente latra
sopra la gente che quivi è sommersa.
Li occhi ha vermigli, la barba unta e atra,
e 'l ventre largo, e unghiate le mani;
graffia li spiriti, scuoia e disquatra.
Urlar li fa la pioggia come cani:
dell'un de' lati fanno all'altro schermo; 20
volgonsi spesso i miseri profani.
Quando ci scorse Cerbero, il gran vermo,
le bocche aperse e mostrocci le sanne;
non avea membro che tenesse fermo.
Lo duca mio distese le sue spanne,
prese la terra, e con piene le pugna
la gittò dentro alle bramose canne.

CANTO VI

The Third Circle; the Gluttonous; Cerberus; Ciacco

WITH the return of my mind that was shut off before the piteous state of the two kinsfolk, which quite confounded me with grief, new torments and new souls in torment I see about me, wherever I move and turn and set my gaze. I am in the third circle, of eternal, accursed rain, cold and heavy, never changing its measure or its kind; huge hail, foul water and snow pour down through the gloomy air, and the ground that receives it stinks. Cerberus,[1] a beast fierce and hideous, with three throats barks like a dog over the people that are immersed there; he has red eyes, a beard greasy and black, a great belly, and clawed hands, and he scars and flays and rends the spirits. The rain makes them howl like dogs, and the profane wretches often turn themselves, of one side making a shelter for the other.

When Cerberus, the great worm, perceived us, he opened his mouths and showed us the fangs, not one of his limbs keeping still, and my Leader spread his hands, took up earth, and with full fists threw it into the ravenous gullets. As the dog that

Qual è quel cane ch'abbaiando agugna,
  e si racqueta poi che 'l pasto morde,
  chè solo a divorarlo intende e pugna, 30
cotai si fecer quelle facce lorde
  dello demonio Cerbero, che 'ntrona
  l'anime sì, ch'esser vorrebber sorde.
Noi passavam su per l'ombre che adona
  la greve pioggia, e ponavam le piante
  sopra lor vanità che par persona.
Elle giacean per terra tutte quante,
  fuor d'una ch'a seder si levò, ratto
  ch'ella ci vide passarsi davante.
'O tu che se' per questo inferno tratto,' 40
  mi disse 'riconoscimi, se sai:
  tu fosti, prima ch' io disfatto, fatto.'
E io a lei: 'L'angoscia che tu hai
  forse ti tira fuor della mia mente,
  sì che non par ch' i' ti vedessi mai.
Ma dimmi chi tu se' che 'n sì dolente
  loco se' messa ed a sì fatta pena,
  che s'altra è maggio, nulla è sì spiacente.'
Ed elli a me: 'La tua città, ch' è piena
  d'invidia sì che già trabocca il sacco, 50
  seco mi tenne in la vita serena.
Voi cittadini mi chiamaste Ciacco:
  per la dannosa colpa della gola,
  come tu vedi, alla pioggia mi fiacco.
E io anima trista non son sola,
  chè tutte queste a simil pena stanno
  per simil colpa.' E piu non fè parola.
Io li rispuosi: 'Ciacco, il tuo affanno
  mi pesa sì, ch'a lagrimar mi 'nvita;
  ma dimmi, se tu sai, a che verranno 60
li cittadin della città partita;
  s'alcun v' è giusto; e dimmi la cagione
  per che l' ha tanta discordia assalita.'
Ed elli a me: 'Dopo lunga tencione
  verranno al sangue, e la parte selvaggia
  caccerà l'altra con molta offensione.

yelps for greed and becomes quiet when it bites its food, being all absorbed in struggling to devour it, such became these foul visages of the demon Cerberus, who so thunders at the souls that they would fain be deaf.

We passed over the shades that were beaten down by the heavy rain, setting our feet on their emptiness, which seemed real bodies. They were all lying on the ground, except one who sat up as soon as he saw us passing before him.

'O thou who art led through this Hell,' he said to me 'recall me, if thou canst; thou wast begun before I was ended.'

And I said to him: 'The anguish thou hast perhaps takes thee from my memory, so that I do not seem ever to have seen thee; but tell me who thou art, put in a place of such misery and under such a penalty that, if any is greater, none is so loathsome.'

And he said to me: 'Thy city, which is so full of envy that already the sack runs over, held me within it in the bright life, when you citizens called me Ciacco.[2] For the damning fault of gluttony, as thou seest, I lie helpless in the rain; and in my misery I am not alone, for all these are under the same penalty for the same fault.' And he said no more.

I answered him: 'Ciacco, thy distress so weighs on me that it bids me weep. But tell me, if thou canst, what the citizens of the divided city shall come to and whether any there is just, and tell me the cause of such discord assailing it.'

And he said to me: 'After long strife they shall come to blood and the party of the rustics[3] shall drive out the other with much offence; then, by

Poi appresso convien che questa caggia
  infra tre soli, e che l'altra sormonti
  con la forza di tal che testè piaggia.
Alte terrà lungo tempo le fronti, 70
  tenendo l'altra sotto gravi pesi,
  come che di ciò pianga o che n'adonti.
Giusti son due, e non vi sono intesi:
  superbia, invidia e avarizia sono
  le tre faville c' hanno i cuori accesi.'
Qui puose fine al lacrimabil sono;
  e io a lui: 'Ancor vo' che m' insegni,
  e che di più parlar mi facci dono.
Farinata e 'l Tegghiaio, che fuor sì degni,
  Iacopo Rusticucci, Arrigo e 'l Mosca 80
  e li altri ch'a ben far puoser li 'ngegni,
dimmi ove sono e fa ch' io li conosca;
  chè gran disio mi stringe di savere
  se 'l ciel li addolcia, o lo 'nferno li attosca.'
E quelli: 'Ei son tra l'anime più nere:
  diverse colpe giù li grava al fondo:
  se tanto scendi, là i potrai vedere.
Ma quando tu sarai nel dolce mondo,
  priegoti ch'alla mente altrui mi rechi:
  più non ti dico e più non ti rispondo.' 90
Li diritti occhi torse allora in biechi;
  guardommi un poco, e poi chinò la testa:
  cadde con essa a par delli altri ciechi.
E 'l duca disse a me: 'Più non si desta
  di qua dal suon dell'angelica tromba
  quando verrà la nimica podèsta:
ciascun rivederà la trista tomba,
  ripiglierà sua carne e sua figura,
  udirà quel ch' in etterno rimbomba.'
Sì trapassammo per sozza mistura 100
  dell'ombre e della pioggia, a passi lenti,
  toccando un poco la vita futura;
per ch' io dissi: 'Maestro, esti tormenti
  crescerann'ei dopo la gran sentenza,
  o fier minori, o saran sì cocenti?'

force of one who is now manœuvring, that party is destined to fall within three years and the other to prevail, long holding its head high and keeping the first under grievous burdens, for all their tears and shame. Two men are just and are not heeded there. Pride, envy and avarice are the three sparks that have set these hearts on fire.' Here he made an end of his grievous words.

And I said to him: 'I would still learn from thee, and I beg thee to grant me further speech. Farinata and Tegghiaio, men of such worth, Jacopo Rusticucci, Arrigo and Mosca and the rest whose minds were set on well-doing,[4] tell me where they are and give me knowledge of them; for I am pressed with a great desire to know whether they share Heaven's sweetness or the bitterness of Hell.'

And he: 'They are among the blackest souls and different faults weigh them down to the depth; if thou descend so far thou canst see them. But when thou shalt be in the sweet world I pray thee bring me to men's memory. I tell thee no more nor answer thee again.'

With that he turned his direct look askance, gazed at me for a moment, then bent his head and so dropped to the level of the other blind.

And my Leader said to me: 'He wakes no more till the sounding of the angel's trumpet, when the adverse Judge[5] shall come; each shall find again the sad tomb and take again his flesh and form and hear that which echoes in eternity.'

So we passed on through the foul mixture of the shades and the rain with slow steps, touching a little on the life to come. I said therefore: 'Master, will these torments increase after the great judgement, or become less, or continue as fierce as now?'

Ed elli a me: 'Ritorna a tua scïenza,
che vuol, quanto la cosa è più perfetta,
più senta il bene, e così la doglienza.
Tutto che questa gente maladetta
in vera perfezion già mai non vada, 110
di là piu che di qua essere aspetta.'
Noi aggirammo a tondo quella strada,
parlando piu assai ch' io non ridico;
venimmo al punto dove si digrada:
quivi trovammo Pluto, il gran nemico.

1. Guardian of the infernal regions in classical mythology.

2. Ciacco, who died in Dante's 21st year, said to have been a good liver and a wit in Florence; the name, meaning Hog, may have been a nickname.

3. The Whites, the more democratic party in Florence; 'the other' was the Blacks, the aristocratic party.

And he answered me: 'Go back to thy science,[6] which requires that in the measure of a creature's perfection it feels more both of pleasure and of pain. Although these people who are accursed never come to true perfection, they look to be completer then than now.'

We went round that curving road, with much more talk than I repeat, and reached the point where the descent begins. Here we found Plutus, the great enemy.[7]

4. Recent Florentines of note. Arrigo is not mentioned again; the other four appear in Cantos x, xvi, and xxviii.

5. Christ.

6. The teaching of Aristotle, repeated by Aquinas.

7. Plutus, classical god of wealth, perhaps confused here with Pluto, king of the infernal regions.

NOTE

Dante's swoon at the end of the last canto, covering his transition to the third circle, serves as a device for marking off the great scene with the lovers from the violently contrasting scene of the gluttons. Gluttony, the second of the sins of incontinence, is punished lower in Hell than lasciviousness because it is more simply a yielding of the soul to the flesh without any but a fleshly motive; it is a more entirely *beastly* sin, and Dante uses every means of emphasizing its beastliness. Cerberus, the image of gluttony, and the souls grovelling in the mire are compared more than once to dogs, and Virgil and Dante tread on 'the foul mixture of the shades and the rain'. The tearing of the spirits by Cerberus may well express the miseries, continued and magnified in eternity, which are the normal consequences of gluttony, and the din of his triple barking in their ears, their own howling, the bitter, pelting sleet, the stench in which they lie, are all a grotesque contrast to the luxurious banquetings which have been their chief joy. Dante speaks of them as 'profane wretches', with an implied reference, probably, to the 'profane person, as Esau, who for one morsel of meat sold his birthright'.

Ciacco, whom Dante had known in his own youth in Florence, was now disfigured almost out of knowledge by his vice and its punishment; but his portraiture is unmistakably from life, he is no mere type, but a man. His movements and his words are alike abrupt, curt, energetic. He 'sat up as soon as he saw us passing', he recalled with a harsh directness his nickname and told his 'damning fault', he talked of their city with summary bitterness and his speech was brief and grudging, —'he said no more', 'he made an end of his words', and, at the last, 'I tell thee no more, nor answer thee again.' Yet, for all his taciturnity, the world is still for him 'the sweet world' in which he would be 'brought to men's memory'; and then, with a last momentary gaze askance at his townsman,—this surely a personal recollection—he disappears, leaving his likeness indelible in our mind.

By a curious law, not easily explained, the souls in Hell have knowledge of both past and future events on earth, so that Ciacco is able to inform Dante of happenings in Florence later than Easter of 1300, the fictitious date of the poem, which was within a few weeks of the outbreak of party violence when they 'came to blood'. This is one of many instances of Dante's use as matter of prophecy of later events known to himself, and the device helps to give verisimilitude—especially for contemporary readers—to the supernatural conditions of his story. Ciacco was the first Florentine he met in his journey and it was natural that they should talk together of their city and of the events and prospects there. In the fierce party feuds between Blacks and Whites which ruined the peace of Florence Dante shared the 'grievous burdens' of the Whites; when he was already out of the city he was included in the sentence of exile passed on them in 1302, and his wrongs always smouldered in his heart except when they broke into flame against the city he loved still. His words, 'one who is now manœuvring', in Ciacco's account of coming events in Florence are the first of many references to Boniface VIII, the reigning Pope of the time, whose intervention in the affairs of the city was, in Dante's view, a main cause of its miseries.

There has been uncertainty among the commentators about the 'two men' in Florence who 'are just and are not heeded there', and many have thought that Dante meant himself—very soon to be in leading office and activity—for one of them. Perhaps it is better to understand the words as an expression of the desperate moral impoverishment of the city, with a thought, it may be, of Sodom and Gomorrah and their lack of the ten righteous men who might have saved them from destruction. It is, in any case, a confirmation of Ciacco's report of the Florentines of note and credit about whom Dante enquires with concern: 'They are among the blackest souls.' Even 'men of such worth' in the life of Florence had a root of corruption in them.

The recovery of their bodies at the time of the Last Judgement, which the orthodoxy of the time anticipated, is to increase the capacity of these souls for suffering, in reversal of their earthly experience in which their god has been their belly and their chief happiness has been found *there*.

INFERNO

'PAPÈ Satàn, papè Satàn aleppe!'
cominciò Pluto con la voce chioccia;
e quel savio gentil, che tutto seppe,
disse per confortarmi: 'Non ti noccia
la tua paura; chè, poder ch'elli abbia,
non ci torrà lo scender questa roccia.'
Poi si rivolse a quella infiata labbia,
e disse: 'Taci, maladetto lupo:
consuma dentro te con la tua rabbia.
Non è sanza cagion l'andare al cupo: 10
vuolsi nell'alto, là dove Michele
fè la vendetta del superbo strupo.'
Quali dal vento le gonfiate vele
caggiono avvolte, poi che l'alber fiacca,
tal cadde a terra la fiera crudele.
Così scendemmo nella quarta lacca,
pigliando più della dolente ripa
che 'l mal dell'universo tutto insacca.
Ahi giustizia di Dio! tante chi stipa
nove travaglie e pene quant' io viddi? 20
e perchè nostra colpa sì ne scipa?
Come fa l'onda là sovra Cariddi,
che si frange con quella in cui s' intoppa,
così convien che qui la gente riddi.
Qui vidi gente più ch'altrove troppa,
e d'una parte e d'altra, con grand'urli,
voltando pesi per forza di poppa.

CANTO VII

The Fourth Circle; the Avaricious and the Prodigal; Plutus; Fortune; the Fifth Circle; the Wrathful

'PAPE Satan, Pape Satan, aleppe!'[1] began Plutus with clucking voice; and the gentle Sage, who knew all, said for my comfort: 'Do not let thy fear distress thee, for with all his power he shall not hinder us from descending this rock.' Then he turned back on that bloated visage and said: 'Silence, accursed wolf! Consume thyself with thy rage within. Not without cause is his journey to the depth; it is willed on high, where Michael avenged the proud adultery.'[2]

As sails swollen with the wind fall in a heap when the mast snaps, so fell the cruel beast to the ground.

Then we descended into the fourth hollow, passing farther down the dismal slope which ensacks all the evil of the universe. Ah, Justice of God, who crams together all the new toils and pains that I saw? And why does our sin so lay us waste? As do the waves there above Charybdis,[3] one breaking against another when they meet, so must the souls here dance their round. Here I saw far more people than elsewhere both on the one side and the other, with great howls rolling weights by main force of chest; they clashed together when

Percoteansi incontro; e poscia pur lì
si rivolgea ciascun, voltando a retro,
gridando: 'Perchè tieni?' e 'Perchè burli?' 30
Così tornavan per lo cerchio tetro
da ogni mano all'opposito punto,
gridandosi anche loro ontoso metro;
poi si volgea ciascun, quand'era giunto,
per lo suo mezzo cerchio all'altra giostra.
E io, ch'avea lo cor quasi compunto,
dissi: 'Maestro mio, or mi dimostra
che gente è questa, e se tutti fuor cherci
questi chercuti alla sinistra nostra.'
Ed elli a me: 'Tutti quanti fuor guerci 40
sì della mente in la vita primaia,
che con misura nullo spendio ferci.
Assai la voce lor chiaro l'abbaia
quando vegnono a' due punti del cerchio
dove colpa contraria li dispaia.
Questi fuor cherci, che non han coperchio
piloso al capo, e papi e cardinali,
in cui usa avarizia il suo soperchio.'
E io: 'Maestro, tra questi cotali
dovre' io ben riconoscere alcuni 50
che furo immondi di cotesti mali.'
Ed elli a me: 'Vano pensiero aduni:
la sconoscente vita che i fè sozzi
ad ogni conoscenza or li fa bruni.
In etterno verranno alli due cozzi:
questi resurgeranno del sepulcro
col pugno chiuso, e questi coi crin mozzi.
Mal dare e mal tener lo mondo pulcro
ha tolto loro, e posti a questa zuffa:
qual ella sia, parole non ci appulcro. 60
Or puoi veder, figliuol, la corta buffa
de' ben che son commessi alla Fortuna,
per che l'umana gente si rabuffa;
chè tutto l'oro ch' è sotto la luna
e che già fu, di quest'anime stanche
non poterebbe farne posare una.'

they met and then at that point each turned about and rolled his weight back again, shouting: 'Why hoard?' and 'Why squander?' Thus they returned round the gloomy circle on either hand to the opposite point, shouting at each other again their taunting chorus; then, having reached it, each turned back by his half circle to the other joust.

And I, whose heart was as if pierced through, said: 'My Master, show me now who are these people and whether all these tonsured ones on our left were clerics.'

And he said to me: 'Every one of them was so asquint in mind in the first life that they had no right measure in their spending; this they bark out plainly enough when they reach the two points of the circle, where contrary faults divide them. These were clerics whose hair does not cover their heads, both popes and cardinals, in whom avarice shows its mastery.'

And I said: 'Master, among such as these I ought surely to recognize some who were defiled with these offences.'

And he answered me: 'Thou harbourest a vain thought; the undiscerning life that made them foul now makes them obscure to all discernment. They shall come forever to the two buttings; these shall rise from the grave with closed fist, and these with cropped hair;[4] ill-giving and ill-keeping have robbed them of the fair world and set them in this scuffle, —such as it is, I spend no fair words on it. Now mayst thou see, my son, the brief mockery of the wealth committed to fortune, for which the race of men embroil themselves; for all the gold that is beneath the moon, or ever was, could not give rest to one of these weary souls.'

'Maestro,' diss' io lui 'or mi dì anche:
questa Fortuna di che tu mi tocche,
che è, che i ben del mondo ha sì tra branche?'
Ed elli a me: 'Oh creature sciocche, 70
quanta ignoranza è quella che v'offende!
Or vo' che tu mia sentenza ne 'mbocche.
Colui lo cui saver tutto trascende,
fece li cieli e diè lor chi i conduce
sì ch'ogni parte ad ogni parte splende,
distribuendo igualmente la luce:
similemente alli splendor mondani
ordinò general ministra e duce
che permutasse a tempo li ben vani
di gente in gente e d'uno in altro sangue, 80
oltre la difension di senni umani;
per ch'una gente impera ed altra langue,
seguendo lo giudicio di costei,
che è occulto come in erba l'angue.
Vostro saver non ha contasto a lei:
questa provede, giudica, e persegue
suo regno come il loro li altri dei.
Le sue permutazion non hanno triegue:
necessità la fa esser veloce,
sì spesso vien chi vicenda consegue. 90
Quest' è colei ch' è tanto posta in croce
pur da color che le dovrìen dar lode,
dandole biasmo a torto e mala voce;
ma ella s' è beata e ciò non ode:
con l'altre prime creature lieta
volve sua spera e beata si gode.
'Or discendiamo omai a maggior pièta;
già ogni stella cade che saliva
quand' io mi mossi, e 'l troppo star si vieta.'
Noi ricidemmo il cerchio all'altra riva 100
sovr'una fonte che bolle e riversa
per un fossato che da lei deriva.
L'acqua era buia assai più che persa;
e noi, in compagnia dell'onde bige,
entrammo giù per una via diversa.

'Master,' I said to him 'now tell me further, this fortune thou namest to me, who is she that holds the world's wealth thus in her clutches?'

And he said to me: 'O foolish creatures, what ignorance is this that besets you! Now I will have thee feed on my judgement of her. He whose wisdom transcends all made the heavens and gave them guides, so that every part shines to every part, dispersing the light equally.[5] In the same way He ordained for worldly splendours a general minister and guide who should in due time change vain wealth from race to race and from one to another blood, beyond the prevention of human wits, so that one race rules and another languishes according to her sentence which is hidden like the snake in the grass. Your wisdom cannot strive with her. She foresees, judges and maintains her kingdom, as the other heavenly powers do theirs. Her changes have no respite. Necessity makes her swift, so fast men come to take their turn. This is she who is so reviled by the very men that should give her praise, laying on her wrongful blame and ill repute. But she is blest and does not hear it. Happy with the other primal creatures she turns her sphere and rejoices in her bliss.

'Now let us descend to greater wretchedness. Already every star sinks that was rising when I set out[6] and it is forbidden to stay too long.'

We crossed the circle to the other edge, past a spring that boils up and pours over by a trench leading from it, the water of the blackest purple, and following its murky waves we entered the place below by a rough track. This gloomy stream, when

In la palude va c' ha nome Stige
questo tristo ruscel, quand' è disceso
al piè delle maligne piagge grige.
E io, che di mirare stava inteso,
vidi genti fangose in quel pantano, 110
ignude tutte, con sembiante offeso.
Questi si percotean non pur con mano,
ma con la testa e col petto e coi piedi,
troncandosi co' denti a brano a brano.
Lo buon maestro disse: 'Figlio, or vedi
l'anime di color cui vinse l' ira;
e anche vo' che tu per certo credi
che sotto l'acqua ha gente che sospira,
e fanno pullular quest'acqua al summo,
come l'occhio ti dice, u' che s'aggira 120
Fitti nel limo, dicon: "Tristi fummo
nell'aere dolce che dal sol s'allegra,
portando dentro accidïoso fummo:
or ci attristiam nella belletta negra."
Quest' inno si gorgoglian nella strozza,
chè dir nol posson con parola integra.'
Così girammo della lorda pozza
grand'arco tra la ripa secca e 'l mèzzo,
con li occhi volti a chi del fango ingozza:
venimmo al piè d'una torre al da sezzo. 130

1. Apparently a threat against the travellers and a warning to Satan below.
2. The revolt of the rebel angels in Heaven, described, in the language of the Old Testament, as adultery. 'There was war in heaven; Michael and his angels fought against the dragon; . . . and the great dragon was cast out' (*Rev.* xii. 7-9).
3. The whirlpool in the Straits of Messina.

it has reached the foot of the malign grey slopes, enters the marsh which is called Styx;[7] and I, who had stopped to gaze intently, saw muddy people in that bog, all naked and with looks of rage. They were smiting each other not only with the hand but with head and breast and feet and tearing each other piecemeal with their teeth.

The good Master said: 'Son, thou seest now the souls of those whom anger overcame; and I would have thee know for sure also that there are people under the water who sigh and make the water bubble on the surface, as thine eye tells thee wherever it turns. Fixed in the slime they say: "We were sullen in the sweet air that is gladdened by the sun, bearing in our hearts a sluggish smoke; now we are sullen in the black mire." This hymn they gurgle in their throat, for they cannot get the words out plainly.'

Thus we went round a great arc of the filthy pond between the dry bank and the swamp, our eyes bent on those that gorged themselves with the mire; and we came at last to the foot of a tower.

4. A proverbial expression in Italian is that a prodigal spends 'even to the hair of his head'.

5. The reference is to the angelic orders controlling the heavens (*Par.* xxviii).

6. It is now after midnight of Good Friday.

7. One of the rivers of the classical under-world.

NOTE

Plutus, the god of wealth, is in classical mythology a rather attractive figure. All Dante's account of him is the mention of his 'clucking voice' and 'bloated visage', Virgil's calling him 'accursed wolf', and his collapse at Virgil's rebuke. It would seem that Plutus is like the souls that are his captives, all but inarticulate and indistinguishable. The commentators, after much discussion, have not been able to come to any agreement on the meaning of his uncouth greeting of the poets. He is, at any rate, enraged and yet helpless at the challenge of reason and the soul, come to inspect and expose his kingdom.

Dante repeats the lesson he had from Aristotle, that avarice and extravagance, mean hoarding and reckless spending, are opposite forms of the same sin, both being excessive concern with earthly possessions, setting men in unending, furious and fruitless conflict. Familiar with both offences in the rising plutocracy of Florence, he found the chief marks of this kind of sin in its irrationality, its gratuitousness, its vulgar stupidity, its waste and obliteration of personality. This is the only circle in Hell—except among the usurers and in the last depth of treachery—where he cannot distinguish or name anyone, and his first exclamation on reaching it is of amazement at the weary, futile 'scuffle' of these souls, which have now and forever no other character or capacity but to hoard and to squander without end or profit. In his description of them Dante reduplicates his expressions for their rolling of the weights and turning and clashing together, as if to make visible the endlessness of their toil. In this vast scene of indistinguishable humanity, as elsewhere, we have 'Dante's transformation of the elements of reality from the passions of individuals to the representation of the passion itself in its elements, in its unchangeable and eternal effects' (*S. F. Bignone, L.D.*).

He puts the hoarders on the left, a place of more indignity than that of the prodigals, for their sin is more definitely anti-social and unhuman, and it is among them that he finds many of the clergy, as it were the masterpieces in this kind. Among all the sins of his time nothing seemed to Dante so gross and monstrous an unfaithfulness, so plain a spiritual 'adultery' and idolatry, as the avarice of the Church of Christ.

Men's false and vain attempts to dispose of the world's wealth bring him to the subject of God's disposal of it, under the symbolical figure of Fortune; and here Fortune is Plutus's opposite, the minister of God's providence in contrast with the disordered will of men. Dante had written some years before in the *Convito* of wealth, 'in whose coming there is no discrimination, no shining of distributive justice, but almost always sheer wrong'. Here, surely remembering and regretting his own language, he bears his share of Virgil's rebuke of man's ignorance. The common talk of Fortune was all of a capricious fate that 'holds the world's wealth in her clutches', and she was popularly represented as a blinded figure standing on a wheel. Dante now rejects through Virgil that popular, heathenish idea of Fortune and conceives her as of the kindred of the angels, ruling on earth as they in the heavens, seeking always and only God's ends in the souls of men, faithful, irresistible, serene. The late Professor W. P. Ker compared this with Wordsworth's language in the *Ode to Duty*,—'Thou dost preserve the stars from wrong',—which he calls 'no figurative imagination, but vision of the law of the world. Dante thinks in the same way of Fortune, so intensely that he sees her as a goddess, turning her sphere in like manner as the Intelligences move the spheres of the planets. There is nothing like this anywhere else in his verse or prose; nowhere else does allegory or mythology turn into the revelation of an unknown deity.' Disappointed, outcast, and impoverished, Dante had much to tempt him to cynical views; yet this myth of Fortune—not traditional but his own—is his account of Providence. 'It seems blind necessity and is profound and inscrutable reasonableness' (*V. Rossi*). The myth embodies lessons which Dante learned from Boethius's *Consolation of Philosophy*, to which he owns elsewhere his large indebtedness.

The Styx is the second of the rivers of Hell; it 'boils up and pours over' in the circle of avarice and it provides below the place of torment for anger. May the connection—for Dante surely intends a connection—be that suggested by the words of the *Epistle of James*: 'From whence come wars and fightings among you? Come they not hence, even of your lusts that war in your members?'

Here, in the fifth circle, we meet the fourth class of the incontinent, whose sin is that of uncontrolled temper,—the fury of those on the surface of the marsh who attack each other with their whole person, and the sullen resentment of those whose sin is deeper and who are sunk and lost in the depth of the bog. The mire filling their mouths may mean the foulness of speech which is the peculiar and frequent accompaniment and sign of this intemperance of spirit.

Among these sins of weakness it is to be noted that the incontinencies of the flesh do not sink the souls so deep in Hell as those of the spirit, and that the worst of all that class of sins is the sluggish, persistent bitterness of the souls which are so mastered by their resentments that they refuse the light of the sun, the goodness of God.

INFERNO

Io dico, seguitando, ch'assai prima
  che noi fossimo al piè dell'alta torre,
  li occhi nostri n'andar suso alla cima
per due fiammette che i' vedemmo porre,
  e un'altra da lungi render cenno
  tanto, ch'a pena il potea l'occhio tòrre.
E io mi volsi al mar di tutto 'l senno:
  dissi: 'Questo che dice? e che risponde
  quell'altro foco? e chi son quei che 'l fenno?'
Ed elli a me: 'Su per le sucide onde 10
  già scorgere puoi quello che s'aspetta,
  se 'l fummo del pantan nol ti nasconde.'
Corda non pinse mai da sè saetta
  che sì corresse via per l'aere snella,
  com' io vidi una nave piccioletta
venir per l'acqua verso noi in quella,
  sotto il governo d'un sol galeoto,
  che gridava: 'Or se' giunta, anima fella!'
'Flegïàs, Flegïàs, tu gridi a voto'
  disse lo mio signore 'a questa volta: 20
  più non ci avrai che sol passando il loto.'
Qual è colui che grande inganno ascolta
  che li sia fatto, e poi se ne rammarca,
  fecesi Flegïàs nell' ira accolta.
Lo duca mio discese nella barca,
  e poi mi fece intrare appresso lui;
  e sol quand' io fui dentro parve carca.

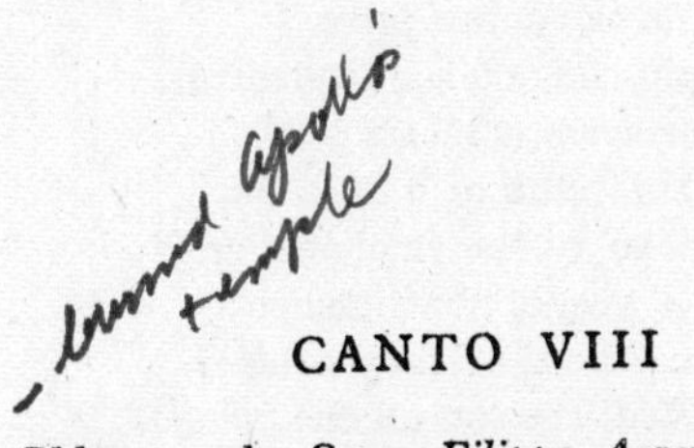

CANTO VIII

Phlegyas; the Styx; Filippo Argenti; the gate of Dis

CONTINUING, I have to tell that long before we were at the foot of the high tower our eyes rose to its top on account of two lights which we saw put there and to which another, so far off that we could hardly make it out, sent back a signal. And I turned to the sea of all wisdom and said: 'What does this mean? And that other fire, what does it answer? And who are they that have made it?'

And he said to me: 'Over the foul waves thou mayst discern already that which we wait for, if the marsh's fumes do not hide it from thee.'

Never string drove arrow from the bow that ran so swiftly through the air as at that moment I saw approaching us a little boat in charge of a single oarsman, who cried: 'Now thou art caught, guilty soul!'

'Phlegyas, Phlegyas,[1] this time thou criest in vain,' said my Lord 'thou shalt have us no longer than the passing of the slough.'

Like one that hears of a great fraud practised on him and then resents it, such Phlegyas became in his pent-up rage.

My Leader went down into the boat, then made me enter after him, and not until I was in did it

Tosto che 'l duca e io nel legno fui,
segando se ne va l'antica prora
dell'acqua più che non suol con altrui. 30
Mentre noi corravam la morta gora,
dinanzi mi si fece un pien di fango,
e disse: 'Chi se' tu che vieni anzi ora?'
E io a lui: 'S' i' vegno, non rimango;
ma tu chi se', che sì se' fatto brutto?'
Rispuose: 'Vedi che son un che piango.'
E io a lui: 'Con piangere e con lutto,
spirito maladetto, ti rimani;
ch' i' ti conosco, ancor sie lordo tutto.'
Allora stese al legno ambo le mani; 40
per che 'l maestro accorto lo sospinse,
dicendo: 'Via costà con li altri cani!'
Lo collo poi con le braccia mi cinse;
baciommi il volto, e disse: 'Alma sdegnosa,
benedetta colei che in te s' incinse!
Quei fu al mondo persona orgogliosa;
bontà non è che sua memoria fregi:
così s' è l'ombra sua qui furïosa.
Quanti si tengon or là su gran regi
che qui staranno come porci in brago, 50
di sè lasciando orribili dispregi!'
E io: 'Maestro, molto sarei vago
di vederlo attuffare in questa broda
prima che noi uscissimo del lago.'
Ed elli a me: 'Avante che la proda
ti si lasci veder, tu sarai sazio:
di tal disïo convien che tu goda.'
Dopo ciò poco vid' io quello strazio
far di costui alle fangose genti,
che Dio ancor ne lodo e ne ringrazio. 60
Tutti gridavano: 'A Filippo Argenti!';
e 'l fiorentino spirito bizzarro
in sè medesmo si volvea co' denti.
Quivi il lasciammo, che più non ne narro;
ma nell'orecchie mi percosse un duolo,
per ch' io avante l'occhio intento sbarro.

seem laden, and as soon as he and I had embarked the ancient prow moved off, cutting deeper into the water than it was wont with others.

While we were running through the stagnant channel there rose up in front of me one covered with mud and said: 'Who art thou that comest before thy time?'

And I said to him: 'If I come I do not stay. But thou, who art thou that art become so foul?'

He answered: 'Thou seest I am one that weeps.'

And I to him: 'In weeping and in misery, accursed spirit, remain; for I know thee, for all thy filth.'

Then he reached out to the boat with both hands; on which the wary Master thrust him off, saying: 'Away there with the other dogs!', then clasped me with his arms about my neck, kissed my cheek and said: 'Indignant soul, blessed is the womb that bore thee! In the world this man was full of arrogance; no good there is to adorn his memory, therefore is his shade here furious. How many above there now account themselves great kings who shall lie here like swine in the mire, leaving of themselves horrible dispraises!'

And I said: 'Master, I should like well to see him soused in this broth before we leave the lake.'

And he to me: 'Before the shore comes in sight thou shalt have satisfaction; in such a wish thou art sure to be gratified.'

Soon after I saw such a rending of him by the muddy crowd that I still give praise and thanks to God for it; all cried: 'At Filippo Argenti!'[2] and the passionate Florentine spirit turned on himself with his teeth. Here we left him, so of him I have no more to tell; but on my ears smote a sound of grief, at which with eyes wide open I looked intently forward.

Lo buon maestro disse: 'Omai, figliuolo,
  s'appressa la città c' ha nome Dite,
  coi gravi cittadin, col grande stuolo.'
E io: 'Maestro, già le sue meschite 70
  là entro certe nella valle cerno,
  vermiglie come se di foco uscite
fossero.' Ed ei mi disse: 'Il foco etterno
  ch'entro l'affoca le dimostra rosse,
  come tu vedi in questo basso inferno.'
Noi pur giugnemmo dentro all'alte fosse
  che vallan quella terra sconsolata:
  le mura mi parean che ferro fosse.
Non sanza prima far grande aggirata,
  venimmo in parte dove il nocchier forte 80
  'Usciteci' gridò: 'qui è l'entrata.'
Io vidi più di mille in su le porte
  da ciel piovuti, che stizzosamente
  dicean: 'Chi è costui che sanza morte
va per lo regno della morta gente?'
  E 'l savio mio maestro fece segno
  di voler lor parlar secretamente.
Allor chiusero un poco il gran disdegno,
  e disser: 'Vien tu solo, e quei sen vada,
  che sì ardito intrò per questo regno. 90
Sol si ritorni per la folle strada:
  pruovi, se sa; chè tu qui rimarrai
  che li ha' iscorta sì buia contrada.'
Pensa, lettor, se io mi sconfortai
  nel suon de le parole maladette,
  chè non credetti ritornarci mai.
'O caro duca mio, che più di sette
  volte m' hai sicurtà renduta e tratto
  d'alto periglio che 'ncontra mi stette,
non mi lasciar' diss' io 'così disfatto; 100
  e se 'l passar più oltre ci è negato,
  ritroviam l'orme nostre insieme ratto.'
E quel signor che lì m'avea menato,
  mi disse: 'Non temer; chè 'l nostro passo
  non ci può tòrre alcun: da tal n' è dato.

The good Master said: 'Now, my son, the city draws near which bears the name of Dis,[3] with its grave citizens and great garrison.'

And I said: 'Master, already I make out distinctly its mosques there within the valley, red as if they had come out of the fire.'

And he said to me: 'The eternal fire which burns within them makes them show red, as thou seest, in this nether Hell.'

We got right into the deep moats entrenching that unhappy city, whose walls seemed to be of iron, and when we had first made a wide circuit we came to a place where the boatman cried loudly: 'Go out here, that is the entrance.'

I saw above the gates more than a thousand of those rained down from Heaven,[4] who cried angrily: 'Who is this that without death goes through the kingdom of the dead?' And the Sage my Master made a sign that he would speak with them apart. Then they restrained a little their fierce resentment and said: 'Come thou alone, and let him go off who has dared thus to enter on this kingdom. Let him return alone on his mad way and see if he knows it, for thou shalt stay here who hast been his guide on that dark road.'

Judge, reader, if I did not lose heart at the sound of the accursed words; for I did not think I should ever return here.

'O my dear Leader, who seven times and more hast restored my confidence and drawn me from great peril confronting me, leave me not' I said 'so undone; and if going farther is denied us, let us quickly retrace our steps together.'

And my Liege who had brought me there said to me: 'Do not fear, for none can hinder our passage, by such an One is it granted us; but wait

Ma qui m'attendi, e lo spirito lasso
  conforta e ciba di speranza bona,
  ch' i' non ti lascerò nel mondo basso.'
Così sen va, e quivi m'abbandona
  lo dolce padre, e io rimango in forse, 110
  che no e sì nel capo mi tenciona.
Udir non potti quello ch'a lor porse;
  ma ei non stette là con essi guari,
  che ciascun dentro a pruova si ricorse.
Chiuser le porte que' nostri avversari
  nel petto al mio segnor, che fuor rimase,
  e rivolsesi a me con passi rari.
Li occhi alla terra e le ciglia avea rase
  d'ogni baldanza, e dicea ne' sospiri:
  'Chi m' ha negate le dolenti case!' 120
E a me disse: 'Tu, perch' io m'adiri,
  non sbigottir, ch' io vincerò la prova,
  qual ch'alla difension dentro s'aggiri.
Questa lor tracotanza non è nova;
  chè già l'usaro a men secreta porta,
  la qual sanza serrame ancor si trova.
Sopr'essa vedestù la scritta morta:
  e già di qua da lei discende l'erta,
  passando per li cerchi sanza scorta,
tal che per lui ne fia la terra aperta.' 130

1. Phlegyas, enraged against Apollo, burned one of his temples.

2. A wealthy noble of Florence, contemporary with Dante.

3. Another name in Roman mythology for Pluto, used by Dante as an alternative name for Satan; here applied to the lower Hell, his fortified city.

for me here and comfort thy weary spirit and feed it with good hope, for I will not forsake thee in the nether world.'

He goes away and leaves me there, the gentle Father, and I remain in doubt, ay and no contending in my head. I could not hear what he put before them; but he was not long there with them when they all ran in headlong, and these our adversaries shut the gates in the face of my Lord, who was left outside and turned back to me with slow steps. His eyes were on the ground and his brow shorn of all boldness and he said between his sighs: 'Who are these to deny me the abodes of pain?' And to me he said: 'Do not thou be dismayed for my vexation, for I shall prevail in the contest, whatever is contrived within to hinder us. This insolence of theirs is not new, for once they showed it at a less hidden gate, which still stands without a bolt. Over it thou sawest the deadly writing,[5] and already within it one descends the steep and passes without escort through the circles, by whom the city shall be opened to us.'

4. The rebel angels.

5. In the legend of the Harrowing of Hell the devils opposed Christ's entry; a passage in the service for Easter Eve runs: 'Today our Saviour burst the bolts and gates of death.'

NOTE

Phlegyas is here the spirit of intemperate anger and as guardian of the marsh he conveys the souls to their appointed places in it. Crossing with furious speed at the signal he hails Dante fiercely as a victim. It is the first time in his journey—it will not be the last—when Dante is claimed by one of the ministers of Hell as one of the damned. For this is just such a sin as he must many a time have been charged with and here he expressly repudiates the charge. It is not himself, but Virgil, that declares him scatheless, and it is in Virgil's company that he is to cross the marsh.

Filippo Argenti was of the class of proud and turbulent nobles who were the plague of Florence and Dante's peculiar abhorrence, and he is introduced here as a typical representative of the incontinence of violent and ungoverned temper. The name Argenti is said to have been given him by the people from his practice of shoeing his horse with silver.

The interview between Filippo and Dante strikes a modern reader with something like disgust at what is felt to be its monstrous inhumanity and moral indecency, and if we are to read it with any understanding it is necessary to put ourselves in imagination at the medieval point of view. In handling the problems of persistent sin and human destiny Dante and the thinking men of his time felt themselves bound to an unrelenting consistency and acceptance of the facts of the spiritual world as they knew it, in its grimmest and most appalling aspects; they were bound, as it were, to take God's part in it. From that point of view, Dante's fierce and savage scorn of Filippo in his misery and his gratification in seeing that misery increased is not in the least, in his own judgement, a momentary lapse into the sin of intemperate anger. It is not an infection from the foul fumes of the marsh nor a sudden surge within him of his lower nature in the presence of sudden temptation, but rather a sign of the pure and righteous anger of a soul to which the will of God is dear, anger directed against such arrogance and insolence as Filippo's which his reason wholly approves. It is the spirit of the Hebrew Psalmist—whatever we may now think of it in the Psalmist or in the Poet—who says: 'Do not I hate them, O Lord, that hate thee, and am not I grieved with those that rise up against thee?' The scene of Dante's outburst and Virgil's embrace of him during the crossing of the marsh is plainly introduced by way of contrasting this high passion with the base, self-centred fury of the sinners in the mire and of showing that there is also an anger which is from above.

The narrative of the approach to the gates of Dis will be better considered after its completion in the next canto.

INFERNO

QUEI color che viltà di fuor mi pinse
   veggendo il duca mio tornare in volta,
   più tosto dentro il suo novo ristrinse.
Attento si fermò com' uom ch'ascolta;
   chè l'occhio nol potea menare a lunga
   per l'aere nero e per la nebbia folta.
'Pur a noi converrà vincer la punga'
   cominciò el, 'se non . . . Tal ne s'offerse:
   oh quanto tarda a me ch'altri qui giunga!'
I' vidi ben sì com'ei ricoperse 10
   lo cominciar con l'altro che poi venne,
   che fur parole alle prime diverse;
ma nondimen paura il suo dir dienne,
   perch' io traeva la parola tronca
   forse a peggior sentenzia che non tenne.
'In questo fondo della trista conca
   discende mai alcun del primo grado,
   che sol per pena ha la speranza cionca?'
Questa question fec' io; e quei 'Dirado
   incontra' mi rispuose 'che di nui 20
   faccia 'l cammino alcun per qual io vado.
Vero è ch'altra fïata qua giù fui,
   congiurato da quella Eritòn cruda
   che richiamava l'ombre a' corpi sui.
Di poco era di me la carne nuda,
   ch'ella mi fece intrar dentr'a quel muro,
   per trarne un spirto del cerchio di Giuda.
Quell' è 'l più basso loco e 'l più oscuro,
   e 'l più lontan dal ciel che tutto gira:
   ben so il cammin; però ti fa sicuro. 30

CANTO IX

The Furies; the Angel; the Sixth Circle; the Heretics

THAT colour which cowardice brought out in me, seeing my Leader turn back, the more quickly repressed the change in his. He stopped attentive as if listening, for the eye could not reach far through the dark air and dense fog. 'Yet we must win this fight,' he began 'or else . . .! Such help was offered us![1] How long it seems till someone comes!'

I saw plainly, as soon as he covered up his beginning with the words that followed, that they were different from the first; but none the less what he said made me afraid, for I drew out his broken phrases to a worse meaning than perhaps he meant.

'Does anyone ever descend to this depth of the dismal hollow from the first circle, where the only penalty is hope cut off?' I asked; and he answered: 'It seldom happens that any of us makes the journey on which I go, but I was down here once before, conjured by that fell Erichtho who recalled shades to their bodies.[2] My flesh was not long naked of me when she made me enter within that wall to draw forth a spirit from the circle of Judas, the deepest and darkest place, farthest from the heaven that encircles all.[3] Well do I know the way, therefore be reassured. This marsh

Questa palude che 'l gran puzzo spira
  cinge dintorno la città dolente,
  u' non potemo intrare omai sanz' ira.'
E altro disse, ma non l' ho a mente;
  però che l'occhio m'avea tutto tratto
  ver l'alta torre alla cima rovente,
dove in un punto furon dritte ratto
  tre furïe infernal di sangue tinte,
  che membra femminine avìeno e atto,
e con idre verdissime eran cinte; 40
  serpentelli e ceraste avean per crine,
  onde le fiere tempie erano avvinte.
E quei, che ben conobbe le meschine
  della regina dell'etterno pianto,
  'Guarda' mi disse 'le feroci Erine.
Quest' è Megera dal sinistro canto;
  quella che piange dal destro è Aletto;
  Tesifone è nel mezzo'; e tacque a tanto.
Con l' unghie si fendea ciascuna il petto;
  battìensi a palme, e gridavan sì alto, 50
  ch' i' mi strinsi al poeta per sospetto.
'Vegna Medusa: sì 'l farem di smalto'
  dicevan tutte riguardando in giuso:
  'mal non vengiammo in Teseo l'assalto.'
'Volgiti in dietro e tien lo viso chiuso;
  chè se il Gorgòn si mostra e tu 'l vedessi,
  nulla sarebbe del tornar mai suso.'
Così disse 'l maestro; ed elli stessi
  mi volse, e non si tenne alle mie mani,
  che con le sue ancor non mi chiudessi. 60
O voi ch'avete li 'ntelletti sani,
  mirate la dottrina che s'asconde
  sotto 'l velame de li versi strani.
E già venìa su per le torbid'onde
  un fracasso d'un suon, pien di spavento,
  per che tremavano amendue le sponde,
non altrimenti fatto che d'un vento
  impetüoso per li avversi ardori,
  che fier la selva e sanz'alcun rattento

exhaling the great stench goes all round the woeful city, which we cannot now enter without contention.'

And he said more, but I do not remember it, for my sight had drawn me wholly to the lofty tower with the glowing summit, where all at once were risen erect three hellish, blood-stained Furies that had the parts and the bearing of women and were girt with hydras of bright green, and for hair they had little serpents and horned snakes twined about the savage temples. And he, who knew well the handmaids of the Queen of everlasting lamentations,[4] said to me: 'See the fierce Erinyes![5] That is Megæra on the left; she wailing on the right is Alecto; Tesiphone is in the middle'; and with that he was silent. Each was rending her breast with her nails; they smote themselves with their palms and cried so loud that I pressed close to the Poet for fear.

'Let Medusa come and we will turn him to stone,'[6] they all cried, looking down; 'we avenged ill the assault of Theseus.'[7]

'Turn thy back and keep thine eyes shut, for should the Gorgon show herself and thou see her there would be no returning above.' My Master said this and himself turned me round and, not trusting to my hands, covered my face with his own also.

Ye that are of good understanding, note the teaching that is hidden under the veil of the strange lines.

And now came over the turbid waves a crashing, fearful sound that set both shores trembling; it was like the noise of a wind violent from conflicting heats which strikes the forest and with unchecked

li rami schianta, abbatte e porta fori; 70
dinanzi polveroso va superbo,
e fa fuggir le fiere e li pastori.
Li occhi mi sciolse e disse: 'Or drizza il nerbo
del viso su per quella schiuma antica
per indi ove quel fummo è più acerbo.'
Come le rane innanzi alla nemica
biscia per l'acqua si dileguan tutte,
fin ch'alla terra ciascuna s'abbica,
vid' io più di mille anime distrutte
fuggir così dinanzi ad un ch'al passo 80
passava Stige con le piante asciutte.
Dal volto rimovea quell'aere grasso,
menando la sinistra innanzi spesso;
e sol di quell'angoscia parea lasso.
Ben m'accorsi ch'elli era da ciel messo,
e volsimi al maestro; e quei fè segno
ch' i' stessi queto ed inchinassi ad esso.
Ahi quanto mi parea pien di disdegno!
Venne alla porta, e con una verghetta
l'aperse, che non v'ebbe alcun ritegno. 90
'O cacciati del ciel, gente dispetta,'
cominciò elli in su l'orribil soglia
'ond'esta oltracotanza in voi s'alletta?
Perchè recalcitrate a quella voglia
a cui non può il fin mai esser mozzo,
e che più volte v' ha cresciuta doglia?
Che giova nelle fata dar di cozzo?
Cerbero vostro, se ben vi ricorda,
ne porta ancor pelato il mento e 'l gozzo.'
Poi si rivolse per la strada lorda, 100
e non fè motto a noi, ma fè sembiante
d'omo cui altra cura stringa e morda
che quella di colui che li è davante;
e noi movemmo i piedi inver la terra,
sicuri appresso le parole sante.
Dentro li entrammo sanz'alcuna guerra;
e io, ch'avea di riguardar disio
la condizion che tal fortezza serra,

course splits the branches, flings them down and carries them away and, driving the dust before it, goes on in pride and puts wild beasts and shepherds to flight.

He freed my eyes and said: 'Strain now thy sight over that ancient scum to the part where the fume is harshest.'

As frogs before their enemy the snake all vanish through the water till each squats on the bottom, so I saw more than a thousand ruined souls flee before one that passed on foot over the Styx dry-shod; he was clearing that gross air from his face, moving often his left hand in front of him, and only of that vexation he seemed weary. Well I perceived that he was one sent from Heaven, and I turned to the Master, who signed to me to keep silence and bow down to him. Ah, how full of indignation he appeared to me! He came to the gate and with a little wand opened it, for there was no resistance.

'O outcasts of Heaven, despised race,' he began on the horrid threshold 'whence this insolence that harbours in you? Why kick against that will whose end can never be frustrate and which has many a time increased your pain? What profits it to butt against the fates? Your own Cerberus—if you rightly remember—still bears his chin and throat peeled for this.'[8] Then he turned back on the filthy way; and he said not a word to us, but had the look of one pressed and spurred by another care than that of those before him. And we moved our steps towards the city, secure after the holy words.

We entered in there without dispute; and I, who was eager to examine the condition of those held within such a stronghold, cast my eye round as

com' io fui dentro, l'occhio intorno invio;
e veggio ad ogne man grande campagna 110
piena di duolo e di tormento rio.
Sì come ad Arli, ove Rodano stagna,
sì com'a Pola, presso del Carnaro
ch' Italia chiude e suoi termini bagna,
fanno i sepulcri tutt' il loco varo,
così facevan quivi d'ogni parte,
salvo che 'l modo v'era più amaro;
chè tra gli avelli fiamme erano sparte,
per le quali eran sì del tutto accesi
che ferro più non chiede verun'arte. 120
Tutti li lor coperchi eran sospesi,
e fuor n'uscivan sì duri lamenti,
che ben parean di miseri e d'offesi.
E io: 'Maestro, quai son quelle genti
che, seppellite dentro da quell'arche,
si fan sentir con li sospir dolenti?'
Ed elli a me: 'Qui son li eresïarche
co' lor seguaci, d'ogni setta, e molto
più che non credi son le tombe carche.
Simile qui con simile è sepolto, 130
e i monimenti son più e men caldi.'
E poi ch'alla man destra si fu volto,
passammo tra i martìri e li alti spaldi.

1. By Beatrice (Canto ii).

2. A Greek sorceress. The reference is possibly to one of the medieval legends about Virgil.

3. The Giudecca (Canto xxxiv).

4. Proserpine, wife of Pluto and Queen of Hell.

5. The Greek Furies.

soon as I was inside, and I saw on every hand a great plain full of pain and cruel torment. Just as at Arles where the Rhone makes a swamp, and at Pola near Quarnero, which bounds Italy and bathes its confines,[9] the graves make the whole place uneven, so they did here on every side, except for their more grievous nature here. For among the tombs were spread flames by which they were made to glow all over hotter than is wanted by any craft. All their lids stood open and such dire lamentations issued from them as plainly came from people wretched and suffering.

And I said: 'Master, who are these people buried within these chests whose groans of pain we hear?'

And he said to me: 'Here are the arch-heretics with their followers of every sect, and the tombs are laden far more than thou thinkest; like is buried with like and the monuments are heated more and less.'

Then, turning to the right, we passed between the torments and the lofty ramparts.

6. Medusa, one of the Gorgon sisters of Greek mythology; the sight of her turned men to stone.

7. Theseus, King of Athens, tried to rescue Proserpine from Hell and was himself rescued by Hercules.

8. Hercules dragged Cerberus from Hell with a chain.

9. At Arles in Provence and at Pola in Istria were ancient burial-places.

NOTE

Having passed through the circles of the upper Hell where the sins of weakness are punished, Dante approaches the deeper Hell of wilful sin, the stronghold of Satan, named after him the city of Dis. The importance of this stage in Dante's journey, the entering of Dis, is indicated both by the large space given to it, equivalent to a whole canto, and still more by its unique quality of crisis and suspense, his whole enterprise standing for a time in question. The approach is marked by signs increasingly terrifying: the mysterious gleam of the distant signal seen dimly through the fog of the marsh, the wailing of the imprisoned souls that 'smote on his ears' as they crossed, Virgil's formal announcement, 'Now, my son, the city draws near', with his solemn irony, 'its grave citizens and great garrison', the ominous red glow of the 'mosques' looming through the gross air, and the host of devils in the gateway shouting defiance at the travellers. It is a studied crescendo of terror.

The whole of the lower Hell is surrounded by a great wall, which is defended by the rebel angels and immediately within which are punished the arch-heretics and their followers. The ancient pagan schemes of human sin which Dante mainly followed in his Hell had, of course, no place either for the lack of Christian faith or for the denial of it, and both of these he must fit into his system. The former, the fatal defect as he must count it of the virtuous heathen, he put just before the sins of weakness; the latter, the sin as he must count it of wilful refusal of the truth of God and the soul, he put here, immediately within the walls of Dis, on the outermost ring of the city of wilful sin; so that the involuntary and the voluntary lack of faith—in scholastic terminology 'negative' and 'positive' unbelief—are linked respectively with the sins of weakness and of will. The character and conduct of the devil-garrison of the city, with the position of the infidels round its walls, at least suggest the idea, which may or may not have been in Dante's mind, that all deliberate and persistent sin, all the forms of violence and fraud found in the city of Satan within and below the wall, are in their real nature a rejection of grace and a contradiction of providence, the soul's refusal to have God in its knowledge, and that Satan himself, depicted by Dante as the complete negative of God, is what Goethe called him, 'the spirit that ever denies'.

The buildings of the city seen by Dante from a distance are called 'mosques', because for his generation to which the Crusades were a recent memory—the seventh and last Crusade was fought in Dante's childhood—the mosque was the very seat and symbol of stubborn and aggressive unbelief.

Virgil, going to parley with the rebel spirits at the gate, is defied for the first time in Hell and the ninth canto begins with his broken and hesitating utterances, very different from his usual language. 'The theme of the first part of this canto is *despair*, and these words of Virgil are obviously intended to lead up to it' (*A. J. Butler*). How much or how little of autobiography there is in this narrative of disablement and fear, it is, of course, impossible to say; but it is in harmony with much else that we know of Dante if we find here the memory of a period in his life when it seemed as if the foundations were removed and when there came to him a new assurance. The scene and mood of the first canto and his first meeting with Virgil on the desert slope are vividly recalled to us.

By the interpolation addressed to the reader—'Note the teaching'—Dante underlines, as it were, the significance of the Furies and the Gorgon, their traditional character as the spirits of remorse and despair. Against the forces of denial and refusal with these dreadful allies the conscience is all but paralysed and reason itself for the time baffled and disabled, and the soul's only safety is to wait on God. Ultimately, the question of salvation is the question of the resources of grace. We cannot, in the last reckoning, *prove* the things of the spirit against the denial of them; the reality, the sufficiency, of grace can be proved only by grace itself in its self-demonstration. Dante's attitude is precisely that of the Psalmist:

> 'Who will show us any good?
> Lord, lift thou up the light of thy countenance upon us.'

The coming of the angel is skilfully prepared for in the narrative. Virgil, stopped by the devils, has a strange, sure premonition of 'one' who has already passed the gate which Christ long ago broke down; then, in his perplexity and impatience, 'he stopped attentive, as if listening'; then, while he shelters Dante from the threatenings of the screaming Furies to bring Medusa, comes a sound as of a rushing mighty wind—surely suggested by the story of Pentecost and the gift of the Spirit; and then, august, serene, untroubled except by the foul fumes of men's earthly passions, 'one sent from Heaven', at whose presence devils and Furies are silent for fear and Virgil and Dante for reverence and at the touch of whose wand the way is open. It is 'the representation in naked simplicity of the victory of divine omnipotence over diabolical insolence' (*V. Rossi*).

The condition of the infidel souls within the walls is the fulfilment of their unbelief. In one way or other they have denied the soul's life; now, imprisoned in eternal tombs, they are only so far alive as to know the God whom they have refused, as a consuming fire. 'The tombs are laden', Virgil says, 'far more than thou thinkest'; for in that age of awakening thought and of warfare and debate for and against the Papacy, with the Inquisition on the watch, far more and graver heresy was suspected than was ever acknowledged or known.

INFERNO

ORA sen va per un secreto calle,
tra 'l muro de la terra e li martìri,
lo mio maestro, e io dopo le spalle.
'O virtù somma, che per li empi giri
mi volvi,' cominciai 'com'a te piace,
parlami, e sodisfammi a' miei disiri.
La gente che per li sepolcri giace
potrebbesi veder? già son levati
tutt' i coperchi, e nessun guardia face.'
Ed elli a me: 'Tutti saran serrati 10
quando di Iosafàt qui torneranno
coi corpi che là su hanno lasciati.
Suo cimitero da questa parte hanno
con Epicuro tutt'i suoi seguaci,
che l'anima col corpo morta fanno.
Però alla dimanda che mi faci
quinc'entro satisfatto sarà tosto,
e al disio ancor che tu mi taci.'
E io: 'Buon duca, non tegno riposto
a te mio cuor se non per dicer poco, 20
e tu m' hai non pur mo a ciò disposto.
'O Tosco che per la città del foco
vivo ten vai così parlando onesto,
piacciati di restare in questo loco.
La tua loquela ti fa manifesto
di quella nobil patrïa natio
alla qual forse fui troppo molesto.'
Subitamente questo suono uscìo
d'una dell'arche; però m'accostai,
temendo, un poco più al duca mio. 30

CANTO X

Farinata; Cavalcante

MY Master now made his way by a hidden track between the wall of the city and the torments, and I close behind him.

'O thou of loftiest virtue,' I began 'who leadest me round as thou wilt through the sinful circles, speak to me and satisfy my desires. The people that lie within the sepulchres, may they be seen, for indeed all the covers are raised and no one keeps guard?'

And he answered me: 'All will be shut in when they return from Jehoshaphat with the bodies they have left above.[1] In this part Epicurus and all his followers, who make the soul die with the body, have their burial-place;[2] but, for thy question to me, thou shalt soon have satisfaction from within there, and for the desire too about which thou art silent.'

And I said: 'Good Leader, I do not keep my heart hidden from thee except to speak less, and to that thou hast before now disposed me.'

'O Tuscan who makest thy way alive through the city of fire and speakest so modestly, may it please thee to stop at this point: thy tongue shows thee native of that noble fatherland to which I was perhaps too harsh.' Suddenly this sound issued from one of the chests, so that in fear I drew a little closer to my Leader.

Ed el mi disse: 'Volgiti: che fai?
  Vedi là Farinata che s'è dritto:
  dalla cintola in su tutto 'l vedrai.'
Io avea già il mio viso nel suo fitto;
  ed el s'ergea col petto e con la fronte
  com'avesse l' inferno in gran dispitto.
E l'animose man del duca e pronte
  mi pinser tra le sepulture a lui,
  dicendo: 'Le parole tue sien conte.'
Com' io al piè della sua tomba fui, 40
  guardommi un poco, e poi, quasi sdegnoso,
  mi dimandò: 'Chi fuor li maggior tui?'
Io ch'era d'ubidir disideroso,
  non lil celai, ma tutto lil'apersi;
  ond'ei levò le ciglia un poco in soso,
poi disse: 'Fieramente furo avversi
  a me e a miei primi e a mia parte,
  sì che per due fïate li dispersi.'
'S'ei fur cacciati, ei tornar d'ogni parte'
  rispuosi lui 'l'una e l'altra fïata; 50
  ma i vostri non appreser ben quell'arte.'
Allor surse alla vista scoperchiata
  un'ombra lungo questa infino al mento:
  credo che s'era in ginocchie levata.
Dintorno mi guardò, come talento
  avesse di veder s'altri era meco;
  e poi che il sospecciar fu tutto spento,
piangendo disse: 'Se per questo cieco
  carcere vai per altezza d' ingegno,
  mio figlio ov' è? perchè non è ei teco?' 60
E io a lui: 'Da me stesso non vegno:
  colui ch'attende là per qui mi mena,
  forse cui Guido vostro ebbe a disdegno.'
Le sue parole e 'l modo della pena
  m'avean di costui già letto il nome;
  però fu la risposta così piena.
Di subito drizzato gridò: 'Come
  dicesti: "Egli ebbe"? non viv'elli ancora?
  non fiere li occhi suoi il dolce lome?'

And he said to me: 'Turn round. What ails thee? See there Farinata who has risen erect; from the middle up thou shalt see his full height.'[3]

Already I had my eyes fixed on his and he was lifting up his breast and brow as if he had great scorn of Hell, and the bold and ready hands of my Leader pushed me between the tombs to him, saying: 'Let thy words be fitting.'

When I was at the foot of his tomb he looked at me for a moment, and then, as if in disdain, asked me: 'Who were thy ancestors?' And I, who was eager to obey, concealed nothing and made all plain to him; at which he raised his eyebrows a little, then said: 'They were fierce enemies to me and to my forebears and to my party, so that twice over I scattered them.'

'If they were driven out' I answered him 'they returned from every quarter both the first time and the second; but yours did not rightly learn that art.'

Then rose to sight beside him a shade showing as far as the chin; I think he had lifted himself on his knees. He looked round about me as if he had a desire to see whether someone was with me, but when his expectation was all quenched he said, weeping: 'If thou goest through this blind prison by height of genius, where is my son and why is he not with thee?'

And I answered him: 'I come not of myself; he that waits yonder is leading me through here, perhaps to her your Guido held in disdain.' His words and the nature of his punishment had already told me his name, so that I replied thus fully.[4]

Suddenly erect, he cried: 'How saidst thou "he held"? Lives he not still? Strikes not the sweet

Quando s'accorse d'alcuna dimora 70
ch' io facea dinanzi alla risposta,
supin ricadde e più non parve fora.
Ma quell'altro magnanimo a cui posta
restato m'era, non mutò aspetto,
nè mosse collo, nè piegò sua costa;
e sè continuando al primo detto,
'S'elli han quell'arte' disse 'male appresa,
ciò mi tormenta più che questo letto.
Ma non cinquanta volte fia raccesa
la faccia della donna che qui regge, 80
che tu saprai quanto quell'arte pesa.
E se tu mai nel dolce mondo regge,
dimmi perchè quel popolo è sì empio
incontr'a' miei in ciascuna sua legge?'
Ond' io a lui: 'Lo strazio e 'l grande scempio
che fece l'Arbia colorata in rosso,
tali orazion fa far nel nostro tempio.'
Poi ch'ebbe sospirato e 'l capo scosso,
'A ciò non fu' io sol,' disse 'nè certo
sanza cagion con li altri sarei mosso. 90
Ma fu' io solo, là dove sofferto
fu per ciascun di torre via Fiorenza,
colui che la difesi a viso aperto.'
'Deh, se riposi mai vostra semenza,'
prega' io lui 'solvetemi quel nodo
che qui ha inviluppata mia sentenza.
El par che voi veggiate, se ben odo,
dinanzi quel che 'l tempo seco adduce,
e nel presente tenete altro modo.'
'Noi veggiam, come quei c' ha mala luce, 100
le cose' disse 'che ne son lontano;
cotanto ancor ne splende il sommo duce.
Quando s'appressano o son, tutto è vano
nostro intelletto; e s'altri non ci apporta,
nulla sapem di vostro stato umano.
Però comprender puoi che tutta morta
fia nostra conoscenza da quel punto
che del futuro fia chiusa la porta.'

light on his eyes?' When he perceived that I made some delay before replying he fell back again and was seen no more.

But that other, the great soul at whose desire I had stopped, did not change countenance, nor move his head, nor bend his form. And continuing the former talk: 'If they have badly learned that art,' he said 'it is worse torment to me than this bed; but not fifty times shall the face of the lady who reigns here be rekindled before thou shalt know for thyself how hard is that art.[5] And, so mayst thou return some time to the sweet world, tell me why that people is so pitiless against my kindred in all its laws.'

To which I answered him: 'The rout and the great slaughter that stained the Arbia red are the cause of such devotions in our temple.'[6]

He sighed and shook his head, then said: 'In that I was not alone, nor without cause, assuredly, would I have moved with the rest; but there I was alone where all agreed to make an end of Florence, the one man to defend her before them all.'[7]

'So may your seed some time have rest, pray loose for me this knot,' I begged of him 'which has here entangled my judgement. It seems, if I hear aright, that you see beforehand what time brings with it, but that in regard to the present it is not so with you.'

'We see, like those with faulty vision, things at a distance from us,' he said 'so much light the Sovereign Lord still grants us; when they draw near or are present our intellect is wholly at fault and unless others bring us word we know nothing of your human state. Thou canst understand, therefore, that all our knowledge will be dead from the moment the door of the future is closed.'[8]

Allor, come di mia colpa compunto,
dissi: 'Or direte dunque a quel caduto 110
che 'l suo nato è co' vivi ancor congiunto;
e s' i' fui, dianzi, alla risposta muto,
fate i saper che 'l feci che pensava
già nell'error che m'avete soluto.'
E già il maestro mio mi richiamava;
per ch' i' pregai lo spirto più avaccio
che mi dicesse chi con lu' istava.
Dissemi: 'Qui con più di mille giaccio:
qua dentro è 'l secondo Federico,
e 'l Cardinale; e delli altri mi taccio.' 120
Indi s'ascose; ed io inver l'antico
poeta volsi i passi, ripensando
a quel parlar che mi parea nemico.
Elli si mosse; e poi, così andando,
mi disse: 'Perchè se' tu sì smarrito?'
E io li sodisfeci al suo dimando.
'La mente tua conservi quel ch'udito
hai contra te' mi comandò quel saggio.
'E ora attendi qui' e drizzò 'l dito:
'quando sarai dinanzi al dolce raggio 130
di quella il cui bell'occhio tutto vede,
da lei saprai di tua vita il vïaggio.'
Appresso volse a man sinistra il piede:
lasciammo il muro e gimmo inver lo mezzo
per un sentier ch'a una valle fiede
che 'nfin là su facea spiacer suo lezzo.

1. The Valley of Jehoshaphat near Jerusalem was regarded as the place of the Last Judgement. 'I will gather all nations and will bring them down into the valley of Jehoshaphat, . . . for there will I sit to judge all the heathen' (*Joel* iii. 2, 12).

2. Epicurus's doctrine of happiness as the chief good was identified with various heresies which may be summed up as materialistic sensualism.

3. Farinata degli Uberti, head of the Florentine Ghibellines when the Guelfs were twice expelled from the city and when they were routed at Montaperti near the river Arbia in 1260, Dante's family being Guelf. To both Farinata and Cavalcante Dante uses the respectful *you*.

4. It is the shade of Cavalcante, a leading Guelf in Florence, whose son Guido was married to Farinata's daughter and was Dante's senior and intimate and a leading poet in Florence; Guido died a few months after the date of the Vision.

Then, being moved with compunction for my fault, I said: 'Will you, now, tell him who fell back that his son is still in the company of the living? And let him know that, if I was silent in response to him before, it is because I was already occupied with the doubt you have cleared for me.'

And now my Master was recalling me; with more haste, therefore, I begged the spirit to tell me who were there with him, and he said to me: 'I lie here with more than a thousand. Within here is the second Frederick[9] and the Cardinal,[10] and of the rest I say nothing.'

With that he hid himself, and I turned my steps to the ancient Poet, thinking over that saying which seemed hostile to me. He set out, and then, as we went, he said to me: 'Why art thou so lost in thought?' And I satisfied his question.

'Keep in thy memory what thou hast heard against thyself,' the Sage bade me 'but now give heed to what is here'; and he pointed with his finger. 'When thou art before her sweet radiance whose fair eyes see all, thou shalt know from her of thy life's journey.'

Then he turned his feet to the left and leaving the wall we went towards the centre by a path that strikes down to a valley from which the stench even up there was offensive.

5. The moon is identified with Proserpine, Queen of Hell. Fifty months after this (1304) a great attempt at the reconciliation and return of the Florentine exiles, Dante among them, was unsuccessful.

6. The repeated decree for the exclusion of the Uberti from Florence was passed probably in the Church of St John, the present Baptistery; such were the 'devotions' of Florence.

7. After Montaperti the Ghibellines proposed to destroy Florence.

8. When time ends with the Judgement Day.

9. Emperor (1212–1250), charged with sensualism and materialism.

10. Cardinal Ottaviano degli Ubaldini, of a great Ghibelline family, is reported to have said: 'If there is a soul, I have lost mine a thousand times for the Ghibellines.'

NOTE

The opening lines of the tenth canto put a fresh emphasis on Dante's docility to Virgil—'I close behind him'—'O thou of loftiest virtue who leadest me round as thou wilt'. It is the docility, indeed, of personal confidence and affection, for Virgil never ceases to be Virgil, but it is also the soul's docility, after its deliverance from despair, to reason that is subject to the divine prompting, and this, significantly, in the place where rebellious reason bears its penalty.

But here the allegory gives place to a dramatic scene in which Virgil has little share and in which the parts are taken by Dante himself and two other Florentines, both of the generation immediately before his own. The two belonged severally and prominently to the two parties whose strife had rent the public and private life of Florence for more than a generation,—as if Dante would show that the heresy punished here was no monopoly of the imperialist, anti-papal Ghibellines, as their Guelf enemies were ready to make out.

'The desire about which he was silent' to Virgil might well be Dante's desire to know if Farinata was there. Farinata degli Uberti was the first of the 'men of such worth, whose minds were set on well-doing', about whom he had questioned Ciacco and of whom Ciacco had said they were 'among the blackest souls' below (Canto vi). The great Ghibelline had been the leader of his party in Florence in their last struggles, before and after the middle of the century, against the rising power of the Guelf burghers in the commune. In the shifting fortunes of the civil war his party was in possession of Florence when he died there in the year before Dante's birth, two years before they were finally defeated and expelled. Brought up as Dante was in a Guelf family which had suffered repeatedly during the recent troubles and in a Florence intensely conscious and jealous of its Guelf liberties, the name and fame of Farinata, and in particular the story of Montaperti, would be very familiar to him, and in Dante's eighteenth year Farinata and his wife were retrospectively convicted of heresy by the Inquisition, their bones scattered, and the family property confiscated.

Farinata's gaunt and tragic figure is one of the most imposing creations of Dante's *Inferno*, 'the greatest of Dante's colossal sculptures' (*E. G. Parodi*). His voice breaks suddenly through the groans from the tombs, prompted by the sound of the tongue of Florence, and Dante, shrinking before the towering, ghostly presence and yet gazing at it with fascination, is challenged abruptly by the great noble: 'Who were thy ancestors?' When Dante names his family, Farinata, 'raising his eyebrows a little', recollecting with an effort a family of the minor nobility, remembers that he 'twice scattered them'. He is wholly unmoved by the paternal agony of his Guelf compatriot and companion in misery which interrupts for a moment their talk, though the two families were closely allied. And yet he loves his 'noble fatherland' more than he hates his Florentine enemies. He learns now the cause of his city's unrelenting hatred of his family who were by repeated decrees expressly excluded from permission to return, and he almost yields to plead with Dante —himself soon to be an outcast—against it. The scene culminates in his claim to have saved Florence in the hour of her extreme peril, he 'the one man to defend her before them all'. The line is an echo of the actual words of Farinata at the Ghibelline council after Montaperti, as they are reported by the old historian: 'Whoever he be that would destroy her, while life is in my body I shall defend her sword in hand'. 'All, victors and victims, overwhelmed by party passion, he alone the heroic victor over his passion for love of his country' (*V. Rossi*).

It is for that greatness of soul that Dante honours Farinata. 'In the years when he was writing the first cantos of the *Inferno* he had already formed his political ideas, which were neither Guelf nor Ghibelline in the common sense of the words. He condemned both parties and would have Church and Empire, instead of striving with each other, to return each to its proper office, factions to disappear, injustices and persecutions to be ended, and peace to flourish again' (*M. Barbi*). The dramatic and personal quality of the whole scene is shot through with Dante's plea for civil and religious reconciliation and peace. It is as the Guelf of 1300 that Dante recalls against Farinata 'the slaughter that stained the Arbia red' forty years before. 'That was the deed which Farinata's enemies, these Guelfs to whom Dante was not yet ashamed to belong, adduced in justification of their legislative perfidy. But the poet of the *Comedy*, who is Dante no longer of Florence, the citizen of the world for whom the world is his country as for the fish the sea, revolts against the prolonged iniquity and enters his protest in the name of justice trampled down; it is the Dante of the New Testament who withstands the Dante of the Old' (*M. Scherillo, L.D.*).

In strong contrast with Farinata is Cavalcante beside him, whose absorbing passion is his fatherly affection and pride and who falls back in despair at the thought that his son Guido is no longer alive. In the *Vita Nuova* Dante refers to Guido Cavalcanti as 'the first among my friends' and in the *Purgatorio* as a poet of distinction. The son of an 'Epicurean', distinguished as much in philosophy as in poetry, reputed a sceptic in religion, Guido would seem to Dante to be on a perilous road. His 'disdain' for Beatrice must, in the context, mean his repudiation of that which for Dante was divine truth and his contempt for the spiritual aspiration which alone—and not 'height of genius'—could fit him for such a journey as Dante's. For himself Dante claims only that he is being led by Virgil 'perhaps to her'. He dare not yet claim more than the hope, but it is that hope that makes him follow Virgil through Hell. How much Dante meant by this reference to Guido we cannot tell, and it has been much discussed, but surely something of essential divergence and moral estrangement between the two old friends. His words 'your Guido held', which Cavalcante misunderstood, come naturally from Dante's recollection of his youth and intimacy with Guido in Florence; and in reporting the message which he left for the father that 'his son is still in the company of the living' he must be supposed to have had vividly in his mind the fact that Guido was then lying sick in Florence and was within a few months of death.

CANTO X

From Farinata Dante has the first warning of his own coming exile and of his finding it hard to return to Florence, and when Farinata says that 'not fifty times shall the face of the lady who reigns here be rekindled' before his words are fulfilled it is not meant merely that this will happen within fifty months, but that that dark time for Dante is to be measured in relation to the powers and the course of Hell. In his bewilderment Virgil bids him wait to know of his life's journey from Beatrice, to know, in knowing better the truth of God, the meaning of his own life. It is the repudiation on his own account of the doctrine here current, which 'makes the soul die with the body' and has only an earthly measure for human good and ill, and his declaration that the worth and gain of his days, the darkest of them, is to be made plain in the context of God's purposes and in her radiance 'whose fair eyes see all'.

The law by which the lost are limited in their knowledge of earthly events to the past and the future is partly based on the current theological teaching of the time, but as here defined it is largely Dante's own invention. The device not only gives opportunity in the poem for the forecasting of events known to Dante himself at the time of writing, but adds a singularly grim feature to all the penalties of Hell. The 'light' granted to the souls there by the Sovereign Lord is that they look forward through the years to a door which is some time to close on them, so that then they will be left with only their eternal memories.

IN su l'estremità d'un'alta ripa
che facevan gran pietre rotte in cerchio,
venimmo sopra più crudele stipa;
e quivi per l'orribile soperchio
del puzzo che 'l profondo abisso gitta,
ci raccostammo in dietro ad un coperchio
d'un grand'avello, ov' io vidi una scritta
che dicea: 'Anastasio papa guardo,
lo qual trasse Fotin della via dritta.'
'Lo nostro scender conviene esser tardo, 10
sì che s'ausi un poco in prima il senso
al tristo fiato; e poi no i fia riguardo.'
Così 'l maestro; e io 'Alcun compenso'
dissi lui 'trova, che 'l tempo non passi
perduto.' Ed elli: 'Vedi ch'a ciò penso.'
'Figliuol mio, dentro da cotesti sassi'
cominciò poi a dir 'son tre cerchietti
di grado in grado, come que' che lassi.
Tutti son pien di spirti maladetti;
ma perchè poi ti basti pur la vista, 20
intendi come e perchè son costretti.
D'ogni malizia ch'odio in cielo acquista
ingiuria è 'l fine, ed ogni fin cotale
o con forza o con frode altrui contrista.
Ma perchè frode è dell'uom proprio male,
più spiace a Dio; e però stan di sutto
li frodolenti e più dolor li assale.
De' vïolenti il primo cerchio è tutto;
ma perchè si fa forza a tre persone,
in tre gironi è distinto e costrutto. 30

CANTO XI

The Plan of Hell

ON the edge of a great steep made by a circle of huge broken rocks we came above a more cruel pen, and here, for the horrible excess of stench thrown up by the profound abyss, we drew back behind the cover of a great vault on which I saw an inscription that said: 'I hold Pope Anastasius, whom Photinus drew from the straight path.'[1]

'We must delay our descent, that the sense may first get used a little to the vile breath, and then we shall not heed it.' Thus the Master; and I: 'Find some compensation, that the time may not be lost'; and he: 'Thou shalt see it is my own thought.'

'My son,' he began then 'within these cliffs are three lesser circles, one below another, like those thou art leaving; all are full of spirits accursed, but, that afterwards the sight itself may suffice thee, understand how and why they are confined there. Every kind of wickedness that gains the hatred of Heaven has injustice for its end, and every such end afflicts someone either by force or fraud;[2] but because fraud is a sin peculiar to man it is more offensive to God, and for that reason the fraudulent have their place lower and more pain assails them. All the first circle is of the violent; but since violence is done to three persons, it is formed of three

A Dio, a sè, al prossimo si pòne
  far forza, dico in loro ed in lor cose,
  come udirai con aperta ragione.
Morte per forza e ferute dogliose
  nel prossimo si danno, e nel suo avere
  ruine, incendi e tollette dannose;
onde omicide e ciascun che mal fiere,
  guastatori e predon, tutti tormenta
  lo giron primo per diverse schiere.
Puote omo avere in sè man vïolenta 40
  e ne' suoi beni; e però nel secondo
  giron convien che sanza pro si penta
qualunque priva sè del vostro mondo,
  biscazza e fonde la sua facultade,
  e piange là dov'esser de' giocondo.
Puossi far forza nella deitade,
  col cuor negando e bestemmiando quella,
  e spregiando natura e sua bontade;
e però lo minor giron suggella
  del segno suo e Soddoma e Caorsa 50
  e chi spregiando Dio col cor favella.
La frode, ond'ogni coscïenza è morsa,
  può l'omo usare in colui che 'n lui fida
  ed in quel che fidanza non imborsa.
Questo modo di retro par ch'uccida
  pur lo vinco d'amor che fa natura;
  onde nel cerchio secondo s'annida
ipocrisia, lusinghe e chi affattura,
  falsità, ladroneccio e simonia,
  ruffian, baratti, e simile lordura. 60
Per l'altro modo quell'amor s'oblia
  che fa natura, e quel ch' è poi aggiunto,
  di che la fede spezïal si cria;
onde nel cerchio minore, ov' è 'l punto
  dell' universo in su che Dite siede,
  qualunque trade in etterno è consunto.'
E io: 'Maestro, assai chiara procede
  la tua ragione, ed assai ben distingue
  questo baratro e 'l popol ch'e' possiede.

separate rounds. Force may be used against God, against oneself, against a neighbour—in themselves, that is, or in things that are theirs, as I shall make plain to thee. Violent death and painful wounds are inflicted on a neighbour, and on his substance devastations, burnings, and wrongful exactions; therefore homicides and everyone that wounds in malice, pillagers and plunderers, the first round torments them all in different troops. A man may lay violent hands on himself or on his own possessions, and therefore in the second round must repent in vain whoever robs himself of your world or gambles away and dissipates his wealth, lamenting where he should rejoice. Violence may be done to the Godhead by denying and blaspheming Him in the heart and by despising nature and her bounty, and therefore the smallest round stamps with its seal both Sodom[3] and Cahors[4] and him that speaks despitefully in his heart against God.[5] Fraud, which always stings the conscience, a man may practise on one who confides in him or on one who does not so place his confidence; it is evident that this latter way destroys simply the bond of love which nature makes, so that in the next circle hypocrisy, flatteries, sorceries, falsifications, theft, and simony, panders, jobbers, and like filth have their nest. By the other way both that love which nature makes is forgotten and that also which is added to it and which creates a special trust; therefore in the smallest circle, at the central point of the universe and seat of Dis, every traitor is consumed eternally.'

And I said: 'Master, thy account is quite clear thus far and makes very plain the distinctions in this abyss and among the people it holds; but tell

Ma dimmi: quei della palude pingue, 70
  che mena il vento, e che batte la pioggia,
  e che s' incontran con sì aspre lingue,
perchè non dentro dalla città roggia
  sono ei puniti, se Dio li ha in ira?
  e se non li ha, perchè sono a tal foggia?'
Ed elli a me: 'Perchè tanto delira'
  disse 'lo 'ngegno tuo da quel che sòle?
  o ver la mente dove altrove mira?
Non ti rimembra di quelle parole
  con le quai la tua Etica pertratta 80
  le tre disposizion che 'l ciel non vole,
incontinenza, malizia e la matta
  bestialitade? e come incontinenza
  men Dio offende e men biasimo accatta?
Se tu riguardi ben questa sentenza,
  e rechiti alla mente chi son quelli
  che su di fuor sostegnon penitenza,
tu vedrai ben perchè da questi felli
  sien dipartiti, e perchè men crucciata
  la divina vendetta li martelli.' 90
'O sol che sani ogni vista turbata,
  tu mi contenti sì quando tu solvi,
  che, non men che saver, dubbiar m'aggrata.
Ancora un poco in dietro ti rivolvi,'
  diss' io 'là dove di' ch'usura offende
  la divina bontade, e 'l groppo solvi.'
'Filosofia,' mi disse 'a chi la 'ntende,
  nota non pur in una sola parte
  come natura lo suo corso prende
da divino intelletto e da sua arte; 100
  e se tu ben la tua Fisica note,
  tu troverai, non dopo molte carte,
che l'arte vostra quella, quanto pote,
  segue, come 'l maestro fa il discente;
  sì che vostr'arte a Dio quasi è nepote.
Da queste due, se tu ti rechi a mente
  lo Genesì dal principio, convene
  prender sua vita ed avanzar la gente;

me, those of the slimy bog, those the wind drives, those the rain beats on, and those that encounter with such bitter tongues, why are they not punished within the red city if God holds them in His wrath? And if He does not why are they in such a plight?'

And he said to me: 'Why do thy thoughts wander so from their wont, or where else is thy mind looking? Rememberest thou not the words with which thy *Ethics*[6] expounds the three dispositions which are against the will of Heaven, incontinence, malice, and mad brutishness, and how incontinence offends God less and incurs less blame? If thou consider well this teaching and call to mind who are those that bear their penalty above outside thou shalt see clearly why they are separated from these wicked spirits and why divine vengeance smites them with less wrath.'

'O Sun that healest all troubled sight, so dost thou satisfy me with the resolving of my doubts that it is no less grateful to me to question than to know. Turn back again a little' I said 'to the point where thou saidst that usury offends against the Divine Goodness, and loose that knot.'

'Philosophy, for one who understands,' he said to me 'notes, not in one place only, how nature takes her course from the divine mind and its art;[7] and if thou note well thy *Physics* thou wilt find, not many pages on, that your art, as far as it can, follows nature as the pupil the master, so that your art is to God, as it were, a grandchild. By these two, if thou recall to mind *Genesis* near the beginning,[8] it behoves mankind to gain their livelihood and their advancement, and because the usurer

e perchè l'usuriere altra via tene,
per sè natura e per la sua seguace 110
dispregia, poi ch' in altro pon la spene.
Ma seguimi oramai, che 'l gir mi piace;
chè i Pesci guizzan su per l'orizzonta,
e 'l Carro tutto sovra 'l Coro giace,
e 'l balzo via là oltra si dismonta.'

1. In medieval tradition Pope Anastasius (5th century) was persuaded by Photinus, a deacon of Thessalonica, to deny the divine birth of Christ.

2. 'Thou hatest all workers of iniquity' (*Ps.* v. 5). Cicero divided wilful sins into those of violence and those of fraud.

3. Sodomites; *Gen.* xix. 5.

4. Usurers, for whom the French town was notorious, so that they were known as Caorsines.

takes another way he despises nature both in herself and in her follower, setting his hope elsewhere.

But now follow me, for I would go; the Fishes are quivering on the horizon and all the Wain lies over Caurus[9] and farther on there is the descent of the cliff.'

5. 'The fool hath said in his heart, There is no God' (*Ps.* xiv. 1).

6. *Ethics,* Philosophy and *Physics* below mean Aristotle's.

7. 'Art' in the sense of operation or workmanship; nature is God's 'art'.

8. Man's material resources are nature and industry. 'God blessed them and said, . . . Replenish the earth and subdue it. . . . And God said, Behold I have given you every herb, . . . to you it shall be for meat' (*Gen.* i. 28–29).

9. The Constellation of the Fishes rises in that season shortly before the sun; Caurus is the N.W. wind; it is now early morning of Holy Saturday.

NOTE

The position of Anastasius's tomb in the circle of the infidels, almost on the edge of the pit and within reach of the stench rising from the fouler sins below, indicates how great an outrage on truth itself Dante reckoned an unbelieving pope to be. It is in the shelter of his tomb, as it were in that context, that Dante learns the plan of the lower Hell.

The canto is the most prosaic in the *Inferno*, being little more than a verbal diagram. Its plan is taken partly from Cicero and partly from Aristotle, the authority of the latter being hardly less for Dante than that of Scripture. Cicero's 'force', or violence, is taken as equivalent to Aristotle's 'mad brutishness', Cicero's 'fraud' to Aristotle's 'malice', and 'incontinence' is named only by Aristotle. Fraud, as compared with violence, 'is a sin peculiar to man'; it is specifically an abuse of man's specific gift of reason and by its nature a conscious and deliberate offence, which 'always stings the conscience', and is therefore the more damning; and of all fraud treachery, the breach of trust, offends the most. Still before the travellers, therefore, are the three great circles of violence, simple fraud, and treachery.

It has been suggested that the surprising sharpness of Virgil's rebuke of Dante for his question about the incontinent outside the city of Dis is connected with a Stoic view held by some Christian sects and regarded as heretical, that all sins are of equal guilt and subject to the same penalties. Dante's outburst of gratitude for Virgil's explanation indicates the importance in his mind of the broad distinction between the sins of weakness and those of will, a distinction represented by the fiery city wall.

It is by a very curious piece of medieval thinking that sins so different as blasphemy, sodomy, and usury are grouped together as forms of violence against God, directed respectively against God Himself, against nature, God's 'art', and against human art or industry, which springs from nature and follows it. The lending of money for interest, though it was increasingly practised and was, indeed, inevitable in the commercial development of Florence, lay under the formal condemnation of the Church and, as it was practised, often deserved its condemnation, being the breeding of money from money by the deliberate abuse of men's weakness or neediness. That injurious sucking of private advantage out of men's necessities Dante regarded as an outrage on the divine order of society in material things and, even more than blasphemy itself, an offence against the goodness of God.

There were various Christian sects, considered heretical, which were active in thirteenth century Italy, Waldensians, Catharists and others, and it has been thought that Dante's silence about them here may be due to the fact that they had sprung up, in general, as protests against the existing corruptions of the Church and as appeals for a purer Christianity; for in Dante's measure of right and wrong the intention is always fundamental. In the whole descending scale of sins, from incontinence to treachery, he observes 'that high principle of justice, but little known, in truth, in the fourteenth century, that the sole criterion for estimating the moral and juridical responsibility of human actions is the intention that has determined them, and not the material effect they have produced' (*V. Vaturi, L.D.*).

INFERNO

Era lo loco, ov'a scender la riva
  venimmo, alpestro e, per quel ch' iv'er'anco,
  tal ch'ogni vista ne sarebbe schiva.
Qual è quella ruina che nel fianco
  di qua da Trento l'Adice percosse,
  o per tremoto o per sostegno manco,
che da cima del monte, onde si mosse,
  al piano è sì la roccia discoscesa,
  ch'alcuna via darebbe a chi su fosse;
cotal di quel burrato era la scesa; 10
  e 'n su la punta della rotta lacca
  l' infamïa di Creti era distesa
che fu concetta nella falsa vacca;
  e quando vide noi, sè stesso morse,
  sì come quei cui l' ira dentro fiacca.
Lo savio mio inver lui gridò: 'Forse
  tu credi che qui sia 'l duca d'Atene,
  che su nel mondo la morte ti porse?
Partiti, bestia: chè questi non vene
  ammaestrato dalla tua sorella, 20
  ma vassi per veder le vostre pene.'
Qual è quel toro che si slaccia in quella
  c' ha ricevuto già 'l colpo mortale,
  che gir non sa, ma qua e là saltella,
vid' io lo Minotauro far cotale;
  e quello accorto gridò: 'Corri al varco:
  mentre ch' è in furia è buon che tu ti cale.'

CANTO XII

The Seventh Circle; the Violent; the Minotaur; the First Round; the Violent against others; the Centaurs; the Phlegethon

THE place where we came for the descent of the steep was alpine, and besides, because of what was there, a place every eye would shun. Like the landslip that struck the flank of the Adige on this side Trent on account of earthquake or lack of support, where from the mountain-top from which it started to the plain the rocks are so shattered that they would give some footing for one above, such was the descent of that ravine; and on the edge of the broken chasm was outstretched the infamy of Crete that was conceived in the pretended cow.[1] And when he saw us he gnawed himself, like one that bursts with inward rage.

My Sage cried to him: 'Thou thinkest, perhaps, that the Duke of Athens is here, who in the world above gave thee thy death. Get thee gone, beast, for this man does not come tutored by thy sister, but is on his way to see your pains.'

Like the bull that breaks loose the moment it has received its mortal stroke and cannot go on but plunges this way and that, so I saw the Minotaur do, and my Guide, perceiving it, cried: 'Run to the passage; it is well thou descend while he is in fury.'

Così prendemmo via giù per lo scarco
di quelle pietre, che spesso moviensi
sotto i miei piedi per lo novo carco. 30
Io gìa pensando; e quei disse: 'Tu pensi
forse in questa ruina ch' è guardata
da quell' ira bestial ch' i' ora spensi.
Or vo' che sappi che l'altra fïata
ch' i' discesi qua giù nel basso inferno,
questa roccia non era ancor cascata;
ma certo poco pria, se ben discerno,
che venisse colui che la gran preda
levò a Dite del cerchio superno,
da tutte parti l'alta valle feda 40
tremò sì, ch' i' pensai che l'universo
sentisse amor, per lo qual è chi creda
più volte il mondo in caòs converso;
ed in quel punto questa vecchia roccia
qui e altrove tal fece riverso.
Ma ficca li occhi a valle, chè s'approccia
la riviera del sangue in la qual bolle
qual che per vïolenza in altrui noccia.'
Oh cieca cupidigia e ira folle,
che sì ci sproni nella vita corta, 50
e nell'etterna poi sì mal c' immolle!
Io vidi un'ampia fossa in arco torta,
come quella che tutto 'l piano abbraccia,
secondo ch'avea detto la mia scorta;
e tra 'l piè della ripa ed essa, in traccia
corrìen Centauri, armati di saette,
come solìen nel mondo andare a caccia.
Veggendoci calar, ciascun ristette,
e della schiera tre si dipartiro
con archi e asticciuole prima elette; 60
e l'un gridò da lungi: 'A qual martiro
venite voi che scendete la costa?
Ditel costinci; se non, l'arco tiro.'
Lo mio maestro disse: 'La risposta
farem noi a Chiron costà di presso:
mal fu la voglia tua sempre sì tosta.'

CANTO XII

So we took our way down that scree of stones, which often moved under my feet with the new weight.

I was going on in thought when he said: 'Thou are thinking, perhaps, of this ruined cliff that is guarded by that bestial rage I quenched just now; know then that the other time I came down here into the nether Hell this rock had not yet fallen. But surely, if I reckon rightly, it was a little before he came who carried off from Dis the great spoil of the highest circle that the deep, foul valley trembled on every side[2] so that I thought the universe felt love, by which, as some believe, the world has many times been turned to chaos;[3] and at that moment this ancient rock, here and elsewhere, was thrown down thus. But fix thine eyes below, for the river of blood draws near in which are boiling those that by violence do injury to others.'

O blind covetousness and foolish anger, which in the brief life so goad us on and then, in the eternal, steep us in such misery! I saw a broad moat bent in a curve so as to encircle the whole level, just as my Escort had said, and between it and the foot of the scarp ran centaurs in line armed with arrows, as they were accustomed on earth to follow the chase. Seeing us coming down they all stopped and three left the troop with bows and shafts which they first selected, and one cried from a distance: 'To what torment do you come, you that descend the slope? Tell us from there; if not, I draw my bow.'

My Master said: 'We will give our answer to Chiron beside thee there. Thy will was ever thus hasty, to thy hurt.' Then he touched me and said:

Poi mi tentò, e disse: 'Quelli è Nesso,
  che morì per la bella Deianira
  e fè di sè la vendetta elli stesso.
E quel di mezzo, ch'al petto si mira, 70
  è il gran Chiron, il qual nodrì Achille;
  quell'altro è Folo, che fu sì pien d' ira.
Dintorno al fosso vanno a mille a mille,
  saettando qual anima si svelle
  del sangue più che sua colpa sortille.'
Noi ci appressammo a quelle fiere snelle:
  Chiron prese uno strale, e con la cocca
  fece la barba in dietro alle mascelle.
Quando s'ebbe scoperta la gran bocca,
  disse a' compagni: 'Siete voi accorti 80
  che quel di retro move ciò ch'el tocca?
Così non soglion far li piè de' morti.'
  E 'l mio buon duca, che già li era al petto,
  dove le due nature son consorti,
rispuose: 'Ben è vivo, e sì soletto
  mostrar li mi convien la valle buia:
  necessità 'l ci 'nduce, e non diletto.
Tal si partì da cantare alleluia
  che mi commise quest'officio novo:
  non è ladron, nè io anima fuia. 90
Ma per quella virtù per cu' io movo
  li passi miei per sì selvaggia strada,
  danne un de' tuoi, a cui noi siamo a provo,
e che ne mostri là dove si guada,
  e che porti costui in su la groppa,
  chè non è spirto che per l'aere vada.'
Chiron si volse in su la destra poppa,
  e disse a Nesso: 'Torna, e sì li guida,
  e fa cansar s'altra schiera v' intoppa.'
Or ci movemmo con la scorta fida 100
  lungo la proda del bollor vermiglio,
  dove i bolliti facìeno alte strida.
Io vidi gente sotto infino al ciglio;
  e 'l gran Centauro disse: 'E' son tiranni
  che dier nel sangue e nell'aver di piglio.

'That is Nessus, who died for the fair Dejanira and himself avenged himself;[4] and he in the middle that looks down on his breast is the great Chiron, who brought up Achilles; and that other is Pholus, who was so full of anger. Round the moat they go by thousands, directing their arrows at any soul that draws itself out of the blood farther than its guilt allots to it.'

We drew near to these agile beasts and Chiron took a dart and with the notch put his beard back on his jaws, and when he had uncovered his great mouth he said to his companions: 'Have you observed that the one behind moves what he touches? The feet of the dead are not wont to do so.'

And my good Leader, who was now at his breast where the two natures are joined, replied: 'He is indeed alive and, alone as he is, I must show him the gloomy valley. Necessity brings him here, not pleasure. It was one that left her singing of hallelujahs who laid on me this new task. He is no robber, nor I a thievish spirit; but, by that Power by which I move my steps on so wild a track, give us one of thy band whom we may keep beside, that he may show us where the ford is and carry this man over on his back, for he is not a spirit to go through the air.'

Chiron bent round on his right breast and said to Nessus: 'Go back and guide them then, and if you meet another troop make it keep off.'

We moved on then with the trusty guide along the margin of the red boiling, in which the boiled made piercing shrieks. I saw people sunk to the eyebrows, and the great Centaur said: 'They are tyrants who gave their hands to blood and plunder;

Quivi si piangon li spietati danni;
quivi è Alessandro, e Dïonisio fero,
che fè Cicilia aver dolorosi anni.
E quella fronte c' ha 'l pel così nero,
è Azzolino; e quell'altro ch' è biondo, 110
è Opizzo da Esti, il qual per vero
fu spento dal figliastro su nel mondo.'
Allor mi volsi al poeta, e quei disse:
'Questi ti sia or primo, e io secondo.'
Poco più oltre il Centauro s'affisse
sovr'una gente che 'nfino alla gola
parea che di quel bulicame uscisse.
Mostrocci un'ombra dall'un canto sola,
dicendo: 'Colui fesse in grembo a Dio
lo cor che 'n su Tamici ancor si cola.' 120
Poi vidi gente che di fuor del rio
tenean la testa ed ancor tutto il casso;
e di costoro assai riconobb' io.
Così a più a più si facea basso
quel sangue, sì che cocea pur li piedi;
e quindi fu del fosso il nostro passo.
'Sì come tu da questa parte vedi
lo bulicame che sempre si scema'
disse 'l Centauro 'voglio che tu credi
che da quest'altra a più a più giù prema 130
lo fondo suo, infin ch'el si raggiunge
ove la tirannia convien che gema.
La divina giustizia di qua punge
quell'Attila che fu flagello in terra
e Pirro e Sesto; ed in etterno munge
le lagrime, che col bollor diserra,
a Rinier da Corneto, a Rinier Pazzo,
che fecero alle strade tanta guerra.'
Poi si rivolse, e ripassossi 'l guazzo.

here they lament their ruthless crimes. Here is Alexander and cruel Dionysius, he that gave woeful years to Sicily;[5] and that brow with the hair so black is Ezzelino, and that other that is fair Obizzo of Este, who was indeed made an end of by his step-son in the world above.'[6]

Then I turned to the Poet, and he said: 'Let him be first with thee now and me second.'

A little farther on the Centaur stopped above a crowd who appeared as far as the throat issuing from that boiling stream, and he pointed out to us a shade on one side alone and said: 'That one clove in God's bosom the heart which still drips on the Thames.'[7]

Then I saw people who had the head and also the whole chest out of the river, and of these I recognized many. So, more and more, the blood there became shallow till it cooked only the feet; and here was our passage of the moat.

'As on this side thou seest the boiling stream diminish continually,' said the Centaur 'so I would have thee know that on the other, more and more, it deepens its bed till it comes again to the place where tyranny must groan. There Divine Justice stings that Attila who was a scourge on earth,[8] and Pyrrhus, and Sextus,[9] and eternally milks the tears, unlocked by the boiling, from Rinier of Corneto and Rinier Pazzo, who on the highways made such strife.'[10]

Then he turned back and crossed the ford again.

1. The Minotaur, for Dante a bull with a human head, was the fruit of the passion of Pasiphae, wife of King Minos of Crete, for a bull when she concealed herself in the wooden figure of a cow. It devoured an annual tribute of youths and maidens from Athens and was killed by Theseus of Athens, helped by his mistress Ariadne, the Minotaur's half-sister.

2. The Harrowing of Hell (Canto iv) and the earthquake at the Crucifixion (*Matt.* xxvii. 50–51).

3. Empedocles was supposed to have taught that the material order of the world was due to the discord of the elements and that when they are brought into harmony by 'love' the world loses its variety and the result is 'chaos'.

4. Nessus having offered violence to Dejanira, Hercules, her husband, shot him with a poisoned arrow; dying, he left his shirt, stained with his poisoned blood, to Dejanira as a charm; later she gave it to Hercules and it caused his death. Chiron was the son of Saturn and famed for his wisdom. Little is said of Pholus in classical literature.

5. Alexander of Macedon and Dionysius of Syracuse, tyrants of antiquity.

6. Two notoriously cruel tyrants in North Italy in the 13th century, respectively Guelf and Ghibelline. There were rumours of Obizzo's murder.

7. Guy de Montfort of England avenged in 1272 the death of his father Simon, by stabbing his cousin, the nephew of Henry III of England, in a church in Viterbo during the elevation of the host; the heart of the murdered man was supposed to be preserved in a casket in Westminster Abbey.

8. Attila the Hun, known as 'the Scourge of God', invaded Italy in the 5th century.

9. Pyrrhus of Epirus and Sextus, son of Pompey, enemies of Rome.

10. Robber nobles of the time.

NOTE

On the brink of the steep that leads down to the various classes of the violent, the monster Minotaur represents 'mad brutishness' in general, which is punished in the three rounds of the seventh circle. He was the fruit of an unnatural lust and he fed on human flesh. His helpless and senseless fury when reminded by Virgil of his death at the hands of Theseus marks the limit of the brute before the challenge of reason.

The earthquake of the Crucifixion, by which the precipitous sides of the great pit containing the lower Hell were broken at parts into great screes on which Dante can descend, was a shudder and convulsion of the world at the greatest of all crimes, committed against the supreme love. The kingdom of Satan was shaken and the effects are seen especially in those parts of Hell, here and farther down, where violence and hypocrisy are punished, the sins which joined in the Crucifixion to do their worst.

Virgil's curiously hesitating reference to the curious doctrine ascribed to Empedocles about the effect of the thrill of 'love' on the material order of the universe seems a mere philosophic irrelevance, and the question rises why it is here at all. May that irrelevance itself be Dante's method of indicating the incapacity of reason for coping with the redemptive operation of grace? Virgil knows that something happened then which is beyond his scope—'I thought the universe felt love'—and he can talk of it only in the language of wonder and bewilderment.

The Centaurs, of composite brute and human natures like the Minotaur, are set in charge of the violent against their fellows, who are tormented by the blood they have shed. And yet, while they are thus closely associated with the spirit of violence, the Centaurs alone among the guardian monsters of the infernal circles and in contrast with all the rest are attractive, dignified and courteous figures, to whose leaders Virgil expressly defers for guidance, and in modelling them and giving them life and grace Dante shows something of the creative delight of a sculptor. Another peculiar feature of this canto is that here alone in the *Inferno* Dante maintains an attitude of complete detachment in relation both to the guardians and to the suffering souls, without any hint of pity or scorn or disgust or fear; he simply has nothing to say, after the one general exclamation about covetousness and anger. The late Professor Rossi speaks of 'the fine serenity which is the very singular character of this canto', and Professor Torraca notes that this is the only scene of serenity in all Hell, from Limbo downwards; it is a temper the stranger for its contrast with the sins of hot blood which are described here. The whole atmosphere of this first round of the seventh circle is markedly different from that of any other part of Hell, and it is safe to suppose that Dante meant it to be different and meant the difference to be significant for his readers.

Several of the earliest and best of Dante's commentators in the fourteenth century understood the Centaurs here to be representative or symbolical of the *condottieri* of the time, the hired soldiers of the tyrants and communes of Italy, 'the instruments of their own oppression thus becoming their chastisement' (*E. G. Gardner*); and if we accept this identification it may help to explain the situation. Dante, knowing the refinement, in many respects, of many of the petty Italian courts, in some of which he had been a familiar guest, and the personal dignity of many such military employees, makes here, perhaps, his ironical comment on that whole situation of ordered anarchy, in the dignified, half-brute forms of the Centaurs. However dignified and friendly and, on occasion, serviceable, they are half-brutes after all. Ministers of divine justice as they are, like the other monsters, and ready to talk about it, they are also, like the rest, representative of the sins they punish, as were the tyrants and their mercenaries, in that 'sultry air, dense with the fumes of blood and the smoke of conflagrations, which still lies heavy, like the stench of Phlegethon, on the history of Italy in that horrible age' (*G. Mazzoni, L.D.*). (The greatest portrayal of an Italian *condottiere*, of a later age, Verrocchio's famous equestrian bronze of Colleone in Venice, might stand for one of the Centaurs, the very ideal of a free-lance.) If Dante had anything of this intention in the peculiar character of the canto, his irony is the keener for his own marked and unusual silence and detachment in the narrative. It was a grimly judicial observer that went along the river bank with Virgil and Nessus, keeping his own counsel. When Virgil says of Nessus to Dante: 'Let him be first with thee now and me second', may it be as if he said: 'You may take it from him; he knows all there is to know of oppression and plunder and bloody death'? In the account of the bolgia of the Thieves in the twenty-fifth canto we are to meet with another centaur, the fierce fantastic creature Cacus, and we are told there that he is separated from 'his brothers', the centaurs of this circle, 'for his fraud'; apart from that they are of the same breed.

In any case Phlegethon is Dante's challenge to military adventure and public violence, with all their glory and gain; here they share the penalty of footpads and cut-throats.

NON era ancor di là Nesso arrivato,
  quando noi ci mettemmo per un bosco
  che da nessun sentiero era segnato.
Non fronda verde, ma di color fosco;
  non rami schietti, ma nodosi e 'nvolti;
  non pomi v'eran, ma stecchi con tosco:
non han sì aspri sterpi nè sì folti
  quelle fiere selvagge che in odio hanno
  tra Cecina e Corneto i luoghi colti.
Quivi le brutte Arpìe lor nidi fanno, 10
  che cacciar delle Strofade i Troiani
  con tristo annunzio di futuro danno.
Ali hanno late, e colli e visi umani,
  piè con artigli, e pennuto il gran ventre;
  fanno lamenti in su li alberi strani.
E 'l buon maestro 'Prima che più entre,
  sappi che se' nel secondo girone'
  mi cominciò a dire, 'e sarai mentre
che tu verrai nell'orribil sabbione:
  però riguarda ben; sì vederai 20
  cose che torrìen fede al mio sermone.'
Io sentìa d'ogni parte trarre guai,
  e non vedea persona che 'l facesse;
  per ch' io tutto smarrito m'arrestai.
Cred' ïo ch'ei credette ch'io credesse
  che tante voci uscisser tra quei bronchi
  da gente che per noi si nascondesse.

CANTO XIII

The Second Round; the Violent against themselves; the Suicides; the barren wood; Piero delle Vigne

NESSUS had not yet reached the other side again when we set out through a wood which was not marked by any path. No green leaves, but of dusky hue; no smooth boughs, but knotted and warped; no fruits were there, but poisonous thorns. No brakes so harsh and dense have these savage beasts that hate the tilled lands between the Cecina and Corneto.[1] Here make their nests the loathsome Harpies that drove the Trojans from the Strophades with dismal presage of future ill;[2] they have wide wings and human necks and faces, feet clawed and their great bellies feathered, and they make lamentations on the strange trees.

And the good Master began to speak to me: 'Before thou go farther know that thou art in the second round and shalt be until thou come to the horrible sand; look well, therefore, and thou shalt see things which would discredit my telling of them.'

I heard from every side wailings poured forth and saw none that made them, so that, all bewildered, I stopped. I think he thought I thought that all these voices among the trunks came from people who were hiding from us, so the Master

Però disse 'l maestro: 'Se tu tronchi
qualche fraschetta d'una d'este piante,
li pensier c' hai si faran tutti monchi.' 30
Allor porsi la mano un poco avante,
e colsi un ramicel da un gran pruno;
e 'l tronco suo gridò: 'Perchè mi schiante?'
Da che fatto fu poi di sangue bruno,
ricominciò a dir: 'Perchè mi scerpi?
non hai tu spirto di pietà alcuno?
Uomini fummo, e or siam fatti sterpi:
ben dovrebb'esser la tua man più pia,
se state fossimo anime di serpi.'
Come d'un stizzo verde ch'arso sia 40
dall'un de' capi, che dall'altro geme
e cigola per vento che va via,
sì della scheggia rotta usciva inseme
parole e sangue; ond' io lasciai la cima
cadere, e stetti come l'uom che teme.
'S'elli avesse potuto creder prima,'
rispuose 'l savio mio 'anima lesa,
ciò c' ha veduto pur con la mia rima,
non averebbe in te la man distesa;
ma la cosa incredibile mi fece 50
indurlo ad ovra ch'a me stesso pesa.
Ma dilli chi tu fosti, sì che 'n vece
d'alcun'ammenda tua fama rinfreschi
nel mondo su, dove tornar li lece.'
E 'l tronco: 'Sì col dolce dir m'adeschi,
ch' i' non posso tacere; e voi non gravi
perch' io un poco a ragionar m' inveschi.
Io son colui che tenni ambo le chiavi
del cor di Federigo, e che le volsi,
serrando e diserrando, sì soavi, 60
che dal secreto suo quasi ogn'uom tolsi:
fede portai al glorïoso offizio,
tanto ch' i' ne perde' li sonni e' polsi.
La meretrice che mai dall'ospizio
di Cesare non torse li occhi putti,
morte comune, delle corti vizio,

said: 'If thou break off any little branch from one of these trees, all thy present thoughts will prove mistaken.'

Then I put out my hand a little and plucked a twig from a great thorn, and its trunk cried: 'Why dost thou tear me?' And when it had turned dark with blood it began again: 'Why manglest thou me? Hast thou no spirit of pity? We were men and now are turned to stocks; thy hand might well have been more pitiful had we been souls of serpents.' As a green brand that is burning at one end drips from the other and hisses with the escaping wind, so from the broken splinter came forth words and blood together; at which I let fall the tip and stood as one afraid.

'If he could have believed before, wounded soul, what he had never seen but in my lines,[3] he would not have stretched forth his hand against thee,' my Sage replied 'but the thing being incredible made me prompt him to the deed which grieves myself. But tell him who thou wast, so that, for some amends, he may revive thy fame in the world above, where he is permitted to return.'

And the trunk said: 'Thou so allurest me with thy gentle speech that I cannot be silent, and let it not burden you if I am beguiled into talk for a little. I am he that held both the keys of Frederick's heart and turned them, locking and unlocking, so softly that I kept nearly every other man from his secrets; and I brought such faithfulness to the glorious office that I lost for it sleep and strength.[4] The harlot that never turned her shameless eyes from Caesar's household, the common bane and the vice of courts,[5] inflamed all minds against me,

infiammò contra me li animi tutti;
e li 'nfiammati infiammar sì Augusto,
che' lieti onor tornaro in tristi lutti.
L'animo mio, per disdegnoso gusto, 70
credendo col morir fuggir disdegno,
ingiusto fece me contra me giusto.
Per le nove radici d'esto legno
vi giuro che già mai non ruppi fede
al mio signor, che fu d'onor sì degno.
E se di voi alcun nel mondo riede,
conforti la memoria mia, che giace
ancor del colpo che 'nvidia le diede.'
Un poco attese, e poi 'Da ch'el si tace'
disse 'l poeta a me 'non perder l'ora; 80
ma parla, e chiedi a lui, se più ti piace.'
Ond' io a lui: 'Domanda tu ancora
di quel che credi ch'a me satisfaccia;
ch' i' non potrei, tanta pietà m'accora!'
Perciò ricominciò: 'Se l'uom ti faccia
liberamente ciò che 'l tuo dir priega,
spirito incarcerato, ancor ti piaccia
di dirne come l'anima si lega
in questi nocchi; e dinne, se tu puoi,
s'alcuna mai di tai membra si spiega.' 90
Allor soffiò il tronco forte, e poi
si convertì quel vento in cotal voce:
'Brievemente sarà risposto a voi.
Quando si parte l'anima feroce
dal corpo ond'ella stessa s' è disvelta,
Minòs la manda alla settima foce.
Cade in la selva, e non l' è parte scelta;
ma là dove fortuna la balestra,
quivi germoglia come gran di spelta.
Surge in vermena ed in pianta silvestra: 100
l'Arpìe, pascendo poi delle sue foglie,
fanno dolore, ed al dolor fenestra.
Come l'altre verrem per nostre spoglie,
ma non però ch'alcuna sen rivesta;
chè non è giusto aver ciò ch'om si toglie.

and those inflamed so inflamed Augustus that happy honours turned to dismal woes. My mind, in scornful temper thinking by dying to escape from scorn, made me, just, unjust to myself. By the new roots of this tree I swear to you, never did I break faith with my lord, who was so worthy of honour; and if either of you return to the world let him establish my memory, which still lies under the blow that envy gave it.'

The Poet waited a little, then said to me: 'Since he is silent do not miss the chance but speak if thou wouldst question him further.' To which I answered him: 'Do thou ask him again of what thou thinkest will satisfy me; for I cannot, such pity fills my heart.'

He began again therefore: 'So may the man do freely for thee what thou askest of him, may it please thee, imprisoned spirit, to tell us further how the soul is bound in these knots, and tell us, if thou canst, whether from such members any is ever set free.'

Then the trunk blew hard, and soon that wind turned into a voice: 'You shall be answered briefly. When the fierce soul leaves the body from which it has uprooted itself, Minos sends it to the seventh depth. It falls into the wood, not in a place chosen for it but where fortune flings it. It sprouts there like a grain of spelt and rises to a sapling and to a savage tree; then the Harpies, feeding on its leaves, cause pain and for the pain an outlet. Like the rest we shall go for the cast-off flesh we have left, but not so that any of us will be clothed in it again, for it is not just that one should have that of which he robs himself. We shall drag them here

Qui le strascineremo, e per la mesta
selva saranno i nostri corpi appesi,
ciascuno al prun dell'ombra sua molesta.'
Noi eravamo ancora al tronco attesi,
credendo ch'altro ne volesse dire, 110
quando noi fummo d'un romor sorpresi,
similemente a colui che venire
sente il porco e la caccia alla sua posta,
ch'ode le bestie, e le frasche stormire.
Ed ecco due dalla sinistra costa,
nudi e graffiati, fuggendo sì forte
che della selva rompìeno ogni rosta.
Quel dinanzi: 'Or accorri, accorri, morte!'
E l'altro, cui pareva tardar troppo,
gridava: 'Lano, sì non furo accorte 120
le gambe tue alle giostre dal Toppo!'
E poi che forse li fallìa la lena,
di sè e d'un cespuglio fece un groppo.
Di retro a loro era la selva piena
di nere cagne, bramose e correnti
come veltri ch'uscisser di catena.
In quel che s'appiattò miser li denti,
e quel dilaceraro a brano a brano;
poi sen portar quelle membra dolenti.
Presemi allor la mia scorta per mano, 130
e menommi al cespuglio che piangea,
per le rotture sanguinenti, in vano.
'O Giacomo' dicea 'da Santo Andrea,
che t' è giovato di me fare schermo?
che colpa ho io della tua vita rea?'
Quando 'l maestro fu sovr'esso fermo,
disse: 'Chi fosti, che per tante punte
soffi con sangue doloroso sermo?'
Ed elli a noi: 'O anime che giunte
siete a veder lo strazio disonesto 140
c' ha le mie fronde sì da me disgiunte,
raccoglietele al piè del tristo cesto.
I' fui de la città che nel Batista
mutò il primo padrone; ond' e' per questo

and through the dismal wood our bodies will be hung, each on the bush of its injurious shade.'

We were still intent on the trunk, thinking it had more to tell us, when we were surprised by a noise, like one aware of the boar and the chase approaching his post when he hears the beasts and the crashing of the branches; and there on our left were two, naked and scarred and flying so fast that they broke through every entanglement of the wood. He in front cried: 'Now come, come quickly, death!', and the other, who seemed to be falling behind: 'Thy legs were not so nimble, Lano, at the jousts of the Toppo,' and, perhaps because breath failed him, he crouched close in beside a bush.[6] Behind them the wood was full of black bitches, ravenous and swift like hounds loosed from the chain; on him that squatted there they set their teeth and tore him apart piecemeal, then carried off these suffering members.

My Escort then took me by the hand and led me to the shrub, which was making vain laments through the bleeding fractures. 'O Giacomo da Sant' Andrea,' it said 'how has it served thee to make a screen of me? What blame have I for thy guilty life?'

When the Master stopped over it he said: 'Who wast thou that through so many wounds blowest forth woeful speech with blood?'

And it said to us: 'O souls that have arrived to see the shameful havoc that has thus torn my leaves from me, gather them again at the foot of the wretched bush. I was of the city that changed for the Baptist its first patron, who for this will

sempre con l'arte sua la farà trista;
e se non fosse che 'n sul passo d'Arno
rimane ancor di lui alcuna vista,
que' cittadin che poi la rifondarno
sovra 'l cener che d'Attila rimase,
avrebber fatto lavorare indarno. 150
Io fei giubbetto a me delle mie case.'

1. The marshy, wooded and malarious district of the Maremma on the west coast of Italy, between the river Cecina and the town of Corneto.

2. The Harpies drove Aeneas's company from the Strophades, islands in the Ionian Sea, defiling their banquet and foretelling their starvation.

3. There is a similar incident in the *Aeneid.*

4. Piero delle Vigne, for many years chief adviser of the Emperor Frederick II (Canto x), became his Chancellor and was a poet; accused of treason, he was blinded and imprisoned and committed suicide in 1249. He 'held both the keys'—of mercy and of judgement.

always afflict it with his art; and were it not that at the passage of the Arno there yet remains some semblance of him, those citizens who afterwards rebuilt it on the ashes left by Attila would have laboured in vain.[7] I made a gibbet for myself of my house.'

5. Envy.

6. Lano of Siena and Giacomo of Padua, notorious spendthrift nobles of the 13th century; Lano was killed in battle on the river Toppo in 1288.

7. Florentines said that Mars, supplanted as patron of the city, plagued it with war and was only partly conciliated by the preservation of his statue, or its remains, at the head of the Ponte Vecchio. Florence was mistakenly supposed to have been destroyed by Attila.

NOTE

From the impersonal quality of the twelfth canto, in which Dante is mere observer and narrator, we pass into the eerie horror of the thirteenth, with Dante emotionally at the centre of the scene.

The trackless, withered, thorny wood, the vile birds, the mysterious wailings through the solitude, represent together life poisoned at the heart and issuing in chosen, desperate death. The Harpies, of brute-human form like the Minotaur and the Centaurs, are the embodiment of fears that threaten and appal with 'dismal presage of coming ill', and the whole is a picture of the soul's abandonment to despair, its defeat and surrender in the spiritual contest which is faith. They have 'uprooted themselves' from their bodies, and 'this unnatural separation, which in life is the work of a single moment of blind passion, and the wound which the suicide inflicts on himself, Dante renders eternal. The soul violently separated from the body . . . remains enclosed in a body strange to it and of lower nature, in a plant that will feel every hour the violence which the suicide wrought on himself in life. . . . The hell of the suicides is suicide itself repeated every moment to eternity' (*F. De Sanctis*). After the Judgement their bodies will hang on their branches, an addition to their misery, a lasting sign and memory of the life they have cast away. Here, as on the bank of Phlegethon, Dante is silent—except for saying to Virgil that he cannot speak, 'such pity fills my heart',—but this is a different silence; that, of detached observation, this, of fear and horror, as men are silent in a charnel-house. His mind stammers —'I think he thought I thought'—and when the bleeding trunk hisses into speech he 'lets fall the tip and stands as one afraid'.

The pity and horror of the scene are greatly heightened by the presence of the Emperor Frederick's famous Chancellor, who died sixteen years before Dante was born and who is now imprisoned in a great thorn-tree. Piero delle Vigne was of humble origin and became the most influential statesman of his time in western Europe, and for more than twenty years he was the Emperor's chief adviser in the struggle with the Papacy which ended only with the Emperor's death in 1250. His story opens with the studied courtesy and is continued with something of the verbal ingenuity and literary artifice which were characteristic of his day and of the cultivated imperial court in Naples. 'He had many titles to Dante's sympathy: his literary teaching, his poetic gift, the high offices he had borne, his tragic fall, and, more than all, the relentless struggle he maintained in defence of lay authority against the arrogant pretensions of the Church' (*A. Medin, L.D.*). The story, as it is told here, is in effect Dante's vindication of Piero's memory from the charges of treason for which he had suffered and under which, after half a century, his name lay still; and the best proof of his faithfulness, as Dante represents him, is in the tone of his references to his old master. In a few lines he names the Emperor four times with increasing honour and affection: 'Frederick'—'Caesar'—'Augustus'—'my lord who was so worthy of honour'. Blinded, publicly disgraced, and imprisoned, he is said to have dashed out his brains on the wall of his cell. After a life of integrity and splendid service he failed—so Dante judged and was bound to judge—in the last test. 'In this plant one thing only of human remains alive and present, his memory on earth' (*F. De Sanctis*), and for that one thing he pleads.

The sin of the spendthrifts who are hunted through the wood is distinguished from the mere slack extravagance of the wastrels in the fourth circle (Canto vii) as a deliberate and ostentatious ruining of themselves which is itself a kind of suicide; that is a sin of weakness, this of will. As they were driven by their own folly to scatter their substance on earth, the furious hell-hounds now hunt them and waste and scatter their members, and one of them groups himself with the shrub of a suicide as if to identify himself with the other's crime; for, according to Aristotle, the dissipation of the means of life is equivalent to self-destruction. The two spendthrifts and the hounds after them come with a noise and disappear; their life is a flash in the pan.

The second example of suicide, in contrast with Piero, is insignificant, as if to leave no glamour of greatness about suicide itself. According to Boccaccio he was one of many Florentine suicides of the time, and perhaps he is not meant for any one of them in particular. He had hanged himself from his own house, and that a house in Florence; 'and for a man to have so little respect for his own house, his family name and traditions, as to turn it into a gibbet, is to a proud Florentine like Dante, who gloried even in Paradise in the nobility of his blood, a proof of no ordinary baseness' (*J. S. Carroll*).

The suicide's reference to the Florentine superstition about the statue of Mars is Dante's taunt against his own turbulent city for its confidence in the heathen forces of strife and for its divided loyalty, given at once to the witness to Christ and to the god of war, who 'will always afflict it with his art'. The devil-ridden city was the fitting environment in which this man 'made a gibbet of his house'. It is his poor excuse.

INFERNO

POI che la carità del natìo loco
mi strinse, raunai le fronde sparte,
e rende'le a colui, ch'era già fioco.
Indi venimmo al fine ove si parte
lo secondo giron dal terzo, e dove
si vede di giustizia orribil arte.
A ben manifestar le cose nove,
dico che arrivammo ad una landa
che dal suo letto ogni pianta rimove.
La dolorosa selva l' è ghirlanda 10
intorno, come 'l fosso tristo ad essa:
quivi fermammo i passi a randa a randa.
Lo spazzo era una rena arida e spessa,
non d'altra foggia fatta che colei
che fu da' piè di Caton già soppressa.
O vendetta di Dio, quanto tu dei
esser temuta da ciascun che legge
ciò che fu manifesto alli occhi miei!
D'anime nude vidi molte gregge
che piangean tutte assai miseramente, 20
e parea posta lor diversa legge.
Supin giacea in terra alcuna gente;
alcuna si sedea tutta raccolta,
e altra andava continüa-mente.
Quella che giva intorno era più molta,
e quella men che giacea al tormento,
ma più al duolo avea la lingua sciolta.

CANTO XIV

The Third Round; the Violent against God, nature and art; the burning sand; the Blasphemers; Capaneus; the Old Man of Crete

SINCE love of my native place constrained me, I gathered up the scattered leaves and restored them to him, who was already hoarse.

Then we came to the boundary between the second round and the third, where is seen a fearful device of justice. To make the new things clear, I have to tell that we reached a plain that rejects every plant from its bed; the doleful wood is a garland round it, as round the wood the dismal moat. Here, at the very edge, we stayed our steps. The ground was a dry, deep sand, much like that once trod by the feet of Cato.[1] O vengeance of God, how must thou be feared by everyone who reads what was plain before my eyes! I saw many herds of naked souls who were all lamenting most miserably, and different laws seemed to be laid on them, some lying supine on the ground, some sitting all crouched up, and some moving on continually; those going about were the greatest number and those lying in torment fewest but their tongues most loosed

Sovra tutto 'l sabbion, d'un cader lento,
piovean di foco dilatate falde,
come di neve in alpe sanza vento. 30
Quali Alessandro in quelle parti calde
d' Indïa vide sopra 'l süo stuolo
fiamme cadere infino a terra salde;
per ch'ei provide a scalpitar lo suolo
con le sue schiere, acciò che lo vapore
mei si stingeva mentre ch'era solo:
tale scendeva l'etternale ardore;
onde la rena s'accendea, com'esca
sotto focile, a doppiar lo dolore.
Sanza riposo mai era la tresca 40
delle misere mani, or quindi or quinci
escotendo da sè l'arsura fresca.
I' cominciai: 'Maestro, tu che vinci
tutte le cose, fuor che' demon duri
ch'all'entrar della porta incontra uscinci,
chi è quel grande che non par che curi
lo 'ncendio e giace dispettoso e torto,
sì che la pioggia non par che 'l maturi?'
E quel medesmo che si fu accorto
ch' io domandava il mio duca di lui, 50
gridò: 'Qual io fui vivo, tal son morto.
Se Giove stanchi 'l suo fabbro da cui
crucciato prese la folgore aguta
onde l'ultimo dì percosso fui;
o s'elli stanchi li altri a muta a muta
in Mongibello alla focina negra,
chiamando "Buon Vulcano, aiuta, aiuta!",
sì com'el fece alla pugna di Flegra,
e me saetti con tutta sua forza;
non ne potrebbe aver vendetta allegra.' 60
Allora il duca mio parlò di forza
tanto, ch' i' non l'avea sì forte udito:
'O Capaneo, in ciò che non s'ammorza
la tua superbia, se' tu piu punito:
nullo martiro, fuor che la tua rabbia,
sarebbe al tuo furor dolor compito.'

by the pain. Over all the great sand, falling slowly, rained down broad flakes of fire, as of snow in the mountains without wind. As Alexander, in the torrid Indian parts, saw flames falling on his host unbroken to the ground, for which he had the soil trampled by his troops to extinguish the vapours better before they spread,[2] so the eternal fire was descending there and the sand was kindled by it like tinder under the flint, to redouble the pain. There was no pause in the dance of the wretched hands, now here, now there, beating off from them the fresh burning.

I began: 'Master, thou who overcomest all things save the stubborn demons that came out against us at the entrance of the gate, who is that great one who seems as if he did not heed the fire and lies disdainful and scowling so that the rain seems not to soften him?'

And he himself, who had perceived that I was asking my Leader about him, cried: 'What I was living, that am I dead. Though Jove wear out his smith from whom in rage he seized the keen bolt with which, the last day, I was smitten—though he wear out the rest by turns at the black smithy in Mongibello, shouting "Help, help, good Vulcan!" as once on the field of Phlegra, and hurl his shafts at me with all his force, he should not so have the joy of vengeance.'[3]

Then my Leader spoke with such force as I had not heard him use before: 'Ah, Capaneus, in that thy pride is unquenched thou art punished the more; no torment but thy own raving would be pain to match thy fury.' Then he turned to me

Poi si rivolse a me con miglior labbia
dicendo: 'Quei fu l'un de' sette regi
ch'assiser Tebe; ed ebbe e par ch'elli abbia
Dio in disdegno, e poco par che 'l pregi; 70
ma, com' io dissi lui, li suoi dispetti
sono al suo petto assai debiti fregi.
Or mi vien dietro, e guarda che non metti
ancor li piedi nella rena arsiccia;
ma sempre al bosco tien li piedi stretti.'
Tacendo divenimmo là 've spiccia
fuor della selva un picciol fiumicello,
lo cui rossore ancor mi raccapriccia.
Quale del Bulicame esce ruscello
che parton poi tra lor le peccatrici, 80
tal per la rena giù sen giva quello.
Lo fondo suo ed ambo le pendici
fatt'eran pietra, e' margini da lato;
per ch' io m'accorsi che 'l passo era lici.
'Tra tutto l'altro ch' i' t' ho dimostrato,
poscia che noi entrammo per la porta
lo cui sogliare a nessuno è negato,
cosa non fu dalli tuoi occhi scorta
notabile come 'l presente rio,
che sovra sè tutte fiammelle ammorta.' 90
Queste parole fuor del duca mio;
per ch' io 'l pregai che mi largisse il pasto
di cui largito m'avea il disio.
'In mezzo mar siede un paese guasto'
diss'elli allora, 'che s'appella Creta,
sotto 'l cui rege fu già il mondo casto.
Una montagna v' è che già fu lieta
d'acqua e di fronde, che si chiamò Ida:
or è diserta come cosa vieta.
Rea la scelse già per cuna fida 100
del suo figliuolo, e per celarlo meglio,
quando piangea, vi facea far le grida.
Dentro dal monte sta dritto un gran veglio,
che tien volte le spalle inver Damiata
e Roma guarda come süo speglio.

again with gentler look and said: 'That was one of the seven kings who laid siege to Thebes and held, and seems to hold God in disdain and seems to esteem Him lightly; but his own revilings, as I told him, most fittingly adorn his breast. Come now after me, and watch still not to put thy feet on the scorching sand but keep them always close to the wood.'

In silence we came to where there gushes forth from the wood a little stream whose redness makes me shudder yet. As issues from the Bulicame a rivulet which the sinful women then divide among them,[4] so this took its way down across the sand; its bed and both its banks were of stone, with the margins alongside, from which I perceived that the passage was there.

'In all the rest that I have shown thee since we entered by the gate whose threshold is denied to none nothing has been given to thy eyes of such note as this stream here, which quenches all the flames above it.' These were my Leader's words, so that I begged him to grant me the food for which he had granted me the appetite.

'In mid-sea lies a waste land named Crete,' he said then 'under whose king the world once was pure.[5] A mountain is there, once glad with leaves and waters, which was called Ida; now it is deserted like a thing outworn. Rhea chose it once as the trusty cradle of her child, and there, to conceal him better when he cried, she made them raise an uproar. Within the mountain stands a great old man, who keeps his back turned to Damietta and gazes on Rome as on his mirror; his head is fashioned

La sua testa è di fino oro formata,
  e puro argento son le braccia e il petto,
  poi è di rame infino alla forcata;
da indi in giuso è tutto ferro eletto,
  salvo che 'l destro piede è terra cotta;   110
  e sta 'n su quel più che 'n su l'altro eretto.
Ciascuna parte, fuor che l'oro, è rotta
  d'una fessura che lagrime goccia,
  le quali, accolte, foran quella grotta.
Lor corso in questa valle si diroccia:
  fanno Acheronte, Stige e Flegetonta;
  poi sen van giù per questa stretta doccia
infin là ove più non si dismonta:
  fanno Cocito; e qual sia quello stagno,
  tu lo vedrai; però qui non si conta.'   120
E io a lui: 'Se 'l presente rigagno
  si diriva così dal nostro mondo,
  perchè ci appar pur a questo vivagno?'
Ed elli a me: 'Tu sai che 'l luogo è tondo;
  e tutto che tu sie venuto molto
  pur a sinistra, giù calando al fondo,
non se' ancor per tutto il cerchio volto:
  per che, se cosa n'apparisce nova,
  non de' addur maraviglia al tuo volto.'
E io ancor: 'Maestro, ove si trova   130
  Flegetonta e Letè? chè dell'un taci,
  e l'altro di' che si fa d'esta piova.'
'In tutte tue question certo mi piaci'
  rispuose; 'ma 'l bollor dell'acqua rossa
  dovea ben solver l'una che tu faci.
Letè vedrai, ma fuor di questa fossa,
  là dove vanno l'anime a lavarsi
  quando la colpa pentuta è rimossa.'
Poi disse: 'Omai è tempo da scostarsi
  dal bosco; fa che di retro a me vegne: 140
  li margini fan via, che non son arsi,
e sopra loro ogni vapor si spegne.'

of fine gold, his breast and arms are pure silver, then to the fork he is of brass, and from there down all of choice iron except that the right foot is baked clay, and he rests more on this than on the other. Every part except the gold is cleft by a fissure that drips with tears, which gather and force their way down through the cavern there, then take their course from rock to rock into this depth. They form Acheron and Styx and Phlegethon, then, going down by this narrow channel to where there is no more descent, they form Cocytus,[6] and what kind of pond that is thou shalt see, so that here I do not speak of it.'

And I said to him: 'If the stream here flows down thus from our world, why does it appear to us only at this boundary?'

And he to me: 'Thou knowest that the place is round, and although thou hast come far, always to the left in the descent to the bottom, thou hast not yet gone round the whole circle; so that if anything new appears to us it need not bring wonder to thy face.'

And I again: 'Master, where are Phlegethon and Lethe,[7] for about the one thou art silent and the other, thou sayest, comes from this rain of tears?'

'I am pleased indeed with all thy questions,' he replied 'but the boiling of the red water might well have solved one thou askest.[8] Lethe thou shalt see, but there beyond this abyss where the souls go to bathe themselves when their repented guilt is removed.'[9]

Then he said: 'Now it is time to go on from the wood; see that thou follow behind me. The margins, which are not on fire, make a path and above them all the flames are quenched.'

INFERNO

1. Cato of Utica, in N. Africa, fighting in the Civil War against Caesar.

2. An incident in the medieval version of Alexander's invasion of N.W. India.

3. In the siege of Thebes Capaneus mounted the wall and defied Jove, who struck him down with a thunderbolt; Vulcan, Jove's 'smith', had his 'smithy' in the interior of Etna ('Mongibello'), where, by help of the one-eyed Cyclopes, he forged Jove's bolts. At Phlegra the Giants, having attacked Olympus, were destroyed by Jove.

4. A well-known hot sulphurous spring near Viterbo, whose water was led to the houses of ill-fame in the neighbourhood.

5. The reign of Saturn, mythical King of Crete, was the world's Golden Age. He devoured his own children, and Rhea, his wife, preserved their child Jupiter by having him brought up secretly on Mount Ida.

6. The lowest part of Hell (Canto xxxii).

7. Rivers of the classical under-world; Lethe is the river of forgetfulness.

8. In the *Aeneid* Phlegethon is described as a fiery stream.

9. On the summit of Purgatory (*Purg.* xxviii and xxxi).

NOTE

In accordance with the plan of the lower Hell outlined in the eleventh canto the sins punished in the third round of the seventh circle, on the burning plain, are: violence directly against God—blasphemy, violence against nature, God's child —sodomy, and violence against art or industry, 'to God, as it were, a grandchild'—usury; and the first idea we get of the whole round is that of *barrenness*, it is 'a plain that rejects every plant from its bed'. The blasphemers who confronted God in their insolence now confront Him forever in their agony; the sodomites are driven about by the unrest of their old, corrupt passion; the usurers crouch permanently over their money-bags; and such sins leave the soul sterile. These sins, in one way or other directed specifically against the divine ordering of human life, are all regarded as in a peculiar sense sins against God, so that they are punished by that which is the special symbol of God's anger, such a 'fire from the Lord out of heaven' as destroyed Sodom and Gomorrah.

The references to Cato and Alexander serve to give verisimilitude to the scene by supposed historical analogies; but it is at least possible that Dante intended also a larger relevancy. Cato trod the sands of Africa as the armed enemy of Julius Caesar, that is, of the Empire; and Alexander, in his vast campaigns, 'tried' Dante says elsewhere 'to trip up his Roman rival in the race', so that God 'snatched him from the contest'. They, two of the greatest, set themselves, like these fruitless souls in hell, against God's high providence for the world, and it was wholly in vain.

Of these three classes of sinners the blasphemers are the least numerous, for open blasphemy is rare; but, having been loud-mouthed against God, they are the loudest now in their cries of pain. The furious insolence of Capaneus, the only blasphemer named, whose whole being is now absorbed in the remembrance of 'the last day' of his defiance, the taunts he flings at God, the only god he can conceive of, a god of mere brute force, are only a kind of noisy pretence. He only 'seems as if he did not heed the fire'—the word 'seems' is used about him four times, Virgil repeating it after Dante—and his rage only adds to his torment. His is 'the impotent fury of the denial of an unescapable reality, venting itself in a vain parade of its arrogance. Quite other is the greatness of Farinata; that is a moral greatness which rises above the torment of his bed of fire, while confessing to it' (*V. Rossi*).

When Dante recalls Virgil's insufficiency before the 'stubborn demons' at the gate of Dis, does he mean to ask how reason is to meet the challenge of defiant blasphemy? If so, Virgil's reply is his contemptuous exposure of the violent *un*reason of Capaneus's impudent pretences. When Carlyle heard Margaret Fuller say that she 'accepted the universe', 'Gad, you'd better!' he said.

It is fitting that it should be when they have reached this fiery desert, symbolizing men's rejection of all the divine purpose and order for their life, that Dante learns from Virgil of the Old Man of Crete, the symbol of human history and decadence. The island itself was regarded in antiquity and is described in the *Aeneid* as the cradle of the Trojan, therefore of the Roman, race, and as having been, under Saturn, the centre of the world's Golden Age. 'It was the heathen Garden of Eden' (*J. S. Carroll*), and its actual ruin, by the time of Dante, under the wasting tyranny of Venice gave analogy and support to the symbolism of the Old Man. There is a pathetic longing for the past imagined innocence and happiness of the world in the 'once' which Virgil uses three times with regard to it. The figure is taken from the dream of Nebuchadnezzar (*Dan*. ii. 31–33) with some suggestions from the ancient Latin poets, the whole being adapted to Dante's purposes. The four metals represent the successive degenerating ages of history. The figure looks away from Egypt (Damietta), from the ancient east, and on Rome 'as on its mirror', seeing there, in imagination and expectancy, its own perfection. The iron legs on which it rests are the imperial and ecclesiastical authorities and the one foot of clay on which it chiefly leans the existing degenerate Papacy. Below the golden head it is cloven with sin, of which the stream of tears running into and through all the depths of Hell is the consequence. That river, which we afterwards find to be stained with blood, the stream of all the misery caused by men to men through the ages of sin, returns on the sinful and impenitent souls themselves, appearing in Hell at different points and under different names as means of their punishment: Acheron, the river of death; Styx, the marsh of anger; Phlegethon, the hot blood of murder and rapine; and farthest down, Cocytus, the frozen lake of treachery. The symbolism is elaborate and artificial; but the Old Man is a form 'mysterious and majestic, whose profound poetry of pain and human pity supersedes its obvious allegorical intentions' (*V. Rossi*).

Dante asks Virgil about Lethe, the river of forgetfulness, familiar to him as a part of the classical under-world; but its boon is not given to the impenitent. To remember forever is a part of their doom.

Twice Virgil draws Dante's attention to the fact, mentioned a third time at the beginning of the next canto, that the little stream, the overflow of Phlegethon crossing the sandy plain, quenches the flames above it; and he does so the first time with so much emphasis that we are bound to ask the meaning of the fact, which he does not explain. Partly it is the Poet's device for their safe passage across the burning sand; but symbolically it must be more, and probably the interpretation given by Rossi and some others is the right one: that this stream of all the tears and blood shed by the whole race which is incurably afflicted by the guilt of Adam, not being here an instrument of punishment but only an evidence of age-long human agony, softens in its presence the rigour of divine justice. It is the Virgilian sense of tears in mortal things breaking in on the grim consistency of retribution as it was conceived by medieval Christendom.

ORA cen porta l'un de' duri margini;
  e 'l fummo del ruscel di sopra aduggia,
  sì che dal foco salva l'acqua e li argini.
Quale i Fiamminghi tra Guizzante e Bruggia,
  temendo il fiotto che 'nver lor s'avventa,
  fanno lo schermo perchè 'l mar si fuggia;
e quale i Padovan lungo la Brenta,
  per difender lor ville e lor castelli,
  anzi che Chiarentana il caldo senta;
a tale imagine eran fatti quelli, 10
  tutto che nè sì alti nè sì grossi,
  qual che si fosse, lo maestro felli.
Già eravam dalla selva rimossi
  tanto, ch' i' non avrei visto dov'era,
  perch' io in dietro rivolto mi fossi,
quando incontrammo d'anime una schiera
  che venìan lungo l'argine, e ciascuna
  ci riguardava come suol da sera
guardare uno altro sotto nuova luna;
  e sì ver noi aguzzavan le ciglia 20
  come 'l vecchio sartor fa nella cruna.
Così adocchiato da cotal famiglia,
  fui conosciuto da un, che mi prese
  per lo lembo e gridò: 'Qual maraviglia!'
E io, quando 'l suo braccio a me distese,
  ficca' i li occhi per lo cotto aspetto,
  sì che 'l viso abbruciato non difese
la conoscenza sua al mio intelletto;
  e chinando la mia alla sua faccia,
  rispuosi: 'Siete voi qui, ser Brunetto?' 30

CANTO XV

The Sodomites; Brunetto Latini

NOW one of the hard margins bears us on and the vapour from the stream makes a shade above so that it shelters the water and the banks from the fire. As the Flemings between Wissant and Bruges, fearing the flood rushing in on them, make their bulwark to drive back the sea, and as the Paduans do along the Brenta to protect their towns and castles before Chiarentana feels the heat,[1] these were made of the same fashion, except that the builder, whoever he was, made them neither so high nor so broad.

Already we had got so far from the wood that I should not have seen where it was if I had turned backward, when we met a troop of souls who were coming alongside the bank, and each looked at us as men look at one another under a new moon at dusk, and they puckered their brows on us like an old tailor on the eye of his needle.

Eyed thus by that company, I was recognized by one who took me by the hem and cried: 'How marvellous!' And I, when he reached out his arm to me, fixed my eyes on his baked looks so that the scorched features did not keep my mind from recognizing him and, bending my face to his, I answered: 'Are you here, Ser Brunetto?'[2]

E quelli: 'O figliuol mio, non ti dispiaccia
se Brunetto Latini un poco teco
ritorna in dietro e lascia andar la traccia.'
I' dissi lui: 'Quanto posso, ven preco;
e se volete che con voi m'asseggia,
faròl, se piace a costui che vo seco.'
'O figliuol,' disse 'qual di questa greggia
s'arresta punto, giace poi cent'anni
sanz'arrostarsi quando 'l foco il feggia.
Però va oltre: i' ti verrò a' panni; 40
e poi rigiugnerò la mia masnada,
che va piangendo i suoi etterni danni.'
I' non osava scender della strada
per andar par di lui; ma 'l capo chino
tenea com' uom che reverente vada.
El cominciò: 'Qual fortuna o destino
anzi l'ultimo dì qua giù ti mena?
e chi è questi che mostra 'l cammino?'
'Là su di sopra, in la vita serena,'
rispuos' io lui 'mi smarri' in una valle, 50
avanti che l'età mia fosse piena.
Pur ier mattina le volsi le spalle:
questi m'apparve, tornand' io in quella,
e reducemi a ca per questo calle.'
Ed elli a me: 'Se tu segui tua stella,
non puoi fallire a gloriöso porto,
se ben m'accorsi nella vita bella;
e s' io non fossi sì per tempo morto,
veggendo il cielo a te così benigno,
dato t'avrei all'opera conforto. 60
Ma quello ingrato popolo maligno
che discese di Fiesole ab antico,
e tiene ancor del monte e del macigno,
ti si farà, per tuo ben far, nemico:
ed è ragion, chè tra li lazzi sorbi
si disconvien fruttar lo dolce fico.
Vecchia fama nel mondo li chiama orbi;
gent' è avara, invidiosa e superba:
dai lor costumi fa che tu ti forbi.

And he: 'O my son, let it not displease thee if Brunetto Latini turn back with thee a little and let the train go on.'

I said to him: 'With all my heart I beg it of you, and if you wish me to sit with you I will, if it please him here with whom I go.'

'O son,' he said 'whoever of this flock stops one moment lies afterwards for a hundred years without shielding himself when the fire strikes him. Go on, therefore; I shall come at thy skirt and later rejoin my band who go mourning their eternal loss.'

I durst not descend from the track to go on his level, but I kept my head bent down as one that walks with reverence, and he began: 'What chance or destiny brings thee down here before thy last day, and who is this that shows the way?'

'Up above there in the bright life,' I answered him 'before my age was at the full,[3] I lost my way in a valley. Only yesterday morning I turned my back on it. He appeared to me when I was returning to it and by this road he leads me home.'

And he said to me: 'If thou follow thy star thou canst not fail of a glorious haven, if I discerned rightly in the fair life, and had I not died too soon, seeing heaven so gracious to thee I would have strengthened thee in thy work. But that thankless and malignant folk which came down of old from Fiesole and still keeps something of the mountain and the rock[4] shall become, for thy well-doing, thine enemy,—and with reason, for among the bitter sorbs it is not natural the sweet fig should come to fruit. Old fame in the world calls them blind, a people avaricious, envious and proud; see thou cleanse thyself from their ways. Thy fortune

La tua fortuna tanto onor ti serba 70
  che l'una parte e l'altra avranno fame
  di te; ma lungi fia dal becco l'erba.
Faccian le bestie fiesolane strame
  di lor medesme, e non tocchin la pianta,
  s'alcuna surge ancora in lor letame,
in cui riviva la sementa santa
  di que' Roman che vi rimaser quando
  fu fatto il nido di malizia tanta.'
'Se fosse tutto pieno il mio dimando,'
  rispuosi lui 'voi non sareste ancora 80
  dell'umana natura posto in bando;
chè 'n la mente m' è fitta, e or m'accora,
  la cara e buona imagine paterna
  di voi quando nel mondo ad ora ad ora
m'insegnavate come l'uom s'etterna:
  e quant' io l'abbia in grado, mentr' io vivo
  convien che nella mia lingua si scerna.
Ciò che narrate di mio corso scrivo,
  e serbolo a chiosar con altro testo
  a donna che saprà, s' a lei arrivo. 90
Tanto vogl' io che vi sia manifesto,
  pur che mia coscïenza non mi garra,
  che alla Fortuna, come vuol, son presto.
Non è nuova alli orecchi miei tal arra:
  però giri Fortuna la sua rota
  come le piace, e 'l villan la sua marra.'
Lo mio maestro allora in su la gota
  destra si volse in dietro, e riguardommi;
  poi disse: 'Bene ascolta chi la nota.'
Nè per tanto di men parlando vommi 100
  con ser Brunetto, e dimando chi sono
  li suoi compagni più noti e più sommi.
Ed elli a me: 'Saper d'alcuno è bono;
  delli altri fia laudabile tacerci,
  chè 'l tempo sarìa corto a tanto sòno.
In somma sappi che tutti fur cherci
  e litterati grandi e di gran fama,
  d'un peccato medesmo al mondo lerci.

holds for thee such honour that the one party and the other shall be ravenous against thee, but the grass shall be far from the goat. Let the Fiesolan beasts make fodder of themselves and not touch the plant—if on their dung-heap any yet springs up—in which there lives again the holy seed of those Romans who remained there when it became the nest of such wickedness.'

'Were all my prayers fulfilled' I answered him 'you had not yet been banished from humanity; for in my memory is fixed, and now goes to my heart, the dear and kind paternal image of you when many a time in the world you taught me how man makes himself immortal; and how much I am grateful for it my tongue, while I live, must needs declare. That which you tell of my course I write and keep with another text for comment by a lady who will know, if I reach her.[5] This much I would have plain to you, that, so my conscience do not chide me, I am ready for Fortune as she wills. Such earnest of my lot is not new to my ears. Turn Fortune her wheel then as she list—and the clown his mattock!'

On that my Master turned his head backward on the right and looked at me, then said: 'He is a good listener who takes note.'

None the less I continued talking with Ser Brunetto and asked him who of his companions were of most note and dignity.

And he said to me: 'Of some it is well to know; of the rest it will be more creditable to be silent, for the time would not serve for so much talk. Know in a word that they were all clerks and great and famous scholars, defiled in the world by one and the same sin. Priscian[6] goes on with that

Priscian sen va con quella turba grama,
e Francesco d'Accorso; anche vedervi, 110
s'avessi avuto di tal tigna brama,
colui potei che dal servo de' servi
fu trasmutato d'Arno in Bacchiglione,
dove lasciò li mal protesi nervi.
Di più direi; ma 'l venire e 'l sermone
più lungo esser non può, però ch' i' veggio
là surger novo fummo del sabbione.
Gente vien con la quale esser non deggio:
sieti raccomandato il mio Tesoro
nel qual io vivo ancora, e più non cheggio.' 120
Poi si rivolse, e parve di coloro
che corrono a Verona il drappo verde
per la campagna; e parve di costoro
quelli che vince, non colui che perde.

1. Before the snow melts in the hills.

2. Brunetto Latini (c. 1210–1294), notary and Guelf leader in Florence; his *Treasure*, in French, is a kind of encyclopedia; his *Little Treasure*, in Italian verse, tells of an allegorical journey which may have suggested Dante's poem. 'Ser' was the customary form of address for a notary, and Dante addresses him with the courteous *you*.

3. Maturity was reckoned from the 35th year (Canto i).

4. Traditionally, Caesar destroyed the hill-town of Fiesole and founded Florence on the river below with a mixed population of Romans and Fiesolans. Much of Florence was built of stone quarried at Fiesole.

wretched crowd, and Francesco d'Accorso;[7] and if thou hast a craving for such scurf, him thou mightst see there that was translated by the Servant of the Servants from the Arno to the Bacchiglione, where he left his sin-strained nerves.[8] I would say more, but I cannot go farther talking with thee, for I see there a new cloud rising from the sand; people are coming with whom I must not be. Let my *Treasure*, in which I yet live, be commended to thee; and I ask no more.'

Then he turned about and seemed like one of those that run for the green cloth in the field at Verona,[9] and he seemed not the loser among them, but the winner.

5. 'Another text' is Farinata's prophecy in Canto x, which Virgil bade Dante refer to Beatrice for explanation.

6. Famous grammarian of the 6th century whose Latin Grammar was in common use in the Middle Ages.

7. Noted lawyer and teacher in Bologna University and later at Oxford in the 13th century.

8. Andrea de' Mozzi, of a noble Florentine family, Bishop of Florence in Dante's youth, transferred for scandalous life to Vicenza on the Bacchiglione, where he died soon after. 'Servant of the Servants of God', an ancient title of the Pope, here used in irony for Boniface VIII.

9. Annual foot-race in Verona with naked runners, in which prizes were given to the first and the last.

NOTE

Relieved to escape from the horror of the wood, Dante has leisure to compare the built banks of the stream with the two famous water-dikes in the north and south of Europe and then to observe with something like amusement the troop peering at Virgil and himself from the sand in the dim light. Then, in an instant, with a flood of conflicting feelings on the one side and the other, comes the mutual recognition of Dante and Brunetto, taking not only themselves with amazement but, as it would as much, Dante's first readers. In the fiction the two friends had been parted by death six years; in fact, when Dante wrote, much longer. They see one another as they talk by the dusky gleam of the flames falling slowly on the sand and on Brunetto's naked form, and throughout their interview there is an undercurrent of pity and agony unexpressed and continuous. For Brunetto, Dante is 'my son'; for Dante, Brunetto recalls 'the dear and kind paternal image' he knew in Florence.

Brunetto was Dante's senior by some fifty years and for Dante and his contemporaries in Florence he represented as no one else could the older and wiser generation who had made their city great and among whom he was one of the most distinguished; a man of large experience and high authority in the city's government in changing and difficult times, the interpreter by his writings and his speech of the wisdom of old Rome and the translator of Cicero, a scholar and thinker who had gathered authority with his years, and in his old age the friend and most revered counsellor of Dante in his youth. He died in Dante's twenty-ninth year, after Dante had gained some note in Florence as a poet and shortly before—under the influence, we must believe, of Brunetto's example and teaching—he began to take active part in the affairs of the republic. Dante's whole poem is, in one aspect of it, his vindication of himself under the challenge of slander and exile, and, in another, his judgement of Florence and the world of his day; and for a Florentine of his generation no vindication could be more effective than that from the old man to whom, even in that depth of Hell, he uses all the language of courtesy and reverence and grateful affection, as no judgement of Florence could be more damning than one from the lips of her great servant. Brunetto promises him, along with his high destiny, the 'honour' of being the object of the ravenous enmity of both parties in Florence, as Dante himself, in one of his shorter poems, 'holds his exile for an honour'; 'but the grass shall be far from the goat'—the words sound proverbial—for he will be beyond their reach, in Verona or elsewhere. It is after Brunetto's prophecy and appeal to his manhood that Dante breaks forth in defiance: 'Turn Fortune her wheel then as she list—and the clown his mattock!', and refers to the heavenly wisdom which is Beatrice the interpretation one day of his earthly lot, and it is then that Virgil turns to him and commends him for his 'good listening'. Dante had already heard, more briefly and obscurely, from Farinata of what was before him, and when he was 'lost in thought' Virgil had bidden him 'hold in memory' Farinata's words and had promised that Beatrice would tell him of his 'life's journey'.

Brunetto's reference to the mixed population of Florence contains Dante's implicit claim to be himself of 'the holy seed' of Rome there—of the succession, that is, of those to whom is entrusted the one divine and human cause of civilization, the cause to which he has given all his faith and service. For it is in that service that he is now preparing to descend into the depths of human fraud and treachery and to utter judgement on the last corruptions of the world. 'Just as in Limbo he had been consecrated by the noble company of the ancient poets as the restorer of classic art, so here he has himself recognized, for his natural aptitudes, for the favours of heaven to him, for his nobleness of blood, as worthy to go forth, an apostle of moral and civil regeneration to Italy and to the world. Such is the meaning, respectively, of the two scenes, which are intended to confer authority with his contemporaries on the voice raised at the bidding of divine providence in rebuke of all human perversities and in prophecy of a new era of justice and of peace, in a supreme work of poetry' (*V. Rossi, L.D.*).

At the end of the canto Brunetto tells, grudgingly and with contempt, of some of his associates there, and there is a peculiar horror in the discovery that such a man as Brunetto Latini is grouped by the grossness of his sin with 'such scurf' as the unnamed churchman whom both he and Dante had known as Bishop of Florence. Their offence appears to have been extraordinarily prevalent at that time and place, especially in the learned professions, among scholars, teachers, and clergy, to whose class Brunetto belonged, and nothing could have demonstrated its vileness more convincingly than its bringing of men of the quality of Brunetto down to the level of such companions.

How was it possible for Dante at once so to honour his old master and so to blacken his memory? The question is inevitable and has been repeatedly discussed. He had carried through the years imperishable memories of hours spent with Brunetto in the time of his own youth and hopefulness, and in proportion to his reverence and affection had been the shock when he learned of the corrosive lust that had accompanied Brunetto's great qualities and services. Something of that pain is expressed in his first exclamation: 'Are you here, Ser Brunetto?'—the 'you' is emphatic. It is both unnecessary and impossible to suppose that Brunetto's offence was unknown to Dante's readers when the canto was written and that Dante was here informing the world of it. Rather, this was a strange and terrible instance, known already both to Dante and to his contemporaries, of a noble nature inwardly disfigured, and he dared not refuse to speak of it because the man had been his friend, as if he should measure men by their relation to himself. Here if anywhere vindicated anew in his moral authority, Dante is bound by the measures of good and evil which lie for him in the eternal nature of things. It is as if he had said: 'For all the shame that has fallen on Brunetto's name, his service to Florence and to me remains; still he stands for the best that Florence has been and might be; let him be judge now between Florence and me.' It is this underlying conflict of motive that gives such singular dramatic tension to the whole scene of the meeting of the two Florentines.

Then, 'from the lyrical exaltation of the canto we pass insensibly to a deeply felt melancholy, which becomes more intense and full of thought when the two personages, bound to one another with so close ties of filial and paternal affection and so fitted for mutual understanding, give each other that last farewell, both turning back to follow their inexorable destiny. (*E. G. Parodi*).

INFERNO

GIÀ era in loco onde s' udìa 'l rimbombo
dell'acqua che cadea nell'altro giro,
simile a quel che l'arnie fanno rombo,
quando tre ombre insieme si partiro,
correndo, d' una torma che passava
sotto la pioggia dell'aspro martiro.
Venìan ver noi, e ciascuna gridava:
'Sostati tu ch'all'abito ne sembri
essere alcun di nostra terra prava.'
Ahimè, che piaghe vidi ne' lor membri, 10
ricenti e vecchie, dalle fiamme incese!
Ancor men duol pur ch' i' me ne rimembri.
Alle lor grida il mio dottor s'attese;
volse 'l viso ver me, e disse: 'Aspetta:
a costor si vuol essere cortese.
E se non fosse il foco che saetta
la natura del loco, i' dicerei
che meglio stesse a te che a lor la fretta.'
Ricominciar, come noi restammo, ei
l'antico verso; e quando a noi fuor giunti, 20
fenno una rota di sè tutti e trei,
qual sogliono i campion far nudi e unti,
avvisando lor presa e lor vantaggio,
prima che sien tra lor battuti e punti;
e sì rotando, ciascuno il visaggio
drizzava a me, s, che'm còntrario il collo
faceva e i piè continüo vïaggio.
E 'Se miseria d'esto loco sollo
rende in dispetto noi e nostri prieghi'
cominciò l' uno 'e 'l tinto aspetto e brollo, 30

CANTO XVI

The three Florentines; the edge of the pit

I WAS already at a point where the resounding of the water that fell into the next circle was heard like the hum of beehives, when three shades set out together running from a crowd which was passing under the rain of fierce torment. They came towards us, each crying: 'Stop thou, who by thy dress seemest to be one from our degenerate city.' Ah me, what wounds old and new I saw in their members, burnt in by the flames! It grieves me still only to remember them.

My Teacher listened to their cries, then turned his face to me and said: 'Wait, to these we must show courtesy, and were it not for the fire which the nature of the place discharges I would say that haste is more fitting for thee than for them.'

As soon as we stopped they resumed their former pace, and when they reached us all three made a wheel of themselves as champions are used to do, naked and oiled, watching their advantage for a grip before the exchange of thrusts and blows; and thus wheeling each kept directing his face towards me, so that they had both their neck and their feet in continual movement.

And one began: 'If the misery of this sandy place and our aspect blackened and hairless bring us and our petitions into contempt, may our fame incline

la fama nostra il tuo animo pieghi
  a dirne chi tu se', che i vivi piedi
  così sicuro per lo 'nferno freghi.
Questi, l'orme di cui pestar mi vedi,
  tutto che nudo e dipelato vada,
  fu di grado maggior che tu non credi:
nepote fu della buona Gualdrada;
  Guido Guerra ebbe nome, ed in sua vita
  fece col senno assai e con la spada.
L'altro, ch'appresso me la rena trita, 40
  è Tegghiaio Aldobrandi, la cui voce
  nel mondo su dovrìa esser gradita.
E io, che posto son con loro in croce,
  Iacopo Rusticucci fui; e certo
  la fiera moglie più ch'altro mi noce.'
S' i' fossi stato dal foco coperto,
  gittato mi sarei tra lor di sotto,
  e credo che 'l dottor l'avrìa sofferto;
ma perch' io mi sarei bruciato e cotto,
  vinse paura la mia buona voglia 50
  che di loro abbracciar mi facea ghiotto.
Poi cominciai: 'Non dispetto, ma doglia
  la vostra condizion dentro mi fisse
  tanta che tardi tutta si dispoglia,
tosto che questo mio segnor mi disse
  parole per le quali i' mi pensai
  che qual voi siete, tal gente venisse.
Di vostra terra sono, e sempre mai
  l'ovra di voi e li onorati nomi
  con affezion ritrassi e ascoltai. 60
Lascio lo fele, e vo per dolci pomi
  promessi a me per lo verace duca;
  ma infino al centro pria convien ch' i' tomi.'
'Se lungamente l'anima conduca
  le membra tue,' rispuose quelli ancora
  'e se la fama tua dopo te luca,
cortesia e valor dì se dimora
  nella nostra città sì come sòle,
  o se del tutto se n'è gita fora;

thy mind to tell us who thou art that thus securely movest living feet through Hell. He in whose steps thou seest me tread, though he goes naked and peeled, was of greater station than thou thinkest; he was grandson of the good Gualdrada, Guido Guerra by name,[1] and in his life he did much with counsel and with sword. The other, pressing the sand behind me, is Tegghiaio Aldobrandi, whose voice should have been heeded in the world above; and I who am put with them in torment was Jacopo Rusticucci,[2] and truly my savage wife, more than all else, has wrought me ill.'

Had I been sheltered from the fire I would have thrown myself down among them and I think my Teacher would have suffered it; but since I should have been burnt and baked, fear overcame my good-will which made me eager to embrace them. Then I began: 'Not contempt, but grief, your condition fixed within me so deep that it will be long before it wholly leaves me, as soon as the words of my lord here made me think that such men as you were coming. I am of your city, and your deeds and honoured names I have always recounted and heard with affection. I am leaving the gall and going on for the sweet fruits promised me by my truthful Leader; but first I must go down to the centre.'

'So may the soul long direct thy members and thy fame shine after thee,' he replied in turn 'tell us if courtesy and valour abide in our city as they did, or if they are quite gone from it; for

chè Guiglielmo Borsiere, il qual si dole 70
  con noi per poco e va là coi compagni,
  assai ne cruccia con le sue parole.'
'La gente nova e' subiti guadagni
  orgoglio e dismisura han generata,
  Fiorenza, in te, sì che tu già ten piagni.'
Così gridai con la faccia levata;
  e i tre, che ciò inteser per risposta,
  guardar l' un l'altro com' al ver si guata.
'Se l'altre volte sì poco ti costa'
  rispuoser tutti 'il satisfare altrui, 80
  felice te se sì parli a tua posta!
Però, se campi d'esti luoghi bui
  e torni a riveder le belle stelle,
  quando ti gioverà dicere "I' fui",
fa che di noi alla gente favelle.'
  Indi rupper la rota, ed a fuggirsi
  ali sembiar le gambe loro snelle.
Un amen non sarìa potuto dirsi
  tosto così com'e' furo spariti;
  per che al maestro parve di partirsi. 90
Io lo seguiva, e poco eravam iti,
  che 'l suon dell'acqua n'era sì vicino
  che per parlar saremmo a pena uditi.
Come quel fiume c' ha proprio cammino
  prima da Monte Veso inver levante,
  dalla sinistra costa d'Apennino,
che si chiama Acquaqueta suso, avante
  che si divalli giù nel basso letto,
  e a Forlì di quel nome è vacante,
rimbomba là sovra San Benedetto 100
  dell'Alpe per cadere ad una scesa
  ove dovrìa per mille esser recetto;
così, giù d'una ripa discoscesa,
  trovammo risonar quell'acqua tinta,
  sì che 'n poc' ora avrìa l'orecchia offesa.
Io avea una corda intorno cinta,
  e con essa pensai alcuna volta
  prender la lonza alla pelle dipinta.

Guglielmo Borsiere,[3] who has been a short time in pain with us and goes yonder with our company, afflicts us greatly with his words.'

'The new people and the sudden gains have begot in thee, Florence, arrogance and excess so that already thou weepst for it!' This I cried with lifted face; and the three, taking it for answer, looked at each other as men stare on hearing the truth. 'If other times it costs thee as little to satisfy others,' they all replied 'happy art thou, speaking thus at thy pleasure. Therefore if thou escape from these dark regions and return to see again the beauty of the stars, when it will rejoice thee to say "I was there", do thou speak of us to men.'

Then they broke the wheel and in their flight their nimble legs seemed wings; an *Amen* could not have been said so quickly as they vanished. It seemed good to the Master, therefore, to go on. I followed him, and we had gone only a little way when the sound of the water was so near that we could scarcely have heard each other speak. As that river which is the first to hold its own course from Monte Veso eastward on the left slope of the Apennines—called the Acquacheta above, before it pours into its lower bed and loses that name at Forli—reverberates there over San Benedetto dell'Alpe by falling at one bound where there might well have been a thousand;[4] thus, down a precipitous bank, we found that dark water resounding so that before long it would have stunned our ears.

I had a cord girt about me, with which I once thought to take the leopard with the painted skin.[5]

Poscia che l'ebbi tutta da me sciolta,
sì come 'l duca m'avea comandato, 110
porsila a lui aggroppata e ravvolta.
Ond'ei si volse inver lo destro lato,
e alquanto di lunge dalla sponda
la gittò giuso in quell'alto burrato.
'E' pur convien che novità risponda'
dicea fra me medesmo 'al novo cenno
che 'l maestro con l'occhio sì seconda.'
Ahi quanto cauti li uomini esser dienno
presso a color che non veggion pur l'ovra,
ma per entro i pensier miran col senno! 120
El disse a me: 'Tosto verrà di sovra
ciò ch' io attendo e che il tuo pensier sogna:
tosto convien ch'al tuo viso si scovra.'
Sempre a quel ver c' ha faccia di menzogna
de' l' uom chiuder le labbra fin ch'el pote,
però che sanza colpa fa vergogna;
ma qui tacer nol posso; e per le note
di questa comedìa, lettor, ti giuro,
s'elle non sien di lunga grazia vote,
ch' i' vidi per quell'aere grosso e scuro 130
venir notando una figura in suso,
maravigliosa ad ogni cor sicuro,
sì come torna colui che va giuso
talora a solver l'ancora ch'aggrappa
o scoglio o altro che nel mare è chiuso,
che 'n su si stende, e da piè si rattrappa.

1. All three were among the Guelf leaders in Florence of the generation before Dante. 'The good Gualdrada,' remembered for her beauty and modesty, was ancestress of the great Conti Guidi family of Dante's time.

2. Two of the Florentines about whom Dante questioned Ciacco (Canto vi). If Tegghiaio's advice had been taken by the Guelfs in 1260 they would not have gone to their defeat at Montaperti (Canto x).

After I had loosed it from me completely as my Leader bade, I passed it to him coiled and knotted together; then, swinging round on his right side, he flung it some distance out from the edge down into the depth of the abyss.

'Surely' I said within myself 'something strange must answer the strange signal which the Master so follows with his eye.'

Ah, how careful men should be with those who not only see the deed but look with understanding into the thoughts! He said to me: 'Soon will come up what I look for and what thy mind dreams of; soon it must be discovered to thy sight.'

A man should always close his lips, as far as he can, to the truth that has the face of a lie, since without fault it brings him shame, but here I cannot be silent; and by the strains of this Comedy—so may they not fail of lasting favour—I swear to thee, reader, that I saw come swimming up through that gross and murky air a figure amazing to the stoutest heart, even as he returns who goes down some time to loose the anchor that is caught on a reef or something else hid in the sea, stretching upward and drawing in his feet.

3. Said to have been a Florentine purse-maker of the time.

4. The Acquacheta ('Quiet Water'), a mountain stream making a fall in time of flood near the old monastery of San Benedetto dell' Alpe and farther down joining the Montone, 'the first' south of the Po to enter the Adriatic.

5. Canto i.

NOTE

It is a startling judgement on Florence of the generation just before Dante's that is suggested by the fact that in this round of the sodomites all the four with whom he talks have been men of his city and of note and dignity in it. The three who hail him as a fellow-citizen cherish still their old fame as men of affairs in Florence and plead for its continuance; they are jealous for whatever remains of courtesy and valour, the virtues of civil life and of war, in 'our degenerate city', and they are distressed at the denunciation which Dante addresses to it 'with lifted face', as it were in the direction of Florence itself. 'For the first time the traveller rises up in fierce judgement of contemporary life. The consecration of his civic Florentine virtue which he has just before received from Brunetto gives him now the right to do this, and a singularly fitting occasion for it is offered to him by the presence of the three spirits who had lived on the earth in a time the memory of which is, for Dante, a reproach to the present wickedness' (*V. Rossi*).

With this union in one mood and moment of a passionate love for Florence with the denouncing of its corruptions there is an equally dramatic contrast between Dante's deference to these men at Virgil's bidding for their 'deeds and honoured names' and the lurid background of their sin and its penalty against which he sees them; the outrage and indecency of their sin is measured by the greatness of the men. The most moving thing in the whole canto is the tragic conflict which it illustrates between the force of deep human loyalties, on the one hand, and the inevitable moral imperatives, on the other.

The deafening roar of the river of tears and blood, draining from all the circles of incontinence and of violence and now pouring into the abyss of fraud, is, at this point of transition, a reminder of the accumulated volume of human sin and misery, even while they have not yet reached their worst.

No commentator has been able to give a completely satisfactory explanation of the symbolism—a symbolism plainly intended by Dante—of the cord that was taken from his person and thrown as a signal into the depth below. There is an early story, which may well be true, that in his youth Dante became a novice of the Franciscan Order and later withdrew from it, and in that case—even in any case—the cord probably meant the restraint of vows and of an external discipline with which he had once thought to overcome the temptations of the flesh, 'the leopard with the painted skin'. Now, having seen that evil power in its full working and result, he is hardened and inwardly secured against it and needs no such outward security, so that Virgil can throw the cord away. Why then it should be a sign to Geryon, the monster of fraud, it is harder to say. May the discarded cord, 'coiled and knotted together', represent the challenge which a soul, now secure in its purity and trusting to its reason and conscience, presents to fraud to come out of its hiding and disclose itself for what it is?

The devices at the end of the canto to prepare the reader's mind for the vision of fraud make it more credible by first calling it incredible; and when he tells of the appearance of 'a figure amazing to the stoutest heart', as if of something not to be imagined till it has been seen, he plainly means that human fraud, in its processes and consequences in the soul and in the world, is a monstrous perversion and mystery of iniquity, sunk and hidden in darkness far below all the depths of violence. The vivid comparison to the diver and the studied vagueness of the whole passage leave us in a mood of wonder and suspense for what may follow.

INFERNO

'Ecco la fiera con la coda aguzza,
che passa i monti, e rompe i muri e l'armi;
ecco colei che tutto 'l mondo appuzza!'
Sì cominciò lo mio duca a parlarmi;
e accennolle che venisse a proda
vicino al fin de' passeggiati marmi.
E quella sozza imagine di froda
sen venne, ed arrivò la testa e 'l busto,
ma 'n su la riva non trasse la coda.
La faccia sua era faccia d' uom giusto, 10
tanto benigna avea di fuor la pelle,
e d' un serpente tutto l'altro fusto;
due branche avea pilose infin l'ascelle;
lo dosso e 'l petto e ambedue le coste
dipinti avea di nodi e di rotelle:
con più color, sommesse e sopraposte
non fer mai drappi Tartari nè Turchi,
nè fuor tai tele per Aragne imposte.
Come tal volta stanno a riva i burchi,
che parte sono in acqua e parte in terra, 20
e come là tra li Tedeschi lurchi
lo bivero s'assetta a far sua guerra,
così la fiera pessima si stava
su l'orlo che, di pietra, il sabbion serra.
Nel vano tutta sua coda guizzava,
torcendo in su la venenosa forca
ch'a guisa di scorpion la punta armava.
Lo duca disse: 'Or convien che si torca
la nostra via un poco insino a quella
bestia malvagia che colà si corca.' 30

CANTO XVII

Geryon; the Usurers; the descent to Malebolge

"Lo, the beast with the pointed tail, that passes mountains and breaks through walls and arms! Lo, he that infects all the world!' Thus my Leader began to speak to me, and he beckoned him to come ashore near the end of the stony causeway; and that foul image of fraud came on and landed his head and chest, but did not draw his tail on to the bank. His face was the face of a just man, so gracious was its outward aspect, and all the rest was a serpent's trunk; he had two paws, hairy to the armpits, and the back and breast and both the flanks were painted with knots and circlets—Tartars or Turks never made stuffs with more colours in ground and embroidery, nor were such webs laid by Arachne on the loom.[1] As boats sometimes lie at the shore, part in the water and part on land, and as there among the German gluttons the beaver settles itself to take its prey,[2] so the vile brute lay on the rim that bounds the great sand with stone. All his tail was quivering in the void, twisting upwards the poisonous fork that armed the point like a scorpion's.

My Leader said: 'Now we must bend our way a little, as far as that malignant beast that couches there.'

Però scendemmo alla destra mammella,
e diece passi femmo in su lo stremo,
per ben cessar la rena e la fiammella.
E quando noi a lei venuti semo,
poco più oltre veggio in su la rena
gente seder propinqua al luogo scemo.
Quivi 'l maestro:'Acciò che tutta piena
esperïenza d'esto giron porti,'
mi disse 'va, e vedi la lor mena.
Li tuoi ragionamenti sian là corti: 40
mentre che torni, parlerò con questa,
che ne conceda i suoi omeri forti.'
Così ancor su per la strema testa
di quel settimo cerchio tutto solo
andai, dove sedea la gente mesta.
Per li occhi fora scoppiava lor duolo;
di qua, di là soccorrìen con le mani,
quando a' vapori e quando al caldo suolo:
non altrimenti fan di state i cani,
or col ceffo or col piè, quando son morsi 50
o da pulci o da mosche o da tafani.
Poi che nel viso a certi li occhi porsi,
ne' quali il doloroso foco casca,
non ne conobbi alcun; ma io m'accorsi
che dal collo a ciascun pendea una tasca
ch'avea certo colore e certo segno,
e quindi par che 'l loro occhio si pasca.
E com' io riguardando tra lor vegno,
in una borsa gialla vidi azzurro
che d' un leone avea faccia e contegno. 60
Poi, procedendo di mio sguardo il curro,
vidine un'altra come sangue rossa,
mostrando un'oca bianca più che burro.
E un, che d' una scrofa azzurra e grossa
segnato avea lo suo sacchetto bianco,
mi disse: 'Che fai tu in questa fossa?
Or te ne va; e perchè se' vivo anco,
sappi che 'l mio vicin Vitalïano
sederà qui dal mio sinistro fianco.

We descended, therefore, on our right and went ten paces along the edge, so as to keep well away from the sand and the flames; and when we reached him I saw people beyond sitting on the sand, near where it falls away.

Here the Master said to me: 'That thou mayst carry away full experience of this round, go and see their condition. Let thy talk there be brief. Till thou return I will speak with this creature that he may lend us his strong shoulders.'

So I went by myself still farther along the extreme edge of that seventh circle to where the unhappy folk were seated. Through the eyes their pain was bursting forth; on one side and the other they defended themselves with their hands, sometimes from the flames, sometimes from the burning soil, like dogs in summer that ply, now snout, now paw, when they are bitten by fleas or gnats or gad-flies. When I set my eyes on the faces of some on whom the grievous fire was falling, I did not know one of them; but I observed that from the neck of each hung a pouch of a certain colour and device, and on these they seemed to feast their eyes. And when I came among them, looking about, I saw, azure on a yellow purse, the face and form of a lion; then, continuing my inspection, I saw another, blood-red, which showed a goose whiter than butter. And one that had a sow azure and gravid stamped on his white wallet[3] said to me: 'What dost thou in this pit? Take thyself off, and, since thou art still in life, know that my townsman Vitaliano[4] will sit here on my left. Among these Florentines I am

Con questi fiorentin son padovano: 70
  spesse fïate m' intronan li orecchi,
  gridando: "Vegna il cavalier sovrano,
che recherà la tasca coi tre becchi!" '
  Qui distorse la bocca e di fuor trasse
  la lingua come bue che 'l naso lecchi.
E io, temendo no 'l più star crucciasse
  lui che di poco star m'avea 'mmonito,
  torna' mi in dietro dall'anime lasse.
Trova' il duca mio ch'era salito
  già su la groppa del fiero animale, 80
  e disse a me: 'Or sie forte e ardito.
Omai si scende per sì fatte scale:
  monta dinanzi, ch' i' voglio esser mezzo,
  sì che la coda non possa far male.'
Qual è colui che sì presso ha 'l riprezzo
  della quartana c' ha già l' unghie smorte,
  e triema tutto pur guardando il rezzo,
tal divenn' io alle parole porte;
  ma vergogna mi fè le sue minacce,
  che innanzi a buon segnor fa servo forte. 90
I' m'assettai in su quelle spallacce:
  sì volli dir, ma la voce non venne
  com' io credetti: 'Fa che tu m'abbracce.'
Ma esso, ch'altra volta mi sovvenne
  ad altro forse, tosto ch' io montai
  con le braccia m'avvinse e mi sostenne;
e disse: 'Gerïon, moviti omai:
  le rote larghe, e lo scender sia poco:
  pensa la nova soma che tu hai.'
Come la navicella esce di loco 100
  in dietro in dietro, sì quindi si tolse;
  e poi ch'al tutto si sentì a gioco,
là 'v'era il petto la coda rivolse,
  e quella tesa, come anguilla, mosse,
  e con le branche l'aere a sè raccolse.
Maggior paura non credo che fosse
  quando Fetòn abbandonò li freni,
  per che 'l ciel, come pare ancor, si cosse;

of Padua; many a time they din my ears, shouting: "Let the sovereign knight come, who will bring the pouch with the three goats!" '[5] Then he writhed his mouth and thrust out his tongue, like an ox that licks its nose, and I, fearing lest a longer stay should anger him who had warned me to make it short, turned back from the weary souls.

I found my Leader already mounted on the croup of the savage brute, and he said to me: 'Now be strong and bold. The descent henceforth is by such stairs as this. Mount in front, for I wish to be between that the tail may not harm thee.'

As one so near the shivering-fit of the quartan that his nails are already blue and he trembles all over at the mere sight of shade, such I became at these words of his; but shame threatened me, which makes a servant brave before a good master, and I settled myself on those great shoulders. I wished to say, but the voice did not come as I thought, 'See that thou embrace me!' But he who succoured me another time in another peril clasped me in his arms as soon as I mounted and supported me, then said: 'Geryon,[6] now move; let the circles be wide and the descent slow; remember the new burden thou hast.'

As the bark backs out little by little from its place, so Geryon drew out thence and, when he felt himself quite clear, turned his tail where his breast had been and, stretching it out, moved it like an eel and gathered in the air with his paws. No greater fear, I think, had Phaeton[7] when he let go the reins and the sky was scorched as it

nè quando Icaro misero le reni
  sentì spennar per la scaldata cera, 110
  gridando il padre a lui: 'Mala via tieni!',
che fu la mia, quando vidi ch' i' era
  nell'aere d'ogni parte, e vidi spenta
  ogni veduta fuor che della fera.
Ella sen va notando lenta lenta;
  rota e discende, ma non me n'accorgo
  se non ch'al viso e di sotto mi venta.
Io sentìa già dalla man destra il gorgo
  far sotto noi un orribile scroscio,
  per che con li occhi 'n giù la testa sporgo. 120
Allor fu' io più timido allo scoscio,
  però ch' i' vidi fuochi e senti' pianti;
  ond' io tremando tutto mi raccoscio.
E vidi poi, chè nol vedea davanti,
  lo scendere e 'l girar per li gran mali
  che s'appressavan da diversi canti.
Come 'l falcon ch'è stato assai su l'ali,
  che sanza veder logoro o uccello
  fa dire al falconiere: 'Ohmè, tu cali!',
discende lasso onde si mosse snello, 130
  per cento rote, e da lunge si pone
  dal suo maestro, disdegnoso e fello;
così ne puose al fondo Gerïone
  al piè al piè della stagliata rocca
  e, discarcate le nostre persone,
si dileguò come da corda cocca.

1. Arachne, famed for her weaving, challenged Minerva to a contest and was changed by the goddess into a spider.

2. Beavers were supposed to sit with their tails in the water so as to attract the fish they caught for food.

3. These are the arms of various Florentine and Paduan families.

4. Not otherwise known.

shows still, nor wretched Icarus[8] when he felt his sides losing their wings by the melting wax and his father cried to him: 'Thou takest the wrong way', than was mine when I saw that I was in the air on every side and saw everything lost to sight except the beast. He goes swimming slowly on, wheeling and descending, but I am not conscious of it except for the wind blowing in my face and from below. I heard now on our right the torrent making a hideous roar below us, at which I stretched forth my head and looked down; then I was more afraid for the dismounting, for I saw fires and heard wailings, so that I cowered back all trembling. And I saw then—for I had not seen it before—our descent and circling by the great torments that drew near on every side.

As the falcon that has been long on the wing and without sight of lure or bird makes the falconer cry: 'Alack, thou stoopest!' descends weary, with a hundred wheels, to where it set out swiftly, and alights, angry and sullen, at a distance from its master, so Geryon set us down at the bottom, close to the foot of the jagged rock, and, relieved of our weight, vanished like an arrow from the string.

5. Buiamonte, a leading Florentine money-lender.

6. Geryon, a monster killed by Hercules, represented in medieval legend as enticing strangers to be his guests and killing them.

7. Phaeton, entrusted by his father Apollo with the chariot of the sun for a day, misguided it and the Milky Way shows where the sky was scorched.

8. Daedalus fixed wings on his son Icarus with wax; when Icarus flew too near the sun the wax melted and he fell into the sea.

NOTE

Geryon is another of Dante's composite creatures and far more brute than human, for fraud is the deliberate use of the distinctively human powers for inhuman ends. He has his name from the classical monster, his treacherous character from the medieval story, and some of his features from the locusts of the *Apocalypse*. 'Their faces were as the faces of men . . . and they had tails like unto scorpions, and there were stings in their tails.' (*Rev.* ix. 7–10). But essentially he is Dante's own invention, one live creature with the obvious attributes of fraud—the gracious human face as of a just man, the predacious clawed feet, the body of the subtle serpent marked with enticing knots and circlets, the ready, swinging tail pointed with a sting. The exceptional descent of the pilgrims to the right on the edge of the sand—like their turning right on entering the city of Dis (Canto xi)—is probably their confronting of evil with the soul's integrity, with the same idea continued in their 'ten paces', for the Decalogue, along the edge of the pit.

It is at this point, when they have reached the monster of fraud, that they come in sight of the usurers on the burning sand, 'near where it falls away'. For usury, as Dante knew it and judged it in Italy, though not formally fraudulent, was always by the nature of it on the edge of fraud. In a time of rapid economic change, with a new demand in the city for capital and with new chances, especially in Florence, of 'sudden gains' and their moral consequences, it is not to be supposed that Dante, with no commercial experience and with quite other traditions and sympathies, would discriminate fairly between the rights and wrongs of lending and borrowing in trade, and 'he seems to have regarded as sinful the mere fact of living and profiting by the lending of money' (*D. Mantovani, L.D.*). But what he had in view, plainly, was the practice of oppressive and unscrupulous usury on the part of men of rank and wealth, which he reckoned a breach of the social bond of industry, 'God's grandchild', and so a kind of blasphemy to be punished with fire. It was in a special sense the anti-social use of the intelligence, and for Dante sins are base in the measure in which they are anti-social. He looks at these noble usurers, one by one, with a kind of contemptuous curiosity—'I set my eyes on the faces of some'—'I came among them, looking about'—'continuing my inspection of them'—much as he had looked at them in the streets of Florence and Padua. These men of great family, born to high obligations, have now no recognizable personality left—'I did not know one of them'; he had almost overlooked them altogether and Virgil takes nothing to do with them; 'Dante had no need of instructions for knowing what to think of sinners like these' (*D. Mantovani, L.D.*). Their family arms, once honourable, are now no more than marks, a kind of shop-signs, on the money-bags on which they still feast their eyes, and their old wrangling rivalries continue in Hell, Florentines shouting at Paduans that they have the biggest usurer of all coming soon to join them. They are quite the worst-mannered souls Dante has yet met with in Hell and he does not condescend to speak to any of them. The sting in the mention of their various arms is that the families owning them, and their money-lending members, especially the two still alive in 1300, were well known to Dante's first readers.

When Virgil bids Dante, on his return, mount on Geryon, 'The descent henceforth' he says 'is by such stairs as this.' For fraud, seeking by its nature to disguise and conceal itself, in the last resort and by the nature of things *shows itself* to be fraud, and it belongs peculiarly and inevitably to the penalty of fraud to be found out. Geryon, cheated like the falcon of his prey, is 'angry and sullen', but he is wholly at Virgil's bidding.

The vast descent into the pit, on which Dante uses all the resources of his art, tells of the far deeper degradation of the soul in the sins of fraud than in those of violence. The comparison with Phaeton and Icarus is not merely a picturesque illustration from ancient literature of supernatural flight; it is

Dante's comparison of his own flight with that of heathen and disastrous presumption. He is like Phaeton and Icarus in their bewilderment and terror; but his security in a world of fraud, where 'everything is lost to sight except the beast'—a security which for the moment he does not feel—is all the time in Virgil's clasp.

But here as always the power of the narrative is not in its mere allegorical ingenuity, but in its reality, its imaginative conviction. 'The miracle of art in this canto is its representation of what I should call the mobile plasticity of the monster, its singular vitality up to the moment of its disappearance. Geryon's unstable couching between earth and air, its slow backing out from the bank and its agile movements as soon as it expatiates freely in the breadth of the void, are delineated with such precision and concreteness that prodigies and unlikelihoods take the aspect of what is natural and real; and Dante's experience, when he is seated on these great shoulders, of aerial navigation, by which he is made to share in the conditions of the monster swimming in the air, seems a pledge of truth. . . . With an amazing intuition of the facts, Dante almost succeeds in making us believe in his experience and share it ourselves, so intense and clear is his imaginative vision' (*V. Rossi*).

INFERNO

LUOGO è in inferno detto Malebolge,
tutto di pietra di color ferrigno,
come la cerchia che dintorno il volge.
Nel dritto mezzo del campo maligno
vaneggia un pozzo assai largo e profondo,
di cui *suo loco* dicerò l'ordigno.
Quel cinghio che rimane adunque è tondo
tra 'l pozzo e 'l piè dell'alta ripa dura,
e ha distinto in dieci valli il fondo.
Quale, dove per guardia delle mura 10
più e più fossi cingon li castelli,
la parte dove son rende figura,
tale imagine quivi facean quelli;
e come a tai fortezze da' lor sogli
alla ripa di fuor son ponticelli,
così da imo della roccia scogli
movìen che ricidìen li argini e' fossi
infino al pozzo che i tronca e racco'gli.
In questo luogo, della schiena scossi
di Gerïon, trovammoci; e 'l poeta 20
tenne a sinistra, e io dietro mi mossi.
Alla man destra vidi nova pièta,
novo tormento e novi frustatori,
di che la prima bolgia era repleta.
Nel fondo erano ignudi i peccatori:
dal mezzo in qua ci venìen verso 'l volto,
di là con noi, ma con passi maggiori,

CANTO XVIII

The Eighth Circle; the Fraudulent; the Malebolge; the First Bolgia; the Panders and Seducers; Caccianemico; the Second Bolgia; the Flatterers

THERE is a place in Hell called Malebolge,[1] all stone of iron colour like the wall that goes round it. Right in the middle of the baleful space yawns a pit of great breadth and depth, of whose structure I shall tell in its own place, so that the belt left between the pit and the high rocky bank is round, and its bottom is divided into ten valleys. As, where successive moats encircle a castle to guard its walls, the space they occupy presents a ground-plan, such was the design these made there; and as such fortresses have bridges from their thresholds to the outside bank, so from the base of the rock ran ridges that struck across the dikes and ditches as far as the pit, which cuts them short and gathers them in. In this place we found ourselves, dropped from Geryon's back, and the Poet held to the left and I came on behind.

On our right hand I saw new anguish, new torments and new scourgers, for with these the first ditch was full. The sinners at the bottom were naked. On this side of the middle they came facing us, and on the other along with us but with greater

come i Roman per l'essercito molto,
  l'anno del giubileo, su per lo ponte
  hanno a passar la gente modo colto, 30
che dall' un lato tutti hanno la fronte
  verso 'l castello e vanno a Santo Pietro;
  dall'altra sponda vanno verso il monte.
Di qua, di là, su per lo sasso tetro
  vidi demon cornuti con gran ferze,
  che li battìen crudelmente di retro.
Ahi come facean lor levar le berze
  alle prime percosse! già nessuno
  le seconde aspettava nè le terze.
Mentr' io andava, li occhi miei in uno 40
  furo scontrati; e io sì tosto dissi:
  'Già di veder costui non son digiuno';
Per ch' io a figurarlo i piedi affissi:
  e 'l dolce duca meco si ristette,
  e assentìo ch'alquanto in dietro gissi.
E quel frustato celar si credette
  bassando il viso; ma poco li valse,
  ch' io dissi: 'O tu che l'occhio a terra gette,
se le fazion che porti non son false,
  Venedico se' tu Caccianemico: 50
  ma che ti mena a sì pungenti salse?'
Ed elli a me: 'Mal volontier lo dico;
  ma sforzami la tua chiara favella,
  che mi fa sovvenir del mondo antico.
I' fui colui che la Ghisolabella
  condussi a far la voglia del Marchese,
  come che suoni la sconcia novella.
E non pur io qui piango bolognese;
  anzi n'è questo luogo tanto pieno
  che tante lingue non son ora apprese 60
a dicer "sipa" tra Sàvena e Reno;
  e se di ciò vuoi fede o testimonio,
  rècati a mente il nostro avaro seno.'
Così parlando il percosse un demonio
  della sua scurïada, e disse: 'Via,
  ruffian! qui non son femmine da conio.'

strides—just as on account of the great throng in the year of the Jubilee the Romans took measures for the people to pass over the bridge, so that all on the one side of it faced towards the Castle and went to Saint Peter's and on the other they went towards the Mount.[2] On this side and on that along the gloomy rock I saw horned demons with great whips lashing them cruelly behind. Ah, how they made them lift their heels at the first strokes! Truly none waited for the second or the third.

While I was going on my eyes were met by one of them, and I said quickly: 'Of him there I once saw enough'; so that I held back my steps to make him out and my gentle Leader stopped with me and gave me leave to go back a little. And that scourged soul thought to conceal himself, lowering his face; but to little purpose, for I said: 'Thou casting thy eyes on the ground, if the features thou bearest do not deceive me, art Venedico Caccianemico.[3] But what brings thee into such a biting pickle?'[4]

And he answered me: 'Unwillingly I tell it; but thy plain speech, which makes me remember the old world, compels me. It was I who brought Ghisolabella to do the will of the Marquis, however the vile story is told. And I am not the only Bolognese lamenting here; in truth this place is so full of them that not so many tongues have learned to say *sipa* between the Savena and the Reno,[5] and if thou wouldst have evidence and confirmation of this, recall to mind our avaricious hearts.'

While he was speaking a demon smote him with his scourge and said: 'Off, pander! here are no women to coin.'

I' mi raggiunsi con la scorta mia;
poscia con pochi passi divenimmo
là 'v' uno scoglio della ripa uscìa.
Assai leggeramente quel salimmo; 70
e volti a destra su per la sua scheggia,
da quelle cerchie etterne ci partimmo.
Quando noi fummo là dov'el vaneggia
di sotto per dar passo alli sferzati,
lo duca disse: 'Attienti, e fa che feggia
lo viso in te di quest'altri mal nati,
ai quali ancor non vedesti la faccia
però che son con noi insieme andati.'
Del vecchio ponte guardavam la traccia
che venìa verso noi dall'altra banda, 80
e che la ferza similmente scaccia.
E 'l buon maestro, sanza mia dimanda,
mi disse: 'Guarda quel grande che vene,
e per dolor non par lagrima spanda:
quanto aspetto reale ancor ritene!
Quelli è Iasòn, che per cuore e per senno
li Colchi del monton privati fène.
Ello passò per l' isola di Lenno,
poi che l'ardite femmine spietate
tutti li maschi loro a morte dienno. 90
Ivi con segni e con parole ornate
Isifile ingannò, la giovinetta
che prima avea tutte l'altre ingannate.
Lasciolla quivi, gravida, soletta;
tal colpa a tal martiro lui condanna;
e anche di Medea si fa vendetta.
Con lui sen va chi da tal parte inganna:
e questo basti della prima valle
sapere e di color che 'n sè assanna.'
Già eravam là 've lo stretto calle 100
con l'argine secondo s' incrocicchia,
e fa di quello ad un altr'arco spalle.
Quindi sentimmo gente che si nicchia
nell'altra bolgia e che col muso scuffa,
e sè medesma con le palme picchia.

I rejoined my Escort; then, with a few steps, we came to where a ridge went out from the bank. This we ascended without difficulty and turning to the right on its crags we left these eternal circlings.[6]

When we were at the place where it yawns beneath to give passage to those under the lash the Leader said: 'Stop, and let the sight of these other ill-born souls fall on thee, whose faces thou hast not yet seen because they were going our way.'

From the ancient bridge we looked at the train coming towards us on the other side, driven with whips like the first; and the good Master, without my asking, said to me: 'Look at that great one coming, who for all his pain does not seem to shed a tear. How kingly is his aspect still! He is Jason, who by courage and craft bereft the men of Colchis of the Fleece.[7] He passed by the isle of Lemnos when the bold and pitiless women had given all their men to death, and there with tokens and fair words he beguiled Hypsipyle, the maid who before had beguiled all the rest. He left her there pregnant and forlorn. Such guilt condemns him to such torment, and Medea too is avenged. With him go all who deceive in like fashion, and let this suffice for knowledge of the first valley and of those it holds in its jaws.'

We were now at the place where the narrow track cuts across the second dike and makes of that the abutment to another arch. Here we heard people moaning in the next ditch, puffing with their snouts and smiting themselves with their palms. The

Le ripe eran grommate d'una muffa,
per l'alito di giu che vi s'appasta,
che con li occhi e col naso facea zuffa.
Lo fondo è cupo sì, che non ci basta
luogo a veder sanza montare al dosso 110
dell'arco, ove lo scoglio più sovrasta.
Quivi venimmo; e quindi giù nel fosso
vidi gente attuffata in uno sterco
che dalli uman privadi parea mosso.
E mentre ch' io là giù con l'occhio cerco,
vidi un col capo sì di merda lordo,
che non parea s'era laico o cherco.
Quei mi sgridò: 'Perchè se' tu sì 'ngordo
di riguardar più me che li altri brutti?'
E io a lui: 'Perchè, se ben ricordo, 120
già t' ho veduto coi capelli asciutti,
e se' Alessio Interminei da Lucca:
però t'adocchio più che li altri tutti.'
Ed elli allor, battendosi la zucca:
'Qua giù m' hanno sommerso le lusinghe
ond' io non ebbi mai la lingua stucca.'
Appresso ciò lo duca 'Fa che pinghe'
mi disse 'il viso un poco più avante,
sì che la faccia ben con l'occhio attinghe
di quella sozza e scapigliata fante 130
che là si graffia con l' unghie merdose,
e or s'accoscia, e ora è in piedi stante.
Taidè è, la puttana che rispose
al drudo suo quando disse "Ho io grazie
grandi appo te?": "Anzi maravigliose!"
E quinci sian le nostre viste sazie.'

1. Literally, Evil Pouches.

2. The Jubliee of the Church was instituted by Boniface VIII in 1300 and brought great crowds of pilgrims to Rome. The bridge leading from the city to St Peter's points one way to the Castle of St Angelo and the other to Monte Giordano, a small rising on the left bank of the Tiber.

3. Senicr contemporary of Dante, member of a leading Guelf family of Bologna, who served as Governor of several cities in N. Italy. Various reports were current of his betrayal of his sister to one of the Marquises of Este.

4. The word for 'pickles', *salse*, is also the name of a ravine near Bologna into which the bodies of criminals were thrown.

banks were crusted by the exhalation from below with a mould that sticks on them and is repugnant to eyes and nose, and the bottom is so hollowed out that there is no place from which to see it except by mounting to the crown of the arch, where the ridge overhangs most. We went there, and thence in the moat below I saw people plunged in a filth which seemed to have come from human privies, and searching down there with my eyes I saw one with his head so befouled with ordure that it did not appear whether he was layman or cleric. He shouted at me: 'Why lookest thou so greedily at me more than at the others in their filth?'

And I answered: 'Because, if I remember rightly, I saw thee once with dry hair, and thou art Alessio Interminei of Lucca;[8] therefore I eye thee more than all the rest.'

Then he, beating on his crown: 'Down here my flatteries have sunk me with which my tongue was never cloyed.'

After that the Leader said to me: 'Try to thrust thy head a little farther forward, so as to get a right view of the face of that foul and dishevelled drab who is scratching herself there with her filthy nails and is now squatting, now standing up. It is Thais, the whore who answered her lover when he said: "Have I much favour with thee?", "Nay, beyond measure!"[9] And with that let our sight be satisfied.'

5. Between these rivers is Bologna, and *sipa* is Bolognese dialect for *sì* (yes); there are more Bolognese here than in Bologna itself.

6. Possibly a reference to the medieval custom by which criminals made the 'circuit' of the city before execution.

7. Jason, chief of the Argonauts' voyage in search of the Golden Fleece, seduced and abandoned Hypsipyle, Princess of Lemnos, who had concealed and saved her father when the women of Lemnos agreed to kill all the men,—and later Medea, Princess of Colchis, who had helped him to secure the Fleece.

8. Not otherwise known.

9. An incident in a comedy of Terence.

NOTE

When Dante has to tell of the quality and the consequences of fraud his language is unusually explicit, detailed and matter-of-fact—'There is a place in Hell called Malebolge'—as if he would put past all question the discovery and exposure of fraud's lurking-places; it is all as plain as that. In his account of the Malebolge, which occupies thirteen cantos, he has especially in view the meanness and abjectness of such sins, their self-imprisoning effect on the soul, and the multiplicity and intricacy and ultimate futility of their devices. The fraudulent, who have abused their human privilege of reason, are sunk in the gloomy ditches which are the moats of Satan's stronghold; and the stone of iron colour of which all their prison is formed tells of the hardening and moral insensibility which comes of persistent fraud.

He is at pains, here and in the following cantos, to make the topography of Malebolge quite clear, though it is useless to look for any consistency of scale: the ten concentric 'valleys' or 'moats' or 'ditches' between the outer encircling cliff and the central 'well' or 'pit', with a number of ridges, like spokes of a wheel, 'striking across the dikes and ditches', forming series of arched bridges and rising above the level of the dikes at each point of intersection, with each successive ditch lower than the preceding and the whole general level of Malebolge tending downward as they approach the central depth. If he had any comprehensive principle of order in the allotment of the various classes of the fraudulent to the ten sections of Malebolge, it can hardly be said that his commentators have been able to make it plain.

In the first ditch the two trains of panders and seducers, circling opposite ways but alike in their betrayal of innocence to lust, are driven by the scourges of horned demons, horns being traditionally associated with adultery and their sin keeping them in eternal unrest.

When the double file of sinners is compared with the vast throngs attracted to Rome for Pope Boniface's celebration of the Church's Jubilee and being drilled by the Pope's police on the Tiber bridge at the very time when Dante and Virgil are visiting the Malebolge, it is doubtful if we should take it as a mere neutral illustration, and it would be much in Dante's vein, in view of the contemporary reputation of Rome, to suggest a far closer resemblance between the pilgrims on the bridge and the panders and seducers in the ditch.

Bologna was then a great centre of learning, and its university, where Dante had probably been a student, was of European fame. Its place-names—Salce, Savena, Reno—and its dialect —*sipa*—were as familiar to him as its vices, which are here certified and represented by one of its distinguished citizens.

The great Jason represents, as it were at its height, the crime of seduction—'a magnificent Don Juan, with a baseness that contrasts with his knightly figure' (*K. Vossler*)—and it is in character for Virgil to tell 'without my asking' of the famous hero of antiquity. Jason is driven with whips like the others; his offence is the meaner for his greatness.

The second is the ditch of the flatterers and nothing less than its vile circumstances could express the nausea, emphasized by the unusual brevity of his account of it, that is felt by one of Dante's temper for their sin. We know hardly anything more of Alessio Interminei, but how obnoxious he was to Dante is made plain by his giving him Thais for company.

On the whole canto Rossi's comment is the best: 'Plainly, this is not a canto of passion. The misbegotten breed of these paltry offenders guilty of private crimes awakes no storm in the lofty moral consciousness of the Poet. He feels towards them an olympic, one might almost say a serene, contempt, which holds the mean between indifference and disgust and allows him to abandon himself to the pleasure of creation, varying his tone and his art and rising from the satiric comedy of Venedico to the majesty of Jason and plunging down from that to the fetid degradation of Interminei and Thais.'

INFERNO

O SIMON mago, o miseri seguaci
    che le cose di Dio, che di bontate
    deon essere spose, voi rapaci
per oro e per argento avolterate;
    or convien che per voi suoni la tromba,
    pero che nella terza bolgia state.
Già eravamo alla seguente tomba,
    montati dello scoglio in quella parte
    ch'a punto sovra mezzo il fosso piomba.
O somma sapïenza, quanta è l'arte   10
    che mostri in cielo, in terra e nel mal mondo,
    e quanto giusto tua virtu comparte!
Io vidi per le coste e per lo fondo
    piena la pietra livida di fori,
    d'un largo tutti e ciascun era tondo.
Non mi parean men ampi nè maggiori
    che que' che son nel mio bel San Giovanni,
    fatti per luogo di battezzatori;
l'un delli quali, ancor non è molt'anni,
    rupp'io per un che dentro v'annegava: 20
    e questo sia suggel ch'ogn' uomo sganni.
Fuor della bocca a ciascun soperchiava
    d' un peccator li piedi e delle gambe
    infino al grosso, e l'altro dentro stava.
Le piante erano a tutti accese intrambe;
    per che sì forte guizzavan le giunte,
    che spezzate averìen ritorte e strambe.

CANTO XIX

The Third Bolgia; the Simonists; Pope Nicholas III

Ah, Simon Magus,[1] and you his wretched followers, who, rapacious, prostitute for gold and silver the things of God which should be brides of righteousness, now must the trumpet sound for you, for your place is in the third pouch.

We were now at the next tomb and had climbed to that part of the ridge which hangs right over the middle of the ditch. O Wisdom Supreme, how great is the art Thou showest, in Heaven, on earth, and in the evil world, and how justly does Thy power dispense! I saw along the sides and on the bottom the livid stone full of holes all of one size, and each was round. They seemed to me of a width not more or less than those that were made in my beautiful Saint John[2] as fonts for baptism, one of which, not many years ago, I broke for one that was drowning in it—and to this I set my seal, to clear the mind of everyone. From the mouth of each projected the feet of a sinner and the legs as far as the calf, and the rest was inside; all of them had both soles on fire, from which their joints writhed with such violence that they would have snapped withies or

Qual suole il fiammeggiar delle cose unte
  muoversi pur su per la strema buccia,
  tal era lì dai calcagni alle punte. 30
'Chi è colui, maestro, che si cruccia
  guizzando più che li altri suoi consorti,'
  diss' io 'e cui più roggia fiamma succia?'
Ed elli a me: 'Se tu vuo' ch' i' ti porti
  là giù per quella ripa che più giace,
  da lui saprai di sè e de' suoi torti.'
E io: 'Tanto m'è bel, quanto a te piace:
  tu se' segnore, e sai ch' i' non mi parto
  dal tuo volere, e sai quel che si tace.'
Allor venimmo in su l'argine quarto; 40
  volgemmo e discendemmo a mano stanca
  là giù nel fondo foracchiato e arto.
Lo buon maestro ancor della sua anca
  non mi dipuose, sì mi giunse al rotto
  di quel che sì piangeva con la zanca.
'O qual che se' che 'l di su tien di sotto,
  anima trista come pal commessa,'
  comincia' io a dir, 'se puoi, fa motto.'
Io stava come 'l frate che confessa
  lo perfido assessin, che poi ch'è fitto, 50
  richiama lui, per che la morte cessa.
Ed el gridò: 'Se' tu già costì ritto,
  se' tu già costì ritto, Bonifazio?
  Di parecchi anni mi mentì lo scritto.
Se' tu sì tosto di quell' aver sazio
  per lo qual non temesti torre a 'nganno
  la bella donna, e poi di farne strazio?'
Tal mi fec' io quai son color che stanno,
  per non intender ciò ch'è lor risposto,
  quasi scornati, e risponder non sanno. 60
Allor Virgilio disse: 'Dilli tosto:
  "Non son colui, non son colui che credi" ';
  e io rispuosi come a me fu imposto.
Per che lo spirto tutti storse i piedi;
  poi, sospirando e con voce di pianto,
  mi disse: 'Dunque che a me richiedi?

ropes. As flame on oily things moves only over the outer surface, so it did there from the heels to the toes.

'Who is that one, Master, that writhes in his torment more than any of his fellows' I said 'and is licked by a redder flame?'

And he answered me: 'If thou wilt have me carry thee down there by that more sloping bank,[3] thou shalt know from himself of him and of his misdeeds.'

And I: 'All is well for me that is thy pleasure. Thou art my Lord and knowest that I depart not from thy will; thou knowest too what I do not speak.'

Then we came on to the fourth dike, turned and descended on our left down to the pitted and narrow bottom, and the good Master did not set me down from his haunch till he brought me to the hole of him that so lamented with his shanks.

'Whoever thou art,' I began 'unhappy soul that art held upside down, planted like a post, if thou art able, speak.'

I stood there, like the friar that shrives the treacherous assassin who after being fixed calls him back so that he delays his death,[4] and he cried: 'Standest thou there already, standest thou there already, Boniface? By several years the writing lied to me. Art thou so soon sated with these gains for which thou didst not fear to take by guile the Lady Beautiful and then to do her outrage?'[5]

I became like those that stand as if mocked, not comprehending the reply made to them, and know not what to answer; then Virgil said: 'Tell him quickly, "I am not he, I am not he thou thinkest" '; and I answered as I was bidden.

At that the spirit twisted his feet together, then, sighing and with lamenting voice, he said to me: 'What dost thou want with me then? If to know

Se di saper ch' i' sia ti cal cotanto
 che tu abbi però la ripa corsa,
 sappi ch' i' fui vestito del gran manto;
e veramente fui figliuol dell'orsa, 70
 cupido sì per avanzar li orsatti,
 che su l'avere, e qui me misi in borsa.
Di sotto al capo mio son li altri tratti
 che precedetter me simoneggiando,
 per le fessure della pietra piatti.
Là giù cascherò io altressì quando
 verrà colui ch' i' credea che tu fossi
 allor ch' i' feci 'l subito dimando.
Ma più è 'l tempo già che i piè mi cossi
 e ch' io son stato così sottosopra, 80
 ch'el non starà piantato coi piè rossi:
chè dopo lui verrà di più laida opra
 di ver ponente un pastor sanza legge,
 tal che convien che lui e me ricopra.
Nuovo Iasòn sarà, di cui si legge
 ne' Maccabei; e come a quel fu molle
 suo re, così fia lui chi Francia regge.'
I' non so s' i' mi fui qui troppo folle,
 ch' i' pur rispuosi lui a questo metro:
 'Deh, or mi dì: quanto tesoro volle 90
Nostro Segnore in prima da san Pietro
 ch'ei ponesse le chiavi in sua balia?
 Certo non chiese se non "Viemmi retro".
Nè Pier nè li altri tolsero a Mattia
 oro od argento, quando fu sortito
 al luogo che perdè l'anima ria.
Però ti sta, chè tu se' ben punito;
 e guarda ben la mal tolta moneta
 ch'esser ti fece contra Carlo ardito.
E se non fosse ch'ancor lo mi vieta 100
 la reverenza delle somme chiavi
 che tu tenesti nella vita lieta,
io userei parole ancor più gravi;
 chè la vostra avarizia il mondo attrista,
 calcando i buoni e sollevando i pravi.

who I am concerns thee so much that thou hast come down the bank for it, know that I was invested with the great mantle; but in truth I was a son of the she-bear, so greedy to advance the whelps that above I pursed my gains, and here myself.[6] Beneath my head are dragged the others who went before me in simony, flattened through the fissures of the rock, and down there I shall fall in my turn when he comes for whom I took thee when I put my hasty question. But longer already is the time I have roasted my feet and stood thus inverted than he shall stay planted with his feet red; for after him shall come a lawless shepherd from the west of yet fouler deeds, one fit to cover both him and me.[7] He shall be a new Jason, like him we read of in the *Maccabees*,[8] and as with that one his king dealt softly, so shall he that rules France do with him.'

I do not know if on that I was overbold when all my answer to him was in this strain: 'Pray tell me now, how much treasure did our Lord require of Saint Peter before He gave the keys into his charge? Surely He asked nothing but "Follow me", nor did Peter or the others take gold or silver from Matthias when he was chosen for the place lost by the guilty soul.[9] Stay there then, for thou art rightly punished, and look well to the ill-got gain that made thee bold against Charles.[10] And were it not that reverence for the supreme keys which thou didst hold in the glad life still forbids it to me, I should use yet harder words; for your avarice afflicts the world, trampling on the good and exalting

Di voi pastor s'accorse il Vangelista,
quando colei che siede sopra l'acque
puttaneggiar coi regi a lui fu vista;
quella che con le sette teste nacque,
e dalle diece corna ebbe argomento, 110
fin che virtute al suo marito piacque.
Fatto v'avete Dio d'oro e d'argento:
e che altro è da voi all' idolatre,
se non ch'elli uno, e voi ne orate cento?
Ahi, Costantin, di quanto mal fu matre,
non la tua conversion, ma quella dote
che da te prese il primo ricco patre!'
E mentr' io li cantava cotai note,
o ira o coscïenza che 'l mordesse,
forte spingava con ambo le piote. 120
I' credo ben ch'al mio duca piacesse,
con sì contenta labbia sempre attese
lo suon delle parole vere espresse.
Però con ambo le braccia mi prese:
e poi che tutto su mi s'ebbe al petto,
rimontò per la via onde discese.
Nè si stancò d'avermi a sè distretto,
sì men portò sovra 'l colmo dell'arco
che dal quarto al quinto argine è tragetto.
Quivi soavemente spuose il carco, 130
soave per lo scoglio sconcio ed erto
che sarebbe a le capre duro varco.
Indi un altro vallon mi fu scoperto.

1. Simon of Samaria (*Acts* viii. 9–24), the sorcerer—*Magus* in the Vulgate—who offered money to the Apostles for their spiritual powers and from whom the sin of simony is named.

2. The Baptistery of Florence had holes, probably used as fonts, in the wall of the marble basin. Dante seems to have been blamed for sacrilege on account of the incident.

3. The whole of the Malebolge inclining to the centre, the inner side of each ditch had a shorter and easier slope than the outer.

4. Hired assassins were buried alive head downward.

5. 'The Lady Beautiful' is the Church. Boniface was believed to have procured by fraud the abdication of Pope Celestine (Canto iii) and his own election; he died in 1303, so that 'the writing', the book of the future, known to the dead, showed that he was not due for three years.

6. The speaker, Pope Nicholas III (1277–1280), had in 1300 been 20 years in Malebolge; he was of the Orsini, whose crest was a she-bear.

the wicked. You shepherds it was the Evangelist had in mind when she that sitteth upon the waters was seen by him committing fornication with the kings, she that was born with the seven heads and had her strength from the ten horns so long as her bridegroom took pleasure in virtue.[11] You have made you a god of gold and silver, and what is there between you and the idolaters but that they worship one and you a hundred?[12] Ah, Constantine, to how much evil gave birth, not thy conversion, but that dower the first rich Father had from thee!'[13] And while I sang this song to him, whether bitten by anger or conscience he kicked out hard with both feet.

I believe indeed it pleased my Leader, he listened all the time with so satisfied a look to the words of truth I uttered. He took me, therefore, in both his arms and when he had me right up on his breast remounted by the way he had come down, and he did not tire of holding me close to him but carried me up to the summit of the arch that crosses from the fourth dike to the fifth. Here he gently set down his burden, gently for the ruggedness and steepness of the ridge, which would be a hard passage for goats. From it another valley was disclosed to me.

7. Clement V (1305–1314), a Gascon, owed his election to Philip of France and continued to be Philip's creature; he removed the Papal See from Rome to Avignon. Boniface would have 11 years to wait for Clement.

8. Jason 'supplanted his brother in the high priesthood, having promised to the king three hundred and three score talents of silver' (2 *Macc.* iv. 7).

9. Matthias, chosen apostle in place of Judas (*Acts* i. 15–26).

10. Charles of Anjou, brother of St Louis and King of Sicily, against whom Nicholas was supposed to have been bribed into joining a conspiracy.

11. The imagery of the Apocalypse (*Rev.* xvii. 1–3) is applied to the corrupted Papacy; the 'bridegroom' of the Church is the Pope, 'the seven heads' the gifts of the Spirit or the Sacraments, 'the ten horns' the Commandments.

12. Possibly a reference to the golden calf.

13. The Emperor Constantine, when he removed the Imperial Government to Byzantium in the 4th century, was supposed to have endowed the Church in the person of Pope Sylvester with the Imperial dominion in the west; the belief was based on the ancient forgery known as the Donation of Constantine.

NOTE

The last canto dealt with private wrongs; this deals with a public wrong, in Dante's judgement the greatest of all public wrongs, that done against the holiest of all public interests, the Church of Christ; and his mood—his mood as narrator—changes abruptly from something like indifference and contempt to anger at once lofty and impassioned. The canto begins, like no other in the *Inferno*, with a sudden, unexplained outburst—'Ah, Simon Magus'—as if this were a sin at the sight or thought of which he could not restrain himself. The abuse of sacred things for sordid ends was a monstrous evil of the time, and it was represented at its worst by three of the popes of Dante's lifetime—Nicholas III, in his boyhood; Boniface VIII, during his active public life; and Clement V, when he was writing the *Comedy* in exile. It was, in his view, a crescendo of iniquity, a kind of inverted apostolical succession, from Nicholas, reputed the first of the papal simonists and a great one, through Boniface, the protagonist in his age of the most inordinate pretensions of the Church to political predominance, a worldly, unscrupulous and powerful ecclesiastic, and incidentally the corrupter of the public life of Florence and the cause of Dante's exile, to Clement, treacherous, lecherous, and servile to France, the leader of the Church into its seventy years of shameful 'exile' in Avignon. By a thrilling dramatic device the name of Boniface comes from the hole in the rocky floor, bewildering Dante as much as his reader and seeming to make the fate of the great Pope a thing not so much asserted as determined and beyond question. 'The Poet's judgement takes the aspect of a fearful judgement of God and the most intimate and intense subjectivity takes the form of objective fatality', while 'the judge feigns ignorance and is mistaken for the criminal' (*V. Rossi*). At Virgil's bidding Dante flings off like an insult the suggestion that he himself is Boniface, 'I am not he, I am not he thou thinkest.' There are many references in the *Comedy* to Boniface, but here only, by the voice of his predecessor who waits for him in Hell, he is called by his name.

Dante's profound reverence for 'the supreme keys' held by these men only deepens his contempt and kindles his wrath the more against the men themselves. Among all the simonists there 'along the sides and on the bottom' Pope Nicholas 'writhes in his torment more than any of his fellows' and 'is licked by a redder flame', and Dante takes no heed of any other besides the Pope, as if to indicate that in this kind the sin of the Church's head represents and includes that of all the rest.

Simony is the worship in the Church of 'gold and silver'—the phrase occurs three times in the canto—it is the heathenism of the Church, and this *reversal* of all that the Church of Christ should mean is represented by the deliberately grotesque penalty of the third bolgia, with 'its singular pedestrian expression of feeling' (*V. Rossi*), while the flames that lick the sinners' upturned soles are another example of fire as the peculiar expression of God's wrath with regard to sins specially directed against Himself, simony being a kind of blasphemy.

Is it straining the relevancy to suppose that in recalling the incident in his 'beautiful Saint John', where he had broken the sacred furnishings to save a life, Dante is declaring that life is more sacred than all outward sanctities and defending himself in anticipation from the charge of speaking evil of dignities?

A singular and significant feature of the canto is that Dante is not merely led and instructed by Virgil here as elsewhere, but, after an ardent declaration of his discipleship, he is *carried* down to Nicholas and up again and the narrative stresses Virgil's carefulness in the act. For here peculiarly Dante claims to be identified with a reason which is not merely his own reason but is reason itself. Virgil, besides, represents the Empire, the righteous ordering of the earthly life of humanity; and the Empire's independence of the Church, the distinctiveness of its sphere of authority under God and its high obligation to guard the frontiers of its jurisdiction against ecclesiastical encroachment were fundamental in Dante's thinking and are the main matter of the *De Monarchia*. Against all these principles of world-order the worldly policies and private rapacities of these simoniacal popes, and of Boniface in particular, were a direct and grievous offence. When Dante, a layman, stoops over the degenerate Pope and hears his abject report of the crimes of the Papacy and compares himself to a friar taking the last confession of 'the treacherous assassin', layman and cleric changing places, he is the spokesman of the lay conscience of the world, the voice of the 'indignant soul' of humanity measuring the Church by the Church's own standards, the words of Christ and the practice of the Apostles. Constantine's endowment of the Church with imperial rights, which Dante did not question as a matter of history, he regarded as injurious to the Empire, invalid even for an Emperor, and corrupting to the Church itself. 'Constantine had no power to alienate the imperial dignity, nor had the Church power to receive it' (*De Monarchia*). And when he had spoken these 'words of truth' Virgil 'took him in both his arms'.

INFERNO

DI nova pena mi conven far versi
  e dar matera al ventesimo canto
  della prima canzon, ch'è de' sommersi.
Io era già disposto tutto quanto
  a riguardar nello scoperto fondo,
  che si bagnava d'angoscioso pianto;
e vidi gente per lo vallon tondo
  venir, tacendo e lagrimando, al passo
  che fanno le letane in questo mondo.
Come 'l viso mi scese in lor più basso, 10
  mirabil-mente apparve esser travolto
  ciascun tra 'l mento e 'l principio del casso;
chè dalle reni era tornato il volto,
  ed in dietro venir li convenìa,
  perchè 'l veder dinanzi era lor tolto.
Forse per forza già di parlasia
  si travolse così alcun del tutto;
  ma io nol vidi, nè credo che sia.
Se Dio ti lasci, lettor, prender frutto
  di tua lezione, or pensa per te stesso 20
  com' io potea tener lo viso asciutto,
quando la nostra imagine di presso
  vidi sì torta, che 'l pianto delli occhi
  le natiche bagnava per lo fesso.
Certo io piangea, poggiato a un de' rocchi
  del duro scoglio, sì che la mia scorta
  mi disse: 'Ancor se' tu delli altri sciocchi?

CANTO XX

The Fourth Bolgia; the Diviners; Manto; the origin of Mantua

OF new pain I must make verses and find matter for the twentieth canto of the first book, which is of those in the depths. I was now wholly set on looking into the bottom disclosed there, which was bathed with tears of anguish, and I saw people along the great circular valley coming, silent and weeping, at the pace made by the litanies in this world. As my sight went lower on them, each seemed to be strangely twisted between the chin and the beginning of the chest, for the face was turned towards the loins and they had to come backwards, since seeing forward was denied them. Perhaps some time by stroke of palsy a man has been thus twisted right round, but I have not seen it nor believe it possible.

So God grant thee, reader, to gather fruit of thy reading, think now for thyself how I could keep my cheeks dry when I saw close at hand our form so contorted that the tears from the eyes bathed the buttocks at the cleft. I wept indeed, leaning on one of the rocks of the rugged ridge, so that my Escort said to me: 'Art thou too as witless as

Qui vive la pietà quand'è ben morta:
  chi è più scellerato che colui
  che al giudicio divin passion porta? 30
Drizza la testa, drizza, e vedi a cui
  s'aperse alli occhi de' Teban la terra,
  per ch'ei gridavan tutti: "Dove rui,
Anfiarao? perchè lasci la guerra?"
  E non restò di ruinare a valle
  fino a Minòs che ciascheduno afferra.
Mira c' ha fatto petto delle spalle:
  perchè volle veder troppo davante,
  di retro guarda e fa retroso calle.
Vedi Tiresia, che mutò sembiante 40
  quando di maschio femmina divenne,
  cangiandosi le membra tutte quante;
e prima, poi, ribatter li convenne
  li duo serpenti avvolti, con la verga,
  che rïavesse le maschili penne.
Aronta è quei ch'al ventre li s'atterga,
  che ne' monti di Luni, dove ronca
  lo Carrarese che di sotto alberga,
ebbe tra' bianchi marmi la spelonca
  per sua dimora onde a guardar le stelle 50
  e 'l mar non li era la veduta tronca.
E quella che ricuopre le mammelle,
  che tu non vedi, con le treccie sciolte,
  e ha di là ogni pilosa pelle,
Manto fu, che cercò per terre molte,
  poscia si puose là dove nacqu' io;
  onde un poco mi piace che m'ascolte.
Poscia che 'l padre suo di vita uscìo,
  e venne serva la città di Baco,
  questa gran tempo per lo mondo gìo. 60
Suso in Italia bella giace un laco,
  a piè de l'Alpe che serra Lamagna
  sovra Tiralli, c' ha nome Benaco.
Per mille fonti, credo, e più si bagna,
  tra Garda e Val Camonica, Apennino
  dell'acqua che nel detto laco stagna.

the rest? Here pity lives when it is quite dead.[1] Who is more guilty than he that makes the divine counsel subject to his will?

'Raise, raise thy head and see him for whom the earth opened before the eyes of the Thebans, so that they all shouted: "Where art thou rushing to, Amphiaraus?[2] Why dost thou quit the fight?" And he did not stop in his plunge into the depth as far as Minos, who seizes everyone. Look how he has made a breast of his shoulders; because he would see too far ahead he looks behind and makes his way backwards.

'See Tiresias,[3] who changed semblance when from male he turned female, being transformed in every member, and must strike the two twined serpents again with his staff before he could resume his manly plumes.

'He that backs up to the other's belly is Aruns,[4] who in the hills of Luni, where the Carrarese that live below till the ground, had a cave among the white marbles for his dwelling; looking from it at the stars and the sea his prospect was without bound.

'And she that covers her breasts, which thou dost not see, with her loose tresses and has on that side all her hairy parts was Manto,[5] who searched through many lands, then settled in the place where I was born; and on this I would have thee hear me for a little. After her father had parted from life and the city of Bacchus was enslaved[6] she went for a long time about the world. Above in fair Italy, at the foot of the mountains that bound Germany over Tyrol, lies a lake which is called Benaco.[7] By a thousand springs and more, I suppose, Apennino[8] is bathed between Garda and Val Camonica by the water that settles in the lake there,

Luogo è nel mezzo là dove 'l Trentino
pastore e quel di Brescia e 'l Veronese
segnar porìa, se fesse quel cammino.
Siede Peschiera, bello e forte arnese 70
da fronteggiar Bresciani e Bergamaschi,
ove la riva intorno più discese.
Ivi convien che tutto quanto caschi
ciò che 'n grembo a Benaco star non pò,
e fassi fiume giù per verdi paschi.
Tosto che l'acqua a correr mette co,
non più Benaco, ma Mencio si chiama
fino a Governol, dove cade in Po.
Non molto ha corso, ch'el trova una lama,
nella qual si distende e la 'mpaluda; 80
e suol di state talor esser grama.
Quindi passando la vergine cruda
vide terra nel mezzo del pantano,
sanza coltura e d'abitanti nuda.
Lì, per fuggire ogni consorzio umano,
ristette con suoi servi a far sue arti,
e visse, e vi lasciò suo corpo vano.
Li uomini poi che 'ntorno erano sparti
s'accolsero a quel luogo, ch'era forte
per lo pantan ch'avea da tutte parti. 90
Fer la città sovra quell'ossa morte;
e per colei che 'l luogo prima elesse,
Mantua l'appellar sanz'altra sorte.
Già fuor le genti sue dentro più spesse,
prima che la mattia da Casalodi
da Pinamonte inganno ricevesse.
Però t'assenno che se tu mai odi
originar la mia terra altrimenti,
la verità nulla menzogna frodi.'
E io: 'Maestro, i tuoi ragionamenti 100
mi son sì certi e prendon sì mia fede,
che li altri mi sarìen carboni spenti.
Ma dimmi, della gente che procede,
se tu ne vedi alcun degno di nota;
chè solo a ciò la mia mente rifiede.'

and in the middle of it is a spot where the pastors of Trent and Brescia and Verona, if they went that way, might give their blessing.[9] Peschiera, a strong and beautiful fortress to confront the Brescians and the Bergamese, lies at the lowest point of the surrounding shore, and there all that cannot remain in the bosom of Benaco must fall and becomes a river flowing down through green pastures. As soon as the water starts to run it is called no longer Benaco, but Mincio, as far as Governolo where it falls into the Po, and after a short course it comes to a level where it spreads and makes a marsh that is sometimes noisome in summer. Passing that way, the cruel virgin saw land in the middle of the fen, untilled and without inhabitants; there, to avoid all human intercourse, she stopped with her minions to ply her arts and lived and left there her empty body. Afterwards the people that were scattered round about gathered on that spot, which was strong because of the bog it had on every side, and they built the city over those dead bones, and from her who first chose the place called it Mantua, without other augury. Once the people within it were more numerous, before the folly of Casalodi was tricked by Pinamonte.[10] I charge thee, therefore, that if ever thou hear of another origin of my city thou let no false tale pervert the truth.'

And I said: 'Master, thy account is so sure for me and so holds my confidence that any other would be for me dead embers. But tell me of the people that are passing, if thou see any who are worthy of note, for to that alone my mind reverts.'

Allor mi disse: 'Quel che dalla gota
porge la barba in su le spalle brune,
fu, quando Grecia fu di maschi vota
sì ch'a pena rimaser per le cune,
augure, e diede 'l punto con Calcanta 110
in Aulide a tagliar la prima fune.
Eurìpilo ebbe nome, e così 'l canta
l'alta mia tragedìa in alcun loco:
ben lo sai tu che la sai tutta quanta.
Quell'altro, che ne' fianchi è così poco,
Michele Scotto fu, che veramente
delle magiche frode seppe il gioco.
Vedi Guido Bonatti; vedi Asdente,
ch'avere inteso al cuoio ed allo spago
ora vorrebbe, ma tardi si pente. 120
Vedi le triste che lasciaron l'ago,
la spuola e 'l fuso, e fecersi 'ndivine;
fecer malie con erbe e con imago.
Ma vienne omai; chè già tiene 'l confine
d'amendue li emisperi e tocca l'onda
sotto Sobilia Caino e le spine;
e già iernotte fu la luna tonda:
ben ten de' ricordar, chè non ti nocque
alcuna volta per la selva fonda.'
Sì mi parlava, ed andavamo introcque. 130

1. It is merciful to be merciless to such a sin.

2. Greek augur, one of the Seven Kings who besieged Thebes; foreseeing his own death, he hid himself, and his wife Eriphyle was induced by a bribe to betray him; approaching Thebes, he was swallowed up by the earth.

3. Famous soothsayer of Thebes; having parted two coupling serpents with his staff, he was transformed into a woman, and 7 years after, having done the same again, was restored to his manhood.

4. Etruscan soothsayer who foretold the Civil War that ended with Caesar's victory.

5. Theban prophetess, daughter of Tiresias.

6. Bacchus, child of a Theban princess, was worshipped in Thebes.

7. Modern Lake Garda.

8. A spur of the Rhoetian Alps.

9. A chapel on an island in the lake was under the common jurisdiction of the three bishops, any one of whom might hold service there.

Then he said to me: 'He that from his cheeks spreads his beard over his swarthy shoulders was augur when Greece was left so empty of males that scarcely any remained for the cradles, and with Calchas he gave the moment for cutting the first cable in Aulis.[11] Eurypylus was his name, and thus my high tragedy[12] sings of him in a certain passage —as thou knowest well, who knowest it altogether.

'That other, so spare in the flanks, was Michael Scot,[13] who assuredly knew the game of magic frauds.

'See Guido Bonatti;[14] see Asdente, who now would fain have given his mind to the leather and the thread, but repents too late.

'See the wretched women who gave up the needle, the shuttle, and the distaff and turned fortune-tellers; they wrought spells with herbs and images.[15]

'But come now, for Cain with his thorns already holds the confines of both hemispheres and touches the waves below Seville,[16] and already last night the moon was round. Thou must remember it well, for it helped thee sometimes in the depth of the wood.'

While he talked thus with me we went on our way.

10. Count Casalodi, Guelf Lord of Mantua, was persuaded to exile the nobles by Pinamonte, a Ghibelline citizen, who then raised the people against Casalodi and seized his power, in 1272.

11. All the men of Greece had gone to the Trojan War; returning, they sent Eurypylus to consult the Oracle of Apollo on the time for sailing.

12. The *Aeneid* is called a tragedy as a poem in a lofty style.

13. Michael Scot, a famous Scotch scholar of the early 13th century at the court of Frederick II.

14. Bonatti, a famous writer on astrology of the later 13th century, private astrologer to Guido of Montefeltro (Canto xxvii). Asdente ('Toothless') was the nickname of a cobbler of Parma with a reputation for sooth-saying.

15. Herbs were used for love-philtres and poisons. The piercing or melting of human images of wax or silver was supposed to be fatal to the originals.

16. The moon was supposed to set beyond Spain, where the land hemisphere ended westward.

NOTE

There is a curious deliberation, as of one taking breath for his task, in the first words of the canto: 'Of new pain I must make verses and find matter for the twentieth canto of the first book.' Dante may well have wondered how he was to deal with the sins of divination under Virgil's guidance, and there is here something of tension between the travellers which indicates a perplexity felt and overcome.

On the one hand, the whole business of divination, much practised and honoured in Dante's time, the mystery-traffic of them that peep and mutter, their pretentious learning and fantastic trickeries and intermeddlings with conscience and with providence, their show of penetration into the regions of human freewill and divine purpose, the sham-religious solemnity of their proceedings recalled in the backward shufflings of these contorted shades 'coming at the pace made by the litanies in this world'—all that method of approach to life's meanings and undertakings was, for one of Dante's high sanity, intellectual integrity, and profound sense of the sacredness of freewill and of the moral unity of human life, wholly obnoxious and profane, a gratuitous perversion and looking the wrong way for the guidance of men's affairs. Much was admitted and maintained by Dante and by everyone as to the influences of the stars on men's natural tempers and dispositions, but he followed Aquinas in regarding such influences as essentially secondary to the unpredictable and unfathomable workings of the divine and human wills, and he would have agreed with Sir Thomas Browne on judicial astrology: 'If there be a truth therein, it doth not injure Divinity. If to be born under Mercury disposeth us to be witty, under Jupiter to be wealthy, I do not owe a Knee unto these, but unto that merciful Hand that hath ordered my indifferent and uncertain nativity unto such benevolous Aspects' (*Religio Medici*). The attempt to spell out the mysteries of the stars and the supposed magical properties of things so as to forecast or control events and bend the ways of providence was condemned both by Scripture and by Aquinas as a manifest impiety, and it is punished here in a way which recalls the language of the *Book of Isaiah*, where it is said that the Lord, the redeemer, that maketh all things, is He 'that frustrateth the tokens of the liars and maketh diviners mad, that turneth wise men backward and maketh their knowledge foolish'. Magic and the practices allied to it are, in a word, the religion of the irreligious and the negative of a Christian faith. And the sins of simony and sorcery are kindred neighbours; Simon, the type of simony, was also *Magus*, 'to whom all gave heed, from the least to the greatest, saying: This man is the great power of God' (*Acts* viii. 10). The venal churchman is not far from the trader in mysteries.

'St Thomas and Dante, almost alone, lift their voices against the superstitious practices of astrology; but their voices, however lofty and powerful, are lost in the immense clamour of voices invoking its aid. . . . Princes and communes kept astrologers in their service; chairs of astrology had their place in the universities; a medical man was not reckoned to be qualified who was not at the same time an astrologer; philosophers and scientists of distinction were among the most ardent supporters and publishers of astrology, on which they wrote volumes' (*E. G. Parodi, L.D.*). Astrology was used 'to determine the moment for starting an enterprise, for deciding on war or peace, for engaging in battle, for laying the first stone of a building' (*V. Rossi*). In this matter Dante was taking his stand against a great stream.

On the other hand, not only was divination not reprobated, it was honoured, in that ancient literature which Dante reverenced only less than Scripture, and it is possible that his compassion for the diviners, which Virgil so sharply rebukes, means that he did at one time share in that regard for them. In the old story the engulfing of Amphiaraus was, in fact, his rescue from a hostile spear by Jupiter and his being immortalized, so that he was later held as a god and consulted by oracle. Tiresias was consulted by the gods and endowed by Jupiter with the gift of prophecy. Aruns was summoned to Rome in a time of anxiety to forecast the issue of the Civil War. And Virgil himself in his great poem attributed the founding of his native city to the son of the prophetess Manto. She was indeed another Manto from the Manto of Thebes, Tiresias's daughter, and Virgil's story in the *Aeneid* is plainly contradictory of his account of Manto and Mantua given here with so much circumstance and deliberation and occupying more than a third of the canto. Dante, in fact, corrects Virgil by making Virgil correct himself. Here, the origin of Mantua is represented as thoroughly natural, the waters gathering from many mountain springs in Lake Garda and flowing down through the green Lombard country to form a marsh which provides a place secure from attack for the building of the city by the people gathered there, and 'the cruel virgin', hating and hateful to humanity, giving nothing to the city but her 'empty body' and 'those dead bones' and her name, 'without other augury', with no taint of the magic of her arts. The energy and insistence of Virgil's repudiation of magic in all its many shapes, his rebuke of Dante's grief over the distortion of the dumb oracles beneath them, who 'make the divine counsel subject to their will', his care to clear the name of his own city from an ancient stigma, the fact that it is Virgil himself who gives account of all the sorcerers there, ancient and modern, his words constituting, quite exceptionally, nearly the whole canto, and the irony which puts a new colouring on the stories of these famous ancient diviners; all is, in effect, Dante's own declaration that the way of wisdom for men is wholly separate from that way of spells and incantations and prognostications which men have trusted in their ignorance and practised in their guile, and that it is to be found only in the discipline of reason and conscience, of which Virgil is his chosen symbol. 'It reflects the highest honour on the character and critical spirit of Dante to have condemned with so strict severity that which everyone then approved and admired' (*E. G. Parodi, L.D.*).

It is noted by Parodi that in the four soothsayers first named Dante has chosen a personage from each of the four long Latin poems known to him—Virgil's *Aeneid*, Ovid's *Metamorphoses*, Statius's *Thebais* and Lucan's *Pharsalia*. 'Since the Latin poets especially are full of diviners, augurs, works of magic, and since, with their high authority and with the charm of their art, they could delude and misdirect men's minds, he selects from each of the greatest works of Latin poetry known to him a characteristic example and calls to his deluded contemporaries in the tones of his immortal verse: "See the destiny merited by the Amphiaraus and Tiresias and Aruns and Manto whom you recall and quote in your support—the wrath of God and the scorn of men." '

The canto is at the same time the clearing of Virgil's own name; for one element in the extraordinary character of Virgil in medieval legend and popular fancy is that he was regarded as himself a magician and that his writings were used in an established method of divination known as *sortes virgilianae.* For Dante, that way of regarding his great master was intolerable and he makes Virgil 'protest, indirectly but effectively, against his own reputation for magic' (*F. D'Ovidio*). The tone of the canto recalls the contrast noted in the second canto between the visit of the pagan Aeneas to the world of the dead and the journey of the Christian Dante. It is a Christian re-interpretation of pagan story.

The moon, just past full, is setting, so that it is now shortly after sunrise of Saturday in Holy Week; for the time is told in Hell only from the moon, never from the sun, the visible image of God, not to be named in the place of darkness.

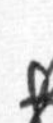

INFERNO

Così di ponte in ponte, altro parlando
che la mia comedìa cantar non cura,
venimmo, e tenavamo il colmo, quando
restammo per veder l'altra fessura
di Malebolge e li altri pianti vani;
e vidila mirabil-mente oscura.
Quale nell'arzanà de' Viniziani
bolle l' inverno la tenace pece
a rimpalmare i legni lor non sani,
—chè navicar non ponno, e in quella vece 10
chi fa suo legno novo e chi ristoppa
le coste a quel che più vïaggi fece;
chi ribatte da proda e chi da poppa;
altri fa remi e altri volge sarte;
chi terzeruolo e artimon rintoppa—
tal, non per foco, ma per divin' arte,
bollìa là giuso una pegola spessa,
che 'nviscava la ripa d'ogni parte.
I' vedea lei, ma non vedea in essa
mai che le bolle che 'l bollor levava, 20
e gonfiar tutta, e riseder compressa.
Mentr' io là giù fisamente mirava,
lo duca mio, dicendo: 'Guarda, guarda!',
mi trasse a sè del loco dov' io stava.
Allor mi volsi come l'om cui tarda
di veder quel che li convien fuggire
e cui paura subita sgagliarda,
che, per veder, non indugia 'l partire;
e vidi dietro a noi un diavol nero
correndo su per lo scoglio venire. 30

CANTO XXI

The Fifth Bolgia; the Barrators; Malacoda

THUS from bridge to bridge, talking of other things of which my Comedy is not concerned to sing, we came on and reached the summit, when we stopped to see the next fissure of Malebolge and the next vain tears; and I saw it strangely dark. As in the Arsenal of the Venetians[1] they boil the viscous pitch in winter to caulk their unsound ships—for they cannot sail then, and instead one builds himself a new ship and another plugs the ribs of his that has made many voyages, one hammers at the prow and another at the stern, this one makes oars, that one twists ropes, another patches jib and mainsail; so, not by fire but by divine art, a thick tar was boiling below there which stuck to the bank on every side. I saw it, but saw in it nothing but the bubbles raised by the boiling and the whole swelling up and settling together again.

While I was gazing fixedly down there, my Leader, saying: 'Beware, beware!', drew me to him from where I stood; then I turned like one that is eager to see what he must escape and is unmanned with sudden fear and while looking does not stay his flight, and I saw behind us a black devil come running up the ridge. Ah, how savage was his

Ahi quant'elli era nell'aspetto fero!
  e quanto mi parea nell'atto acerbo,
  con l'ali aperte e sovra i piè leggero!
L'omero suo, ch'era aguto e superbo,
  carcava un peccator con ambo l'anche,
  e quei tenea de' piè ghermito il nerbo.
Del nostro ponte disse: 'O Malebranche,
  ecco un delli anzïan di santa Zita!
  Mettetel sotto, ch' i' torno per anche
a quella terra ch' i' ho ben fornita: 40
  ogn' uom v'è barattier, fuor che Bonturo;
  del no per li denar vi si fa ita.'
Là giù il buttò, e per lo scoglio duro
  si volse; e mai non fu mastino sciolto
  con tanta fretta a seguitar lo furo.
Quel s'attuffò, e tornò su convolto;
  ma i demon che del ponte avean coperchio,
  gridar: 'Qui non ha luogo il Santo Volto:
qui si nuota altrimenti che nel Serchio!
  Però, se tu non vuo' di nostri graffi, 50
  non far sopra la pegola soverchio.'
Poi l'addentar con più di cento raffi,
  disser: 'Coverto convien che qui balli,
  sì che, se puoi, nascosamente accaffi.'
Non altrimenti i cuoci a' lor vassalli
  fanno attuffare in mezzo la caldaia
  la carne con li uncin, perchè non galli.
Lo buon maestro 'Acciò che non si paia
  che tu ci sia,' mi disse 'giù t'acquatta
  dopo uno scheggio, ch'alcun schermo t'aia; 60
e per nulla offension che mi sia fatta,
  non temer tu, ch' i' ho le cose conte,
  e altra volta fui a tal baratta.'
Poscia passò di là dal co del ponte;
  e com' el giunse in su la ripa sesta,
  mestier li fu d'aver sicura fronte.
Con quel furore e con quella tempesta
  ch'escono i cani a dosso al poverello
  che di subito chiede ove s'arresta,

aspect and how fierce he seemed to me in his action, with open wings and light on his feet! His shoulder, which was sharp and high, was laden with both thighs of a sinner and he held him clutched by the tendons of his feet.

He spoke from our bridge: 'You Malebranche,[2] here is one of the Ancients of Santa Zita;[3] put him under, while I go back for more to that city, which is well stocked with them. Every man there is a barrator, all but Bonturo;[4] there *No* is made *Ay* for cash.'

He flung him down and turned back on the flinty ridge, and never was unleashed mastiff in such haste to follow the thief. The sinner plunged in and rose again doubled up, but the demons that were covered by the bridge cried: 'The Holy Face is not here for thee.[5] Here the swimming is not like that in the Serchio;[6] so, unless thou wouldst taste of our hooks, do not come out above the pitch.' Then they caught at him with more than a hundred gaffs and said: 'Thou must dance here under cover and pilfer out of sight, if thou canst.' Just so cooks make their scullions plunge the meat down into the cauldrons with their forks that it may not float.

The good Master said to me: 'That thou mayst not be seen to be here, crouch down behind a rock that may give thee some shelter, and for any outrage that may be offered to me do not thou be afraid, for I know about things here and was in a fray of the kind another time.'[7]

Then he went on past the head of the bridge, and as soon as he came on to the sixth bank he had need to show a bold front. With the fury and uproar of dogs that rush out on a mendicant who suddenly begs where he stops these rushed out from under

usciron quei di sotto al ponticello, 70
e porser contra lui tutt' i runcigli;
ma el gridò: 'Nessun di voi sia fello!
Innanzi che l' uncin vostro mi pigli,
traggasi avante l' un di voi che m'oda,
e poi d'arruncigliarmi si consigli.'
Tutti gridaron: 'Vada Malacoda!';
per ch' un si mosse—e li altri stetter fermi—
e venne a lui dicendo: 'Che li approda?'
'Credi tu, Malacoda, qui vedermi
esser venuto' disse 'l mio maestro 80
'sicuro già da tutti vostri schermi,
sanza voler divino e fato destro?
Lascian' andar, chè nel cielo è voluto
ch' i' mostri altrui questo cammin silvestro.'
Allor li fu l'orgoglio sì caduto,
che si lasciò cascar l' uncino a' piedi,
e disse alli altri: 'Omai non sia feruto.'
E 'l duca mio a me: 'O tu che siedi
tra li scheggion del ponte quatto quatto,
sicuramente omai a me tu riedi.' 90
Per ch' io mi mossi, ed a lui venni ratto;
e i diavoli si fecer tutti avanti,
sì ch' io temetti ch'ei tenesser patto:
così vid' io già temer li fanti
ch' uscivan patteggiati di Caprona,
veggendo sè tra nemici cotanti.
I' m'accostai con tutta la persona
lungo 'l mio duca, e non torceva li occhi
dalla sembianza lor ch'era non bona.
Ei chinavan li raffi e 'Vuo' che 'l tocchi' 100
diceva l' un con l'altro 'in sul groppone?'
E rispondìen: 'Sì, fa che lile accocchi!'
Ma quel demonio che tenea sermone
col duca mio, si volse tutto presto,
e disse: 'Posa, posa, Scarmiglione!'
Poi disse a noi: 'Più oltre andar per quest
iscoglio non si può, però che giace
tutto spezzato al fondo l'arco sesto.

the bridge and turned all their hooks against him. But he cried: 'Let there be no mischief from any of you. Before you catch me with your forks one of you come forward and hear me; then consult about hooking me.'

All cried: 'Let Malacoda go.' So one moved, the rest standing still, and came to him, saying: 'What good will it do him?'

'Thinkest thou, Malacoda,' said my Master 'thou seest me come here secure thus far against all your defences without Divine Will and propitious fate? Let us pass, for it is willed in Heaven that I show another this savage way.'

Then his insolence was so fallen that he let the fork drop at his feet and said to the rest: 'He must not be touched then.'

And my Leader said to me: 'Thou that sittest crouching down among the rocks of the bridge, it is safe now for thee to come back to me.' And on that I rose and came to him quickly, and the devils all pushed forward so that I feared for their keeping of the compact; thus I once saw the soldiers that marched out of Caprona[8] under treaty afraid at seeing themselves among so many enemies. I drew near my Leader, pressing close to him, and did not turn my eyes from their looks, which were not pleasant; and they lowered their prongs, one saying: 'Wilt thou that I touch him on the rump?' and another answering: 'Ay, let him have it.' But that demon who held speech with my Leader turned round sharply and said: 'Hold, hold, Scarmiglione!'

Then he said to us: 'To go farther by this ridge is not possible, for the sixth arch lies all broken up at the bottom, but if it is still your pleasure to

E se l'andare avante pur vi piace,
andatevene su per questa grotta; 110
presso è un altro scoglio che via face.
Ier, più oltre cinqu'ore che quest'otta,
mille dugento con sessanta sei
anni compiè che qui la via fu rotta.
Io mando verso là di questi miei
a riguardar s'alcun se ne sciorina:
gite con lor, che non saranno rei.'
'Tra'ti avante, Alichino, e Calcabrina,'
cominciò elli a dire, 'e tu, Cagnazzo;
e Barbariccia guidi la decina. 120
Libicocco vegn'oltre e Draghignazzo,
Ciriatto sannuto e Graffiacane
e Farfarello e Rubicante pazzo.
Cercate intorno le boglienti pane:
costor sian salvi infino all'altro scheggio
che tutto intero va sopra le tane.'
'Ohmè, maestro, che è quel ch' i' veggio?'
diss' io 'Deh, sanza scorta andianci soli,
se tu sa' ir; ch' i' per me non la cheggio.
Se tu se' sì accorto come suoli 130
non vedi tu ch'e' digrignan li denti,
e con le ciglia ne minaccian duoli?'
Ed elli a me: 'Non vo' che tu paventi:
lasciali digrignar pur a lor senno,
ch'e' fanno ciò per li lessi dolenti.'
Per l'argine sinistro volta dienno;
ma prima avea ciascun la lingua stretta
coi denti verso lor duca per cenno;
ed elli avea del cul fatto trombetta.

1. The Venetian Arsenal, enlarged in Dante's time, was one of the most famous in Europe.

2 Literally *Evil-claws*, a general name for the devils here.

3. Lucca, here named from its patron-saint, a maidservant who died in 1275; the Ancients of Lucca were the chiefs of its Council.

4. 'Barrator' here means swindler in public office; Bonturo was a notorious barrator of Lucca, still living in 1300.

go on make your way along this rocky dike; there is another ridge near which gives a passage. Yesterday, five hours later than now, completed a thousand, two hundred and sixty-six years since the road here was broken.[9] I am sending that way some of my company here, to look if any is out taking the air. Go with them, for they will not molest you. Come forward, Alichino and Calcabrina,' he went on 'and thou Cagnazzo, and let Barbariccia direct the squad; let Libicocco come too, and Draghignazzo, Ciriatto with the tusks, and Graffiacane, and Farfarello, and mad Rubicante. Scout round the boiling tar. Let these be safe as far as the next ridge that goes unbroken all the way over the dens.'

'Ah me, Master,' I said 'what is that I see? Pray, if thou know the way, let us go alone without escort; for on my part I want none. If thou art as wary as thou art wont, dost thou not see them grinding their teeth and threatening mischief to us with their brows?'

And he said to me: 'I will not have thee fearful. Let them go on grinding as they please, for they do it on account of the boiled wretches.'

They wheeled round by the dike on the left; but first each pressed his tongue between his teeth at their leader for a signal and he made a trumpet of his rear.

5. Ancient Byzantine crucifix in Lucca Cathedral.
6. The river near Lucca.
7. 'I was down here once before' (Canto ix).
8. A castle near Pisa, taken by the troops of Florence and Lucca in 1298.
9. The earthquake at the Crucifixion (Canto xii) happened, by Dante's reckoning, in A.D. 34, 1266 years before 1300 and at noon of Good Friday; it is now 7 a.m of Holy Saturday.

(This canto will be considered along with the next.)

INFERNO

Io vidi già cavalier muover campo,
 e cominciare stormo, e far lor mostra,
 e tal volta partir per loro scampo;
corridor vidi per la terra vostra,
 o Aretini, e vidi gir gualdane,
 fedir torneamenti, e correr giostra;
quando con trombe, e quando con campane,
 con tamburi e con cenni di castella,
 e con cose nostrali e con istrane;
nè già con sì diversa cennamella 10
 cavalier vidi muover nè pedoni,
 nè nave a segno di terra o di stella.
Noi andavam con li diece demoni:
 ahi fiera compagnia! ma nella chiesa
 coi santi, ed in taverna co' ghiottoni.
Pur alla pegola era la mia intesa,
 per veder della bolgia ogni contegno
 e della gente ch'entro v'era incesa.
Come i dalfini, quando fanno segno
 a' marinar con l'arco della schiena, 20
 che s'argomentin di campar lor legno,
talor così, ad alleggiar la pena,
 mostrav' alcun de' peccatori il dosso,
 e nascondea in men che non balena.
E come all'orlo dell'acqua d'un fosso
 stanno i ranocchi pur col muso fori,
 sì che celano i piedi e l'altro grosso,
sì stavan d'ogne parte i peccatori;
 ma come s'appressava Barbariccia,
 così si ritraèn sotto i bollori. 30

CANTO XXII

Ciampolo and the devils

I HAVE seen before now horsemen move camp, and open the attack, and make their muster, and at times go off in flight; I have seen scouts over your land, Aretines;[1] and I have seen the movements of raiding-parties, clash of tournaments and running of jousts, now with trumpets and now with bells, with drums and with castle-signals and devices our own and foreign; and never yet have I seen horsemen move at so strange a bugle, nor footmen, nor ship sailing by mark of land or star.

We went with the ten demons; savage company indeed, but 'in church with saints and with guzzlers in the tavern.' My attention was all on the pitch, to see every feature of the moat and of the people that were burning in it. Like dolphins when with their arching back they give sailors a sign to take measures for saving their ship,[2] so from time to time one of the sinners would show his back to ease his pain and hide it again quicker than a lightning-flash; and as frogs lie in a ditch at the water's edge with only the muzzle out so as to hide their feet and the rest of their bulk, the sinners were lying all about, but as soon as Barbariccia came near they drew back under the boiling. I

I' vidi, e anco il cor me n'accapriccia,
uno aspettar così, com'elli 'ncontra
ch'una rana rimane ed altra spiccia;
e Graffiacan, che li era più di contra,
li arruncigliò le 'mpegolate chiome
e trassel su, che mi parve una lontra.
I' sapea già di tutti quanti il nome,
sì li notai quando fuorono eletti,
e poi ch'e' si chiamaro, attesi come.
'O Rubicante, fa che tu li metti 40
li unghioni a dosso, sì che tu lo scuoi!'
gridavan tutti insieme i maladetti.
E io: 'Maestro mio, fa, se tu puoi,
che tu sappi chi è lo sciagurato
venuto a man delli avversari suoi.'
Lo duca mio li s'accostò a lato,
domandollo ond'ei fosse, ed ei rispose:
'I' fui del regno di Navarra nato.
Mia madre a servo d'un segnor mi pose,
che m'avea generato d'un ribaldo, 50
distruggitor di sè e di sue cose.
Poi fui famiglia del buon re Tebaldo;
quivi mi misi a far baratteria,
di ch' io rendo ragione in questo caldo.'
E Ciriätto, a cui di bocca uscìa
d'ogni parte una sanna come a porco,
li fè sentir come l' una sdrucìa.
Tra male gatte era venuto il sorco;
ma Barbariccia il chiuse con le braccia,
e disse: 'State in là, mentr' io lo 'nforco.' 60
E al maestro mio volse la faccia:
'Domanda' disse 'ancor, se più disii
saper da lui, prima ch'altri 'l disfaccia.'
Lo duca dunque: 'Or dì: delli altri rii
conosci tu alcun che sia latino
sotto la pece?' E quelli: 'I' mi partii,
poco è, da un che fu di là vicino:
così foss' io ancor con lui coperto,
ch' i' non temerei unghia nè uncino!'

saw—and my heart yet shudders at it—one linger thus, as it chances when one frog remains and another dives, and Graffiacane, who was just opposite him, hooked him by the tarry locks and drew him up, so that he seemed to me an otter.

I already knew the names of all of them, I had noted them so well when they were chosen and then observed what they called each other.

'See thou get thy claws on him, Rubicante, and take the skin off him,' the accursed creatures shouted all together; and I said: 'My Master, pray learn, if thou canst, who is the hapless wretch that has fallen into the hands of his enemies.'

My Leader went beside him and asked him whence he was, and he replied: 'I was born in the Kingdom of Navarre.[3] My mother put me in the service of a lord, for she had borne me to a wastrel who made an end of himself and of his fortune; then I was in the household of the good King Thibault[4] and there gave myself to the practice of barratry, for which I pay the reckoning in this heat.'

And Ciriatto, from whose mouth came out a tusk on each side like a boar's, let him feel how one of them could rip. The mouse had fallen among wicked cats, but Barbariccia caught him in his arms and said: 'Stand off while I grip him', then turned his face to my Master and said: 'Ask on, if thou wouldst learn more from him before another mangles him.'

My Leader said therefore: 'Tell us then, of the other sinners beneath the pitch knowest thou any that is Italian?' And he: 'I parted just now from one that was a neighbour of theirs. Would I were still under cover with him so that I should not fear claw or hook!'

E Libicocco 'Troppo avem sofferto' 70
disse; e preseli 'l braccio col runciglio,
sì che, stracciando, ne portò un lacerto.
Draghignazzo anco i volle dar di piglio
giuso alle gambe; onde 'l decurio loro
si volse intorno intorno con mal piglio.
Quand'elli un poco rappaciati foro,
a lui, ch'ancor mirava sua ferita,
domandò 'l duca mio sanza dimoro:
'Chi fu colui da cui mala partita
di' che facesti per venire a proda?' 80
Ed ei rispuose: 'Fu frate Gomita,
quel di Gallura, vasel d'ogne froda,
ch'ebbe i nemici di suo donno in mano,
e fè sì lor che ciascun se ne loda.
Danar si tolse, e lasciolli di piano,
sì com' e' dice; e nelli altri offici anche
barattier fu non picciol, ma sovrano.
Usa con esso donno Michel Zanche
di Logodoro; e a dir di Sardigna
le lingue lor non si sentono stanche. 90
Ohmè, vedete l'altro che digrigna:
i' direi anche, ma i' temo ch'ello
non s'apparecchi a grattarmi la tigna.'
E 'l gran proposto, volto a Farfarello
che stralunava li occhi per fedire,
disse: 'Fatti 'n costà, malvagio uccello.'
'Se voi volete vedere o udire'
ricominciò lo spaurato appresso
'Toschi o Lombardi, io ne farò venire;
ma stieno i Malebranche un poco in cesso, 100
sì ch'ei non teman delle lor vendette;
e io, seggendo in questo luogo stesso,
per un ch' io son, ne farò venir sette
quand' io suffolerò, com'è nostro uso
di fare allor che fori alcun si mette.'
Cagnazzo a cotal motto levò 'l muso,
crollando il capo, e disse: 'Odi malizia
ch'elli ha pensata per gittarsi giuso!'

And Libicocco said: 'We have borne too much,' and took him by the arm with his gaff so that he tore it and carried off a muscle; Draghignazzo too tried to take hold of him below by the legs, at which their captain wheeled round on them all with ugly looks.

When they were somewhat quieted, my Leader without delay asked him that was still gazing at his wound: 'Who is he from whom, as thou sayest, thou didst part unluckily to come ashore?'

And he replied: 'It was Fra Gomita, he of Gallura, a vessel of every fraud,[5] who had his lord's enemies in his hand and so dealt with them that all speak well of him; he "took the cash and let them off quietly", as he says, and in other affairs too he was no small barrator but a lordly one. Don Michael Zanche of Logodoro[6] keeps company with him and in talking of Sardinia their tongues are never weary. Oh me, see that other grinding his teeth! I would tell thee more, but I fear he is preparing to scratch my scurf.'

And the great marshal, turning to Farfarello who was rolling his eyes to strike, said: 'Take thyself off there, villainous bird!'

'If you would see or hear Tuscans or Lombards,' the frightened spirit then began again 'I will make some of them come; but let the Malebranche hold back a little so that they may not fear their vengeance, and I, remaining on this same spot, for one that I am will make seven come when I whistle, as our custom is when any of us gets out.'

Cagnazzo, when he heard that, lifted his snout and shook his head, saying: 'Hear the trick he has thought of for throwing himself down!' To which,

Ond'ei, ch'avea lacciuoli a gran divizia,
 rispuose: 'Malizioso son io troppo, 110
 quand' io procuro a' miei maggior tristizia.'
Alichin non si tenne, e, di rintoppo
 alli altri, disse a lui: 'Se tu ti cali,
 io non ti verrò dietro di gualoppo,
ma batterò sovra la pece l'ali:
 lascisi 'l collo, e sia la ripa scudo,
 a veder se tu sol più di noi vali.'
O tu che leggi, udirai nuovo ludo:
 ciascun dall'altra costa li occhi volse;
 quel prima ch'a ciò fare era più crudo. 120
Lo Navarrese ben suo tempo colse;
 fermò le piante a terra, ed in un punto
 saltò e dal proposto lor si sciolse.
Di che ciascun di colpa fu compunto,
 ma quei più che cagion fu del difetto;
 però si mosse e gridò: 'Tu se' giunto!'
Ma poco i valse: chè l'ali al sospetto
 non potero avanzar: quelli andò sotto,
 e quei drizzò volando suso il petto:
non altrimenti l'anitra di botto, 130
 quando 'l falcon s'appressa, giù s'attuffa,
 ed ei ritorna su crucciato e rotto.
Irato Calcabrina della buffa,
 volando dietro li tenne, invaghito
 che quei campasse per aver la zuffa;
e come 'l barattier fu disparito,
 così volse li artigli al suo compagno,
 e fu con lui sopra 'l fosso ghermito.
Ma l'altro fu bene sparvier grifagno
 ad artigliar ben lui, ed amendue 140
 cadder nel mezzo del bogliente stagno.
Lo caldo sghermitor subito fue;
 ma però di levarsi era neente,
 sì avieno inviscate l'ali sue.
Barbariccia, con li altri suoi dolente,
 quattro ne fè volar dall'altra costa
 con tutt' i raffi, ed assai prestamente

having great store of devices, he replied: 'I am over-tricky indeed, in getting more trouble for my friends!'

Alichino could not hold in, but in spite of the others said to him: 'If thou drop down I will come after thee, not at a gallop but swooping on my wings over the pitch. Let us leave the top and make a screen of the dike and see if by thyself thou art more than a match for us.'[7]

Now, reader, thou shalt hear new sport. All turned their eyes towards the other slope, he first that had been most loth to consent. The Navarrese chose his time well, planted his feet on the ground, and with a sudden leap broke away from the marshal; at which they were all smitten with self-reproach, but he most that was the cause of the blunder, so that he started out, crying: 'Thou art caught!' But it availed him little, for wings could not outstrip terror. The one went under and the other lifted his breast, flying upward. Just so the wild duck instantly plunges under on the approach of the falcon, which turns upward again, vexed and dispirited. Calcabrina went flying after him, furious at the trick but eager for the sinner to escape so as to have a scuffle, and as soon as the barrator had disappeared he turned his claws on his fellow and got to grips with him over the ditch; but the other was indeed a full-grown hawk to claw him well and both fell into the middle of the boiling pond. The heat unclutched them in a moment; but yet there was no getting out, they had so beglued their wings. Barbariccio, lamenting with the rest, made four of them fly to the other bank, each with his fork, and with all speed they descended

di qua, di là, discesero alla posta:
porser li uncini verso li 'mpaniati,
ch'eran già cotti dentro dalla crosta; 150
e noi lasciammo lor così 'mpacciati.

1. Probably a reference to the defeat of Arezzo by Florence and Lucca in 1298 when Dante may have been present.

2. Dolphins were taken for a sign of storm.

3. Not otherwise known, but named Ciampolo by the early commentators.

on this side and that to their posts. They pushed out their gaffs to the two that were limed, who were already cooked within their crust; and we left them in that broil.

4. Thibault II of Navarre (1253–1270).

5. Deputy of Nino Visconti, Judge of Gallura (*Purg.* viii), a division of Sardinia; hanged for his knavery.

6. Judge of Logodoro, another division of Sardinia.

7. They were to cross to the inner side of the dike, overlooking the next bolgia.

NOTE

Virgil's last words in the twentieth canto recalled Dante's experience 'in the depth of the wood' where all his light had been the broken gleams of the moon. Then, at the beginning of the twenty-first, we are told that the travellers came on, 'talking of other things of which my Comedy is not concerned to sing'—the same things, we may fairly suppose, to which Virgil had referred, the bitterness and bewilderment of the period of Dante's life represented by the dark wood, which he must not dwell on here but which is always in his memory. When he wrote these cantos one of the bitterest of his memories was the charge of barratry during his term of office as Prior in the Florentine Government, the charge that was flung after him by the authorities of Florence in the early years of his exile. It was a charge which probably not even his worst enemies believed to be just and which he never condescended to deny, unless, as it were in spite of himself, in these two cantos. More space is given to barratry than to any other single sin in Hell, nearly two and a half cantos, as if it had a great place in Dante's experience and in his knowledge of the petty communes of Italy, and as if he found his relief in treating it as extravagant farce. This is the one place in Hell where he is personally threatened by the fiends, and it is here more than anywhere else that he needs and finds his protection and security in Virgil, from the first scene on the bridge to the final escape reported in the twenty-third canto. 'Although hunted as a criminal, not a drop of the boiling pitch lights upon him, nor do the rakes and hooks of the Evil-claws as much as graze his skin' (*E. G. Gardner*).

The swift, vivid description of the great Venetian Arsenal, 'a picture of life sharply contrasted with a picture of death' (*D. Guerri, L.D.*), gives, like all Dante's similes, a strange, convincing reality to his imaginary scene. The sin of barratry, the equivalent in the State of simony in the Church, is shown in the condition of the souls there, hidden and held in the black, glutinous fluid, their 'dance' and 'pilfering' covered in the heaving and subsiding mass, which is, as it were, the outward show presented by their system of government. For barratry is, in fact, a sin which works under the surface and *sticks* to men and keeps them as busy, in their own way, as the workers in a dockyard.

In the miracle-plays of the Middle Ages the spirit of farce found its opportunity whenever the scene was in Hell or when devils occupied the stage, and in the bolgia of the barrators Dante 'reflects, as nowhere else, the popular Christian conception of Hell' (*C. H. Grandgent*). Note, for example, the farcical mock-solemnity of the exordium of the twenty-second canto on the 'strange bugle' to which the escort of devils starts out. In these cantos the grim horror of the doom of the sinners is almost forgotten in the grotesque and exuberant vitality of the devils, in whose malicious ribaldry and riotous vulgarity Dante sets forth the domination of the barrators by their sin which keeps them immersed in the vile *milieu* they have chosen. In the whole account the devils have a much larger place than their victims, the sin itself than the sinners, the general corruption of public life than the particular offences. They are organized, as jobbery has to be, taking orders from each other, yet quarrelsome and filled with a sort of mad fury, swift, scheming, knavish, merciless, falling into cross-purposes, getting entangled in their own devices, talking only in threats and jibes. 'I think' says Ruskin 'the twenty-first and twenty-second books of the *Inferno* the most perfect portraiture of fiendish nature which we possess.'

The names of the devils, as uncouth as their persons and conduct, are not traditional names but inventions. Some of them suggest their own meanings; Malacoda, Evil-tail—Barbariccia, Curlybeard—Cagnazzo, Low Hound—Draghignazzo, Vile Dragon—Ciriatto, Swineface—Graffiacane, Scratchdog—Rubicante, Redface—Scarmiglione, Tousletop; and these suggestions are quite consistent with an idea which is favoured both by some of the names themselves and by its notable fitness to Dante, that they are grotesque perversions of personal and family names well known in contemporary Italy and especially in Florence.

For some reason the government of Lucca is taken as an outstanding example of the prevalence of barratry and this gives opportunity for the choice taunt and paradox of calling the city by the name of Santa Zita, a maidservant recently adopted by Lucca as its patron saint after a lifetime of faithful service. In similar vein is the devils' jeering reference to the Holy Face of Lucca, the invocation of which had saved some of these souls in the pitch, or saved their credit, sometimes in the earthly life. The unhappy Lucchese, who has come to the surface of the pitch 'doubled up', is mocked by the devils as if he were still, by force of old habit, bowing to the Holy Face, which 'is not here for him'. He is now in the same case with all the others there, who, when they emerge from their own element as it were into relative decency, 'to ease their pain', are liable at any moment to be caught in a shameful exposure which is a worse agony and from which they escape, if they can, under cover of the pitch again.

Malacoda, in his conference with Virgil, tells him truthfully that the bridge immediately ahead is broken, but falsely that the other bridges over the sixth bolgia are whole. It is his characteristic device for getting the pilgrims entrapped among the demons of barratry. For Malacoda is the plausible rascally official, civil and submissive to superior authority, circumstantial and convincing in his lies—giving the date and hour of the fall of the bridge—restraining his underlings in their brutal rashness so as to gain his end, exercising his authority in selecting the squad with dignity and deliberation.

Barbariccia is the N.C.O., called 'captain' (*decurio,* leader of a squad of ten, in the old Latin form) and 'the great marshal' for mock dignity. He is on easy terms with his troop and answers their grimace with his characteristic starting-signal. In the end he is cheated like the rest.

Ciampolo, who had sharpened his wit from his youth up in the practice of barratry, can beat the devils at their own game. He talks volubly to Virgil and gains time by giving him much superfluous information while laying his plans and playing on the malice and assurance of the devils, to get out of their hands by means of an ingenious and circumstantial lie.

The last comment is that the devils by their very devilishness quite over-reach themselves, and the pilgrims 'leave them in that broil'.

'If it be true, as it probably is, that Dante, making game of the devils and the barrators, intended an ironical allusion to his own condemnation for barratry, the devils would be his accusers and persecutors, whose perfidy he described with bitter mockery; and the barrators, with whom, according to the charge, he would have been a confrere, he treats as they deserve, in the manner of one who is their superior, with no violent outbursts, pouring out on them now scorn and now a cheerful irony and putting them on familiar terms with the devils in a contest of tricks and frauds, as if to say, "The one lot are as good as the other, equal in my contempt"' (*E. G. Parodi*).

INFERNO

TACITI, soli, sanza compagnia
  n'andavam l'un dinanzi e l'altro dopo,
  come i frati minor vanno per via.
Volt'era in su la favola d' Isopo
  lo mio pensier per la presente rissa,
  dov'el parlò della rana e del topo;
chè più non si pareggia 'mo' e 'issa'
  che l' un con l'altro fa, se ben s'accoppia
  principio e fine con la mente fissa.
E come l' un pensier dell'altro scoppia, 10
  così nacque di quello un altro poi,
  che la prima paura mi fè doppia.
Io pensava così: 'Questi per noi
  sono scherniti con danno e con beffa
  sì fatta, ch'assai credo che lor nòi.
Se l' ira sovra 'l mal voler fa gueffa,
  ei ne verranno dietro più crudeli
  che 'l cane a quella lievre ch'elli acceffa.'
Già mi sentìa tutti arricciar li peli
  della paura, e stava in dietro intento, 20
  quand' io dissi: 'Maestro, se non celi
te e me tostamente, i' ho pavento
  de' Malebranche: noi li avem già dietro:
  io li 'magino sì, che già li sento.'
E quei: 'S' i' fossi di piombato vetro,
  l' imagine di fuor tua non trarrei
  più tosto a me, che quella d'entro impetro.
Pur mo venìeno i tuo' pensier tra' miei,
  con simile atto e con simile faccia,
  sì che d' intrambi un sol consiglio fei. 30

CANTO XXIII

The Sixth Bolgia; the Hypocrites; Fra Catalano

SILENT, alone, without escort, we went on, one before and the other after, as Friars Minor take their way. My thoughts were turned by the present quarrel on the fable of Aesop where he told of the frog and the mouse;[1] for *mo* and *issa*[2] are not more alike than the one case and the other, if we compare the beginning and the end attentively. And as one thought springs out of another, so from that one another was born in turn which redoubled my former fear. I thought, they are fooled because of us, and with such hurt and mockery as, I believe, must greatly vex them, and if anger is added to ill-will they will come after us savager than a dog snapping at a leveret. Already I felt my hair all bristling with fear and I stood looking back intently, when I said: 'Master, unless thou quickly hide thyself and me I am in terror of the Malebranche; we have them after us already. I so imagine them that already I hear them.'

And he said: 'Were I of leaded glass[3] I should not draw to me thy outward semblance sooner than I receive thy inward; just now thy thoughts joined with mine, being alike in action and aspect, so that of both I have made one sole

S'elli è che sì la destra costa giaccia,
  che noi possiam nell'altra bolgia scendere,
  noi fuggirem l' imaginata caccia.'
Già non compiè di tal consiglio rendere,
  ch' io li vidi venir con l'ali tese
  non molto lungi, per volerne prendere.
Lo duca mio di subito mi prese,
  come la madre ch'al romore è desta
  e vede presso a sè le fiamme accese,
che prende il figlio e fugge e non s'arresta, 40
  avendo più di lui che di sè cura,
  tanto che solo una camicia vesta;
e giù dal collo della ripa dura
  supin si diede alla pendente roccia,
  che l' un de' lati all'altra bolgia tura.
Non corse mai sì tosto acqua per doccia
  a volger ruota di molin terragno,
  quand'ella più verso le pale approccia,
come 'l maestro mio per quel vivagno,
  portandosene me sovra 'l suo petto, 50
  come suo figlio, non come compagno.
A pena fuoro i piè suoi giunti al letto
  del fondo giù, ch' e' furono in sul colle
  sovresso noi; ma non li era sospetto;
chè l'alta provedenza che lor volle
  porre ministri della fossa quinta,
  poder di partirs' indi a tutti tolle.
Là giù trovammo una gente dipinta
  che giva intorno assai con lenti passi,
  piangendo e nel sembiante stanca e vinta. 60
Elli avean cappe con cappucci bassi
  dinanzi alli occhi, fatte della taglia
  che in Clugnì per li monaci fassi.
Di fuor dorate son, sì ch'elli abbaglia;
  ma dentro tutte piombo, e gravi tanto,
  che Federigo le mettea di paglia.
Oh in etterno faticoso manto!
  Noi ci volgemmo ancor pur a man manca
  con loro insieme, intenti al tristo pianto;

counsel. If it be that the slope on the right lies so that we can descend into the next ditch, we shall escape from the chase we imagine.'

He had not yet finished telling me his plan when I saw them coming with outstretched wings, not far off, meaning to take us. My Leader caught me instantly, like a mother who is wakened by the noise and sees beside her the flames kindled and catches up her child and flies and, more concerned for him than herself, does not stay even to put on a shift; and down from the ridge of the stony bank, lying on his back, he let himself go on the sloping rock that encloses the next ditch on one side. Never ran water so fast through a sluice to turn the wheel of a land-mill when coming nearest to the blades, as my Master went down that bank, bearing me along with him on his breast not as a companion but as his child. Hardly had his feet reached the bed of the depth below when they were on the height right over us; but there was nothing to fear, for the high providence which willed to set them as ministers of the fifth ditch deprives them all of power to leave it.

There below we found a painted people who were going round with very slow steps, weeping and looking weary and overcome. They had cloaks with cowls down over their eyes, of the cut that is made for the monks of Cluny,[4] so gilded outside that they were dazzling, but within all lead and so heavy that those Frederick imposed were of straw.[5] O toilsome mantle for eternity!

We turned again, still to the left, along with them, intent on their wretched weeping, but on

ma per lo peso quella gente stanca 70
venìa sì pian, che noi eravam novi
di compagnia ad ogni mover d'anca.
Per ch' io al duca mio: 'Fa che tu trovi
alcun ch'al fatto o al nome si conosca,
e li occhi, sì andando, intorno movi.'
E un che 'ntese la parola tosca,
di retro a noi gridò: 'Tenete i piedi,
voi che correte sì per l'aura fosca!
Forse ch'avrai da me quel che tu chiedi.'
Onde 'l duca si volse e disse: 'Aspetta, 80
e poi secondo il suo passo procedi.'
Ristetti, e vidi due mostrar gran fretta
dell'animo, col viso, d'esser meco;
ma tardavali 'l carco e la via stretta.
Quando fuor giunti, assai con l'occhio bieco
mi rimiraron sanza far parola;
poi si volsero in sè, e dicean seco:
'Costui par vivo all'atto della gola;
e s'e' son morti, per qual privilegio
vanno scoperti della grave stola?' 90
Poi disser me: 'O Tosco, ch'al collegio
dell' ipocriti tristi se' venuto,
dir chi tu se' non avere in dispregio.'
E io a loro: 'I' fui nato e cresciuto
sovra 'l bel fiume d'Arno alla gran villa,
e son col corpo ch' i' ho sempre avuto.
Ma voi chi siete, a cui tanto distilla
quant' i' veggio dolor giù per le guance?
e che pena è in voi che sì sfavilla?'
E l'un rispuose a me: 'Le cappe rance 100
son di piombo sì grosse, che li pesi
fan così cigolar le lor bilance.
Frati Godenti fummo, e bolognesi;
io Catalano e questi Loderingo
nomati, e da tua terra insieme presi,
come suole esser tolto un uom solingo
per conservar sua pace; e fummo tali,
ch'ancor si pare intorno dal Gardingo.'

account of the load that weary people came on so slowly that we were in new company with each step we took; I said therefore to my Leader: 'Pray find someone that is known by deed or name, looking round as we go.'

And one who caught the Tuscan speech cried after us: 'Stay your steps, you that haste so through the dusky air; perhaps thou shalt have from me what thou askest.' At which my Leader turned round and said: 'Wait, and then go on at his pace.'

I stopped and saw two showing by their looks the great haste of their mind to join me, but the load and the crowded way delayed them. When they came up they gazed sideways at me for a while without uttering a word, then turned to each other and said: 'This man seems alive, by the working of his throat, and if they are dead by what privilege do they go uncovered with the heavy stole?' Then they said to me: 'O Tuscan, who art come to the assembly of the hypocrites of a sad countenance, do not disdain to tell us who thou art.'

And I said to them: 'I was born and grew up on the fair stream of Arno, in the great city, and am with the body I have always had; but who are you down whose cheeks such pain distils as I see, and what penalty is upon you that glitters so?'

And one of them answered me: 'The orange cloaks are of lead, so thick that the weight makes their balances creak thus. We were Jovial Friars[6] and Bolognese, I Catalano and he Loderingo by name, and we were chosen together by thy city, where it was the custom to take one man alone, to keep the peace, and what we were may still be seen round the Gardingo.'[7]

Io cominciai: 'O frati, i vostri mali . . .';
ma più non dissi, ch'all'occhio mi corse 110
un, crucifisso in terra con tre pali.
Quando mi vide, tutto si distorse,
soffiando nella barba con sospiri;
e 'l frate Catalan, ch'a ciò s'accorse,
mi disse: 'Quel confitto che tu miri,
consigliò i Farisei che convenìa
porre un uom per lo popolo a' martiri.
Attraversato è, nudo, nella via,
come tu vedi, ed è mestier ch'el senta
qualunque passa, come pesa, pria. 120
E a tal modo il socero si stenta
in questa fossa, e li altri dal concilio
che fu per li Giudei mala sementa.'
Allor vid' io maravigliar Virgilio
sovra colui ch'era disteso in croce
tanto vilmente nell'etterno essilio.
Poscia drizzò al frate cotal voce:
'Non vi dispiaccia, se vi lece, dirci
s'alla man destra giace alcuna foce
onde noi amendue possiamo uscirci, 130
sanza costringer delli angeli neri
che vegnan d'esto fondo a dipartirci.'
Rispuose adunque: 'Più che tu non speri
s'appressa un sasso che dalla gran cerchia
si move e varca tutt' i vallon feri,
salvo che 'n questo è rotto e nol coperchia:
montar potrete su per la ruina,
che giace in costa e nel fondo soperchia.'
Lo duca stette un poco a testa china;
poi disse: 'Mal contava la bisogna 140
colui che i peccator di qua uncina.'
E 'l frate: 'Io udi' già dire a Bologna
del diavol vizi assai, tra' quali udi'
ch'elli è bugiardo, e padre di menzogna.'
Appresso il duca a gran passi sen gì,
turbato un poco d' ira nel sembiante;
ond' io dalli 'ncarcati mi parti'
dietro alle poste delle care piante.

I began: 'O Friars, your evil deeds'—but I said no more, for there caught my eye one crucified on the ground with three stakes. When he saw me he writhed all over, blowing in his beard with sighs; and Fra Catalano, observing it, said to me: 'That transfixed one thou art looking at counselled the Pharisees that it was expedient to make one man suffer for the people.[8] He is stretched naked, as thou seest, across the way and must feel the weight of each that passes; and in the same fashion his father-in-law is racked in this ditch, and the rest of that council which was a seed of evil for the Jews.'[9]

Then I saw Virgil marvelling over him that was stretched crosswise so vilely in the eternal exile. Then he directed his words to the Friar: 'May it please you, if it is permitted, to tell us if there lies any passage on the right by which we two can go out from here, without requiring some of the black angels to come and take us from this bottom.'

He replied then: 'Nearer than thou hopest is a ridge of rock that starts from the great encircling wall and spans all the cruel valleys, except that at this one it is broken down and does not go over it. You will be able to mount by the ruin that slopes against the side and is piled up on the bottom.'

My Leader stood for a moment with bent head, then said: 'An ill account of the business he gave that hooks the sinners over there.' And the Friar: 'I once heard them tell in Bologna of the Devil's many vices, among which I heard that he is a liar and the father of lies.'

Then my Leader went on with great strides, his looks disturbed somewhat with anger; so I left these burdened souls, following the prints of the dear feet.

1. A fable wrongly ascribed to Aesop. A frog, having proposed to tow a mouse across a stream, dived and tried to drown it and when the mouse struggled a kite seized the frog. Calcabrina may be the frog and Alichino the mouse.

2. Words in Italian dialects, both meaning *now*.

3. A mirror.

4. St Bernard complained that they were lavish and luxurious.

5. Frederick II (Canto x) was said to have punished traitors by wrapping them in leaden cloaks which were then melted on them; but the story is doubtful.

6. Knights of St Mary, a military and religious order founded in 1261 for protection of the weak and mediation in party feuds; popularly known, for their easy life, as the Jovial Friars.

7. The two, Guelf and Ghibelline, were invited as joint Governors to Florence in 1266 to make peace between the parties; afterwards charged with corruption and the destruction, at the Pope's bidding, of the palace of the Uberti (Canto x) in the quarter of Florence called the Gardingo.

8. 'Caiaphas, being the high priest that same year, said unto them, Ye know nothing at all, nor consider that it is expedient for us that one man should die for the people and that the whole nation perish not' (*John* xi. 49–50).

9. Annas, 'father-in-law to Caiaphas' (*John* xviii. 13), and the Jewish Sanhedrin.

NOTE

After the turmoil of the fiends of barratry there is a sudden calm with the opening of the twenty-third canto and Dante is left to his own reflections. Is it a reminiscence from some of the more peaceful and solitary days of his exile when he had left the wrangle of Florentine politics behind him?

But his reflections themselves turned to terror; the devils were after him with their hooks and would convict and exhibit him to the world as a barrator, and his resource is in his integrity. In the laboured medieval way Virgil tells how his mind is a mirror to Dante's, so at one are they; and then, in a passage of dramatic force singular even in the *Divine Comedy*, Dante tells of his passionate committal of himself to his conscience and of being clasped and carried to safety like a child in Virgil's arms. The whole passage seems to require the autobiographical reference to justify it.

The penalty of the hypocrites may have been suggested by the derivation given in a Latin lexicon probably known to Dante, which makes the word *hypocrite* mean, literally, *gilded over*. In any case the symbolism is obvious enough; the monkish gravity of pace and sidelong looks—the outward show as of brocaded copes and the coarse metal beneath the dazzling gilt—the crushing burden, 'making the balances creak', of a deliberate make-believe that has become a laborious and permanent bondage disabling them from any free movement of their souls—the 'sad countenance', once assumed, now inevitable. The language emphasizes the extreme *tiresomeness* of hypocrisy: the souls are 'weary and overcome'—the word weary is used also a second time—with their 'toilsome mantle for eternity'. All their manhood is exhausted in keeping up appearances.

The two Jovial Friars from Bologna were vividly remembered

in Florence from the time of Dante's infancy—whether justly or not need not here concern us—for bad faith and partiality and rapacity in a position of high public trust, and Dante might have put them among the barrators in the pitch. But he reckoned their hypocrisy, their mean impiety and religious pretence, an even more abject and injurious sin, giving them their lower place in Hell.

The startling figure of Caiaphas, inarticulate with shame and fury at his exposure to one redeemed by Christ, abruptly calls away Dante's attention from the Friars, as if to say: 'What is all hypocrisy to this, the supreme crime of history committed in the name of religion and the public good?' By their deed Caiaphas and the rest have gibbeted themselves and must be trodden under foot by the other hypocrites and bear the weight of all *their* shame. The sight and the report were a marvel to Virgil, not intelligible to a pagan and incredible and incomprehensible to sane reason and conscience.

It is now plain that all the bridges over the sixth bolgia were broken down by the earthquake of the Crucifixion, like the great wall of the pit of violence described in the twelfth canto.

Catalano's last speech, commenting on the fraud which the devils put on Virgil about the broken bridges, is characteristic and significant. It combines the Friar's demure and malicious mockery of the simplicity of Virgil in taking a devil at his word with Dante's mimicry of the monkish habit of grave quotation of authorities for a platitude, 'I once heard them tell in Bologna'; and 'there passes over the face of the narrator and creator the malicious smile of irony which is the form in this canto of the profound disdain that broods in such a soul as Dante's' (*V. Rossi*).

INFERNO

IN quella parte del giovanetto anno
  che 'l sole i crin sotto l'Aquario tempra
  e già le notti al mezzo dì sen vanno,
quando la brina in su la terra assempra
  l' imagine di sua sorella bianca,
  ma poco dura alla sua penna tempra;
lo villanello a cui la roba manca,
  si leva, e guarda, e vede la campagna
  biancheggiar tutta; ond'ei si batte l'anca,
ritorna in casa, e qua e là si lagna, 10
  come 'l tapin che non sa che si faccia;
  poi riede, e la speranza ringavagna,
veggendo il mondo aver cangiata faccia
  in poco d'ora, e prende suo vincastro,
  e fuor le pecorelle a pascer caccia.
Così mi fece sbigottir lo mastro
  quand' io li vidi sì turbar la fronte,
  e così tosto al mal giunse lo 'mpiastro;
chè, come noi venimmo al guasto ponte,
  lo duca a me si volse con quel piglio 20
  dolce ch' io vidi prima a piè del monte.
Le braccia aperse, dopo alcun consiglio
  eletto seco riguardando prima
  ben la ruina, e diedemi di piglio.
E come quei ch'adopera ed estima,
  che sempre par che 'nnanzi si proveggia,
  così, levando me su ver la cima
d' un ronchione, avvisava un'altra scheggia
  dicendo: 'Sovra quella poi t'aggrappa;
  ma tenta pria s'è tal ch'ella ti reggia.' 30

CANTO XXIV

The Seventh Bolgia; the Thieves; Vanni Fucci

IN that part of the youthful year when the sun refreshes his locks under Aquarius and already the long nights are moving away to the south,[1] when the rime copies on the ground the likeness of her white sister but her pen does not long keep its point, the peasant who is short of fodder rises and looks out and sees the fields all white, at which he smites his thigh, turns back into the house and goes here and there complaining like a poor wretch that knows not what is to be done, then comes back and gathers hope again when he sees how in a little time the world has changed its face, and grasps his staff and drives forth his sheep to pasture; thus the Master made me lose heart when I saw his brow so clouded and thus quickly came the plaster to the hurt, for as soon as we reached the shattered bridge my Leader turned to me with that sweet look which I saw first at the foot of the mountain. He opened his arms, having chosen some plan in his mind, first examining the ruin well, and took hold of me; and like one that works and reckons and seems always to provide beforehand, so, while lifting me up towards the top of one great boulder, he was looking out another rock, saying: 'Take hold of that next, but try first if it will bear thee.' It was no way for one wearing

Non era via da vestito di cappa,
chè noi a pena, ei lieve e io sospinto,
potavam su montar di chiappa in chiappa;
e se non fosse che da quel precinto
più che dall'altro era la costa corta,
non so di lui, ma io sarei ben vinto.
Ma perchè Malebolge inver la porta
del bassissimo pozzo tutta pende,
lo sito di ciascuna valle porta
che l'una costa surge e l'altra scende: 40
noi pur venimmo al fine in su la punta
onde l'ultima pietra si scoscende.
La lena m'era del polmon sì munta
quand' io fui su, ch' i' non potea più oltre
anzi m'assisi nella prima giunta.
'Omai convien che tu così ti spoltre,'
disse 'l maestro 'chè, seggendo in piuma,
in fama non si vien, nè sotto coltre;
sanza la qual chi sua vita consuma,
cotal vestigio in terra di sè lascia, 50
qual fummo in aere ed in acqua la schiuma.
E però leva su: vinci l'ambascia
con l'animo che vince ogni battaglia,
se col suo grave corpo non s'accascia.
Più lunga scala convien che si saglia;
non basta da costoro esser partito:
se tu m' intendi, or fa sì che ti vaglia.'
Leva'mi allor, mostrandomi fornito
meglio di lena ch' i' non mi sentìa,
e dissi: 'Va, ch' i' son forte e ardito.' 60
Su per lo scoglio prendemmo la via,
ch'era ronchioso, stretto e malagevole,
ed erto più assai che quel di pria.
Parlando andava per non parer fievole;
onde una voce uscì dell'altro fosso,
a parole formar disconvenevole.
Non so che disse, ancor che sovra 'l dosso
fossi dell'arco già che varca quivi:
ma chi parlava ad ira parea mosso.

the mantle, for we—he light and I pushed—could hardly mount from jag to jag, and had it not been that on that dike the slope was shorter than on the other, I do not know for him, but I should have been quite beaten; but since all Malebolge inclines towards the mouth of the nethermost pit, the lie of each of the valleys makes one side higher and the other lower. We did at length come up to the point where the last stone breaks off, and the breath was so spent from my lungs when I was up that I could go no farther, but sat down as soon as I got there.

'Now must thou thus cast off all sloth,' said the Master 'for sitting on down or under blankets none comes to fame, and without it he that consumes his life leaves such trace of himself on earth as smoke in air or foam on the water. Rise, therefore, conquer thy panting with the soul, which conquers in every battle if it sink not with its body's weight. There is a longer stair which must be climbed;[2] it is not enough to have left these spirits. If thou understandest me, act now so that it profit thee.'

I rose then, showing myself better furnished with breath than I felt, and said: 'Go, for I am strong and fearless.'

We took our way up the ridge, which was craggy and narrow and difficult and far steeper than the last, and I talked as I went, so as not to seem faint; at which a voice came forth from the next ditch, not able to articulate. I do not know what it said, though I was already on the crown of the arch that crosses there, but he that spoke seemed to be moved with anger. I had bent downward,

Io era volto in giù, ma li occhi vivi 70
non poteano ire al fondo per lo scuro;
per ch' io: 'Maestro, fa che tu arrivi
dall'altro cinghio e dismontiam lo muro;
chè, com' i' odo quinci e non intendo,
così giù veggio e neente affiguro.'
'Altra risposta' disse 'non ti rendo
se non lo far; chè la dimanda onesta
si de' seguir con l'opera tacendo.'
Noi discendemmo il ponte dalla testa
dove s'aggiugne con l'ottava ripa, 80
e poi mi fu la bolgia manifesta;
e vidivi entro terribile stipa
di serpenti, e di sì diversa mena
che la memoria il sangue ancor mi scipa.
Più non si vanti Libia con sua rena;
chè se chelidri, iaculi e faree
produce, e cencri con anfisibena,
nè tante pestilenzie nè sì ree
mostrò già mai con tutta l'Etïopia
nè con ciò che di sopra al Mar Rosso èe. 90
Tra questa cruda e tristissima copia
correan genti nude e spaventate,
sanza sperar pertugio o elitropia:
con serpi le man dietro avean legate;
quelle ficcavan per le ren la coda
e il capo, ed eran dinanzi aggroppate.
Ed ecco a un ch'era da nostra proda,
s'avventò un serpente che 'l trafisse
là dove 'l collo alle spalle s'annoda.
Nè *o* sì tosto mai nè *i* si scrisse, 100
com'el s'accese ed arse, e cener tutto
convenne che cascando divenisse;
e poi che fu a terra sì distrutto,
la polver si raccolse per sè stessa,
e 'n quel medesmo ritornò di butto.
Così per li gran savi si confessa
che la fenice more e poi rinasce,
quando al cinquecentesimo anno appressa:

but my keen gaze could not reach the bottom for the dark; I said therefore: 'Pray, Master, go on to the next encircling bank and let us descend the wall, for from this point I not only hear without understanding but I look down and distinguish nothing.'

'I give thee no answer' he said 'but to do it, for a fair request should be followed by the deed in silence.'

We descended at the end of the bridge where it joins the eighth bank and then the ditch was plain to me, and there within it I saw a fearful throng of serpents and of kinds so strange that the memory yet chills my blood. Let Lybia with her sands boast no more; for if she breeds chelydri, jaculi and phareae and cenchres with amphisbaena[3] she never showed plagues so many or so malignant, with all Ethiopia and the regions on the Red Sea. Among this cruel and most dismal swarm ran people naked and terrified, without hope of hiding-place or heliotrope.[4] They had their hands tied behind with serpents. These thrust through their loins the head and tail, which were knotted in front.

And lo, on one that was at our bank sprang a serpent which transfixed him at the point where the neck is joined to the shoulders, and never was *I* or *O* written so fast[5] as he took fire and burnt and must sink all turned to ashes; and when he was on the ground thus dissolved the dust drew together of itself and took instantly the same form again. Thus it is agreed by the great sages[6] that the phoenix, when she approaches her five-hundredth year, dies and then is born again; in her

erba nè biada in sua vita non pasce,
ma sol d' incenso lacrime e d'amomo, 110
e nardo e mirra son l'ultime fasce.
E qual è quel che cade, e non sa como,
per forza di demon ch'a terra il tira,
o d'altra oppilazion che lega l'omo,
quando si leva, che 'ntorno si mira
tutto smarrito della grande angoscia
ch'elli ha sofferta, e guardando sospira;
tal era il peccator levato poscia.
Oh potenza di Dio, quant'è severa
che cotai colpi per vendetta croscia! 120
Lo duca il domandò poi chi ello era;
per ch'ei rispuose: 'Io piovvi di Toscana,
poco tempo è, in questa gola fera.
Vita bestial mi piacque e non umana,
sì come a mul ch' i' fui; son Vanni Fucci
bestia, e Pistoia mi fu degna tana.'
E io al duca: 'Dilli che non mucci,
e domanda che colpa qua giù 'l pinse;
ch' io 'l vidi uomo di sangue e di crucci.'
E 'l peccator, che 'ntese, non s' infinse, 130
ma drizzò verso me l'animo e 'l volto,
e di trista vergogna si dipinse;
poi disse: 'Più mi duol che tu m' hai colto
nella miseria dove tu mi vedi,
che quando fui dell'altra vita tolto.
Io non posso negar quel che tu chiedi:
in giù son messo tanto perch' io fui
ladro alla sagrestia de' belli arredi,
e falsamente già fu apposto altrui.
Ma perchè di tal vista tu non godi, 140
se mai sarai di fuor da' luoghi bui,
apri li orecchi al mio annunzio, e odi:
Pistoia in pria de' Neri si dimagra:
poi Fiorenza rinova gente e modi.
Tragge Marte vapor di Val di Magra
ch'è di torbidi nuvoli involuto;
e con tempesta impetüosa e agra

lifetime she feeds neither on herbs nor grain, but only on tears of frankincense and of balsam, and nard and myrrh are her last winding-sheet. And as one that falls, not knowing how, by force of a devil dragging him to the ground or by some vital obstruction that binds a man, and when he rises stares about him all bewildered with the great anguish he has suffered, and sighs as he looks; such was the sinner when he rose. Ah, the power of God, how stern it is, pouring forth such strokes for vengeance!

Then my Leader asked him who he was, to which he answered: 'I rained from Tuscany not long since into this wild gullet. A beast's life pleased me, not a man's, mule as I was. I am Vanni Fucci, the Beast, and Pistoia was my fitting den.'[7]

And I said to my Leader: 'Tell him not to slip off, and ask what crime thrust him down here, for I saw him a man of blood and rage.'

And the sinner, who heard, did not dissemble, but set his mind and his look on me and coloured with wretched shame, then said: 'I suffer more that thou hast caught me in the misery in which thou seest me than when I was taken from the other life. I may not refuse to answer thy question. I am put down so far because I was a thief in the Sacristy of the Fair Ornaments and then it was laid falsely on another.[8] But lest thou rejoice in this sight, if ever thou go forth from the dark regions, open thy ears to what I declare to thee, and hear. Pistoia first thins herself of Blacks, then Florence renews her people and her ways.[9] Mars draws a vapour from Val di Magra, which is wrapt in turbid clouds, and with a violent and bitter

sovra Campo Picen fia combattuto;
ond'ei repente spezzerà la nebbia,
sì ch'ogni Bianco ne sarà feruto. 150
E detto l' ho perchè doler ti debbia!'

1. The sun enters Aquarius (the Waterman) about January 20th, when the nights are shortening in the northern hemisphere and lengthening in the southern.

2. From the earth's centre to the summit of Purgatory.

3. Venomous snakes mentioned by Lucan.

4. Kind of chalcedony supposed to make its wearer invisible.

5. Letters made with a single stroke.

6. The phoenix story is told by several Latin poets, as Ovid and Lucan.

storm battle shall be joined on the field of Piceno, where the fire shall burst of a sudden through the cloud so that every White shall be struck by it. And I have told it that it may grieve thee.'

7. Fucci was the bastard son ('mule') of a Pistoian noble; violent leader of the Blacks of Pistoia, perhaps known as Beast Fucci.

8. The sacristy of Pistoia Cathedral was famed for its treasures; some were stolen in 1293 and an innocent man, it is said, hanged for the theft. Fucci's guilt, apparently, was not known till after his death.

9. The division of the Pistoian Guelfs into Blacks and Whites spread to Florence, where the domination of the Blacks led to Dante's exile. The 'vapour' was the leader of the Blacks, a member of the great Malaspina family, who defeated the Pistoian Whites in 1302.

NOTE

There is something of lassitude in Dante as he appears to us in the twenty-third canto, a mood which follows naturally on the terrors of the ditch of the barrators and his bare escape from the fiends. Walking with the Friars at their creeping pace, he had little to say to them, and when he would have spoken he was struck dumb again by the sight of Caiaphas and then quite lost heart on account of Virgil's looks, 'disturbed somewhat with anger' at the fraud practised on him. As Virgil was perplexed and hindered by the evil spirits of denial before the gate of Dis, so here he is for the moment not only angered but taken aback and at a loss on account of the unreckonable meanness and malice of fraud, which seems to rule the world as if it would baffle him.

Such a mood of uncertainty and discouragement and the recovery from it were as much a part of Dante's actual experience as his terror in the dark wood and his deliverance; and here as there, as if by intentional reminiscence, the note of his recovery is sounded in the word 'Go' to his Guide. That is the meaning of the most Virgilian picture of the peasant's despondency and his relief at the last traces of winter and the first signs of spring, the clearing of Virgil's clouded brow 'with that sweet look which I saw first at the foot of the mountain', and the resurgence of his manhood with which, at Virgil's bidding, the pilgrim 'casts off all sloth', 'conquers his panting', and faces in his mind 'the longer stair which must be climbed'. The road is far harder than before, harder than anywhere else in Hell, and each step seems impossible until it is taken. That is a part of the cost of despondency and the restoring of the soul. The whole scene recalls the passage in the fifteenth canto that tells of Brunetto Latini's high confidence for Dante and Dante's response.

The general character of the seventh bolgia and its penalties will be better considered along with the scenes of the next canto, but the interview with Vanni Fucci belongs to this. One of the most vitally conceived figures in the *Inferno*, Fucci is of the kindred of Capaneus, the defiant blasphemer on the burning sand (Canto xiv), but far more brutal, of a swaggering, cynical insolence, 'pluming himself on wearing the halo of his own savagery' (*V. Rossi*). Dante has known him in life as 'a man of blood and rage', a lawless and turbulent cut-throat, and he is surprised to find him here among the thieves and not either in Styx or Phlegethon, the places of rage and of bloodshed. It is Dante's way of saying that Fucci has earned a place, if it were possible, in all three parts of Hell, by his intemperance of spirit, his 'mad brutishness', and his thieving and lying about it, forms respectively of incontinence, violence and fraud. Shameless as he is, Fucci is thrown into an agony of shame by the forced confession of his deeper disgrace, which was not known at the time of his death and which, by a dramatic fiction, Dante learns only now and from himself. The shrewdness and success of his fraud on earth go here for nothing, and now even on earth his shame will be known.

It is significant that Dante has nothing to say to Fucci directly and that he questions him expressly and only through Virgil. He will not allow this meeting even to seem to be an altercation between Dante, the White, and Fucci, the Black; it is reason's examination of a criminal.

Fucci's rage and malice are vented in retaliation on Dante with a forecast of the disastrous civil strife, spreading from Pistoia to Florence, which is to issue in the defeat of all Dante's hopes for his own city and in his lifelong exile. The violent Black partisan flings the coming discomfiture of the Whites at Dante as one of them 'that it may grieve him'. The bitter prophecy, plunged 'like a dagger in his heart' (*F. Torraca*), is an immediate challenge to Dante to prove that he possesses 'the soul which conquers in every battle'.

AL fine delle sue parole il ladro
  le mani alzò con amendue le fiche,
  gridando: 'Togli, Dio, ch'a te le squadro!'
Da indi in qua mi fuor le serpi amiche,
  perch' una li s'avvolse allora al collo,
  come dicesse: 'Non vo' che più diche';
e un'altra alle braccia, e rilegollo,
  ribadendo sè stessa sì dinanzi,
  che non potea con esse dare un crollo.
Ahi Pistoia, Pistoia, chè non stanzi 10
  d' incenerarti sì che più non duri,
  poi che in mal fare il seme tuo avanzi?
Per tutt' i cerchi dello 'nferno scuri
  non vidi spirto in Dio tanto superbo,
  non quel che cadde a Tebe giù da' muri.
El si fuggì che non parlò più verbo;
  e io vidi un centauro pien di rabbia
  venir chiamando: 'Ov'è, ov'è l'acerbo?'
Maremma non cred' io che tante n'abbia,
  quante bisce elli avea su per la groppa 20
  infin ove comincia nostra labbia.
Sovra le spalle, dietro dalla coppa,
  con l'ali aperte li giacea un draco;
  e quello affuoca qualunque s' intoppa.
Lo mio maestro disse: 'Questi è Caco,
  che sotto il sasso di monte Aventino
  di sangue fece spesse volte laco.
Non va co' suoi fratei per un cammino,
  per lo furto che frodolente fece
  del grande armento ch'elli ebbe a vicino; 30

CANTO XXV

The five Florentines and the serpents

AT the end of his words the thief lifted up his hands with both the figs,[1] crying: 'Take that, God, for at Thee I square them!' From that time forth the serpents were my friends, for one coiled itself then about his neck, as if to say: 'I will not have thee say more', and another about his arms and bound him again, so rivetting itself in front that he could not make a motion with them.

Ah, Pistoia, Pistoia, why dost thou not resolve to burn thyself to ashes and to last no longer, since thou surpassest thy own seed in wickedness?[2] Through all the dark circles of Hell I saw no spirit so arrogant against God, not him that fell from the walls at Thebes.[3]

He fled, not speaking another word, and I saw a centaur full of rage come shouting: 'Where is he, where is the hardened wretch?' Maremma has not, I believe, as many snakes as he had on his croup up to where our form begins, and on his shoulders, behind the nape, lay a dragon with open wings which sets on fire whoever encounters it.

My Master said: 'That is Cacus, who beneath the rock of Mount Aventine made many a time a lake of blood.[4] He does not go in the same road with his brothers, for his fraud in stealing the great herd that lay near him, and for that his crooked

onde cessar le sue opere biece
sotto la mazza d'Ercule, che forse
li ne diè cento, e non sentì le diece.'
Mentre che sì parlava, ed el trascorse
e tre spiriti venner sotto noi,
de' quai nè io nè 'l duca mio s'accorse,
se non quando gridar: 'Chi siete voi?':
per che nostra novella si ristette,
ed intendemmo pur ad essi poi.
Io non li conoscea; ma ei seguette, 40
come suol seguitar per alcun caso,
che l' un nomar un altro convenette,
dicendo: 'Cianfa dove fia rimaso?':
per ch' io, acciò che 'l duca stesse attento,
mi puosi il dito su dal mento al naso.
Se tu se' or, lettore, a creder lento
ciò ch' io dirò, non sarà maraviglia,
chè io che 'l vidi a pena il mi consento.
Com' io tenea levate in lor le ciglia,
e un serpente con sei piè si lancia 50
dinanzi all' uno, e tutto a lui s'appiglia.
Co' piè di mezzo li avvinse la pancia,
e con li anterïor le braccia prese;
poi li addentò e l' una e l'altra guancia;
li diretani alle cosce distese,
e miseli la coda tra 'mbedue,
e dietro per le ren su la ritese.
Ellera abbarbicata mai non fue
ad alber sì, come l'orribil fera
per l'altrui membra avviticchiò le sue. 60
Poi s'appiccar come di calda cera
fossero stati e mischiar lor colore,
nè l'un nè l'altro già parea quel ch'era,
come procede innanzi dall'ardore
per lo papiro suso un color bruno
che non è nero ancora e 'l bianco more.
Li altri due 'l riguardavano, e ciascuno
gridava: 'Ohmè, Agnel, come ti muti!
Vedi che già non se' nè due nè uno.'

ways were ended under the club of Hercules, who gave him, perhaps, a hundred blows, and he felt not ten.'

While he spoke the Centaur ran past and three spirits came beneath us, of whom neither I nor my Leader was aware until they cried: 'Who are you?'; on which our talk broke off and we gave all our heed to them. I did not know them; but it happened, as often happens by some chance, that one had to name another, and he said: 'Where can Cianfa have stopped?' And at that, so that my Leader should remain attentive, I laid my finger from chin to nose.

If, reader, thou art now slow to credit what I shall tell, it will be no wonder, for I who saw it scarcely admit it to myself.

While I kept my eyes on them, lo, a serpent with six feet darts up in front of one and fastens on him all over; with the middle feet it clasped the paunch and with those in front seized the arms, then set its fangs in the one cheek and the other; the hind feet it spread on the thighs and thrust its tail between them and stretched it up over the loins behind. Never was ivy so rooted to a tree as the horrid beast intertwined the other's members with its own; then, as if they had been of hot wax, they stuck together and mixed their colours and neither the one nor the other appeared now what it was before; thus spreads over the paper before the flame a dark colour that is not yet black, and the white dies off. The other two were looking on and each cried: 'O me, Agnello, how thou changest! Lo, thou art now neither two

Già eran li due capi un divenuti, 70
quando n'apparver due figure miste
in una faccia, ov'eran due perduti.
Fersi le braccia due di quattro liste;
le cosce con le gambe e 'l ventre e 'l casso
divenner membra che non fuor mai viste.
Ogni primaio aspetto ivi era casso:
due e nessun l' imagine perversa
parea; e tal sen gìo con lento passo.
Come 'l ramarro sotto la gran fersa
dei dì canicular, cangiando sepe, 80
folgore par se la via attraversa,
sì pareva, venendo verso l'epe
delli altri due, un serpentello acceso,
livido e nero come gran di pepe;
e quella parte onde prima è preso
nostro alimento, all'un di lor trafisse;
poi cadde giuso innanzi lui disteso.
Lo trafitto 'l mirò, ma nulla disse;
anzi, co' piè fermati, sbadigliava
pur come sonno o febbre l'assalisse. 90
Elli 'l serpente, e quei lui riguardava;
l' un per la piaga, e l'altro per la bocca
fummavan forte, e 'l fummo si scontrava.
Taccia Lucano omai là dove tocca
del misero Sabello e di Nassidio,
e attenda a udir quel ch'or si scocca.
Taccia di Cadmo e d'Aretusa Ovidio;
chè se quello in serpente e quella in fonte
converte poetando, io non lo 'nvidio;
chè due nature mai a fronte a fronte 100
non trasmutò sì ch'amendue le forme
a cambiar lor matera fosser pronte.
Insieme si rispuosero a tai norme,
che 'l serpente la coda in forca fesse,
e il feruto ristrinse insieme l'orme.
Le gambe con le cosce seco stesse
s'appiccar sì, che 'n poco la giuntura
non facea segno alcun che si paresse.

nor one!' Now the two heads had become one, when the two shapes appeared to us blended in one face in which the two were lost; two arms were made of the four lengths; the thighs with the legs, the belly and the chest, became such members as were never seen. Each former feature was blotted out; the perverted shape seemed both and neither, and such, with slow pace, it moved away.

As the lizard under the great scourge of the dog-days, passing from hedge to hedge, seems lightning if it cross the way, so appeared, making for the bellies of the other two, a small, fiery serpent, livid, and black as a pepper-corn; and that part by which we first receive our nourishment[5] it transfixed in one of them, then fell down before him stretched out. The one transfixed stared at it, but said nothing, only stood still and yawned, as if sleep or fever had come upon him. He kept looking at the serpent and it at him; the one from the wound, the other from the mouth, smoked violently, and their smoke met. Let Lucan now be silent with his tales of wretched Sabellus and Nasidius,[6] and let him wait to hear what now comes forth! Let Ovid be silent about Cadmus and Arethusa;[7] for if in his lines he turns him into a serpent and her into a fountain, I do not grudge it to him, for two natures face to face he never so transmuted that both kinds were ready to exchange their substance. They responded mutually in such order that the serpent split its tail into a fork and he that was wounded drew his footprints together, the legs with the thighs adhering to each other of themselves so that soon there was no mark of the juncture to be

Togliea la coda fessa la figura
che si perdeva là, e la sua pelle 110
si facea molle, e quella di là dura.
Io vidi intrar le braccia per l'ascelle,
e i due piè della fiera, ch'eran corti,
tanto allungar quanto accorciavan quelle.
Poscia li piè di retro, insieme attorti,
diventaron lo membro che l'uom cela,
e 'l misero del suo n'avea due porti
Mentre che 'l fummo l' uno e l'altro vela
di color novo, e genera il pel suso
per l' una parte e dall'altra il dipela, 120
l'un si levò e l'altro cadde giuso,
non torcendo però le lucerne empie,
sotto le quai ciascun cambiava muso.
Quel ch'era dritto il trasse ver le tempie,
e di troppa matera ch' in là venne
uscir li orecchi delle gote scempie:
ciò che non corse in dietro e si ritenne
di quel soverchio fè naso alla faccia,
e le labbra ingrossò quanto convenne.
Quel che giacea il muso innanzi caccia, 130
e li orecchi ritira per la testa
come face le corna la lumaccia;
e la lingua, ch'avea unita e presta
prima a parlar, si fende, e la forcuta
nell'altro si richiude; e 'l fummo resta.
L'anima ch'era fiera divenuta,
suffolando si fugge per la valle,
e l'altro dietro a lui parlando sputa.
Poscia li volse le novelle spalle,
e disse all'altro: 'I' vo' che Buoso corra, 140
com' ho fatt' io, carpon per questo calle.'
Così vid' io la settima zavorra
mutare e trasmutare; e qui mi scusi
la novità se fior la penna abborra.
E avvegna che li occhi miei confusi
fossero alquanto, e l'animo smagato,
non poter quei fuggirsi tanto chiusi,

seen; the divided tail took the shape that was lost there and its skin turned soft and the other's hard. I saw the arms draw in at the armpits and the brute's two paws, which were short, lengthen as much as these shortened; then the hind-paws, twisted together, became the member man conceals, and from his the wretch had put forth two feet. While the smoke veils the one and the other with new colour and on the one hand brings out the hair and on the other strips it off, the one rose and the other fell down, but neither turned aside the baleful lamps beneath which they exchanged visages. He that was erect drew his towards the temples, and out of the excess of matter that came there the ears issued from the bare cheeks; that which did not run back and was retained made of that excess a nose for the face and thickened the lips to the due size. He that was lying down drives the snout forward and draws back the ears into the head as the snail does its horns, and the tongue, which was whole and fit for speech before, divides, and the forked one of the other joins up, and the smoke stops. The soul that was become a brute fled hissing along the valley, the other talking and spitting after it.[8] Then he turned on it his new shoulders and said to the other shade: 'I'll have Buoso run on all fours, as I have done, along this road.'[9]

Thus I saw the seventh ballast change and interchange, and let the newness of it be my plea if in anything my pen be at fault.

And although my eyes were somewhat confused and my mind bewildered, these could not fly so

ch' i' non scorgessi ben Puccio Sciancato;
ed era quel che sol, de' tre compagni
che venner prima, non era mutato: 150
l'altr'era quel che tu, Gaville, piagni.

1. An obscene gesture.

2. Pistoia was said to have been founded by the remnant of Cataline's conspirators against Rome.

3. Capaneus (Canto xiv).

4. Cacus, a fire-breathing monster, stole cattle from Hercules, dragging them backwards into his cave; Hercules discovered them by their lowing and killed Cacus. 'His brothers' are the Centaurs of Canto xii.

5. The navel.

6. Soldiers in Cato's army, stung by serpents; Sabellus sank in putrefaction; Nasidius swelled and burst his corslet.

secretly that I did not clearly make out Puccio the Cripple, and he was the only one of the three companions that came first who was not changed; the other was he for whom, Gaville, thou dost mourn.

7. Cadmus, founder of Thebes, killed a dragon sacred to Mars and was transformed to a serpent. The nymph Arethusa, pursued by a river-god, called on Artemis and was changed into a fountain.

8. The human spittle was supposed to be poisonous to snakes.

9. The three first met were Agnello, Buoso and Puccio, of noble Florentine families but hardly known to us otherwise. Two Florentines, Cianfa and Francesco Cavalcanti, appear first as serpents, the former attacking Agnello and the latter Buoso. Francesco was killed for his oppressions by the people of the Tuscan village of Gaville and the family avenged his death.

NOTE

The malignant savagery of Fucci reaches its climax at the beginning of the twenty-fifth canto and is a fitting introduction to the scenes that follow in the thieves' ditch. These are distinguished by a fantastic horror which is singular even among the horrors of the Malebolge. They are difficult to reduce to clear moral symbolism, and too little is known of the characters and careers of the five Florentines of the canto—all, probably, senior contemporaries of Dante—for us to discover the special fitness of their several penalties.

The traditional subtlety, furtiveness, malice and deadliness of the serpent, its intelligence, incapable of rising above brute cunning, and its abject earthliness—'upon thy belly shalt thou go and dust shalt thou eat all the days of thy life' (*Gen.* iii. 14)—make it the most obvious and effective image of thieving, and for his purpose Dante conceives of a serpent with legs and claws. 'The serpent is the enemy of all mankind, and therefore in this valley of serpent-thieves Dante sets before us the kind of world which would exist were all bonds of common honesty dissolved, the social confusion and insecurity and fear, no man knowing when he would be attacked by some serpent which might turn out to be one of his own comrades' (*J. S. Carroll*). The peculiarity of the sin lies in the conversion of high human powers into the cunning of the brute for mere material acquisition, the falsifying and submersion of the soul in earthliness, and the waste and loss of human personality itself; and all this perversion, disablement and dissolution of the soul, the fierce rapacity and mutual dispossession and bad faith of a thieving society, are represented in the sudden consumption of Fucci, in the shapeless, brute-human amalgamation of Agnello and Cianfa, with its harping on 'two' and 'one', and in the weird interchange of shapes between Buoso and Francesco, with the mutual hatred and perversion of 'the one' and 'the other'.

Dante found the suggestion of such metamorphoses in some of the Latin poets, especially Lucan and Ovid, to whose stories he refers with something approaching contempt. It is not that he claims merely to do it better than they; he claims to do something different, to show a deeper, stranger mutation of kinds, the man and the beast uniting or interchanging their faculties and functions, the man with the beast's earthliness, the beast with the man's wit. Nothing could be further from the spirit of classical literature as it was known to Dante than the medieval intensity and tragic mystery of the scenes here. There seems to be something of the same irony in his elaborately, as it may appear irrelevantly, picturesque reference to the ancient fable of the phoenix in connection with Fucci's alternate dissolution and revival; as if he had said: 'These are old stories; this is true, it is happening now.'

In apparent contrast with this claim of Dante's his almost naïve apology at the end of the canto—'let the newness of it be my plea if in anything my pen be at fault'—indicates the conflict in his mind between his classical literary standards and his imaginative realism and abundance. Profoundly conscious of old Rome and of his place as Virgil's pupil in literature, Dante was no less a man of the Gothic age.

The wild figure of Cacus pursuing Fucci after his furious outburst seems to combine the attributes of Fucci's offences—the centaur form, like that of 'his brothers' beside the Phlegethon, for violence—the load of serpents for his many thefts—and the fiery dragon for his sacrilege and blasphemy—for he had stolen from the Church.

But the peculiar power of the canto lies in the conception of the whole scene and in its prevailing psychological atmosphere. From the moment when Dante's attention is suddenly caught by the name of a Florentine and he lays his finger on his lips in strained attention, he does not utter a word nor give any sign of his own feeling and nothing is heard from the ditch through the whole fantastic scene but some brief ejaculations and the hiss of the fleeing serpent. 'The serpent, so methodical, we might say so understanding, in its clutch on the body of

Brunelleschi'—Agnello, that is—'the regular co-ordination of the exchanges in the bodies of Buoso and Cavalcanti during their transformation, and the atmosphere of magical fascination in which the double metamorphosis is accomplished, give the fearful impression of a hidden power working consciously and irresistibly in the raw material. . . . The process of the transformations has the solemn inexorableness of a law of nature; in the succession of so many new and unlooked-for prodigies is felt the operative will of the invisible' (*V. Rossi*). The dazed stupor wrought in Francesco by Buoso's serpent-sting, the unmoving stare through the gloom of the 'baleful lamps' between the man and the beast, and the smoke pouring forth from them both all through their exchange, have the effect of a mutual hypnotism or of an incantation which holds them helpless. The idea of bodily transformation is indeed borrowed from the older poets, 'but the sustained realism, the atmosphere of mystery and horror, the uncanny yawn, stare and smoke, are Dante's own' (*C. H. Grandgent*). It is 'the drama of the soul that is lost in the brute body. The precise materialism of these descriptions, the absence of every suggestion of feeling, are nothing but the means by which is thrown into relief the silent death of the spirit. . . . Every sentiment but that of religious horror is dead; that is the fundamental character of the canto' (*Momigliano*, quoted in *Casini-Barbi*).

INFERNO

GODI, Fiorenza, poi che se' sì grande,
che per mare e per terra batti l'ali,
e per lo 'nferno tuo nome si spande!
Tra li ladron trovai cinque cotali
tuoi cittadini onde mi ven vergogna,
e tu in grande orranza non ne sali.
Ma se presso al mattin del ver si sogna,
tu sentirai di qua da picciol tempo
di quel che Prato, non ch'altri, t'agogna.
E se già fosse, non sarìa per tempo: 10
così foss'ei, da che pur esser dee!
chè più mi graverà, com più m'attempo.
Noi ci partimmo, e su per le scalee
che n'avean fatte i borni a scender pria,
rimontò 'l duca mio e trasse mee;
e proseguendo la solinga via,
tra le schegge e tra' rocchi dello scoglio
lo piè sanza la man non si spedìa.
Allor mi dolsi, e ora mi ridoglio
quando drizzo la mente a ciò ch' io vidi, 20
e più lo 'ngegno affreno ch' i' non soglio,
perchè non corra che virtù nol guidi;
sì che, se stella bona o miglior cosa
m' ha dato 'l ben, ch' io stessi nol m' invidi.
Quante il villan ch'al poggio si riposa,
nel tempo che colui che 'l mondo schiara
la faccia sua a noi tien meno ascosa,
come la mosca cede a la zanzara,
vede lucciole giù per la vallea,
forse colà dov' e' vendemmia ed ara; 30

CANTO XXVI

The Eighth Bolgia; the False Counsellors; Ulysses

REJOICE, Florence, since thou art so great that over land and sea thou beatest thy wings and through Hell thy name is spread abroad! Among the thieves I found five such citizens of thine that shame for them comes on me and thou risest not to great honour by them. But if near morning our dreams are true, thou shalt feel ere long that which Prato,[1] not to say others, craves for thee; and were it come already it would not be too soon. Would it were, since indeed it must, for it will weigh the more on me the more I age.

We set out, and, on the stairs which the projecting rocks had made for our descent before, my Leader mounted again and drew me up, and, following the lonely way among the rocks and splinters of the ridge, the foot made no speed without the hand.

I grieved then and grieve now anew when I turn my mind to what I saw, and more than I am wont I curb my powers lest they run where virtue does not guide them, so that, if favouring star or something better have granted me such boon, I may not grudge it to myself.

As many as the fire-flies which the peasant resting on the hill—in the season when he that lights the world least hides his face from us and at the hour when the fly gives place to the gnat[2]—sees along the valley below, in the fields, perhaps, where he gathers the grapes and tills; with so many

di tante fiamme tutta risplendea
l'ottava bolgia, sì com' io m'accorsi
tosto che fui là 've 'l fondo parea.
E qual colui che si vengiò con li orsi
vide 'l carro d'Elia al dipartire,
quando i cavalli al cielo erti levorsi,
che nol potea sì con li occhi seguire,
ch'el vedesse altro che la fiamma sola,
sì come nuvoletta, in su salire;
tal si move ciascuna per la gola 40
del fosso, chè nessuna mostra il furto,
e ogni fiamma un peccatore invola.
Io stava sovra 'l ponte a veder surto,
sì che s' io non avessi un ronchion preso,
caduto sarei giù sanz'esser urto.
E 'l duca, che mi vide tanto atteso,
disse: 'Dentro dai fuochi son li spirti;
ciascun si fascia di quel ch'elli è inceso.'
'Maestro mio,' rispuos' io 'per udirti
son io più certo; ma già m'era avviso 50
che così fosse, e già voleva dirti:
chi è in quel foco che vien sì diviso
di sopra, che par surger della pira
dov' Eteòcle col fratel fu miso?'
Rispuose a me: 'Là dentro si martira
Ulisse e Dïomede, e così inseme
alla vendetta vanno come all' ira;
e dentro dalla lor fiamma si geme
l'agguato del caval che fè la porta
onde uscì de' Romani il gentil seme. 60
Piangevisi entro l'arte per che, morta,
Deïdamìa ancor si duol d'Achille,
e del Palladio pena vi si porta.'
'S'ei posson dentro da quelle faville
parlar,' diss' io 'maestro, assai ten priego
e ripriego, che il priego vaglia mille,
che non mi facci dell'attender niego
fin che la fiamma cornuta qua vegna:
vedi che del disio ver lei mi piego!'

flames the eighth ditch was all gleaming, as I perceived as soon as I came where the bottom was in sight. And as he that was avenged by the bears saw the chariot of Elijah at his departure when the horses reared and rose to heaven, who could not follow it with his eyes so as to see anything but the flame alone like a little cloud mounting up;[3] so each flame moves along the gullet of the ditch, for none shows the theft and every one steals away a sinner.

I was standing on the bridge, having risen up to see, so that if I had not taken hold of a rock I should have fallen below without a push; and my Leader, who saw me so intent, said: 'Within the flames are the spirits; each is swathed in that which burns him.'

'My Master,' I replied 'by hearing thee I am more certain, but already I thought it was so, and I already wished to ask thee who is in that fire which comes so cloven at the top that it seems to rise from the pyre where Eteocles was laid with his brother.'[4]

He answered me: 'Within there are tormented Ulysses and Diomed, and thus together they go under vengeance as once under wrath, and within their flame they groan for the ambush of the horse that made the gateway by which the noble seed of the Romans went forth; they lament within it the craft on account of which Deidamia dead still mourns Achilles, and there is borne the penalty for the Palladium.'[5]

'If they are able to speak within these lights,' I said 'I earnestly pray thee, Master, and pray again that my prayer avail a thousandfold that thou do not forbid me to stay till the horned flame comes near; thou seest how I bend toward it with desire.'

Ed elli a me: 'La tua preghiera è degna 70
di molta loda, e io però l'accetto;
ma fa che la tua lingua si sostegna.
Lascia parlare a me, ch' i' ho concetto
ciò che tu vuoi; ch'ei sarebbero schivi,
perchè fuor greci, forse del tuo detto.'
Poi che la fiamma fu venuta quivi
dove parve al mio duca tempo e loco,
in questa forma lui parlare audivi:
'O voi che siete due dentro ad un foco,
s' io meritai di voi mentre ch' io vissi, 80
s' io meritai di voi assai o poco
quando nel mondo li alti versi scrissi,
non vi movete; ma l' un di voi dica
dove per lui perduto a morir gissi.'
Lo maggior corno della fiamma antica
cominciò a crollarsi mormorando
pur come quella cui vento affatica;
indi la cima qua e là menando,
come fosse la lingua che parlasse,
gittò voce di fuori, e disse: 'Quando 90
mi diparti' da Circe, che sottrasse
me più d'un anno là presso a Gaeta,
prima che sì Enea la nomasse,
nè dolcezza di figlio, nè la pièta
del vecchio padre, nè 'l debito amore
lo qual dovea Penelopè far lieta,
vincer poter dentro da me l'ardore
ch' i' ebbi a divenir del mondo esperto,
e delli vizi umani e del valore;
ma misi me per l'alto mare aperto 100
sol con un legno e con quella compagna
picciola dalla qual non fui diserto.
L' un lito e l'altro vidi infin la Spagna,
fin nel Morrocco, e l' isola de' Sardi,
e l'altre che quel mare intorno bagna.
Io e' compagni eravam vecchi e tardi
quando venimmo a quella foce stretta
dov' Ercule segnò li suoi riguardi,

And he said to me: 'Thy prayer deserves much praise, therefore I consent to it. But do thou restrain thy tongue. Leave it to me to speak, for I have understood what thou wishest; for perhaps, since they were Greeks, they would disdain thy speech.'

After the flame had come where it seemed to my Leader the time and place I heard him speak in these words: 'O ye who are two within one fire, if I deserved of you while I lived, if I deserved of you much or little when in the world I wrote the lofty lines, do not move on, but let the one of you tell where, being lost, he went to die.'

The greater horn of the ancient flame began to toss and murmur just as if it were beaten by the wind, then, waving the point to and fro as if it were the tongue that spoke, it flung forth a voice and said: 'When I parted from Circe,[6] who held me more than a year near Gaeta before Aeneas so named it, not fondness for a son, nor duty to an aged father, nor the love I owed Penelope[7] which should have gladdened her, could conquer within me the passion I had to gain experience of the world and of the vices and the worth of men; and I put forth on the open deep with but one ship and with that little company which had not deserted me. The one shore and the other I saw as far as Spain, as far as Morocco, and Sardinia and the other islands which that sea bathes round. I and my companions were old and slow when we came to that narrow outlet where Hercules set up his

acciò che l'uom più oltre non si metta:
dalla man destra mi lasciai Sibilia, 110
dall'altra già m'avea lasciata Setta.
"O frati," dissi "che per cento milia
perigli siete giunti all'occidente,
a questa tanto picciola vigilia
de' nostri sensi ch'è del rimanente,
non vogliate negar l'esperïenza,
di retro al sol, del mondo sanza gente.
Considerate la vostra semenza:
fatti non foste a viver come bruti,
ma per seguir virtute e canoscenza." 120
Li miei compagni fec' io sì aguti,
con questa orazion picciola, al cammino,
che a pena poscia li avrei ritenuti;
e volta nostra poppa nel mattino,
dei remi facemmo ali al folle volo,
sempre acquistando dal lato mancino.
Tutte le stelle già dell'altro polo
vedea la notte, e 'l nostro tanto basso
che non surgea fuor del marin suolo.
Cinque volte racceso e tante casso 130
lo lume era di sotto dalla luna,
poi che 'ntrati eravam nell'alto passo,
quando n'apparve una montagna, bruna
per la distanza, e parvemi alta tanto
quanto veduta non avea alcuna.
Noi ci allegrammo, e tosto tornò in pianto;
chè della nova terra un turbo nacque,
e percosse del legno il primo canto.
Tre volte il fè girar con tutte l'acque:
alla quarta levar la poppa in suso 140
e la prora ire in giù, com'altrui piacque,
infin che 'l mar fu sopra noi richiuso.'

landmarks so that men should not pass beyond.[8] On my right hand I left Seville, on the other had already left Ceuta. "O brothers," I said "who through a hundred thousand perils have reached the west, to this so brief vigil of the senses that remains to us choose not to deny experience, in the sun's track, of the unpeopled world. Take thought of the seed from which you spring. You were not born to live as brutes, but to follow virtue and knowledge." My companions I made so eager for the road with these brief words that then I could hardly have held them back, and with our poop turned to the morning we made of the oars wings for the mad flight, always gaining on the left. Night then saw all the stars of the other pole and ours so low that it did not rise from the ocean floor. Five times the light had been rekindled and as often quenched on the moon's under-side since we had entered on the deep passage, when there appeared to us a mountain, dim by distance, and it seemed to me of such a height as I had never seen before. We were filled with gladness, and soon it turned to lamentation, for from the new land a storm rose and struck the forepart of the ship. Three times it whirled her round with all the waters, the fourth time lifted the poop aloft and plunged the prow below, as One willed, until the sea closed again over us.'

1. A possible reference to the rebellion of Prato against Florence, to which it was then subject.

2. On a midsummer evening.

3. Elisha saw the ascension of Elijah by 'a chariot of fire and horses of fire'; he was mocked by the children, who were devoured by bears (2 *Kings* ii. 11, 23–24).

4. Two sons of Oedipus, King of Thebes, were rivals and killed each other; their bodies being burned together the flames divided.

5. Ulysses and Diomed, Greek chiefs in the Trojan War, beguiled Achilles to desert Deidamia and join them, concealing the prophecy of his death; their theft of the sacred image of Pallas Athene, the 'Palladium' of Troy, was reckoned fatal to the city and their device of the wooden horse led to the fall of Troy and the escape of Aeneas and his followers to Italy.

6. Enchantress charming men into beasts.

7. Wife of Ulysses.

8. The Pillars of Hercules, the supposed limit of the habitable world, were Gibraltar and Mount Abyla in Africa.

NOTE

In the last canto, from the moment when the familiar Florentine name of Cianfa caught Dante's ear, one thief after another was named, the one by the other, and it turns out, as if by no choice of the Poet but by undesigned accumulation, that all five of them were nobles of Florence, known to Dante. It is as if he could no longer restrain himself when he breaks silence here—as narrator, not as traveller—in his apostrophe to Florence, a blend of ironical praise with scorn and shame and warning and grief. His morning dream is of the world's new age and if that is to come Florence must suffer. What is here set down as prophecy had reference probably to prospective events in Florence later than the writing of these lines and to his hopes for Italy and the world in the recently elected Emperor Henry VII.

The eighth bolgia is that of the evil counsellors, those who have used their high mental gifts for guile, and because of their higher endowment their sin is reckoned greater and their place is lower than that of the thieves. At the sight and thought of them Dante grieves over the vast mis-spending and waste of human greatness. Knowing his own gifts and aware of the dangers of his day for such a man as he, whose counsel was sought in the affairs of Italy, he is warned and 'curbs his powers', taking hold of a rock so as not to fall into this ditch. The main thought is that great mental powers are a great trust and that the expending of them on ends which are not God's is treason and disaster.

The penalty of false counsel may have been suggested by the language of the *Epistle of James*: 'Behold, how great a matter a little fire kindleth! And the tongue is a fire, a world of iniquity: so is the tongue among our members, that it defileth the whole body, and setteth on fire the course of nature:

and it is set on fire of hell.' Of the flames in the ditch 'none showed the theft and every one stole away a sinner'; for the sin is the fraudulent and injurious concealment of the mind, the man's tongue used to conceal the man himself. In false counsel the man *steals himself* from his fellows and the measure of his theft is the power of his counsel. The abuse of such a gift is a kind of sacrilege, punished with the flaming tongue which is the sin itself; 'each is swathed in that which burns him.' It is Dante's version of the words of the *Book of Job* and of St Paul: 'He taketh the wise in their own craftiness.'

On his first sight of the false counsellors Dante compares them with fire-flies seen in a valley from the hill above, for their innumerable insignificance—of so much account, from any height of sanity, are their schemes and concealments now—and with Elijah, the bold and faithful counsellor ascending to heaven in fiery triumph, in contrast with these frustrate ghosts below imprisoned in their flames. In this context Elisha is described as 'he that was avenged by the bears', not with irrelevant wordiness, but for vindication of the succession of true prophecy.

Dante's great story of the last voyage of Ulysses, merely suggested by hints in classical and medieval literature, is essentially an invention of his own, which inspired what are perhaps Tennyson's finest lines. Everything is done to heighten the dignity of Ulysses. When Dante first hears his name he is passionately eager to wait for him. Not Dante himself, the modern Italian—and he was not a humble man—but Virgil, the ancient and greater poet who took for his model the old heroic story, is worthy to speak with the Greek heroes, men of the primeval world, and he does so with studied courtesy and deference. Ulysses makes no personal response to Virgil and does not name either of the poets; he only tells of his own last days, and that with an absorbed passion and in tones of pride and daring in which he lives through them all again from his first resolve to his last hour. The voice is 'flung forth' from the flame and begins without preface as if by the force itself of the remembrance that is always with him. It is 'a brief, condensed, epic story, defining his character with amazing power and exalting it at the same time to be a symbol of sublime humanity, making of it one of those great and rare creations in which the particular shines with so clear a light that it assumes a universal significance' (*V. Rossi*)—the significance, namely, of an eternal and insatiable human hunger and quest after knowledge of the world; and as we read it we forget the sin in contemplation of the sinner's greatness. 'No one of his age was more deeply moved than Dante by the passion to know all that is knowable, and nowhere else has he given such noble expression to that noble passion as in the great figure of Ulysses' (*B. Croce*).

There is much here of the same intimate dramatic identification of the poet himself with a doomed soul as we found in the fifth canto and as we shall find again in the thirty-third. Francesca and Ulysses, different in all else, are alike in their committal to a passion which commands them like a fate, in which they still have their life, a life all of remembrance, and which makes them burn and shine with an equal splendour in the gloom of Hell.

How is it that Dante has at once so glorified Ulysses and so condemned him? There is here conspicuously a tension and unresolved conflict in Dante's mind between the poet and the medieval theologian, more properly between two ideals and motives; on the one hand, of sheer human craving and daring to know all that man, at every mortal cost, can attain to know, and, on the other, of the submission of the spirit to the deeper and still costlier discipline of obedience to providence and to grace. Here, if anywhere, Dante's imagination beats at the bars of his day and creed.

This is the story, as Dante intends it, of an evil counsellor, wrapt, while he tells it, in his tongue of flame—the word *within* is, in Dante's manner, repeated seven times. For Dante, Ulysses was a chief enemy of 'the noble seed of the Romans' which went forth from Troy, an enemy, that is, and unwilling instrument, of God's ordering of humanity. He is described in the *Aeneid* as 'the contriver of crimes'. His great achievements in the war were the achievements of his guile, in which he involved Diomed, his friend, now suffering with him in the same flame; he broke away from all the honourable ties of home, separating himself from the human fellowship, and passed the bounds set for man, tempted, and then driven, by his greatness to his fate; by the example of his own daring and by appeal to their loyalty and heroism he beguiled his companions to join him in his 'mad flight, always gaining on the left'—in the *Paradiso* Dante looks down from the heavens on 'the mad track of Ulysses'; they approached the island-mountain of Purgatory, the place of penitence and redemption—for so the 'new land' is to be understood—but these are no penitents and its gifts are not for them; it is 'from it' that the storm rose so that they could not reach it and their voyage ended in desperate futility and death—an end which 'One willed', for, except in Fucci's blasphemy, God cannot be named by the lost. It is the greatness of Ulysses that makes his doom so overwhelming, and such greatness and such doom together give to this canto more than any other in the *Inferno* of the quality and power of high tragedy. The lofty spirit, uttering its undying memories from within its narrow, flaming prison, telling of its own ranging through the unknown world 'in the sun's track' by the urgency of its hunger for knowledge and experience, and of its end, leaving no trace, is one of the most moving and majestic figures in the *Divine Comedy*.

INFERNO

GIÀ era dritta in su la fiamma e queta
per non dir più, e già da noi sen gìa
con la licenza del dolce poeta,
quand' un'altra, che dietro a lei venìa,
ne fece volger li occhi a la sua cima
per un confuso suon che fuor n'uscìa.
Come 'l bue cicilian che mugghiò prima
col pianto di colui, e ciò fu dritto,
che l'avea temperato con sua lima,
mugghiava con la voce dell'afflitto, 10
sì che, con tutto che fosse di rame,
pur el parea dal dolor trafitto;
così, per non aver via nè forame
dal principio nel foco, in suo linguaggio
si convertìan le parole grame.
Ma poscia ch'ebber colto lor vïaggio
su per la punta, dandole quel guizzo
che dato avea la lingua in lor passaggio,
udimmo dire: 'O tu a cu' io drizzo
la voce e che parlavi mo lombardo, 20
dicendo "Istra ten va; più non t'adizzo",
perch' io sia giunto forse alquanto tardo,
non t' incresca restare a parlar meco:
vedi che non incresce a me, e ardo!
Se tu pur mo in questo mondo cieco
caduto se' di quella dolce terra
latina ond' io mia colpa tutta reco,
dimmi se i Romagnuoli han pace o guerra;
ch' io fui de' monti là intra Urbino
e 'l giogo di che Tever si diserra.' 30

CANTO XXVII

Guido da Montefeltro

Already the flame was erect and still, having ceased to speak, and it was already leaving us with consent of the gentle Poet, when another coming on behind it made us turn our eyes to its point by a confused sound that came from it. As the Sicilian bull which bellowed for the first time—and it was just—with the cry of him who had shaped it with his file used to bellow with the voice of the victim, so that, though it was of brass, it yet seemed pierced with pain;[1] thus, having at first no course or outlet in the fire, the doleful words were transformed into its language. But after they had made their way up through the point, giving it the same vibration that the tongue had given in their passage, we heard it say: 'O thou to whom I direct my voice and who just now spoke in Lombard,[2] saying: "Now go thy way, I do not urge thee more", though I have come, perhaps, somewhat late, let it not irk thee to stay and speak with me; thou seest it irks not me, and I am burning. If thou hast fallen but now into this blind world from that sweet land of Italy whence I bring all my guilt, tell me if the Romagnoles have peace or war; for I was of the mountains there between Urbino and the height where Tiber is released.'[3]

Io era in giuso ancora attento e chino,
quando il mio duca mi tentò di costa,
dicendo: 'Parla tu; questi è latino.'
E io, ch'avea già pronta la risposta,
sanza indugio a parlare incominciai:
'O anima che se' là giù nascosta,
Romagna tua non è, e non fu mai,
sanza guerra ne' cuor de' suoi tiranni;
ma 'n palese nessuna or vi lasciai.
Ravenna sta come stata è molt'anni: 40
l'aguglia da Polenta la si cova,
sì che Cervia ricuopre co' suoi vanni.
La terra che fè già la lunga prova
e di Franceschi sanguinoso mucchio,
sotto le branche verdi si ritrova;
e 'l mastin vecchio e 'l nuovo da Verrucchio,
che fecer di Montagna il mal governo,
là dove soglion fan de' denti succhio.
Le città di Lamone e di Santerno
conduce il lïoncel dal nido bianco, 50
che muta parte dalla state al verno.
E quella cu' il Savio bagna il fianco,
così com'ella sie' tra 'l piano e 'l monte
tra tirannia si vive e stato franco.
Ora chi se', ti priego che ne conte:
non esser duro più ch'altri sia stato,
se 'l nome tuo nel mondo tegna fronte.'
Poscia che 'l foco alquanto ebbe rugghiato
al modo suo, l'aguta punta mosse
di qua, di là, e poi diè cotal fiato: 60
'S' i' credesse che mia risposta fosse
a persona che mai tornasse al mondo,
questa fiamma starìa sanza più scosse;
ma però che già mai di questo fondo
non tornò vivo alcun, s' i' odo il vero,
sanza tema d' infamia ti rispondo.
Io fui uom d'arme, e poi fui cordigliero,
credendomi, sì cinto, fare ammenda;
e certo il creder mio venìa intero,

I was still bent down and intent when my Leader touched me on the side and said: 'Speak thou; he is Italian.'

And I, being at once ready with the answer, began without delay to speak: 'O soul that art hidden down there, thy Romagna is not, nor ever was, without war in the hearts of her tyrants, but openly I left none there now. Ravenna stands as it has done for many a year; the Eagle of Polenta broods over it and covers Cervia with its pinions. The city which once bore long siege and made of the French a bloody heap finds itself again under the Green Claws. Both the Old and the Young Mastiff of Verrucchio who made ill disposal of Montagna drive their fangs where they are wont. The cities on the Lamone and on the Santerno the Young Lion in the White Lair controls, changing party from summer to winter; and the other whose flank the Savio bathes, as it lies between plain and mountain spends its life between tyranny and freedom.[4] Now who art thou, I beg of thee to tell us; be not more grudging than another has been to thee, so may thy name in the world maintain its place.'

After the fire had roared in its fashion for a time, it moved the sharp point to and fro and then gave breath thus: 'If I thought my answer were to one who would ever return to the world, this flame should stay without another movement; but since none ever returned alive from this depth, if what I hear is true, I answer thee without fear of infamy.

'I was a man of arms, and then a corded friar,[5] thinking, so girt, to make amends; and indeed my

se non fosse il gran prete, a cui mal prenda!, 70
che mi rimise nelle prime colpe;
e come e quare, voglio che m' intenda.
Mentre ch' io forma fui d'ossa e di polpe
che la madre mi diè, l'opere mie
non furon leonine, ma di volpe.
Li accorgimenti e le coperte vie
io seppi tutte, e sì menai lor arte,
ch'al fine della terra il suono uscìe.
Quando mi vidi giunto in quella parte
di mia etade ove ciascun dovrebbe 80
calar le vele e raccoglier le sarte,
ciò che pria mi piacea, allor m' increbbe,
e pentuto e confesso mi rendei,
ahi miser lasso!, e giovato sarebbe.
Lo principe de' novi Farisei,
avendo guerra presso a Laterano,
e non con Saracin nè con Giudei,
chè ciascun suo nimico era Cristiano,
e nessun era stato a vincer Acri
nè mercatante in terra di Soldano; 90
nè sommo officio nè ordini sacri
guardò in sè, nè in me quel capestro
che solea fare i suoi cinti più macri.
Ma come Costantin chiese Silvestro
d'entro Siratti a guerir della lebbre;
così mi chiese questi per maestro
a guerir della sua superba febbre:
domandommi consiglio, e io tacetti,
perchè le sue parole parver ebbre.
E' poi ridisse: "Tuo cuor non sospetti; 100
finor t'assolvo, e tu m' insegna fare
sì come Penestrino in terra getti.
Lo ciel poss' io serrare e diserrare,
come tu sai; però son due le chiavi
che 'l mio antecessor non ebbe care."
Allor mi pinser li argomenti gravi
là 've 'l tacer mi fu avviso il peggio,
e dissi: "Padre, da che tu mi lavi

thought had come true but for the Great Priest[6] —may ill befall him!—who put me back in the old sins, and how and wherefore I would have thee hear from me. While I informed the bones and flesh my mother gave me my deeds were those, not of the lion, but of the fox; I knew all wiles and covert ways and so practised their arts that their sound went forth to the end of the world. When I saw myself come to that part of my life when every man should lower the sails and gather in the ropes, that which before had pleased me then grieved me and with repentance and confession I turned friar, and—woe is me!—it would have served. The Prince of the new Pharisees—being at war near the Lateran and not with Saracens or Jews, for every one of his enemies was Christian and none had been at the taking of Acre or trading in the land of the Soldan[7]—regarded neither the supreme office and holy orders in himself nor, in me, that cord which used to make its wearers lean; but as Constantine sought out Sylvester in Soracte to cure his leprosy,[8] so this man sought me out as his physician to cure the fever of his pride. He asked counsel of me, and I was silent, for his words seemed drunken; and then he spoke again: "Do not let thy heart mistrust; I absolve thee henceforth, and do thou teach me how I may cast Palestrina to the ground. I have power to lock and to unlock Heaven, as thou knowest, for the keys are two which my predecessor did not hold dear."[9] Then the weighty arguments drove me to the point where silence seemed to me the worse offence, and I said: "Father, since thou dost cleanse me from

di quel peccato ov' io mo cader deggio,
  lunga promessa con l'attender corto 110
  ti farà triunfar nell'alto seggio."
Francesco venne poi, com' io fu' morto,
  per me; ma un de' neri cherubini
  li disse: "Non portar: non mi far torto.
Venir se ne dee giù tra' miei meschini,
  perchè diede il consiglio frodolente,
  dal quale in qua stato li sono a' crini;
ch'assolver non si può chi non si pente,
  nè pentère e volere insieme puossi
  per la contradizion che nol consente." 120
Oh me dolente! come mi riscossi
  quando mi prese dicendomi: "Forse
  tu non pensavi ch' ïo loico fossi!"
A Minòs mi portò; e quelli attorse
  otto volte la coda al dosso duro;
  e poi che per gran rabbia la si morse,
disse: "Questi è de' rei del foco furo";
  per ch' io là dove vedi son perduto,
  e sì vestito, andando, mi rancuro.'
Quand'elli ebbe 'l suo dir così compiuto, 130
  la fiamma dolorando si partìo,
  torcendo e dibattendo il corno aguto.
Noi passamm'oltre, e io e 'l duca mio,
  su per lo scoglio infino in su l'altr'arco
  che cuopre il fosso in che si paga il fio
a quei che scommettendo acquistan carco.

1. Phalaris, tyrant of Sicily, roasted his victims in a brazen bull made for him by Perillus, who was the first to suffer in it.

2. Virgil, being of Lombardy, is here supposed to speak the Lombard dialect, to which the word *istra* (*now*) which he uses may belong.

3. Guido, Count of Montefeltro, head of the Ghibellines in Romagna and a distinguished soldier in Dante's time; he died in 1298.

4. The rulers of some of the chief cities of Romagna are indicated, partly by their armorial bearings.

5. A Franciscan.

6. Pope Boniface VIII.

this sin into which I must now fall, large promise with scant observance will make thee triumph in the lofty seat." Then, as soon as I was dead, Francis came for me; but one of the black cherubim said to him: "Do not carry him off, do not cheat me; he must come down among my minions because he gave the fraudulent counsel and from then till now I have been by his hair. For he cannot be absolved who repents not, nor can there be repenting and willing at once, for the contradiction does not permit it." O wretched me, how I started when he took me, saying to me: "Perhaps thou didst not think I was a logician." He carried me to Minos, who coiled his tail eight times about his rough back and after biting it in great rage said: "This is one of the wicked for the thievish fire." Therefore I am lost where thou seest and, thus clothed, go in bitterness.'

When he had so ended his words the flame, grieving, departed, twisting and tossing the pointed horn.

We passed on, my Leader and I, over the ridge as far as the next arch, which spans the ditch where their dues are paid by those who, making division, gather their load.

7. Boniface was at feud with the Colonna, whose stronghold was Palestrina near Rome and who had surrendered on terms to the Papal forces; on Guido's advice Boniface broke faith and destroyed Palestrina. Acre, the last stronghold of the Christians in Palestine. fell to the Saracens in 1291, to the scandal of Christendom. An earlier pope had forbidden Christians to trade with Moslems, and Guido means that none of the Pope's Christian enemies had been contumacious.

8. Constantine, punished with leprosy for persecution of Christians, was directed in a dream to recall Pope Sylvester from his refuge in Mount Soracte and, on his conversion, was cured.

9. Pope Celestine V, who 'made the great refusal' (Canto iii).

NOTE

The unexpected image at the beginning of the canto of the Sicilian bull in which its maker was the first to suffer ('and it was just', Dante interjects) suggests the ferocious complacency of the artificer intent, like the false counsellor, on his ingenious operations, devising ill for others and in the end destroying himself, 'taken in his own craftiness'.

Count Guido of Montefeltro, one of the conspicuous figures of thirteenth century Italy and the dominating personality in Romagna during Dante's young manhood, is helpless now for war as for policy, shut up in his flame and reduced to asking a passing stranger for news of his own country, which is still heaving like a troubled sea under brutal and warring tyrannies. For his skill both in war and in affairs Guido was widely known as 'the Fox'. He fought repeatedly as leader of the Ghibelline forces against the Papacy and was excommunicated, and his declared penitence and reconciliation to the Church and his adoption of the austere life of a monk in his last years added a halo to his name. In the *Convito* Dante mentioned him as 'our most noble Italian', perhaps before he knew of Guido's last offence; for it was apparently only after his death that his share in the Pope's fraud came out, and he tells his story only under the delusion that it cannot be known beyond the bounds of Hell.

Romagna was the part of Italy best known to Dante after his native Tuscany and he was 'at once ready with the answer' to Guido's question about it and runs over the particulars with easy familiarity. The so-called 'perpetual peace' in Romagna which Guido had helped to negotiate and about which he enquires of these strangers had lasted exactly a year when Dante spoke and was to last no longer. 'The Eagle of Polenta' —the ruler of Ravenna—was the father of Francesca of Rimini, and Dante's friendly regard for the family, his own protectors in his last years, is indicated in his language here about their benevolent government. 'The city which once bore long siege' is Forlì, which Guido delivered from the assault of the French by a famous victory in 1282. 'The Old and the Young Mastiff of Verrucchio' were, in succession, the cruel and oppressive rulers of Rimini, the father and the half-brother of Giovanni and Paolo Malatesta, who were the husband and the lover of Francesca (Canto v). 'How many images and scenes and pictures, of battles and of victories, of distresses and of triumphs, the voice that came down to Guido from the height of the bridge revived in his memory!' (*F. Torraca.*)

It is in the line of Dante's most characteristic irony that he should find the shrewdest man of his age, the Fox, tricked by the Pope to his damnation, cheated and caught like any fool by his own guile. He was after all only 'a half-baked knave, who did not understand the sacrilegious trickery of the expert in knavery' (*V. Rossi*). Here again as in the ninetenth canto, by the evidence of the damned themselves, Boniface, the reigning Pope, is the blackest villain of the piece. The spiritual head of Christendom is 'the Prince of the new Pharisees', the chief contemporary enemy of Christ, turning his high functions to the meanest ends, fighting for them against his neighbour Christians and heedless of Christ's real enemies and their conquests in Holy Land. For Dante was of the age which still regarded the Crusades as high and urgent Christian enterprises and the Pope's neglect of them in favour of his own struggle for power and possession as the dereliction of a sacred task. The Christian priest, seducing a penitent 'to cure the fever of his pride' by satisfying it, is compared with the pagan Emperor who in humility sought deliverance from his uncleanness at the hands of a true pope. Boniface's reference to his predecessor, who 'did not hold dear' the papal keys, is the gibe of the worldling who had 'taken by guile the Lady Beautiful' against the guileless devotee whom he supplanted in the 'lofty seat'. Recent enquiry seems to have established, if not the justice of Guido's—Dante's—charges against Boniface, at any rate the fact that such charges were widely current in Dante's time, and in particular that the stricter Franciscans were furious against Boniface. The charges were no invention of Dante's.

The idea of a struggle between a good and an evil spirit for possession of a human soul at death was familiar in medieval literature and art and may have arisen from the passage in the *Epistle of Jude* about Michael the archangel, 'when contending with the devil he disputed about the body of Moses'. The contest between saint and devil for Guido repeats and represents the contest that had taken place in Guido's own soul, and its result was strictly a foregone conclusion. St Francis here is not merely the historical and official head of the monastic order of which Guido was a member; he is the representative of the life of penitence and consecration which Guido had sincerely professed and later betrayed. And the 'black cherub' is not merely a devil in general; he is a fallen member of the second order of the angelic hierarchy whose peculiar glory consists in their knowledge of God, that is to say, their intellectual perfection. The black cherubim are fitted as no other devils could be to take to their doom those whose sin has been the abuse and betrayal of the high powers of the mind in false counsel. There is a spiritual logic which is unescapable and which even a devil can teach, and his arguments prove even more 'weighty' than the Pope's. In the issue between these forces of heaven and hell, the monkish cord and papal absolution—in particular, absolution given by Pope Boniface—are a mockery and a lie, adding their own bitterness to his doom. Minos's savage biting of his tail in passing judgement expresses the peculiar sting of Guido's remorse, the shame of the shrewd man who has over-reached himself in trying to make his profit of both worlds and has been beaten at his own game. An Italian proverb says that 'rogues are simpletons in the end'. 'The devil is irony incarnate; no man is such a knave that the devil is not more knave than he and we see that he is not disposed to put himself out of temper for the knaveries of men. One man may cheat another, but he cannot impose on the devil; for the devil is, in the poetic sense, the man himself, his conscience answering his sophistries with a great guffaw, countering his syllogism with another and making game of him—"Perhaps thou didst not think I was a logician" ' (*F. De Sanctis*).

CANTO XXVII

A deliberate complement and contrast to the story of Guido is that of his son Buonconte in the fifth canto of the *Purgatorio*.

These evil counsellors, thinking to lessen their guilt by sharing it, in fact add to their offence; 'making division' they 'gather their load'.

CHI porìa mai pur con parole sciolte
  dicer del sangue e delle piaghe a pieno
  ch' i' ora vidi, per narrar più volte?
Ogne lingua per certo verrìa meno
  per lo nostro sermone e per la mente
  c' hanno a tanto comprender poco seno.
S'el s'aunasse ancor tutta la gente
  che già in su la fortunata terra
  di Puglia fu del suo sangue dolente
per li Troiani e per la lunga guerra 10
  che dell'anella fè sì alte spoglie,
  come Livïo scrive, che non erra,
con quella che sentïo di colpi doglie
  per contastare a Ruberto Guiscardo;
  e l'altra il cui ossame ancor s'accoglie
a Ceperan, là dove fu bugiardo
  ciascun pugliese, e là da Tagliacozzo,
  dove sanz'arme vinse il vecchio Alardo;
e qual forato suo membro e qual mozzo
  mostrasse, d'aequar sarebbe nulla 20
  il modo della nona bolgia sozzo.
Già veggia, per mezzul perdere o lulla,
  com' io vidi un, così non si pertugia,
  rotto dal mento infin dove si trulla:
tra le gambe pendevan le minugia;
  la corata pareva e 'l tristo sacco
  che merda fa di quel che si trangugia.
Mentre che tutto in lui veder m'attacco,
  guardommi, e con le man s'aperse il petto,
  dicendo: 'Or vedi com' io mi dilacco! 30

CANTO XXVIII

The Ninth Bolgia; the Makers of discord; Mahomet; Piero da Medicina

WHO could ever tell, even with words untrammelled and the tale often repeated, of all the blood and the wounds I saw now? Surely every tongue would fail, for our speech and memory have not the capacity to take in so much. Were all the people assembled again who once in the fateful land of Apulia[1] bewailed their blood shed by the Trojans and in the long war which made the high-piled spoil of rings—as Livy writes who does not err—with those who suffered grievous strokes in the struggle with Robert Guiscard and those others whose bones are still in heaps at Ceperano where every Apulian was faithless, and there by Tagliacozzo where old Alardo conquered without arms;[2] and were one to show his wounded limb and another his cut off, it would be nothing to compare with the foul fashion of the ninth ditch.

No cask ever gapes by loss of end-board or stave like him I saw who was ripped from the chin to the part that breaks wind; between the legs hung the entrails; the vitals appeared, with the foul sack that makes excrement of what is swallowed. While I was all absorbed in the sight of him he looked at me and with his hands laid open his breast, saying: 'See now how I split myself; see how

vedi come storpiato è Maometto!
  Dinanzi a me sen va piangendo Alì,
  fesso nel volto dal mento al ciuffetto.
E tutti li altri che tu vedi qui,
  seminator di scandalo e di scisma
  fur vivi, e però son fessi così.
Un diavolo è qua dietro che n'accisma
  sì crudelmente, al taglio della spada
  rimettendo ciascun di questa risma,
quand'avem volta la dolente strada; 40
  però che le ferite son richiuse
  prima ch'altri dinanzi li rivada.
Ma tu chi se' che 'n su lo scoglio muse,
  forse per indugiar d' ire alla pena
  ch'è giudicata in su le tue accuse?'
'Nè morte 'l giunse ancor, nè colpa 'l mena'
  rispuose 'l mio maestro 'a tormentarlo;
  ma per dar lui esperïenza piena,
a me, che morto son, convien menarlo
  per lo 'nferno qua giù di giro in giro: 50
  e quest'è ver così com' io ti parlo.'
Più fuor di cento che, quando l'udiro,
  s'arrestaron nel fosso a riguardarmi,
  per maraviglia oblïando il martiro.
'Or dì a fra Dolcin dunque che s'armi,
  tu che forse vedra' il sole in breve,
  s'ello non vuol qui tosto seguitarmi,
sì di vivanda che stretta di neve
  non rechi la vittoria al Noarese,
  ch'altrimenti acquistar non sarìa leve.' 60
Poi che l'un piè per girsene sospese,
  Maometto mi disse esta parola;
  indi a partirsi in terra lo distese.
Un altro, che forata avea la gola
  e tronco il naso infin sotto le ciglia,
  e non avea mai ch' una orecchia sola,
ristato a riguardar per maraviglia
  con li altri, innanzi alli altri aprì la canna,
  ch'era di fuor d'ogni parte vermiglia,

Mahomet[3] is mangled! Before me goes Ali in tears, his face cleft from chin to forelock; and all the others thou seest here were in life sowers of scandal and schism and therefore are thus cloven. There is a devil behind here that decks us out thus cruelly, putting each of this kind to the edge of the sword again when we have passed round the doleful road; for the wounds have closed again before any comes again in front of him. But who art thou lingering on the ridge, perhaps to delay going to the penalty pronounced on thy own accusations?'[4]

'Neither has death yet reached him nor does guilt bring him for torment,' replied my Master 'but to give him full experience I, who am dead, must bring him down here through Hell from circle to circle; and this is as true as that I speak to thee.'

There were more than a hundred who, when they heard this, stopped in the ditch to look at me, in wonder forgetting the torment.

'Tell Fra Dolcino,[5] then, thou who wilt perhaps see the sun before long, to arm himself with victuals if he would not soon follow me here, so that stress of snow may not give the Novarese the victory which would else be hard to win.' When he had raised one foot to go on Mahomet said this to me, then set it on the ground and left us.

Another, who had his throat pierced, his nose cut off just under the eyebrows, and only one ear left, stopped with the rest to gaze in astonishment and before the others cleared his windpipe, which was all red outside, and said: 'O thou whom guilt

e disse: 'O tu cui colpa non condanna 70
e cu' io vidi in su terra latina,
se troppa simiglianza non m' inganna,
rimembriti di Pier da Medicina,
se mai torni a veder lo dolce piano
che da Vercelli a Marcabò dichina.
E fa sapere a' due miglior da Fano,
a messer Guido e anco ad Angiolello,
che se l'antiveder qui non è vano,
gittati saran fuor di lor vasello
e mazzerati presso alla Cattolica 80
per tradimento d' un tiranno fello.
Tra l' isola di Cipri e di Maiolica
non vide mai sì gran fallo Nettuno,
non da pirate, non da gente argolica.
Quel traditor che vede pur con l' uno,
e tien la terra che tal è qui meco
vorrebbe di vedere esser digiuno,
farà venirli a parlamento seco;
poi farà sì ch'al vento di Focara
non sarà lor mestier voto nè preco.' 90
E io a lui: 'Dimostrami e dichiara,
se vuo' ch' i' porti su di te novella,
chi è colui dalla veduta amara.'
Allor puose la mano alla mascella
d'un suo compagno e la bocca li aperse,
gridando: 'Questi è desso, e non favella.
Questi, scacciato, il dubitar sommerse
in Cesare, affermando che 'l fornito
sempre con danno l'attender sofferse.'
Oh quanto mi parea sbigottito 100
con la lingua tagliata nella strozza
Curïo, ch'a dir fu così ardito!
E un ch'avea l'una e l'altra man mozza,
levando i moncherin per l'aura fosca,
sì che 'l sangue facea la faccia sozza,
gridò: 'Ricordera' ti anche del Mosca,
che dissi, lasso!, "Capo ha cosa fatta",
che fu 'l mal seme per la gente tosca.'

does not condemn and whom I saw above on Italian soil, if too great likeness do not deceive me, remember Piero da Medicina[6] if ever thou return to see the sweet plain that slopes from Vercelli to Marcabò, and make it known to the two chief men of Fano, both Messer Guido and Angiolello, that, unless our foresight here is vain, they shall be thrown out of their ship and drowned near La Cattolica through a fell tyrant's treachery.[7] Between the islands of Cyprus and Majorca Neptune never saw so great a crime, not of pirates nor of men of Greece. That traitor who sees with but one eye and holds the city which one here with me would fain never have seen will bring them to a parley with him and then deal so that for the wind of Focara they shall have no need of vow or prayer.'[8]

And I said to him: 'Point him out to me and explain, if thou wouldst have me carry news of thee above, who he is to whom that sight was bitter.'

Then he laid his hand on the jaw of one beside him and opened the mouth, crying: 'This is the man, and he does not speak; banished, he quenched Caesar's doubts, declaring that one prepared always loses by delay.' Ah, how aghast appeared to me, with tongue slit in the gullet, Curio, who was so bold of speech![9]

And one who had both the one hand and the other cut off, lifting the stumps through the murky air so that the blood befouled his face, cried: 'Thou wilt recall Mosca[10] too, who said, alas: "A thing done has an end!"—which was ill seed for the Tuscan people.'

E io li aggiunsi: 'E morte di tua schiatta';
perch'elli, accumulando duol con duolo, 110
sen gìo come persona trista e matta.
Ma io rimasi a riguardar lo stuolo,
e vidi cosa ch' io avrei paura,
sanza più prova, di contarla solo;
se non che coscïenza m'assicura,
la buona compagnia che l'uom francheggia
sotto l'asbergo del sentirsi pura.
Io vidi certo, ed ancor par ch' io 'l veggia,
un busto sanza capo andar sì come
andavan li altri della trista greggia; 120
e 'l capo tronco tenea per le chiome,
pèsol con mano a guisa di lanterna;
e quel mirava noi, e dicea: 'Oh me!'
Di sè facea a sè stesso lucerna,
ed eran due in uno e uno in due:
com'esser può, quei sa che sì governa.
Quando diritto al piè del ponte fue,
levò 'l braccio alto con tutta la testa,
per appressarne le parole sue,
che fuoro: 'Or vedi la pena molesta 130
tu che, spirando, vai veggendo i morti:
vedi s'alcuna è grande come questa.
E perchè tu di me novella porti,
sappi ch' i' son Bertram dal Bornio, quelli
che diedi al Re giovane i ma' conforti.
Io feci il padre e 'l figlio in sè ribelli:
Achitofèl non fè più d'Absalone
e di Davìd coi malvagi punzelli.
Perch' io parti' così giunte persone,
partito porto il mio cerebro, lasso!, 140
dal suo principio ch'è in questo troncone.
Così s'osserva in me lo contrapasso.'

'—and death to thy stock!' I added then; at which, heaping sorrow on sorrow, he went away like a man crazed with grief.

But I stayed to watch the troop and saw a thing I should fear simply to tell without more proof, but that conscience reassures me, the good companion which emboldens a man under the breastplate of his felt integrity. Verily I saw, and I seem to see it still, a trunk without a head going as were the others of the miserable herd; and it held the severed head by the hair swinging in its hand like a lantern, and that was looking at us and saying: 'Woe is me!' Of itself it made for itself a lamp, and they were two in one and one in two; how it can be He knows who so ordains. When it was just below the bridge it raised its arm high and with it the head so as to bring its words nearer us, and they were: 'See now my grievous punishment, thou who, breathing, goest looking on the dead; see if any other is so great as this. And, that thou mayst bear news of me, know that I am Bertran de Born, he that gave evil backing to the Young King.[11] I made rebellion between the father and the son; Ahithophel did no worse for Absalom and David with his wicked goadings.[12] Because I parted those so joined I carry my brain, alas, parted from its root in this trunk; thus is observed in me the retribution.'

INFERNO

1. 'Apulia' meant south Italy, 'fateful' for decisive battles.

2. The wars of the Trojans who landed under Aeneas; battles in the war with Carthage, in which Hannibal once gathered three bushels of rings from the Roman dead; the Norman war under Guiscard (11th century) against the Greeks and Saracens; and battles of the Empire in Dante's infancy.

3. Mahomet was believed to have been a Christian convert, a priest, a cardinal, an aspirant to the Papacy, then a renegade and schismatic. Ali, his son-in-law and fourth successor, was head of one party in the great Mahometan schism.

4. Canto v.

5. Head of the Apostolic Brothers, a sect supposed to teach community of goods and of women; in the hills near Novara they defied the Papal forces for more than a year but were starved out in time of snow, and Dolcino, with his supposed mistress, was burned alive in 1307.

6. A noble of the neighbourhood of Bologna.

7. The story, not confirmed, was that Malatestino, 'the Young Mastiff', one-eyed Lord of Rimini, got control of Fano by the murder of the two leaders of the opposite parties there in 1313.

8. They will be drowned before reaching that stormy point of the coast.

9. Curio, the time-serving Roman Tribune banished from the city, joined Caesar near Rimini and advised him to cross the Rubicon, beginning the Civil War.

10. Mosca (Canto vi) took a leading part in the family feud in Florence early in the 13th century which was regarded as the origin of the long party strife; a Buondelmonte jilted the daughter of one of the Amidei, and on the advice of Mosca quoted here Buondelmonte was murdered; in the end Mosca's family, the Lamberti, were exiled and wiped out.

11. Bertran de Born, Lord of Hautefort in Provence, famous noble and troubadour of the 12th century, wrote war-poems and a lament for Prince Henry, oldest son of Henry II of England; the Prince, already crowned consort and known as the Young King, is supposed to have been instigated by Bertran to his rebellion.

12. Ahithophel, Absalom's counsellor in his rebellion against King David (2 *Sam.* xv. 12; xvi. 20–xvii. 4).

NOTE

It is natural that the makers of division, the breakers up of the unity of mankind, should be found in the neighbourhood of the evil counsellors.

The long story of human strife suggested by the opening lines, with the accumulated horror of its battle-fields from the beginning of history to Dante's own day, is 'nothing to compare' with the scene here. It is but the outward manifestation of a deeper, darker evil, the root of bitterness in the souls of men, 'the woeful fatality of human discord' (*V. Rossi*), the persistent and multiplied treason to the human cause of the sins punished in the ninth ditch, where the vile carving of the sinners by the presiding devil discriminates among them according to their particular offences.

Islam was regarded as the main force of antichrist in the world of the time, the very spirit of disorder and dispeace, and Mahomet, especially in the character of the greatest renegade from Christianity, as historically the chief divider of humanity; and the comparison of his person to a burst wine-cask, and the butchery of him, described with deliberate coarseness of phrase, butchery completed, as it were, in Ali, express not only Dante's judgement of the enormity of Mahomet's crime, but the common reflection of Christendom on the barbarism and beastliness of an alien faith, regarded as a kind of reversal of Christianity. Any approach to a real historical judgement of Mahomet was, of course, wholly impossible for Dante and for his age, and the effrontery of Mahomet's action and the rudeness of his speech are the marks of a barbarian.

Mahomet supposes, with some satisfaction, that Dante too is a divider and schismatic, unless he is something worse, and Dante was doubtless so estimated by many of his contemporaries, especially for his criticism of the Church and frequent opposition to its policy and claims. Virgil's emphatic assertion of Dante's innocence, along with Dante's own claim, later in the canto, to his good conscience and felt integrity, may well be his reply to such a charge. For no one stood more persistently for the unity of mankind. That is what the Church and the Empire meant for him and his treatise on Empire is a long, reasoned plea for the essential organic unity of men. 'The whole universe is nothing else but a certain footprint of the divine excellence; therefore the human race is well and best disposed when, as far as may be, it is made like God. But the human race is made most like God when it is most one, for the true principle of unity is in Him alone; wherefore it is written: "Hear, O Israel, the Lord thy God is one"' (*De Monarchia*). It was his lofty sense of providence in human affairs in contrast with the actual crying disorders of the public and private life of the world, the division and bitterness and strife everywhere thwarting every divine purpose, that made him condemn so fiercely these makers of discord.

The unseen devil slashes the schismatics anew every time they pass round the circle—'again—again—again' in Mahomet's report—to mark how schism persists and renews itself. There is the same idea in Mahomet's reference to Fra Dolcino, the defiant schismatic, for so he was considered, against whom the Church organized a crusade and in whom the Prophet recognized, half-contemptuously, a kindred spirit; and in Piero's forecast, true or false, of Malatestino's treachery and in his exposure, with brutal gesture and speech, of Curio, as of a spiritual ancestor, who has lost the use of the tongue he once sold to the highest bidder. Dolcino's capture and death in 1307 were, of course, known to Dante when he wrote and, in the fiction, are foreknown to Mahomet, so that his warning to Dolcino is only a gibe.

It is obvious that Dante knew much more about Piero da Medicina than we do and had reasons unknown to us for finding him here. He is punished in the throat, through which he uttered his slanders, the nose, which he thrust into other people's business, and the ear, with which he listened for their secrets. It is the portrait of a malignant and mischievous busybody, and yet his nostalgia for the familiar, remembered places in

Lombardy which he names makes him for the moment a sympathetic figure.

Mosca, having in life raised his hands and the hands of many others in bloodshed, bloodshed which continued to plague Florence and the rest of Tuscany up to Dante's day, is now handless and befouled with his own blood, his sin returning on his head.

Bertran de Born, in life gay, gifted, famous—he is favourably mentioned more than once in Dante's prose writings—had broken by his instigations, Dante believed, the closest human tie, and in his horrifying death-in-life he embodies 'the retribution' which is the common law of Hell. The quality of the sinners seems to rise from figure to figure, from the brutal squalor of Mahomet to the strange dignity of Bertran, as if to show how the spirit of division submerges and ruins some of the noblest of mankind. In the canto 'religious schism lives, bloody and woeful, in Mahomet and Ali, vast civil war in Curio, petty war, interwoven with treacheries, of contemporary Italy in Piero da Medicina, private vendetta, extended and intensified in the accursed Guelf and Ghibelline divisions, in Mosca dei Lamberti, domestic discords which dismay even the fierce spirit of the Middle Ages and mark the very limit of human hatred, in Bertran de Born. And over all that variety of passions and crimes, over this perpetual slaughter of humanity in mutual rebellion, rises supreme, inscrutable and inexorable the justice of "the retribution", a fearful admonition from the pure conscience of the poet to the savages of that century of discord and bloodshed' (*V. Crescini,* quoted in *Casini-Barbi*).

LA molta gente e le diverse piaghe
avean le luci mïe sì inebriate,
che dello stare a piangere eran vaghe;
ma Virgilio mi disse: 'Che pur guate?
perchè la vista tua pur si soffolge
là giù tra l'ombre triste smozzicate?
Tu non hai fatto sì all'altre bolge:
pensa, se tu annoverar le credi,
che miglia ventidue la valle volge.
E già la luna è sotto i nostri piedi: 10
lo tempo è poco omai che n'è concesso,
e altro è da veder che tu non vedi.'
'Se tu avessi' rispuos' io appresso
'atteso alla cagion per ch' io guardava,
forse m'avresti ancor lo star dimesso.'
Parte sen giva, e io retro li andava,
lo duca, già faccendo la risposta,
e soggiugnendo: 'Dentro a quella cava
dov' io tenea or li occhi sì a posta,
credo ch' un spirto del mio sangue pianga 20
la colpa che là giù cotanto costa.'
Allor disse 'l maestro: 'Non si franga
lo tuo pensier da qui innanzi sovr'ello:
attendi ad altro, ed ei là si rimanga:
ch' io vidi lui a piè del ponticello
mostrarti, e minacciar forte col dito,
e udi 'l nominar Geri del Bello.
Tu eri allor sì del tutto impedito
sovra colui che già tenne Altaforte,
che non guardasti in là, sì fu partito.' 30

CANTO XXIX

The Tenth Bolgia; the Personators, Alchemists, etc.; Griffolino; Capocchio

THE many people and the strange wounds had made my eyes so drunken that they were fain to stay and weep; but Virgil said to me: 'What art thou still gazing at? Why does thy look still rest down there among the miserable maimed shades? Thou hast not done this at the other depths. Consider, if thou think to number them, that the valley goes twenty-two miles round and already the moon is beneath our feet. The time is now short that is allowed to us and there is more to see than thou seest here.'

'If thou hadst given heed to my reason for looking,' I answered then 'perhaps thou wouldst have granted me a longer stay.'

Meantime the Leader was going on, and I went after him, already making my reply, and I added: 'Within that den where I held my eyes so intently just now I think a spirit, one of my blood, weeps for the guilt that costs so much down there.'

Then said the Master: 'Let not thy thoughts be distracted about him henceforth, attend to other things and let him stay there; for I saw him below the bridge point at thee and threaten fiercely with his finger, and I heard him called Geri del Bello.[1] Thou wast then so wholly occupied with him who once held Hautefort that thou didst not look that way till he was gone.'

'O duca mio, la vïolenta morte
  che non li è vendicata ancor' diss' io
  'per alcun che dell'onta sia consorte,
fece lui disdegnoso; ond'el sen gìo
  sanza parlarmi, sì com' io estimo:
  ed in ciò m' ha el fatto a sè più pio.'
Così parlammo infino al luogo primo
  che dello scoglio l'altra valle mostra,
  se più lume vi fosse, tutto ad imo.
Quando noi fummo sor l' ultima chiostra 40
  di Malebolge, sì che i suoi conversi
  potean parere alla veduta nostra,
lamenti saettaron me diversi,
  che di pietà ferrati avean li strali;
  ond' io li orecchi con le man copersi.
Qual dolor fora, se delli spedali
  di Valdichiana tra 'l luglio e 'l settembre
  e di Maremma e di Sardigna i mali
fossero in una fossa tutti insembre,
  tal era quivi, e tal puzzo n' usciva 50
  qual suol venir delle marcite membre.
Noi discendemmo in su l' ultima riva
  del lungo scoglio, pur da man sinistra,
  e allor fu la mia vista più viva
giù ver lo fondo, là 've la ministra
  dell'alto sire, infallibil giustizia,
  punisce i falsador che qui registra
Non credo ch'a veder maggior tristizia
  fosse in Egina il popol tutto infermo,
  quando fu l'aere sì pien di malizia 60
che li animali, infino al picciol vermo,
  cascaron tutti, e poi le genti antiche,
  secondo che i poeti hanno per fermo,
si ristorar di seme di formiche;
  ch'era a veder per quella oscura valle
  languir li spirti per diverse biche.
Qual sovra 'l ventre, e qual sovra le spalle
  l'un dell'altro giacea, e qual carpone
  si trasmutava per lo tristo calle.

'O my Leader,' I said 'the violent death which is yet unavenged for him by any that is a partner in his shame made him indignant, and for that reason, as I judge, he went on without speaking to me, and by this he has made me more compassionate with him.'

We talked thus as far as the nearest point which shows the next valley from the ridge, had there been more light, right to the bottom. When we were above the last cloister of Malebolge so that its lay-brothers could be seen by us, strange lamentations assailed me that had their shafts barbed with pity, at which I covered my ears with my hands. As the pain would be if the diseases of the hospitals of Val di Chiana between July and September, and of the Maremma and Sardinia,[2] were all together in one ditch, such was it there, and such stench issued from it as is wont to come from festered limbs. We descended on to the last bank from the long ridge, still keeping to the left, and then my sight was clearer down into the depth, where the handmaid of the Sovereign Lord, unerring justice, punishes the counterfeiters whom she registers here. I do not think the sight of the whole people sick in Aegina was more pitiful, when the air was so full of corruption that all the animals, to the little worm, fell dead, and then, as the poets hold for certain, the ancient tribes were restored again from seed of ants,[3] than was the sight along that dark valley of the spirits languishing in divers heaps. One lay on his belly, one lay on the shoulders of another, and one shifted on all fours along the dismal way.

Passo passo andavam sanza sermone, 70
  guardando e ascoltando li ammalati,
  che non potean levar le lor persone.
Io vidi due sedere a sè poggiati,
  com'a scaldar si poggia tegghia a tegghia,
  dal capo al piè di schianze macolati;
e non vidi già mai menare stregghia
  a ragazzo aspettato dal segnorso,
  nè a colui che mal volentier vegghia,
come ciascun menava spesso il morso
  dell'unghie sopra sè per la gran rabbia 80
  del pizzicor, che non ha più soccorso;
e sì traevan giù l'unghie la scabbia,
  come coltel di scardova le scaglie
  o d'altro pesce che più larghe l'abbia.
'O tu che con le dita ti dismaglie,'
  cominciò 'l duca mio all' un di loro
  'e che fai d'esse tal volta tanaglie,
dinne s'alcun latino è tra costoro
  che son quinc'entro, se l'unghia ti basti
  etternalmente a cotesto lavoro.' 90
'Latin siam noi, che tu vedi sì guasti
  qui ambedue,' rispuose l'un piangendo;
  'ma tu chi se' che di noi dimandasti?'
E 'l duca disse: 'I' son un che discendo
  con questo vivo giù di balzo in balzo,
  e di mostrar lo 'nferno a lui intendo.'
Allor si ruppe lo comun rincalzo;
  e tremando ciascuno a me si volse
  con altri che l'udiron di rimbalzo.
Lo buon maestro a me tutto s'accolse, 100
  dicendo: 'Dì a lor ciò che tu vuoli';
  e io incominciai, poscia ch'ei volse:
'Se la vostra memoria non s' imboli
  nel primo mondo dall'umane menti,
  ma s'ella viva sotto molti soli,
ditemi chi voi siete e di che genti:
  la vostra sconcia e fastidiosa pena
  di palesarvi a me non vi spaventi.'

CANTO XXIX

Step by step we went without speech, watching and listening to the sick, who had not strength to raise themselves. I saw two sitting propped against each other as pan is propped on pan to warm, spotted from head to foot with scabs; and I never saw curry-comb plied by a stable-boy whose master waits for him or by one kept unwillingly awake as each plied on himself continually the bite of his nails for the great fury of the itch that has no other relief, and the nails were scraping off the scabs as the knife does the scales of the bream or other fish that has them larger.

'O thou that dismailest thyself with thy fingers' my Leader began to one of them 'and sometimes makest pincers of them, tell us if there is any Italian among those that are within there, so may thy nails serve thee forever in that employment.'

'We are Italians whom thou seest so disfigured, both of us here,' the one replied weeping 'but who art thou that enquirest of us?'

And the Leader said: 'I am one who descend from level to level with this living man, and my purpose is to show him Hell.'

Then their mutual support was broken and each turned toward me trembling, with others who overheard him.

The good Master drew close to me, saying: 'Tell them what thou wishest.' And, since he wished it, I began: 'So may your memory not pass from the minds of men in the former world but live on under many suns, tell me who you are and of what people; let not your foul and loathsome penalty make you fear to declare yourselves to me.'

'Io fui d'Arezzo, e Albero da Siena'
  rispuose l'un 'mi fè mettere al foco; 110
  ma quel per ch' io mori' qui non mi mena.
Vero è ch' i' dissi lui, parlando a gioco:
  I' mi saprei levar per l'aere a volo;
  e quei, ch'avea vaghezza e senno poco,
volle ch' i' li mostrassi l'arte; e solo
  perch' io nol feci Dedalo, mi fece
  ardere a tal che l'avea per figliuolo.
Ma nell'ultima bolgia delle diece
  me per l'alchimia che nel mondo usai
  dannò Minòs, a cui fallar non lece.' 120
E io dissi al poeta: 'Or fu già mai
  gente sì vana come la sanese?
  Certo non la francesca sì d'assai!'
Onde l'altro lebbroso, che m' intese,
  rispuose al detto mio: 'Tra'mene Stricca
  che seppe far le temperate spese,
e Niccolò che la costuma ricca
  del garofano prima discoperse
  nell'orto dove tal seme s'appicca;
e tra'ne la brigata in che disperse 130
  Caccia d'Ascian la vigna e la gran fronda,
  e l'Abbagliato suo senno proferse.
Ma perchè sappi chi sì ti seconda
  contra i Sanesi, aguzza ver me l'occhio,
  sì che la faccia mia ben ti risponda:
sì vedrai ch' io son l'ombra di Capocchio,
  che falsai li metalli con alchimia:
  e te dee ricordar, se ben t'adocchio,
com' io fui di natura buona scimia.'

1. A cousin of Dante's father, said to have made trouble in the Sachetti family, one of whom murdered him.

2. Places then notoriously unhealthy.

3. The island of Aegina, depopulated by pestilence, was repopulated by Jupiter transforming ants into men.

'I was of Arezzo,' the one replied 'and Albert of Siena had me put in the fire; but that which I died for does not bring me here. It is true I said to him, speaking in jest, that I knew how to raise myself through the air in flight, and he, being curious and of little wit, would have me show him the art; and only because I did not make him a Daedalus he had me burned by one who held him as a son.[4] But to the last ditch of the ten, for the alchemy I practised in the world, Minos, who may not err, condemned me.'

And I said to the Poet: 'Now was ever a people so light as the Sienese? Not the French, surely, by far.' At which the other leper, who heard what I said, rejoined: 'Except Stricca, pray, who knew how to spend in moderation, and Niccolo, who first devised the costly fashion of the clove in the garden where such seed takes root, and except the company in which Caccia of Asciano squandered the vineyard and the great forest and Blunderer displayed his wit.[5] But, that thou mayst know who thus seconds thee against the Sienese, sharpen thy looks on me so that my face may rightly answer thee, and thou shalt see then that I am the shade of Capocchio,[6] who counterfeited metals by alchemy; and thou must recall, if I make thee out aright, how good an ape I was of nature.'

4. Griffolino of Arezzo played on the credulity of Albert, said to have been the natural son of the Bishop, or the Inquisitor, of Siena, by whom Griffolino was burned as a magician. Daedalus invented human flight (Canto xvii).

5. Probably members of the Spendthrift Club, a notorious group of 12 Sienese youths in Dante's time; cp. Lano in Canto xiii. 'The fashion of the clove', an extravagant use of cloves in cooking which readily 'took root' in Siena.

6. Capocchio was burned alive in Siena for alchemy.

NOTE

Contemplating the disastrous and implacable divisions among men, their party furies and family feuds, Dante is 'fain to stay and weep', he is so dismayed and disabled, and not the less when he thinks of one of his own kin who shared that guilt and would involve him in it, and he is rebuked by Virgil for his momentary lethargy and defeat. Merely to linger and mourn over the world's strife and misery is surrender. 'The time is now short that is allowed to us and there is more to see than thou seest here'; and while they talked 'the Leader was going on and I went after him'.

Geri del Bello represents for Dante one of these hereditary blood-feuds which were running sores in the life of Italy and he acknowledges to Virgil the continued hold on his sympathy of his kinsman's unavenged death. There is in his mind a struggle 'between the religious duty of forgiveness, to which he is deeply and sincerely devoted, and an obscure sense of shame for his lack of will and of power to satisfy an obligation from which, according to the common thought and conscience, he could not withdraw, between the free judgement of reason —Virgil—and the sentiment of a man of the Middle Ages' (*V. Rossi*); but in that struggle reason prevails. It is one more example among so many of the moral tension in Dante which makes him, not a mere moral pattern but a living personality, in this as in so much else of the same stock as Bunyan's Pilgrim. As he represents himself here there is in him 'the old man, not abjured but assuaged, and there is the new man, not declared but victorious' (*N. Zingarelli*). The three figures in the scene at the beginning of the canto are representative— 'Virgil, of the ancient imperial civilization, of law and virtue, Geri, of the indiscipline and fury of the commune, Dante, of the nation reconciled and consolidated, renewing itself on the ancient order' (*N. Zingarelli*).

CANTO XXIX

The moon, whose setting was recorded at the end of the twentieth canto, is now just past full and directly beneath the travellers. It is after one p.m. of Holy Saturday, and their pilgrimage through Hell is, for some reason, limited to that day.

They come now to a meaner, paltrier class of sinners, mere 'lay-brothers' in their 'cloister' of Malebolge, tricksters and profiteers of fraud against whose lamentations Dante shuts his ears. They are like the sick tribes of Aegina whose place was filled again 'from seed of ants'. These falsifiers of things are a peculiarly abject and obnoxious crowd and mean and contemptuous comparisons are chosen for them. Addressing two of them Virgil adds a bitter jest to his question and it is only at Virgil's bidding, 'since he wished it', that Dante condescends to ask them who they are.

Griffolino and Capocchio are both punished for the practice of 'alchemy', and it has to be remembered that Aquinas sharply distinguished between two kinds of alchemy; on the one hand, the serious search for a method of transforming lower metals into gold and silver, an early stage of modern chemistry, and, on the other, a rascally quackery which throve on men's ignorance and greed. It is, of course, the latter that is punished here, the pretended production of the precious metals by tricks and mystifications, the art of Dousterswivel in *The Antiquary*. May the emphatic reference to 'the handmaid of the Sovereign Lord, unerring justice', who 'registers here' on earth the counterfeiters, mean that, however men are taken in, the distinction between the true and the false alchemist is plain to the divine judgement—just as 'Minos, who may not err', corrects the Bishop's, the Church's, condemnation of Griffolino for necromancy?

It was such a wealthy, wanton and frivolous society as that of Siena, and especially such a group in it as the Spendthrift Club, that offered the most fruitful field of operations for these 'apes of nature'. The studied elegance and aristocratic refinement of the life, as of the art, of thirteenth and fourteenth century Siena was apt to be despised by the more robust and bourgeois spirit of Florence and Dante does not miss his chance here or elsewhere.

The alchemists suffer from leprosy, which Dante mistakenly

associated with a violent itch. The penalty seems to represent, in the first place, their endless, fruitless, sordid activity in deception, and, in the second, their impious hocus-pocus with nature and masking of it in false appearances. The squalid trickery of the sin corresponds with the traditional uncleanness of the disease.

Nothing is known of Dante's relations with Capocchio and we are left to imagine the reasons for his refusal to respond to Capocchio's jocular and assured claim to old acquaintance. His contempt becomes savage when, in the next canto, he tells of the aggravation of Capocchio's misery.

INFERNO

NEL tempo che Iunone era crucciata
  per Semelè contra 'l sangue tebano,
  come mostrò una e altra fïata,
Atamante divenne tanto insano
  che, veggendo la moglie con due figli
  andar carcata da ciascuna mano,
gridò: 'Tendiam le reti, sì ch' io pigli
  la leonessa e' leoncini al varco';
  e poi distese i dispietati artigli,
prendendo l'un ch'avea nome Learco, 10
  e rotollo e percosselo ad un sasso;
  e quella s'annegò con l'altro carco.
E quando la fortuna volse in basso
  l'altezza de' Troian che tutto ardiva,
  sì che 'nsieme col regno il re fu casso,
Ecuba trista, misera e cattiva,
  poscia che vide Polissena morta,
  e del suo Polidoro in su la riva
del mar si fu la dolorosa accorta,
  forsennata latrò sì come cane; 20
  tanto il dolor le fè la mente torta.
Ma nè di Tebe furie nè troiane
  si vider mai in alcun tanto crude,
  non punger bestie, non che membra umane,
quant' io vidi due ombre smorte e nude,
  che mordendo correvan di quel modo
  che 'l porco quando del porcil si schiude.
L' una giunse a Capocchio, ed in sul nodo
  del collo l'assannò, sì che, tirando,
  grattar li fece il ventre al fondo sodo. 30

CANTO XXX

Schicchi; Master Adam and Sinon

IN the time when Juno was enraged because of Semele against the Theban blood, as she showed once and again, Athamas turned so insane that, seeing his wife go carrying their two children, one in either hand, he cried: 'Let us spread the nets to take the lioness and the whelps as they pass!', then stretched out his pitiless claws, taking the one that was named Learchus, and whirled him round and dashed him on a rock, and she drowned herself with the other burden;[1] and when fortune turned low the loftiness of the Trojans, who dared all, so that the king together with the kingdom was blotted out, Hecuba, sad, forlorn and captive, when she saw Polyxena dead and recognized with anguish her Polydorus on the beach, being out of her wits barked like a dog, so distraught was her mind with grief.[2] But no fury of Thebes or Troy was ever seen so cruel against any, rending beasts and even the limbs of men, as I saw two pallid and naked shades which ran biting like the hog loosed from the sty. The one came at Capocchio and set its fangs in the nape of his neck, then, dragging him, made his belly scrape on the hard bottom.

E l'Aretin, che rimase tremando,
mi disse: 'Quel folletto è Gianni Schicchi,
e va rabbioso altrui così conciando.'
'Oh!' diss' io lui 'se l'altro non ti ficchi
li denti a dosso, non ti sia fatica
a dir chi è pria che di qui si spicchi.'
Ed elli a me: 'Quell'è l'anima antica
di Mirra scellerata, che divenne
al padre fuor del dritto amore amica.
Questa a peccar con esso così venne, 40
falsificando sè in altrui forma,
come l'altro che là sen va, sostenne,
per guadagnar la donna della torma,
falsificare in sè Buoso Donati,
testando e dando al testamento norma.'
E poi che i due rabbiosi fuor passati
sovra cu' io avea l'occhio tenuto,
rivolsilo a guardar li altri mal nati.
Io vidi un, fatto a guisa di lëuto,
pur ch'elli avesse avuta l'anguinaia 50
tronca dall'altro che l'uomo ha forcuto.
La grave idropesì, che sì dispaia
le membra con l'omor che mal converte,
che 'l viso non risponde alla ventraia,
faceva lui tener le labbra aperte
come l'etico fa, che per la sete
l'un verso il mento e l'altro in su rinverte.
'O voi che sanz'alcuna pena sete,
e non so io perchè, nel mondo gramo,'
diss'elli a noi 'guardate e attendete 60
alla miseria del maestro Adamo:
io ebbi vivo assai di quel ch' i' volli,
e ora, lasso!, un gocciol d'acqua bramo.
Li ruscelletti che de' verdi colli
del Casentin discendon giuso in Arno,
faccendo i lor canali freddi e molli,
sempre mi stanno innanzi, e non indarno,
chè l' imagine lor vie più m'asciuga
che 'l male ond' io nel volto mi discarno.

And the Aretine,[3] who was left trembling, said to me: 'That goblin is Gianni Schicchi, and he goes raging and dealing so with the rest.'

'Oh,' I said to him 'so may the other not fix its teeth on thee, be pleased to tell me who it is before it makes off.'

And he answered me: 'That is the ancient spirit of cursed Myrrha, who became dear to her father with more than lawful love.[4] She contrived to sin with him thus, counterfeiting in herself another's person, as the other who goes off there took it upon him, that he might gain the lady of the stud, to counterfeit in himself Buoso Donati, making the will and giving it due form.'[5]

And when the furious two on whom I had kept my eyes were gone, I turned to look at the other ill-born shades and saw one shaped like a lute, if only he had been cut short at the groin from the part where a man is forked. The heavy dropsy which disproportions the members by ill disposal of the humours so that the face does not answer to the belly made him hold his lips apart, like the hectic who, for thirst, curls the one toward the chin and the other upward.

'O you that are free from all punishment, I know not why, in the grim world,' he said to us 'look and give heed to the misery of Master Adam.[6] Alive, I had in plenty all I wished, and now, alas, I crave one drop of water. The little streams that from the green hills of the Casentino flow down to the Arno, making their channels cool and moist, are always before me, and not in vain, for their image parches me far more than the ill that wastes

La rigida giustizia che mi fruga 70
tragge cagion del loco ov' io peccai
a metter più li miei sospiri in fuga.
Ivi è Romena, là dov' io falsai
la lega suggellata del Batista;
per ch' io il corpo su arso lasciai.
Ma s' io vedessi qui l'anima trista
di Guido o d'Alessandro o di lor frate,
per Fonte Branda non darei la vista.
Dentro c'è l'una già, se l'arrabbiate
ombre che vanno intorno dicon vero; 80
ma che mi val, c' ho le membra legate?
S' io fossi pur di tanto ancor leggero
ch' i' potessi in cent'anni andare un'oncia,
io sarei messo già per lo sentero,
cercando lui tra questa gente sconcia,
con tutto ch'ella volge undici miglia,
e men d' un mezzo di traverso non ci ha.
Io son per lor tra sì fatta famiglia:
e' m' indussero a batter li fiorini
ch'avevan tre carati di mondiglia.' 90
E io a lui: 'Chi son li due tapini
che fumman come man bagnate 'l verno,
giacendo stretti a' tuoi destri confini?'
'Qui li trovai—e poi volta non dierno—'
rispuose 'quando piovvi in questo greppo,
e non credo che dieno in sempiterno.
L' una è la falsa ch'accusò Giuseppo;
l'altr'è il falso Sinon greco da Troia:
per febbre aguta gittan tanto leppo.'
E l'un di lor, che si recò a noia 100
forse d'esser nomato sì oscuro,
col pugno li percosse l'epa croia.
Quella sonò come fosse un tamburo;
e mastro Adamo li percosse il volto
col braccio suo, che non parve men duro,
dicendo a lui: 'Ancor che mi sia tolto
lo muover per le membra che son gravi,
ho io il braccio a tal mestiere sciolto.'

my features. The unbending justice which searches me takes occasion from the place where I sinned to make my sighs come faster; there is Romena, where I falsified the currency stamped with the Baptist and for that left above my body burnt. But might I see here the wretched soul of Guido, or of Alessandro, or of their brother,[7] for Fonte Branda I would not give the sight. One is in here already, if the furious shades that go round speak true, but what does it avail me whose limbs are bound? If I were only so light still that I could go an inch in a hundred years I would have set out already on the road seeking him among these misshapen folk, for all it is eleven miles round and a full half-mile across. Through them I am in such a household; they induced me to strike the florins that had three carats of dross.'

And I said to him: 'Who are the two poor wretches that smoke as wet hands do in winter, lying close on thy right boundary?'

'I found them here when I rained into this trough' he replied 'and they have not given a turn since, nor do I think they will to all eternity. The one is the false woman who accused Joseph;[8] the other false Sinon, the Greek from Troy.[9] Burning fever makes them throw off such a reek.'

And one of them, who took it ill, perhaps, to be named so meanly, struck him with his fist on the leathery paunch; it sounded as if it had been a drum. And Master Adam struck him in the face with his arm, which seemed no less hard, saying to him: 'Though I am kept from moving by the weight of my limbs, I have an arm free for such a case.'

Ond'ei rispuose: 'Quando tu andavi
al fuoco, non l'avei tu così presto: 110
ma sì e più l'avei quando coniavi.'
E l' idropico: 'Tu di' ver di questo:
ma tu non fosti sì ver testimonio
là 've del ver fosti a Troia richesto.'
'S' io dissi falso, e tu falsasti il conio,'
disse Sinone; 'e son qui per un fallo,
e tu per più ch'alcun altro demonio!'
'Ricorditi, spergiuro, del cavallo'
rispuose quel ch'avea infiata l'epa;
'e sieti reo che tutto il mondo sallo!' 120
'E te sia rea la sete onde ti criepa'
disse 'l greco 'la lingua, e l'acqua marcia
che 'l ventre innanzi li occhi sì t'assiepa!'
Allora il monetier: 'Così si squarcia
la bocca tua per tuo mal come sòle;
chè s' i' ho sete ed umor mi rinfarcia,
tu hai l'arsura e 'l capo che ti dole,
e per leccar lo specchio di Narcisso,
non vorresti a 'nvitar molte parole.'
Ad ascoltarli er' io del tutto fisso, 130
quando 'l maestro mi disse: 'Or pur mira!
che per poco che teco non mi risso.'
Quand' io 'l senti' a me parlar con ira,
volsimi verso lui con tal vergogna,
ch'ancor per la memoria mi si gira.
Qual è colui che suo dannaggio sogna,
che sognando desidera sognare,
sì quel ch'è, come non fosse, agogna,
tal mi fec' io, non possendo parlare,
che disïava scusarmi, e scusava 140
me tuttavia, e nol mi credea fare.
'Maggior difetto men vergogna lava'
disse 'l maestro 'che 'l tuo non è stato;
però d'ogne trestizia ti disgrava:
e fa ragion ch' io ti sia sempre a lato,
se più avvien che fortuna t'accoglia
dove sien genti in simigliante piato;
chè voler ciò udire è bassa voglia.'

To which he replied: 'Going to the fire[10] thou hadst it not so ready; but thou hadst it as ready, and more, when thou wast coining.'

And the dropsied one: 'Thou speakest truth in this; but thou wast not so true a witness at Troy, where truth was wanted from thee.'

'If I spoke falsely,' said Sinon 'thou too didst falsify the coin, and I am here for one fault and thou for more than any other devil.'

'Remember, perjurer, the horse,' replied he of the inflated paunch 'and may it plague thee that all the world knows of it.'

'And be thou plagued with the thirst that cracks thy tongue' said the Greek 'and the foul water that makes that belly such a hedge before thy eyes.'

Then the coiner: 'Thus thy mouth gapes, as usual, to put thee in the wrong, for if I have thirst and humour stuffs me, thou hast burning fever and aching head and wouldst need little persuasion to lap Narcissus' mirror.'[11]

I was all intent on listening to them, when the Master said to me: 'Now keep looking. A little more and I quarrel with thee.'

When I heard him speak to me in anger I turned to him with such shame that still it haunts my memory. Like one that dreams of harm to himself and, dreaming, wishes it a dream, so that he longs for that which is as if it were not, I became such that, unable to speak, I wished to excuse myself and did excuse myself all the while, not thinking that I did.

'Less shame washes away a greater fault than thine has been,' said the Master 'therefore unload thy heart of all sadness and take account that I am always at thy side if it befall again that fortune bring thee where are people in a like dispute; for the desire to hear it is a base desire.'

INFERNO

1. When Semele, daughter of Cadmus King of Thebes (Canto xxv), was loved by Jupiter Juno took revenge on the Theban house, inflicting madness on Athamas, husband of Semele's sister Ino.

2. Priam of Troy was killed by the Greeks in the sack of the city and his wife Hecuba enslaved; her daughter Polyxena was sacrificed on Achilles's tomb and her son Polydorus murdered by his guardian Polymnestor and his body washed up by the sea; afterwards she tore out Polymnestor's eyes.

3. Griffolino (Canto xxix).

4. Incestuous daughter of the King of Cyprus.

5. Schicchi, of the Cavalcanti family in Florence, a noted mimic, conspired with the nephew of the wealthy Buoso Donati; they concealed Buoso's death and Schicchi, taking the dead man's place in his bed, dictated a will in his name to the lawyer, bequeathing to himself a famous mare known as 'the lady of the stud'.

6. Master Adam of Brescia served the Counts of Romena, a branch of the Conti Guidi. Romena is in the Casentino, the hill country on the upper Arno, where Adam made false coins for his employers, with the figure of the Baptist; he was burned as a coiner in 1281. Fonte Branda was a fountain near Romena.

7. Count Guido died in 1292; the other two were still alive in 1300.

8. Potiphar's wife (*Gen.* xxxix. 6–20).

9. In the siege Sinon pretended to the Trojans he was a deserter from the Greeks, who would offer the wooden horse in compensation for the theft of the Trojan Palladium; its admission led to the fall of Troy (Canto xxvi).

10. When he was bound.

11. The water of the spring in which Narcissus saw his face.

NOTE

Characteristically, Dante recalls classical examples of madness to heighten the impression of that of the personators here; but the madness in the old stories and this in Hell are on quite different levels. That of Athamas and Hecuba was an infliction of the gods and of disastrous fortune and it is set forth with a literary dignity which is in marked ironical contrast with the squalid realism of the present scene. That defeat and overthrow of their minds was a passive and helpless state which at its worst could not compare with the *moral* insanity, the deliberate disowning and discarding of their personality for base ends by Schicchi and Myrrha, whose gross lust and greed liken them to hungry swine. Such passions, served with such cunning, break every social bond and make those possessed by them the common enemies of their kind. In life, they went 'out of themselves' by choice and guile; now, 'pallid and naked shades', they 'run biting' their fellows.

Master Adam, the dominating figure of the canto, was executed by the Florentine authorities when Dante was a youth of sixteen. The case would be a notorious one and Dante may well have known Adam by sight and have been present at the burning. In any case he would know him well by repute, being familiar with the Casentino only some twenty-five miles away, and being on terms of personal friendship with Master Adam's employers, the Counts of Romena; so that the figure of Adam he presents to us is not, probably, a mere invention, but a portrait. He is a *bon vivant* who, in life, 'had in plenty all he wished', surely with a portly person forecasting his grotesque girth in Hell, enjoying his life and circumstances with gusto and sensitive to the beauties of the Casentino, one who harped, as he does here, on the pronoun *I* and valued himself on his professional dignity as 'Master Adam', a man ready on occasion with a gibe or a blow and vindictive to personal enemies, willing to do any turn for his masters so long as they provided his comforts, and, as a Brescian and a foreigner to Florence, willing for his own profit to injure Florence in her tenderest spot and to use its patron-saint for his own purposes. For the gold florin, first issued in 1252 and taking its name from the city or from its lily, was the very symbol of Florentine greatness and a standard of value not only for Florence but for Christendom, so that to counterfeit the florin was a kind of civil sacrilege and a capital offence, the worse if, as is supposed, Master Adam had been employed previously by Florence itself. His monstrous form here, 'shaped like a lute', the trunk stuffed with humours and the head disproportionately small, suggests one who sucked up all material advantages and was the worse for them, and now his old thirst, with the memory of old delights, has become his torment. He is a pitiful figure, and yet his appeal for pity leaves Dante untouched; taking no account of his misery, he merely asks him about the neighbours 'on his boundary', as if he were a country, and we gather that he felt a peculiar repugnance for a personality so thoroughly self-centred, whose 'fundamental character was plebeian vulgarity' (*V. Rossi*).

The other two, who seem so strangely coupled, Potiphar's wife and Sinon the Greek, are not punished merely as verbal liars for their false words, but as those whose words have been cruelly malicious and disastrous to others. Joseph is the type of virtue and innocence and a patriarch of the Hebrews, and Sinon betrayed the Trojans to their doom. The Hebrews and the Trojans were for Dante the two holy races of antiquity, the ancestors, so to speak, of Church and Empire, and the link between the two liars would seem to be that they sinned severally against humanity in its most sacred aspects.

The scene ends, as such a breakdown of all the good faith on which human society rests, such a loosening and abandonment of 'the bond of love which nature makes' (Canto xi), must end, in wrangling and recrimination, aggravating all the miseries of the sinners alike.

Virgil's rebuke of Dante's absorption in the noisy squabble beneath them is in line with his reproof at the beginning of the previous canto. Endlessly interested in his fellows, their heights and depths and interwoven experiences, Dante would often find their quarrels absorbing and turn away from them with a kind of shame. In the Italy of his day fortune would often 'bring him where were people in a like dispute' and he had to learn that there is an interest in such exchanges of railing which is a kind of enjoyment of them, almost a taking part in them, and which is intolerable to a sane conscience.

The fitness of the penalties to the sins of the tenth of the Malebolge is less clear than in most other cases, but the general idea of them is plain enough. The falsifiers of nature, of their own persons, of the currency, and of their word, have all been more essentially the falsifiers of their own souls; they have corrupted and wasted their powers in fraud and now their souls are forever falsified, distorted and disabled by disease.

INFERNO

UNA medesma lingua pria mi morse,
sì che mi tinse l'una e l'altra guancia,
e poi la medicina mi riporse:
così od' io che soleva la lancia
d'Achille e del suo padre esser cagione
prima di trista e poi di buona mancia.
Noi demmo il dosso al misero vallone
su per la ripa che 'l cinge dintorno,
attraversando sanza alcun sermone.
Quiv'era men che notte e men che giorno, 10
sì che 'l viso m'andava innanzi poco;
ma io senti' sonare un alto corno,
tanto ch'avrebbe ogne tuon fatto fioco,
che, contra sè la sua via seguitando,
dirizzò li occhi miei tutti ad un loco.
Dopo la dolorosa rotta quando
Carlo Magno perdè la santa gesta,
non sonò sì terribilmente Orlando.
Poco portai in là volta la testa,
che me parve veder molte alte torri; 20
ond' io: 'Maestro, dì, che terra è questa?'
Ed elli a me: 'Però che tu trascorri
per le tenebre troppo dalla lungi,
avvien che poi nel maginare abborri.
Tu vedrai ben, se tu là ti congiungi,
quanto 'l senso s' inganna di lontano;
però alquanto più te stesso pungi.'
Poi caramente mi prese per mano,
e disse: 'Pria che noi siam più avanti,
acciò che 'l fatto men ti paia strano, 30

CANTO XXXI

The Giants; the descent to Cocytus

ONE self-same tongue first stung me so that it dyed both my cheeks, and then it offered me the medicine; so have I heard that the lance of Achilles and his father brought a gift, first of pain, then of healing.[1]

We turned our back on the wretched valley, going up by the enclosing bank and crossing over it without any speech. Here it was less than night and less than day so that my sight went little ahead, but I heard a blast from a horn so loud that it would have made any thunder-clap seem faint, and it directed my eyes, following back on its course, wholly to one place. After the dolorous rout when Charlemagne lost the sacred army Roland did not sound a blast so terrible.[2] I had not long kept my head turned that way when I seemed to see many lofty towers; I said therefore: 'Master, tell me, what city is this?'

And he said to me: 'It is because thou piercest the dark from too far off that thou strayest in thy fancy, and if thou reach the place thou shalt see plainly how much the sense is deceived by distance; push on, therefore, with more speed.' Then he took me kindly by the hand and said: 'Before we go farther, that the fact may seem less strange to

sappi che non son torri, ma giganti,
  e son nel pozzo intorno dalla ripa
  dall' umbilico in giuso tutti quanti.'
Come quando la nebbia si dissipa,
  lo sguardo a poco a poco raffigura
  ciò che cela il vapor che l'aere stipa,
così forando l'aura grossa e scura,
  più e più appressando ver la sponda,
  fuggìemi errore e crescìemi paura;
però che come su la cerchia tonda 40
  Montereggion di torri si corona,
  così 'n la proda che 'l pozzo circonda
torreggiavan di mezza la persona
  li orribili giganti, cui minaccia
  Giove del cielo ancora quando tona.
E io scorgeva già d'alcun la faccia,
  le spalle e 'l petto e del ventre gran parte,
  e per le coste giù ambo le braccia.
Natura certo, quando lasciò l'arte
  di sì fatti animali, assai fè bene 50
  per torre tali essecutori a Marte.
E s'ella d'elefanti e di balene
  non si pente, chi guarda sottilmente
  più giusta e più discreta la ne tene;
chè dove l'argomento della mente
  s'aggiugne al mal volere ed alla possa,
  nessun riparo vi può far la gente.
La faccia sua mi parea lunga e grossa
  come la pina di San Pietro a Roma,
  e a sua proporzione eran l'altre ossa; 60
sì che la ripa, ch'era perizoma
  dal mezzo in giù, ne mostrava ben tanto
  di sopra, che di giungere alla chioma
tre Frison s'averìen dato mal vanto;
  però ch' i' ne vedea trenta gran palmi
  dal luogo in giù dov'uomo affibbia 'l manto.
'Raphèl maỳ amèch zabì almi'
  cominciò a gridar la fiera bocca,
  cui non si convenìa più dolci salmi.

thee, know that they are not towers, but giants, and they are every one in the pit, round its banks, from the navel downward.'

As, when mist thins off, the sight little by little re-shapes that which the vapour hides that loads the air, so, as I pierced the thick and murky atmosphere and came on nearer to the brink, error fled and fear grew in me; for, as on the circle of its walls Montereggione[3] is crowned with towers, so on the bank encompassing the pit towered with half their bulk the horrible giants whom Jove still threatens from Heaven when he thunders,[4] and I began now to distinguish the face of one, the shoulders and the chest and a great part of the belly and down by his sides both arms. Nature, assuredly, when she gave up the art of making creatures like these, did right well to deprive Mars of such executors; and if she does not repent of elephants and whales, one looking at it carefully will hold her the more just and prudent for it, for where the equipment of the mind is joined to evil will and to power men can make no defence against it. His face appeared to me to have the length and bulk of Saint Peter's pine-cone at Rome[5] and the other bones were in proportion, so that the bank, which was an apron to him from the middle down, still showed so much of him above that three Frieslanders[6] would have boasted in vain of reaching his hair; for I saw thirty great spans of him down from the place where a man buckles his cloak.

'Raphel may amech zabi almi,'[7] began the savage mouth to cry, for which no sweeter psalms were

E 'l duca mio ver lui: 'Anima sciocca, 70
tienti col corno, e con quel ti disfoga
quand' ira o altra passion ti tocca!
Cercati al collo, e troverai la soga
che 'l tien legato, o anima confusa,
e vedi lui che 'l gran petto ti doga.'
Poi disse a me: 'Elli stesso s'accusa;
questi è Nembròt per lo cui mal coto
pur un linguaggio nel mondo non s'usa.
Lasciànlo stare e non parliamo a voto;
chè così è a lui ciascun linguaggio 80
come 'l suo ad altrui, ch'a nullo è noto.'
Facemmo adunque più lungo vïaggio,
volti a sinistra; ed al trar d' un balestro
trovammo l'altro assai più fero e maggio.
A cinger lui qual che fosse 'l maestro,
non so io dir, ma el tenea soccinto
dinanzi l'altro e dietro il braccio destro
d'una catena che 'l tenea avvinto
dal collo in giù, sì che 'n su lo scoperto
si ravvolgea infino al giro quinto. 90
'Questo superbo volle essere sperto
di sua potenza contro al sommo Giove,'
disse 'l mio duca 'ond'elli ha cotal merto.
Fïalte ha nome; e fece le gran prove
quando i giganti fer paura a' Dei:
le braccia ch'el menò già mai non move.'
E io a lui: 'S'esser puote, io vorrei
che dello smisurato Brïareo
esperïenza avesser li occhi miei.'
Ond'ei rispuose: 'Tu vedrai Anteo 100
presso di qui che parla ed è disciolto,
che ne porrà nel fondo d'ogni reo.
Quel che tu vuo' veder, più là è molto,
ed è legato e fatto come questo,
salvo che più feroce par nel volto.'
Non fu tremoto già tanto rubesto,
che scotesse una torre così forte,
come Fïalte a scuotersi fu presto.

fit; and my Leader towards him: 'Stupid soul, keep to thy horn and vent thyself with that when rage or other passion takes thee. Search at thy neck, bewildered soul, and thou shalt find the strap that holds it tied; see how it lies across thy great chest.' Then he said to me: 'He is his own accuser. This is Nimrod, through whose wicked device the world is not of one sole speech.[8] Let us leave him there and not talk in vain, for every language is to him as his to others, which is known to none.'

We made our way, therefore, farther on, turning left, and found the next a bowshot off, far savager and larger. Whose was the master-hand that bound him I cannot tell, but he had the right arm pinioned behind and the other in front with a chain that held him girt from the neck down, so that on the part of him exposed it was wound to the fifth coil.

'This proud spirit chose to try his strength against supreme Jove,' said my Leader 'and he is thus rewarded. Ephialtes he is called, and he made the great attempt when the giants put the gods in fear.[9] The arms he plied he moves no more.'

And I said to him: 'If it is possible, I would my eyes might have sight of the vast Briareus';[10] to which he replied: 'Thou shalt see Antaeus near here, who speaks and is unfettered,[11] and he will set us down in the lowest depth of guilt. He thou wouldst see is much farther on, and he is bound and fashioned like this one except that he seems fiercer by his looks.'

Never did mighty earthquake shake a tower so violently as Ephialtes shook himself of a sudden;

Allor temett' io più che mai la morte,
e non v'era mestier più che la dotta, 110
s' io non avessi viste le ritorte.
Noi procedemmo più avante allotta,
e venimmo ad Anteo, che ben cinque alle,
sanza la testa, uscìa fuor della grotta.
'O tu che nella fortunata valle
che fece Scipïon di gloria reda,
quand'Annibàl co' suoi diede le spalle,
recasti già mille leon per preda,
e che se fossi stato all'alta guerra
de' tuoi fratelli, ancor par che si creda 120
ch'avrebber vinto i figli della terra;
mettine giù, e non ten vegna schifo,
dove Cocito la freddura serra.
Non ci fare ire a Tizio nè a Tifo:
questi può dar di quel che qui si brama;
però ti china, e non torcer lo grifo.
Ancor ti può nel mondo render fama;
ch'el vive e lunga vita ancor aspetta,
se innanzi tempo Grazia a sè nol chiama.'
Così disse 'l maestro; e quelli in fretta 130
le man distese, e prese il duca mio,
ond'Ercule sentì già grande stretta.
Virgilio, quando prender si sentìo,
disse a me: 'Fatti qua, sì ch' io ti prenda';
poi fece sì ch' un fascio era elli e io.
Qual pare a riguardar la Garisenda
sotto 'l chinato, quando un nuvol vada
sovr'essa sì, che ella incontro penda;
tal parve Anteo a me che stava a bada
di vederlo chinare, e fu tal ora 140
ch' i' avrei voluto ir per altra strada.
Ma lievemente al fondo che divora
Lucifero con Giuda, ci sposò;
nè sì chinato lì fece dimora,
e come albero in nave si levò.

then more than ever I was in fear of death, nor was need of more than the terror, had I not seen the fetters.

We went farther then and came to Antaeus, who stood full five ells, not reckoning the head, above the rock.

'O thou who, in the fateful valley which made Scipio heir of glory when Hannibal and his men turned their backs,[12] didst once take for prey a thousand lions, and through whom, hadst thou been with thy brothers in the great war, it seems yet to be believed that the sons of earth would have conquered, set us down below, and do not be disdainful of it, where the cold locks up Cocytus. Do not make us go on to Tityus or to Typhon.[13] This man can give of that which is craved for here. Bend down, therefore, and do not curl thy lip; he can yet restore thy fame in the world, for he lives and expects to live long still, if Grace call him not untimely to itself.'

The Master spoke thus, and the other in haste reached forth the hands of which Hercules once felt the mighty grasp and took my Leader; and Virgil, when he felt himself taken, said to me: 'Come close, that I may take thee', then made one bundle of himself and me.

As appears the Carisenda[14] seen from beneath the leaning side when a cloud passes over it against the direction in which it hangs, so did Antaeus appear to me while I watched to see him bend, and it was such a moment that I would fain have gone by another road. But he set us down lightly on the bottom which engulfs Lucifer with Judas, and he did not stay thus bent, but like the mast in a ship rose up.

INFERNO

1. The spear of Peleus, father of Achilles, healed by a second touch the wound it caused.

2. The *Chanson de Roland* tells how Roland, nephew and chief paladin of Charlemagne, in the crusade against the Saracens in Spain was defeated at Roncesvalle in the Pyrenees and the blast of his ivory horn was heard by Charlemagne 8 miles off.

3. A fortress near Siena.

4. The giants attacked Olympus, seat of the gods, and were overthrown by Jove (Canto xiv); in medieval fancy they were identified with the 'giants in the earth' of *Gen.* vi. 4.

5. A bronze pine-cone then in front of St. Peter's, about 7½ feet high.

6. Famed for their height.

7. Unintelligible sounds.

8. Nimrod, supposed to have been a giant and designer of the Tower of Babel and cause of the confusion of tongues (*Gen.* x. 8–10, xi. 1–9).

9. The giant Ephialtes and his brother tried to pile Mount Pelion on Mount Ossa so as to scale the heavens against the gods.

10. Described in the *Aeneid* as having a hundred arms and fifty heads.

11. Antaeus, giant of Lybia, was not in the war against the gods; he hunted lions and fed on their flesh; in wrestling he retained his strength by contact with Earth, his mother, and Hercules, struggling with him, raised him from the ground and crushed the breath out of him.

12. Scipio saved the Roman Republic by his defeat of Hannibal and the Carthaginians in Lybia.

13. Two giants who offended Jove and were cast into Tartarus.

14. Leaning tower in Bologna which a passing cloud makes appear to be falling.

NOTE

The thirty-first canto stands apart from its immediate context both in subject and in mood. The giants are not specifically related to the sins either of simple fraud or of treachery, and the psychological atmosphere of Dante's account of them has nothing of the moral nausea and scorn that prevail in his description of the Malebolge or of the intensity and bitterness we are to find in his relations with the sinners in Cocytus.

The giants are monsters of earthliness, embodiments of carnal force and arrogance, now defeated and helpless but still passionate and tormented by their old pretensions, and Virgil's attitude to them is that of contempt and irony. About to confront these forces of the flesh, Dante first assures the reader of his complete reconciliation with Virgil, which is confirmed by Virgil's 'taking him kindly by the hand' on first informing him of the giants. In face of the impious materialism of the world he must be wholly committed to his reason and able to see through the world's strength to its weakness; before each of the three giants whom they meet he confesses to his terror and in the end is secure only because Virgil 'made one bundle of himself and me'.

The giants are the body-guard and paladins of Satan, who is imprisoned in the ice at the bottom of the great pit round which they stand. By the linking together of the classical and scriptural mythologies which was characteristic of the time the giants of Greek story were identified with those of *Genesis*; and here, as defeated rebels against the gods, they are associated with Lucifer and share, and in their vast bulk symbolize, his especial sin of pride. They are 'the sons of earth', earthly in all their being, mere masses of incapacity and ignorance, preposterous for their immense futility. Of the three only Nimrod speaks and he only babbles; it is part of their penalty to be ridiculous. In mockery of them there is a vein of comedy through the whole canto. 'Before these three monsters and in sight of the others who tower above the curving bank Virgil has much the air of a father who accompanies his bright boy on a visit to a menagerie and makes him notice the beasts one by one and quiets his fears and restrains his idle curiosity' (*V. Rossi*).

The enormity of earthly pride, its irrational defiance of the whole divine order of things, is set forth with astonishing dramatic force and accumulation of circumstance: Dante, chastened by Virgil's rebuke and comforted by his pardon, following him in absorbed silence through the murky air—the sudden, tremendous horn-blast breaking on them, then the dim, towering figures looming vastly through the fog—Virgil's hand-clasp and, as they approach, the gradual emergence, part by part, of the huge form of Nimrod. It is with the same aim and effect, of convincing objectivity, that Dante uses familiar standards to indicate the size of Nimrod and the other giants —the towers, the pine-cone, the Frieslanders, the great span, the Flemish ell; we feel him scanning them up and down, trying to measure them through the dusk with his eye, and in the failure of his guesses lies their effectiveness. 'There is no point of view from which to see their figures entire. The imagination is excited and must create a whole out of visible fragments and from measurements. It is the impossibility of seeing them that makes the giants impressive' (*K. Vossler*).

Nimrod is described in *Genesis* as 'a mighty hunter before the Lord', and the words doubtless suggested his horn here and that again Roland's blast. The reference to the Christian hero in the most famous of the tales of chivalry, fighting God's battles for the order and unity of the world, brings before us an extreme contrast to Nimrod's self-centred, stupefying pride and his 'wicked device' which made the members of the human family strangers and foreigners to each other. Now he is a senseless survival from a barbarous age, inarticulate, capable only of making a noise in the world, 'his heroic sounding of the horn only the pastime of an imbecile' (*V. Rossi*), too stupid to find his horn again when he has blown it—that is the last mark of his imbecility. Virgil directs his speech 'towards' Nimrod as he might towards a mountain, not with any idea of being understood and rather in apostrophe than address. Virgil is hardly interested in him and he discourages Dante's curiosity about 'the vast Briareus'. As with Roland and Nimrod, there is an implied contrast later, in Virgil's ironically respectful address to Antaeus, between great Scipio who served and saved the sacred cause of Rome and the famous wrestler, catching lions to satisfy his savage appetite, the contrast between one measure of greatness and another.

The comparison of the giants to towers is persistent. The word occurs five times in the canto; Dante's first impression of the giants is of a towered city, mention is made of Montereggione with its towered walls and of the Carisenda in Bologna and there is a hint of the tower of Babel. It has been reasonably suggested that Dante means to recall here one of the most conspicuous and sinister features of Italy, the towers of the warring nobles and cities with which the land bristled in his day and which were the public signs of brute-force and arrogance and treason against every divine purpose. The imprisoned giants are, as it were, a comment on the towers which were the pride and the plague of Italy. 'They are not towers, but giants', Virgil says to Dante; in the eye of reason the towers of Italy are not mere towers, but embodiments of a spirit which is monstrous and irrational.

Antaeus, though he had no part in the war against the gods and is therefore not bound like the others, appears in classical story as very much of a savage and a bully; of enormous strength, which was maintained only by contact with his mother Earth, safely challenging every stranger to wrestle with him and killing them when he had them down, and defeated and destroyed, and the world well rid of him, by the mightier grasp of Hercules, the son of Jove. His character here is consistent with his old record; he is stupidly vain and greedy of public note and easily persuaded by Virgil's studied flatteries to serve the travellers' convenience.

The real subject of the canto is the disastrous confusion wrought in the world by 'the equipment of the mind joined to evil will and to power', and, in the judgement of reason, its ultimate feebleness and futility.

INFERNO

S' IO avessi le rime aspre e chiocce,
  come si converrebbe al tristo buco
  sovra 'l qual pontan tutte l'altre rocce,
io premerei di mio concetto il suco
  più pienamente; ma perch' io non l'abbo,
  non sanza tema a dicer mi conduco;
chè non è impresa da pigliare a gabbo
  discriver fondo a tutto l' universo,
  nè da lingua che chiami mamma o babbo:
ma quelle donne aiutino il mio verso 10
  ch'aiutaro Anfíone a chiuder Tebe,
  sì che dal fatto il dir non sia diverso.
Oh sovra tutte mal creata plebe
  che stai nel luogo onde parlare è duro,
  mei foste state qui pecore o zebe!
Come noi fummo giù nel pozzo scuro
  sotto i piè del gigante assai più bassi,
  e io mirava ancora all'alto muro,
dicere udi'mi: 'Guarda come passi;
  va sì che tu non calchi con le piante 20
  le teste de' fratei miseri lassi.'
Per ch' io mi volsi, e vidimi davante
  e sotto i piedi un lago che per gelo
  avea di vetro e non d'acqua sembiante.
Non fece al corso suo sì grosso velo
  di verno la Danoia in Osterlic,
  nè Tanaì là sotto il freddo cielo,

CANTO XXXII

The Ninth Circle; the Treacherous; Caina; the Treacherous to kindred; Antenora; the Treacherous to country or cause

HAD I the harsh and grating rhymes that would be fitting for the dismal hole on which all the other rocks bear down I would press out more completely the sap of my conception; but since I have not it is not without fear I bring myself to speak, for to describe the bottom of all the universe is no enterprise to undertake in sport or for a tongue that cries *mamma* and *babbo*. But may those ladies aid my verse who aided Amphion to wall in Thebes,[1] so that the telling may not be diverse from the fact. O beyond all others misbegotten crowd who are in the place it is hard to speak of, better had you here been sheep or goats!

When we were down in the dark well, far below the giants' feet, and I was still gazing up at the lofty wall, I heard said to me: 'Look to thy steps; move so that thy feet do not tread on the heads of the wretched weary brothers.' At which I turned and saw before me and under my feet a lake which through frost had the appearance of glass and not of water. Never did Danube in Austria or far-off Don under its frigid sky make in winter so thick

com'era quivi; che se Tambernic
vi fosse su caduto, o Pietrapana,
non avrìa pur dall'orlo fatto cric. 30
E come a gracidar si sta la rana
col muso fuor dell'acqua, quando sogna
di spigolar sovente la villana;
livide, insin là dove appar vergogna
eran l'ombre dolenti nella ghiaccia,
mettendo i denti in nota di cicogna.
Ognuna in giù tenea volta la faccia:
da bocca il freddo, e dalli occhi il cor tristo
tra lor testimonianza si procaccia.
Quand' io m'ebbi dintorno alquanto visto, 40
volsimi a' piedi, e vidi due sì stretti
che 'l pel del capo avìeno insieme misto.
'Ditemi, voi che sì strignete i petti,'
diss' io 'chi siete?' E quei piegaro i colli;
e poi ch'ebber li visi a me eretti,
li occhi lor, ch'eran pria pur dentro molli,
gocciar su per le labbra, e 'l gelo strinse
le lacrime tra essi e riserrolli.
Con legno legno spranga mai non cinse
forte così; ond'ei come due becchi 50
cozzaro insieme, tanta ira li vinse.
E un ch'avea perduti ambo li orecchi
per la freddura, pur col viso in giùe,
disse: 'Perchè cotanto in noi ti specchi?
Se vuoi saper chi son cotesti due,
la valle onde Bisenzo si dichina
del padre loro Alberto e di lor fue.
D'un corpo usciro; e tutta la Caina
potrai cercare, e non troverai ombra
degna più d'esser fitta in gelatina; 60
non quelli a cui fu rotto il petto e l'ombra
con esso un colpo per la man d'Artù;
non Focaccia; non questi che m' ingombra
col capo sì ch' i' non veggio oltre più,
e fu nomato Sassol Mascheroni;
se tosco se', ben sai omai chi fu.

a veil on its course as was here; for had Tambernic fallen on it, or Pietrapana,[2] it would not even at the edge have given a creak. And as the frog sits with its muzzle out of the water to croak when the peasant-girl dreams often of her gleaning, so, livid up to where the flush of shame appears, the suffering shades were in the ice, setting their teeth to the note of the stork.[3] Each kept his face bent down; by the mouth the cold and by the eyes the misery of the heart finds evidence among them.

When I had looked round me for a time I turned to my feet and saw two pressed so close together that they had the hair of their heads intermingled.

'Tell me,' I said 'you that so strain your breasts together, who are you?'

And they bent back their necks; and when they had raised their faces to me their eyes, which before were moist only within, gushed over at the lids, and the frost bound the tears between and locked them up again, never did clamp bind beam on beam so hard; whereupon they butted together like two goats, such fury mastered them

And one who had lost both his ears by the cold said, with his face still down: 'Why dost thou mirror thyself in us so long? If thou wouldst know who are these two, the valley down which the Bisenzio flows was their father Albert's and theirs.[4] They issued from one womb, and all Caina[5] thou mayst search and not find a shade more fit to be set in jelly, not him whose breast and shadow were pierced with a single blow from Arthur's hand,[6] nor Focaccia,[7] nor him here who so obstructs me with his head that I do not see past him and who was called Sassol Mascheroni;[8] if thou art Tuscan

E perchè non mi metti in più sermoni,
sappi ch' io fu' il Camicion de' Pazzi;
e aspetto Carlin che mi scagioni.'
Poscia vid' io mille visi cagnazzi 70
fatti per freddo; onde mi vien riprezzo,
e verrà sempre, de' gelati guazzi.
E mentre ch'andavamo inver lo mezzo
al quale ogni gravezza si rauna,
e io tremava nell'etterno rezzo;
se voler fu o destino o fortuna,
non so; ma, passeggiando tra le teste,
forte percossi il piè nel viso ad una.
Piangendo mi sgridò: 'Perchè mi peste?
se tu non vieni a crescer la vendetta 80
di Montaperti, perchè mi moleste?'
E io: 'Maestro mio, or qui m'aspetta,
sì ch' io esca d'un dubbio per costui;
poi mi farai, quantunque vorrai, fretta.'
Lo duca stette, e io dissi a colui
che bestemmiava duramente ancora:
'Qual se' tu che così rampogni altrui?'
'Or tu chi se' che vai per l'Antenora,
percotendo' rispuose 'altrui le gote,
sì che, se fossi vivo, troppo fora?' 90
'Vivo son io, e caro esser ti pote,'
fu mia risposta 'se dimandi fama,
ch' io metta il nome tuo tra l'altre note.'
Ed elli a me: 'Del contrario ho io brama;
lèvati quinci e non mi dar più lagna,
chè mal sai lusingar per questa lama!'
Allor lo presi per la cuticagna,
e dissi: 'El converrà che tu ti nomi,
o che capel qui su non ti rimagna.'
Ond'elli a me: 'Perchè tu mi dischiomi, 100
nè ti dirò ch' io sia, nè mosterrolti,
se mille fiate in sul capo mi tomi.'
Io avea già i capelli in mano avvolti,
e tratti li n'avea più d'una ciocca,
latrando lui con li occhi in giù raccolti,

thou knowest well now who he was. And, that thou put me to no further talk, know that I was Camicion de' Pazzi,[9] and I wait for Carlino to exonerate me.'

After that I saw a thousand faces made dog-like with the cold, so that shuddering comes over me, and always will, at frozen pools; and while we were going towards the centre at which all gravity converges and I was shivering in the eternal chill, whether it was will or fate or chance I do not know, but, walking among the heads, I struck my foot hard in the face of one.

Weeping, he shouted at me: 'Why dost thou trample on me? Unless thou comest to add to the revenge for Montaperti,[10] why dost thou molest me?'

And I: 'My Master, now wait for me here, that through him I may be cleared of a doubt; then thou shalt make me hasten as thou wilt.'

The Leader stopped, and I said to him who kept on cursing violently: 'Who art thou, reviling one so?'

'Nay, who art thou' he answered 'that goest through Antenora[11] striking one's cheeks harder than if thou wert alive?'

'I am alive,' was my reply 'and it may be worth much to thee, if thou ask for fame, that I note thy name among the rest.'

And he said to me: 'What I crave for is the opposite. Take thyself hence and do not vex me further, for thou ill knowest how to flatter in this depth.'

Then I took him by the scalp and said: 'Thou must name thyself, or not a hair will be left on thee here.'

At which he said to me: 'Though thou strip me bald I will not tell thee who I am, nor show thee if thou fall upon my head a thousand times.'

I already had his hair twisted in my hand and had torn out more than one tuft of it, he barking

quando un altro gridò: 'Che hai tu, Bocca?
non ti basta sonar con le mascelle,
se tu non latri? qual diavol ti tocca?'
'Omai' diss' io 'non vo' che tu favelle,
malvagio traditor; ch'alla tua onta 110
io porterò di te vere novelle.'
'Va via,' rispuose 'e ciò che tu vuoi conta;
ma non tacer, se tu di qua entro eschi,
di quel ch'ebbe or così la lingua pronta.
El piange qui l'argento de' Franceschi:
"Io vidi" potrai dir "quel da Duera
là dove i peccatori stanno freschi."
Se fossi domandato altri chi v'era,
tu hai da lato quel di Beccheria
di cui segò Fiorenza la gorgiera. 120
Gianni de' Soldanier credo che sia
più là con Ganellone e Tebaldello,
ch'aprì Faenza quando si dormìa.'
Noi eravam partiti già da ello,
ch' io vidi due ghiacciati in una buca,
sì che l' un capo all'altro era cappello;
e come 'l pan per fame si manduca,
così 'l sovran li denti all'altro pose
là 've 'l cervel s'aggiugne con la nuca:
non altrimenti Tideo si rose 130
le tempie a Menalippo per disdegno,
che quei faceva il teschio e l'altre cose.
'O tu che mostri per sì bestial segno
odio sovra colui che tu ti mangi,
dimmi 'l perchè,' diss' io 'per tal convegno,
che se tu a ragion di lui ti piangi,
sappiendo chi voi siete e la sua pecca,
nel mondo suso ancora io te ne cangi,
se quella con ch' io parlo non si secca.'

and with his eyes held down, when another cried: 'What ails thee, Bocca? Art thou not satisfied with the music of thy jaws, but thou must bark? What devil is at thee?'

'Now,' said I 'I do not want thee to speak, vile traitor, for in spite of thee I shall carry of thee a true report.'

'Be off,' he answered 'and tell what tale thou wilt; but do not be silent, if thou get out from here, about him that had his tongue so ready just now. Here he laments the Frenchman's silver. "I saw" thou canst say "him of Duera[12] in the place where the sinners are put to cool." If thou art asked who else was there, thou hast beside thee him of Beccheria, whose gullet Florence slit;[13] Gianni de' Soldanier[14] is, I think, farther on, with Ganelon,[15] and with Tribaldello, who opened Faenza while it slept.'[16]

We had already left him when I saw two frozen in one hole so that the one head was a hood to the other, and, as bread is devoured for hunger, the one above set his teeth in the other at the place where the brain joins the nape; Tydeus gnawed the temples of Menalippus for rage[17] just as he was doing with the skull and the other parts.

'O thou who by so bestial a token showest thy hatred against him thou eatest, tell me the cause,' I said 'on this agreement, that if thou hast reason in thy complaint against him I, knowing who you are and what his sin, shall yet requite thee in the world above, if this tongue I talk with be not withered.'

1. Amphion, by help of the Muses, charmed the mountain-rocks with his lyre to build the walls of Thebes.

2. Mountains, Tambernic not identified, Pietrapana in Tuscany.

3. Like the sound made by the stork with its bill.

4. Sons of a Tuscan noble, who disputed the inheritance and killed each other.

5. Caina—from Cain—the outermost zone of Cocytus, where traitors to kindred are punished.

6. King Arthur killed his traitorous nephew Mordred with so violent a blow of his lance that daylight was seen through the body.

7. Noble of Pistoia whose treacherous murder of his uncle led to the feuds of Blacks and Whites in Tuscany.

8. A Florentine who murdered his nephew for his inheritance.

9. Not known, but the Pazzi were Tuscan nobles; cp. Rinier Pazzo (Canto xii); his nephew Carlino betrayed a castle he held for the Florentine Whites in 1302; he will be punished in Antenora and his deeper guilt will, by comparison, 'exonerate' Camicion.

10. Where the Florentine Guelfs were routed by the Ghibellines in 1260 (Canto x); Bocca, a Ghibelline fighting in the Guelf ranks, cut off the hand of the Guelf standard-bearer and caused a panic.

11. The second zone of Cocytus—from Antenor, the Trojan, believed to have betrayed Troy to the Greeks—where traitors to their country or cause are punished.

12. Buoso of Duera, Ghibelline leader believed to have been bribed to give free passage to the French invading Italy in 1265.

13. Papal Legate in Florence in 1258, executed there on the charge of plotting with the exiled Ghibellines against the Guelf government.

14. Ghibelline noble of Florence who, when his party was expelled, sided with the Guelfs for his own advantage.

15. Ganelon betrayed the cause of Charlemegne and caused the defeat and death of Roland at Roncesvalle.

16. Tribaldello of Faenza betrayed Ghibelline refugees there by opening the gates to their Guelf enemies.

17. Tydeus, one of the seven kings who besieged Thebes, was mortally wounded by Menalippus, whom he killed and gnawed the head with rage.

(This canto will be considered along with the next.)

INFERNO

LA bocca sollevò dal fiero pasto
  quel peccator, forbendola a' capelli
  del capo ch'elli avea di retro guasto.
Poi cominciò: 'Tu vuo' ch' io rinovelli
  disperato dolor che 'l cor mi preme
  già pur pensando, pria ch' io ne favelli.
Ma se le mie parole esser dien seme
  che frutti infamia al traditor ch' i' rodo,
  parlare e lacrimar vedrai inseme.
Io non so chi tu se' nè per che modo 10
  venuto se' qua giù; ma fiorentino
  mi sembri veramente quand' io t'odo.
Tu dei saper ch' i' fui conte Ugolino,
  e questi è l'arcivescovo Ruggieri:
  or ti dirò perch' i son tal vicino.
Che per l'effetto de' suo' mai pensieri,
  fidandomi di lui, io fossi preso
  e poscia morto, dir non è mestieri;
pero quel che non puoi avere inteso,
  ciò è come la morte mia fu cruda, 20
  udirai, e saprai s' e' m' ha offeso.
Breve pertugio dentro dalla muda
  la qual per me ha il titol della fame,
  e 'n che conviene ancor ch'altrui si chiuda,
m'avea mostrato per lo suo forame
  più lune già, quand' io feci 'l mal sonno
  che del futuro mi squarciò 'l velame.
Questi pareva a me maestro e donno,
  cacciando il lupo e' lupicini al monte
  per che i Pisan veder Lucca non ponno. 30

CANTO XXXIII

Ugolino; Ptolomea; the Treacherous to guests; Fra Alberigo

THAT sinner lifted his mouth from the savage meal, wiping it on the hair of the head he had wasted behind, then began: 'Thou wilt have me renew desperate grief which even to think of already wrings my heart before I speak of it; but if my words are to be seed that may bear fruit of infamy to the traitor I gnaw, thou shalt see me speak and weep together. I know not who thou art nor by what means thou hast come down here, but indeed thou seemest to me Florentine when I hear thee. Thou art to know that I was Count Ugolino[1] and this is the Archbishop Ruggieri. I shall tell thee now why I am such a neighbour to him. How by means of his evil devices, confiding in him, I was taken and then killed, there is no need to tell; but what thou canst not have learnt, that is, how cruel was my death, thou shalt hear and shalt know if he has done me wrong.

'A little opening within the mew which because of me has the title of Hunger and in which others are yet to be shut up, had already shown me through its slit several moons, when I had the bad dream which rent for me the veil of the future. This man appeared to me as master and lord hunting the wolf and the whelps on the mountain for which the Pisans cannot see Lucca. With hounds lean,

Con cagne magre, studiose e conte
Gualandi con Sismondi e con Lanfranchi
s'avea messi dinanzi dalla fronte.
In picciol corso mi parieno stanchi
lo padre e' figli, e con l'agute scane
mi parea lor veder fender li fianchi.
Quando fui desto innanzi la dimane,
pianger senti' fra 'l sonno i miei figliuoli
ch'eran con meco, e domandar del pane.
Ben se' crudel, se tu già non ti duoli 40
pensando ciò che 'l mio cor s'annunziava;
e se non piangi, di che pianger suoli?
Già eran desti, e l'ora s'appressava
che 'l cibo ne solea essere addotto,
e per suo sogno ciascun dubitava;
e io senti' chiavar l'uscio di sotto
all'orribile torre; ond' io guardai
nel viso a' mie' figliuoi sanza far motto.
Io non piangea, sì dentro impetrai:
piangevan elli; e Anselmuccio mio 50
disse: "Tu guardi sì, padre! che hai?"
Perciò non lacrimai nè rispuos' io
tutto quel giorno nè la notte appresso,
infin che l'altro sol nel mondo uscìo.
Come un poco di raggio si fu messo
nel doloroso carcere, e io scorsi
per quattro visi il mio aspetto stesso,
ambo le man per lo dolor mi morsi;
ed ei, pensando ch' i' 'l fessi per voglia
di manicar, di subito levorsi 60
e disser: "Padre, assai ci fia men doglia
se tu mangi di noi: tu ne vestisti
queste misere carni, e tu le spoglia."
Queta'mi allor per non farli più tristi;
lo dì e l'altro stemmo tutti muti;
ahi dura terra, perchè non t'apristi?
Poscia che fummo al quarto dì venuti,
Gaddo mi si gettò disteso a' piedi,
dicendo: "Padre mio, chè non m'aiuti?"

trained and eager he had sent the Gualandi, the Sismondi and the Lanfranchi to the front before him, and after a short run the father and sons seemed to me spent and with the sharp fangs I seemed to see their flanks torn open. When I awoke before morning I heard my children, who were with me, crying in their sleep and asking for bread. Thou art cruel indeed if thou grieve not now, thinking what my heart foreboded, and, if thou weep not, at what dost thou ever weep?

'They were now awake and the hour approached when our food used to be brought to us, and each was afraid because of his dream, and I heard below the door of the horrible tower nailed up; at which I looked in the faces of my sons without a word. I did not weep, I so turned to stone within. They wept, and my little Anselm said: "Thou lookest so, father, what ails thee?" At that I shed no tears nor answered all that day nor the night after, till another sun came forth on the world. As soon as a little ray made its way into the doleful prison and I discerned in four faces my own look, I bit both hands for grief; and they, thinking I did it from a desire to eat, rose up suddenly and said: "Father, it will be far less pain for us if thou eat of us. Thou didst clothe us with this wretched flesh and do thou strip us of it." I calmed myself then, not to make them more unhappy. That day and the next we stayed all silent.—Ah, hard earth, why didst thou not open?—When we had come to the fourth day Gaddo threw himself outstretched at my feet, saying: "My father, why dost thou not help me?"

Quivi morì; e come tu mi vedi, 70
  vid' io cascar li tre ad uno ad uno
  tra 'l quinto dì e 'l sesto; ond' io mi diedi,
già cieco, a brancolar sovra ciascuno,
  e due dì li chiamai, poi che fur morti:
  poscia, più che 'l dolor, potè 'l digiuno.'
Quand'ebbe detto ciò, con li occhi torti
  riprese 'l teschio misero co' denti,
  che furo all'osso, come d' un can, forti.
Ahi Pisa, vituperio delle genti
  del bel paese là dove 'l sì sona, 80
  poi che i vicini a te punir son lenti,
muovasi la Capraia e la Gorgona,
  e faccian siepe ad Arno in su la foce,
  sì ch'elli annieghi in te ogni persona!
Chè se 'l conte Ugolino aveva voce
  d'aver tradita te delle castella,
  non dovei tu i figliuoi porre a tal croce.
Innocenti facea l'età novella,
  novella Tebe, Uguiccione e 'l Brigata
  e li altri due che 'l canto suso appella. 90
Noi passammo oltre, là 've la gelata
  ruvidamente un'altra gente fascia,
  non volta in giù, ma tutta riversata.
Lo pianto stesso lì pianger non lascia,
  e 'l duol, che truova in su li occhi rintoppo,
  si volge in entro a far crescer l'ambascia;
chè le lagrime prime fanno groppo,
  e sì come visiere di cristallo,
  rïempion sotto 'l ciglio tutto il coppo.
E avvegna che, sì come d' un callo, 100
  per la freddura ciascun sentimento
  cessato avesse del mio viso stallo,
già mi parea sentire alquanto vento;
  per ch' io: 'Maestro mio, questo chi move?
  non è qua giù ogne vapore spento?'
Ed elli a me: 'Avaccio sarai dove
  di ciò ti farà l'occhio la risposta,
  veggendo la cagion che 'l fiato piove.'

There he died, and, as thou seest me, I saw the three drop one by one during the fifth day and the sixth; therefore I gave myself, now blind, to groping over each and for two days called on them after they were dead. Then fasting had more power than grief.'

When he had said this, with eyes askance he took hold of the wretched skull again with his teeth, which were strong on the bone like a dog's.

Ah, Pisa, shame of the peoples of the fair land where sounds the *sì*,[2] since thy neighbours are slow to punish thee may Capraia and Gorgona shift and put a bar on Arno's mouth so that it drown every soul in thee![3] What if Count Ugolino had the name of betraying thy strongholds, thou shouldst not have put his children to such torment. Their youthful years, thou new Thebes,[4] made them innocent, Uguccione and Brigata and the other two named already in my song.

We passed on farther, where the ice roughly swathes another tribe, who were not face downward but all turned up. The very weeping there does not let them weep and the pain which finds a barrier in the eyes turns inward to increase the anguish; for the first tears form a cluster and, like a crystal visor, fill up all the hollow under the brows. And although from the cold all feeling had left my face as in a callus, I seemed now to feel some wind, so that I said: 'My master, who causes this? Is not all heat quenched down here?'[5]

And he said to me: 'Thou shalt soon be where the eye shall give thee the answer, seeing the cause that drives down the blast.'

E un de' tristi della fredda crosta
  gridò a noi: 'O anime crudeli, 110
  tanto che dato v'è l' ultima posta,
levatemi dal viso i duri veli,
  sì ch' ïo sfoghi 'l duol che 'l cor m' impregna,
  un poco, pria che il pianto si raggeli.'
Per ch' io a lui: 'Se vuo' ch' i' ti sovvegna,
  dimmi chi se', e s' io non ti disbrigo,
  al fondo della ghiaccia ir mi convegna.'
Rispuose adunque: 'I' son frate Alberigo;
  io son quel dalle frutta del mal orto,
  che qui riprendo dattero per figo.' 120
'Oh!' diss' io lui 'or se' tu ancor morto?'
  Ed elli a me: 'Come 'l mio corpo stea
  nel mondo su, nulla scïenza porto.
Cotal vantaggio ha questa Tolomea,
  che spesse volte l'anima ci cade
  innanzi ch'Atropòs mossa le dea.
E perchè tu più volontier mi rade
  le 'nvetriate lacrime dal volto,
  sappie che tosto che l'anima trade
come fec' io, il corpo suo l' è tolto 130
  da un demonio, che poscia il governa
  mentre che 'l tempo suo tutto sia volto.
Ella ruina in sì fatta cisterna;
  e forse pare ancor lo corpo suso
  dell'ombra che di qua dietro mi verna.
Tu 'l dei saper, se tu vien pur mo giuso:
  elli è ser Branca d'Oria, e son più anni
  poscia passati ch'el fu sì racchiuso.'
'Io credo' diss' io lui 'che tu m' inganni;
  chè Branca d'Oria non morì unquanche, 140
  e mangia e bee e dorme e veste panni.'
'Nel fosso su' diss'el 'de' Malebranche,
  là dove bolle la tenace pece,
  non era giunto ancora Michel Zanche,
che questi lasciò il diavolo in sua vece
  nel corpo suo, ed un suo prossimano
  che 'l tradimento insieme con lui fece.

And one of the wretches of the frozen crust cried to us: 'O souls so cruel that there is given you the last station, lift from my face the hard veils, that I may give vent for a little to the misery that swells my heart, before the tears freeze up again.'

So I said to him: 'If thou wouldst have my help, tell me who thou art, and if I do not relieve thee may I have to go to the bottom of the ice.'

He replied then: 'I am Fra Alberigo; I am he of the fruit of the bad garden, and here I am paid date for fig.'[6]

'Oh,' I said to him, 'then art thou dead already?'

And he to me: 'How my body fares in the world above I have no knowledge. This Ptolomea[7] is so privileged that many a time the soul falls down here before Atropos[8] sends it forth; and that thou mayst more willingly clear the glazing of tears from my face, know that as soon as the soul betrays as I did, its body is taken from it by a devil, who controls it henceforth till its full time comes round. The soul falls headlong into this tank here, and perhaps the body still appears above of the shade that is wintering here behind me; thou must know, if thou art just come down. He is Ser Branca d'Oria[9] and many years have passed since he was thus enclosed.

'I believe thou art deceiving me,' I said to him 'for Branca d'Oria never died, but eats and drinks and sleeps and puts on clothes.'

'In the ditch above of the Malebranche,' he said 'where the sticky pitch boils, Michael Zanche had not yet arrived when this man left a devil instead of himself in his body, as did a near kinsman of his who wrought the treachery along with him.

Ma distendi oggimai in qua la mano;
  aprimi li occhi.' E io non lil' apersi;
  e cortesia fu lui esser villano. 150
Ahi Genovesi, uomini diversi
  d'ogne costume e pien d'ogni magagna,
  perchè non siete voi del mondo spersi?
Chè col peggiore spirto di Romagna
  trovai di voi un tal, che per sua opra
  in anima in Cocito già si bagna,
ed in corpo par vivo ancor di sopra.

1. For a time head of the Guelf government of Pisa; the Archbishop, leader of the Ghibellines there, prompted the chief Ghibelline families to rise against Ugolino.

2. The languages of Italy, Provence and Northern France were described by their words for *yes: sì, oc* and *oil*.

3. Pisa, near the mouth of the Arno, looked out on the islands of Capraia and Gorgona.

4. Ancient Thebes was notorious for its atrocities; cp. Athamas (Canto xxx).

5. Winds were supposed to be caused by the sun's heat acting on the vapours of the earth.

But now reach out thy hand here; open my eyes.' And I did not open them for him; and it was courtesy to be a churl to him.

Ah, Genoese, people strange to all good custom and full of all corruption, why are you not driven from the world? For with the worst spirit of Romagna I found one of you such that for his deeds he is in soul already bathed in Cocytus and in body appears still living above.

6. A Jovial Friar (Canto xxiii), of the ruling Guelf family of Faenza. Resenting an injury from his younger brother, he invited him and his son to a banquet and gave signal for their murder in the words, 'Bring the fruit', from which 'the bad fruits of Fra Alberigo' were proverbial. To get date for fig meant, proverbially, to get more than one bargained for.

7. From Ptolemy, Captain of Jericho, who murdered his father-in-law Simon Maccabeus, High Priest, at a banquet, along with his sons; Ptolomea is the third zone of Cocytus, where treachery to guests is punished.

8. Third of the Fates; she determines the time of death.

9. Branca, of the famous Ghibelline family of the d'Oria in Genoa, murdered his father-in-law Zanche (Canto xxii) at a banquet in 1290.

NOTE

Dante's theme is beyond him; but the Muses by whose aid the walls of Thebes, the very home of crime, were built will qualify him to tell of 'the bottom of all the universe'. The extremes of human degradation are within the competence of imagination and of literature.

The account of the giants is ironical and detached, its motive the ridicule of earthly pride and presumption. The first words of the next canto mark a complete change of mood; at once, in this world of treachery, the atmosphere is tense, bitter, personal, dramatic. Nowhere in all the *Inferno* is Dante more vividly realistic, more harshly responsive to the sins, or so savagely antagonized by the sinners. Some of his lines are deliberately 'harsh and grating' in their syllables and far more are so in their sense, which at some points startles and horrifies us. It is his way of demonstrating that treachery, the deliberate and contrived outraging of the closest human ties and the prostitution of the powers of the mind to the cruellest ends, effectually and inevitably cuts off these souls from human consideration and makes them by their choice outcasts from fellowship human and divine. It belongs to their penalty to be bound forever in a fierce *dis*-fellowship even with their fellow-traitors.

The river flowing from the cleft in the symbolical figure of humanity in Crete (Canto xiv), the stream of men's sins and sorrows, their tears and blood, last appeared as Phlegethon, the river of hot blood, associated there with the sins of violence (Canto xii), and it was last mentioned for the roar of its fall into the pit of Malebolge (Canto xvii). Here it settles, frozen, in Cocytus—'and what kind of a pond that is, thou shalt see', Virgil had said to Dante.

For treachery, the sin of cold blood, is a deeper, more inhuman, more paralysing sin than all the forms of violence or of simple fraud, and it is its own penalty, in the numbing, hardening and disabling of the soul with cold. In a sense peculiar to itself treachery *commits* a man, holding him, as these souls are held, clamped in the ice. Of one form of treachery the tenderest of our poets has written:

> 'It hardens a' within
> An' petrifies the feelin'.'

Treachery being the most anti-social of sins, every sinner in Cocytus knows that his fame on earth can only be infamy and he would not willingly be known, and those, the less guilty, in the outer zone have the miserable privilege of holding their faces bent down and concealing their identity. But they are eager to report each other's name and story to the travellers and to gratify their mutual hatred by exposing their neighbour's disgrace. The one inducement to Count Ugolino to tell the story, not of his own sin but of his death, is that his words should 'be seed that may bear fruit of infamy' to his enemy.

The famous Ugolino episode is the longest in the *Inferno*. It stands in marked and intentional contrast and correspondence with Francesca's story in the fifth canto, hers the record of a great love, his of as great a hate. Her love and his hate hold her to her lover and him to his enemy forever in an association which makes their last earthly memories an eternally present agony; each 'speaks and weeps together', and the companion of each suffers in a silence which adds strangely to the poignancy of their stories. These two episodes, with that of Ulysses in the twenty-sixth canto, are the greatest examples of dramatic imagination in the whole poem. Francesca, Ulysses and Ugolino each tell their own tales, of love, of daring, of agony and hate, and in each case, by the power of imaginative sympathy, Dante penetrates to the heart of the sinner so that his sin is forgotten and he is, as it were, restored for his sheer human worth to the human fellowship.

The story itself calls for little comment; the long months reckoned only by the returning brightness of the moon through the window-slit of the prison—the warning dreams and the sudden sound of the nails in the door below—the last days of stony despair and death, and the father, blind, dying, yet with the strength to outlive all his children and bearing with him into Hell all the energy of his hate, which is now his life that cannot die, 'his tenderness and paternal pity being turned to ferocity and rage' (*F. De Sanctis*). The story gains incalculably from its setting in the vast darkness and desolation of Cocytus and in the silent presence of the Archbishop, and through all the telling of it Dante does not intervene with a word. 'Silence and immobility take part in the drama as in no other episode' (*Casini-Barbi*). Then Dante, still speechless to Ugolino, breaks forth on Pisa, which suffered and approved a crime so monstrous.

Nothing is said here of Ugolino's own offence and we are absorbed in the treachery of which he was the victim and is forever the avenger. Yet he too is one of the traitors in the ice, and though we forget his sin in his 'desperate grief' Dante does not allow that even such wrongs exculpate from such guilt as his. Belonging to a leading Ghibelline family of Pisa, he turned Guelf, conspired with the Guelf enemies of the city and gained the chief power in its government, which he shared for a time with his grandson Nino Visconti, Dante's friend whom we shall meet later in the *Purgatorio*. Ugolino was blamed for the disastrous naval defeat of Pisa by Genoa in 1284 and for the surrender of certain Pisan castles to Florence and Lucca. Later, having quarrelled with Nino, he intrigued with the Archbishop, who was Ghibelline leader in Pisa, and had Nino banished from the city. Then, in this competition of mutual knavery and intrigue, Ruggieri moved the people against Ugolino and by fair promises got him into his power with two of his sons and two grandsons, here described for dramatic effectiveness as four sons and for the same reason as children, though some of them were, in fact, grown-up. The end came in 1289, in Dante's twenty-fourth year, when he would share the horror of all Florence at the news from Pisa; for Ugolino's character and record were familiar to Dante and his contemporaries and much could be assumed in writing for them that is not known to us. In addition to the specific guilt of 'betraying Pisa's strongholds', Ugolino is doubtless placed, or found, here by Dante because he 'used the misfortunes of his country for the ends of his own ambition and intrigued with whichever party, Guelf or Ghibelline, promised at the moment to support his power' (*J. S. Carroll*).

For the betrayal of public interests for private advantage was, in Dante's judgement, a deadly offence. That was the consideration which moved him to such cruelty against Bocca, with the ironical offer to him of 'fame' in the world. It was Bocca's treason that brought long-remembered disaster on Florence at Montaperti, when 'the rout and the great slaughter stained the Arbia red' and Farinata barely saved his city from destruction (Canto x). It is significant of Dante's judgement of his age and country that nearly all those he names in this place of treachery are men of his own time or of the generation just before him and belong to 'the fair land where sounds the *sì*', and that they are chosen as much from the one party as the other. Two of them are grouped with the legendary Ganelon because 'his name was a byword in the Middle Ages for treachery' (*P. Toynbee*) and his company is their hall-mark. It was the poisoning of the public life of Italy by the infection of fickleness and bad faith in its princes and peoples that moved him to his outbursts here against Pisa and Genoa. These sins of treachery were not merely individual and occasional offences, they were diffused and endemic.

Dante's singular device for the punishment of treachery to guests, that souls are plunged in Hell while their bodily life continues on earth, was probably suggested by the language of the fifty-fifth Psalm about treacherous friends: 'Let death seize upon them and let them go down quick into hell. Bloody and deceitful men shall not live out half their days', with a further reference to Judas from *John* xiii. 27: 'After the sop Satan entered into him.' 'These violators of hospitality who had broken a faith undertaken by their free choice had made themselves unfit for human fellowship. It was just, therefore, that they should be *ipso facto* excluded from it and that for the time of life remaining to them after their crime it would be human life only in appearance and in reality the life of devils' (*V. Rossi*). Their moral isolation is indicated too by the sealing of their eyes with their frozen tears; they can never again see a human face and their bitter memories gather and stagnate in their hearts.

It is the same idea of inevitable exclusion from all privilege of fellowship that is expressed in Dante's callous deception of Fra Alberigo by the careful equivocation of his promise: 'If I do not relieve thee, may I have to go to the bottom of the ice.' This incident follows, immediately and significantly, on Dante's feeling of the bitter wind from Satan's wings falling chill even on his numbed features, and it means that there, with the full sense and evidence of their offence, any sort of human decency or keeping of faith with souls so abandoned to evil, so cruel and shameless in their falsehood, was impossible. In the inhuman treatment of inhuman sin, the meeting of treachery with treachery, Dante was a man of his age, and in judging his age, as we must, we judge him too; but, dramatically, this induration of the heart in the depth of Hell is justified by its very dreadfulness.

The four concentric zones of Cocytus penalize, respectively, treachery to family; treachery to country or cause, lower in Hell, because the public interest is more sacred than the private; treachery to guests, lower still, because the relationship is a chosen and voluntary one as compared with those of family and country; and treachery to rightful lords and benefactors, lowest of all, because it is essentially rebellion against the ultimate, divine order of the universe, which is, in the last reckoning, the authority of grace. The names of the four zones are mentioned, it seems, casually; but with Dante we may be sure they were not chosen casually, and if we have regard to the particular offences of the four traitors after whom the zones are called we may find a significance in the choice of them which is in the line of Dante's thinking. Cain sinned against his brother Abel; that is, against the intended line of faithful humanity, the holy family of the race. Antenor betrayed the Trojans; that is, the Romans, the people elect of God for government and social order in the world, for the establishment of the Empire. Ptolemy betrayed the High Priest and chief of the Jews, the people elect of God for the knowledge of God among men, for the establishment of the Church. And Judas, from whom the innermost and lowest zone is named Judecca, betrayed Him who is the grace and authority of God on earth. The four names sum up the significance and reach of treachery as the outraging and contradiction of every holiest interest of human life.

INFERNO

'*Vexilla regis prodeunt inferni*
verso di noi; però dinanzi mira'
disse 'l maestro mio 'se tu 'l discerni.'
Come quando una grossa nebbia spira
o quando l'emisperio nostro annotta,
par di lungi un molin che 'l vento gira,
veder mi parve un tal dificio allotta;
poi per lo vento mi ristrinsi retro
al duca mio; chè non li era altra grotta.
Già era, e con paura il metto in metro, 10
là dove l'ombre tutte eran coperte,
e trasparìen come festuca in vetro.
Altre sono a giacere; altre stanno erte,
quella col capo e quella con le piante;
altra, com'arco, il volto a' piè rinverte.
Quando noi fummo fatti tanto avante,
ch'al mio maestro piacque di mostrarmi
la creatura ch'ebbe il bel sembiante,
d' innanzi mi si tolse e fè restarmi,
'Ecco Dite,' dicendo 'ed ecco il loco 20
ove convien che di fortezza t'armi.'
Com' io divenni allor gelato e fioco,
nol dimandar, lettor, ch' i' non lo scrivo,
però ch'ogni parlar sarebbe poco.
Io non mori', e non rimasi vivo:
pensa oggimai per te, s' hai fior d' ingegno,
qual io divenni, d'uno e d'altro privo.
Lo 'mperador del doloroso regno
da mezzo il petto uscìa fuor della ghiaccia;
e più con un gigante io mi convegno, 30

CANTO XXXIV

Judecca; the Treacherous to lords and benefactors; Satan; the departure from Hell

'*VEXILLA regis prodeunt inferni*[1] towards us,' my Master said; 'look forward, therefore, if thou discern him.'

As when a thick fog rises or night falls on our hemisphere appears in the distance a windmill turning with the wind, I seemed to see a structure of the kind; then, for the wind, I drew back behind my Leader, for there was no other shelter there. I was already—and with fear I set it down in verse—where the shades were wholly covered and showed through like straws in glass; some were lying, some erect, this with the head, that with the soles uppermost, another like a bow, bent face to feet.

When we had gone on so far that my Master thought it good to show me the creature who was once so fair,[2] he took himself from before me and made me stop, saying: 'Lo Dis, and the place where thou must arm thee with fortitude.'

How chilled and faint I turned then, do not ask, reader, for I do not write it, since all words would fail. I did not die and I did not remain alive; think now for thyself, if thou hast any wit, what I became, denied both death and life. The Emperor of the woeful kingdom stood forth at mid-breast from the ice, and I compare better with a giant than giants

che giganti non fan con le sue braccia:
  vedi oggimai quant'esser dee quel tutto
  ch'a così fatta parte si confaccia.
S'el fu sì bello com'elli è or brutto,
  e contra 'l suo fattore alzò le ciglia,
  ben dee da lui procedere ogni lutto.
Oh quanto parve a me gran maraviglia
  quand' io vidi tre facce alla sua testa!
  L'una dinanzi, e quella era vermiglia;
l'altr'eran due, che s'aggiugnìeno a questa 40
  sovresso 'l mezzo di ciascuna spalla,
  e sè giugnìeno al luogo della cresta:
e la destra parea tra bianca e gialla;
  la sinistra a vedere era tal, quali
  vegnon di là onde 'l Nilo s'avvalla.
Sotto ciascuna uscivan due grand'ali,
  quanto si convenìa a tanto uccello:
  vele di mar non vid' io mai cotali.
Non avean penne, ma di vispistrello
  era lor modo; e quelle svolazzava, 50
  sì che tre venti si movean da ello:
quindi Cocito tutto s'aggelava.
  Con sei occhi piangea, e per tre menti
  gocciava 'l pianto e sanguinosa bava.
Da ogni bocca dirompea co' denti
  un peccatore, a guisa di maciulla,
  sì che tre ne facea così dolenti.
A quel dinanzi il mordere era nulla
  verso 'l graffiar, che tal volta la schiena
  rimanea della pelle tutta brulla. 60
'Quell'anima là su c' ha maggior pena'
  disse 'l maestro 'è Giuda Scarïotto,
  che 'l capo ha dentro e fuor le gambe mena.
Delli altri due c' hanno il capo di sotto,
  quel che pende dal nero ceffo è Bruto
  —vedi come si storce e non fa motto;
e l'altro è Cassio che par sì membruto.
  Ma la notte risurge, e oramai
  è da partir, chè tutto avem veduto.'

with his arms; see now what that whole must be to answer to such a part. If he was as fair as he is now foul and lifted up his brows against his Maker, well may all sorrow come from him. Ah, how great a marvel it seemed to me when I saw three faces on his head; one in front, and that was red, the two others joined to it just over the middle of each shoulder and all joined at the crown. The right seemed between white and yellow; the left had such an aspect as the people from where the Nile descends. Under each came forth two great wings of size fitting for such a bird, sails at sea I never saw like these; they had no feathers but were like a bat's, and he was beating them so that three winds went forth from him by which all Cocytus was kept frozen. With six eyes he was weeping and over three chins dripped tears and bloody foam. In each mouth he crushed a sinner with his teeth as with a heckle and thus he kept three of them in pain; to him in front the biting was nothing to the clawing, for sometimes the back was left all stripped of skin.

'That soul up there which has the greatest punishment' said the Master 'is Judas Iscariot, who has his head inside and plies his legs without. Of the other two who have their heads below, the one that hangs from the black muzzle is Brutus—see how he writhes and utters not a word—and the other Cassius, who looks so stalwart. But night is rising again and now it is time to go, for we have seen all.'

Com'a lui piacque, il collo li avvinghiai; 70
  ed el prese di tempo e luogo poste;
  e quando l'ali fuoro aperte assai,
appigliò sè alle vellute coste:
  di vello in vello giù discese poscia
  tra 'l folto pelo e le gelate croste.
Quando noi fummo là dove la coscia
  si volge, a punto in sul grosso dell'anche,
  lo duca con fatica e con angoscia
volse la testa ov'elli avea le zanche,
  e aggrappossi al pel com' uom che sale, 80
  sì che 'n inferno i' credea tornar anche.
'Attienti ben, chè per cotali scale'
  disse 'l maestro, ansando com' uom lasso,
  'conviensi dipartir da tanto male.'
Poi uscì fuor per lo foro d'un sasso,
  e puose me in su l'orlo a sedere;
  appresso porse a me l'accorto passo.
Io levai li occhi, e credetti vedere
  Lucifero com' io l'avea lasciato;
  e vidili le gambe in su tenere; 90
e s' io divenni allora travagliato,
  la gente grossa il pensi, che non vede
  qual è quel punto ch' io avea passato.
'Lèvati su' disse 'l maestro 'in piede:
  la via è lunga e 'l cammino è malvagio,
  e già il sole a mezza terza riede.'
Non era camminata di palagio
  là 'v'eravam, ma natural burella
  ch'avea mal suolo e di lume disagio.
'Prima ch' io dell'abisso mi divella, 100
  maestro mio,' diss' io quando fui dritto
  'a trarmi d'erro un poco mi favella:
ov'è la ghiaccia? e questi com'è fitto
  sì sottosopra? e come, in sì poc'ora,
  da sera a mane ha fatto il sol tragitto?'
Ed elli a me: 'Tu imagini ancora
  d'esser di là dal centro, ov' io mi presi
  al pel del vermo reo che 'l mondo fora.

At his bidding I clasped him round the neck; and he watched his chance of time and place and, when the wings were wide open, caught hold of the shaggy flanks, then descended from tuft to tuft between the matted hair and the frozen crusts. When we were where the thigh turns, just on the swelling of the haunch, the Leader with labour and strain brought round his head where his legs had been and grappled on the hair like one climbling, so that I thought we were returning into Hell again.

'Hold fast,' said the Master, panting like one spent, 'for by such stairs must we go forth from so much evil.'

And he passed out through the cleft of a rock and put me on the edge to sit, then reached toward me his cautious step. I raised my eyes and thought to see Lucifer as I had left him, and I saw his legs held upward; and if I became perplexed then let the dull crowd judge who do not see what is the point that I had passed.[3]

'Rise up on thy feet,' said the Master; 'the way is long and the road is hard and already the sun returns to middle tierce.'[4]

It was no palace hall where we were, but a natural dungeon, ill-floored and scant of light.

'Before I extricate myself from the abyss, my Master,' I said when I had risen 'to clear me from perplexity speak to me a little. Where is the ice? And he there, how is he fixed thus upside-down? And how, in so short a time, has the sun made the passage from evening to morning?'

And he said to me: 'Thou imaginest thou art still on the other side of the centre, where I took hold of the hair of the guilty worm that pierces

Di là fosti cotanto quant' io scesi;
quand' io mi volsi, tu passasti 'l punto 110
al qual si traggon d'ogni parte i pesi.
E se' or sotto l'emisperio giunto
ch'è opposito a quel che la gran secca
coverchia, e sotto 'l cui colmo consunto
fu l'uom che nacque e visse sanza pecca:
tu hai i piedi in su picciola spera
che l'altra faccia fa della Giudecca.
Qui è da man, quando di là è sera:
e questi, che ne fè scala col pelo,
fitto è ancora sì come prim'era. 120
Da questa parte cadde giù dal cielo;
e la terra, che pria di qua si sporse,
per paura di lui fè del mar velo,
e venne all'emisperio nostro; e forse
per fuggir lui lasciò qui luogo voto
quella ch'appar di qua, e su ricorse.'
Luogo è là giù da Belzebù remoto
tanto quanto la tomba si distende,
che non per vista, ma per suono è noto
d' un ruscelletto che quivi discende 130
per la buca d' un sasso, ch'elli ha roso
col corso ch'elli avvolge, e poco pende.
Lo duca e io per quel cammino ascoso
intrammo a ritornar nel chiaro mondo;
e sanza cura aver d'alcun riposo
salimmo su, el primo e io secondo,
tanto ch' i' vidi delle cose belle
che porta 'l ciel, per un pertugio tondo;
e quindi uscimmo a riveder le stelle.

1. 'The banners of the King of Hell advance'; parody of an ancient Latin hymn in honour of the Cross, used in Holy Week.

2. Lucifer, the brightest of the Seraphim, raised rebellion in Heaven and he and his followers were defeated and cast out by Michael the archangel, who led the faithful; he became King of Hell. He is named Lucifer, Dis, Beelzebub and Satan by Dante.

3. The earth's centre.

4. Tierce, first of the four canonical divisions of the day after sunrise; 'middle tierce', about 7.30 a.m.

the world. Thou wast on that side so long as I descended; when I turned myself thou didst pass the point to which weights are drawn from every part and art now come beneath the hemisphere opposite to that which covers the great dry land and under whose zenith the Man was done to death who was born and lived without sin.[5] Thou hast thy feet upon a little sphere which forms the other face of Judecca; here it is morning when it is evening there, and he that made a ladder for us with his hair is still fixed as he was before. On this side he fell down from Heaven, and the land which before stood out here made a veil of the sea for fear of him and came to our hemisphere; and perhaps to escape from him that which appears on this side left here the empty space and rushed upwards.'[6]

Down there is a place at the farthest part of his tomb from Beelzebub, which is known, not by sight, but by the sound of a stream that descends there through the hollow of a rock which it has worn in its winding course and gentle slope. The Leader and I entered on that hidden road to return into the bright world, and without caring to have any rest we climbed up, he first and I second, so far that I saw through a round opening some of the fair things that Heaven bears; and thence we came forth to see again the stars.

5. They are now under the southern celestial hemisphere, opposite to that over the terrestrial hemisphere of 'dry land' (*Gen.* i. 9), at the centre of which is Jerusalem (*Ezek.* v. 5), and their time has gone back to that of the antipodes, Holy Saturday morning.

6. The former land of the southern hemisphere fled to the northern, leaving the southern all sea, and the material which once filled the 'natural dungeon', Satan's 'tomb', where they are, rushed up where Satan had plunged down and formed the island-mountain of Purgatory in the southern hemisphere.

NOTE

The account of Judecca, the lowest and innermost zone of Cocytus, has an abstract and impersonal quality in marked contrast with the cantos just preceding. The souls guilty of the ultimate sin of treachery against the authority and grace which are the divine order of the world are finally cut off from all the movements and contacts and communications of human life and imprisoned, each by itself, in their sin; and not one of those in the ice, 'like straws in glass', is even named by Dante or Virgil, to such insignificance and obliteration have they sunk, 'silent and immovable, in agonized and everlasting adoration of the Emperor of the dolorous kingdom' (*E. G. Gardner*). 'Every trace of life has disappeared. The shades, wholly buried and as if petrified in the ice, are deprived of any relief of movement or utterance; Dante is denied by the stony thickness of the ice all communication with them' (*V. Rossi*).

The silence where the poets stand on the icy plain glimmering in the faint light is broken by the stately and familiar words of the triumphal *Hymn of the Cross* adapted by Virgil for the introduction of Dante to the presence-chamber of the King. The stateliness is, of course, ironical, as if in celebration of Hell's triumph, the imprisonment of its King in its deepest dungeon.

The approach of the poets to Satan is described so as to give the reader a cumulative impression of vastness and terror; first, in the higher zone of Ptolomea, Dante 'seemed to feel some wind' driven down on them from above; then, after Virgil's strange announcement, he strains his eyes as through a fog and 'seems to see' a great structure like a whirling windmill and seeks shelter in Virgil from the bitter blast; *then* he is before Satan himself. The comparison with a giant and with Dante's own person is a mere suggestion of Satan's incomparable magnitude.

The figure of Satan is taken in the main from the common stock of medieval iconography, but without the grotesque and meaningless features by which the medieval artists, even Giotto among them, laboured to multiply its horrors. But 'Dante's Lucifer very greatly excels other Lucifers of the same period by the dignity of his aspect and the clear definiteness of the representation. Even when Dante speaks the language of his time, his account shows plainly his familiarity with the language of the classics' (*V. Rossi*). There is a barbarous majesty in the vast silent form, with the inevitable, mechanical working of its great wings and champing jaws suggested in the comparison to the sails of a windmill and to a flax-heckle, and with its sole mark of personality—this wholly Dante's own—in the droppings of tears and bloody foam that tell of his eternal pain and rage.

The significance of Satan here rises out of the earlier part of his myth, to which there are many references in the course of the poem. He was 'created the noblest of all creatures', being the greatest of the Seraphim, 'these devout flames who cowl themselves with their six wings' (*Par*. ix). The Seraphim rank in medieval angelology as the highest and the swiftest of the angelic orders, the glowing spirits of love, the nearest of all to God, His ministers in directing the most spacious of the heavenly spheres. Satan's revolt was the outburst of his pride in the attempt to supplant God Himself; it was he that was 'the first to turn his back on his Maker and from whose envy has come such lamentation' (*Par*. ix). Now his state is a complete reversal of all he ever was—in his 'little sphere' at the deepest point of the universe, farthest from God, held there by his sin, by the frozen cesspool of the world into which drain all the streams of Hell. 'Hell from beneath is moved for thee to meet thee at thy coming. . . . How art thou fallen from heaven, O Lucifer, son of the morning! . . . For thou hast said in thy heart. . . . I will exalt my throne above the stars of God. . . . Yet thou shalt be brought down to hell, to the sides of the pit' (*Isaiah* ix. 12–15). Instead of his ancient radiance his form is that of a monstrous brute, clawed, hairy and bat-winged, and his three faces on the one head are a blasphemous travesty of the Holy Trinity against whom he had risen. As the Trinity of Father, Son and Spirit signified in medieval thinking the unity of the divine power and wisdom and love—as in the inscription on the gate of Hell (Canto iii)—so the red-flushed face of Satan represents his hatred, the sickly white and yellow face his impotence, and the black face his ignorance, the last enforced by the reference to the barbarians of unknown Africa; and from his six wings, recalling his old seraphic form, three blasts send out these influences as blights on the life of men, the winds keeping Cocytus hard frozen, making his own prison more secure, and moving men to be traitors to God and to their race.

Of the three sinners named here for their bad pre-eminence, Judas betrayed his master with a kiss and Brutus and Cassius murdered—so Dante would conceive it—their rightful lord and benefactor, the chosen founder of the Empire. Their sins, that is to say, were not mere examples of personal treachery; they were unexampled treason against Church and Empire, refusals and denials of the whole divine order, and it is for that reason that they are punished deepest of all in Hell, where 'the Emperor devoured those who served him best' (*J. S. Carroll*). Satan is here conceived, not so much as a personal sinner, but rather as the last and greatest of Hell's monsters, the embodied forces of evil; it is their sin itself that is the imprisonment and the torment of the three basest offenders against God and man.

Before going on, Dante, at Virgil's bidding, looks full at Satan and 'arms himself with fortitude'. He meets the last challenge of sin and though it makes him 'chilled and faint' he holds by his reason still and, clasping Virgil by the neck, is brought by means of the very person of Satan to a place of safety, 'for by such stairs must we go forth from so much evil'; Virgil expresses the idea three times. Knowing now all the worst that sin can do in its power and in its impotence, he is enabled by that knowledge which has cost him so dear to cling to his reason, still the vicegerent of grace, and to leave Satan and all his works beneath his feet. Here again, as on the back of Geryon and in the grasp of Antaeus, Virgil is *between* Dante and the power of evil.

The mistaken idea that gravity is most powerful at the earth's centre, so that Virgil, passing the centre, 'panted like one spent', serves Dante's purpose of marking the 'labour and strain' of this defiance of evil and deliverance of the soul from the obsession of sin. Three times in these last cantos he refers expressly and in similar terms to this pull of gravity, this drawing to the centre where Satan's seat is, as operative all through the earth: 'the dismal hole on which all the other rocks bear down'—'the centre at which all gravity converges'—'the point to which weights are drawn from every part'. It is an insistent repetition, peculiarly in Dante's manner, by which he declared the downward drag of every kind of sin, the hold of Satan on the impenitent, the bond of its own earthliness on the soul that has lost its liberty.

Just before leaving Cocytus Virgil said that night was rising; it was then the evening of Holy Saturday. Now, when they have passed the centre, he says: 'The sun returns to middle tierce.' It is the first occasion since 'the beginning of the morning' before they entered Hell, 'when the sun was mounting with those stars which were with it when divine love first set in motion these fair things', on which the time is indicated by reference to the sun or to the services of the Church. For Dante is now, even in that depth, in a new relation to the heavens, under a new sky, and his reckoning henceforth is by the conditions, not of Hell, but of Purgatory, the place of redemption, the mountain which rises into the sunshine and resounds with praise, where it is now *morning* of the same Saturday, the eve of Easter Day. Their descent from the gate of Hell has taken twenty-four hours and the climb by the other way from Satan to the surface is to take about the same time. Dante's long ascent, to end in God's presence, has begun.

The description of Satan's fall from Heaven and its effects on the earth is a bold and singular piece of myth-making. By the convulsion of the earth's frame his 'dungeon' was hollowed out in it and a passage left from the antipodes of the present inhabited world, as Dante knew it, to the centre, while a great mountain was raised from the sea at the point of Satan's fall, on the summit of which stood afterwards the Garden of Eden, so that, passing right through the earth, Dante and Virgil are to emerge on the shore of Purgatory.

The stream whose sound the poets hear in the hollow of the

rock as they climb is commonly understood to be Lethe, the river of forgetfulness, which Virgil has told Dante he will see in Purgatory. On the summit of Purgatory it clears the memory of the penitents of their forgiven sinfulness; here it adds to Cocytus, carrying that old sinfulness back to its source in Hell.

And now, despite all the surging evil of the world with its insolence of defiance and denial, Dante returns from the depths, still, as from the beginning, following his reason, 'he first and I second', with a cleared and assured conviction of the reality, distant but undimmed, of the things of God, seeing, first, only 'some of the fair things which Heaven bears', then 'the stars'. The *Inferno*, like the *Purgatorio* and the *Paradiso*, ends with the word *stars*; for the stars mean for Dante all the good that is beyond the world, all the perfect order and the working providence of God, and it is into obedience to that order and assurance of that providence that all his experience and all the leading of Virgil and the memory and the hope of Beatrice are bringing him.

Aristotle's classic statement of the function of tragedy, to purge the soul by pity and terror, applies with singular fitness to Dante's *Inferno*. All the pity and terror of his journey, met and borne in Virgil's leading and companionship, have purged his soul of that fear of sin in which he was yesterday being driven back by the wolf 'step by step to where the sun is silent' and which is the soul's surrender and defeat. He has still far to go and a greater purgation to bear; but now he sees again the stars.